THE PHOENIX PENCIL COMPANY

A Novel

ALLISON KING

WILLIAM MORROW

An Imprint of HarperCollinsPublishers

HarperCollins books may be purchased for educational, business, or sales promotional use. For information, please email the Special Markets Department at SPsales@harpercollins.com.

FIRST EDITION

Designed by Nancy Singer
Illustrations © Smulsky/stock.adobe.com

Library of Congress Cataloging-in-Publication Data has been applied for.

ISBN 978-0-06-344623-6
ISBN 978-0-06-344792-9 (international edition)

25 26 27 28 29 LBC 5 4 3 2 1

For 外公 and 外婆, grandparents extraordinaire

CHAPTER 1

From the diary of Monica Tsai,
backed up on five servers spanning
three continents

August 11, 2018 (2018-08-11T22:54:30.218542)
Swarthmore, Pennsylvania. United States of America
(39.9058546,75.3562615)

I met a girl today who gave me a pencil.

It was a real journey to get to her too. Not only because she lived across the river in New Jersey and I had to borrow Prof. Logan's stupidly nice car, or because she made me nervous, in a heart-racing kind of way. But because I had already been looking for a year. My goal wasn't her or the pencil, exactly. Really, I was trying to help my grandmother reconnect with her cousin, the one she rarely talks about, who she grew up with at the family pencil company, back in Shanghai.

It all started a year ago, when me, grandmother, and grandfather were celebrating grandmother's ninetieth birthday at her favorite restaurant, Arby's. I was feeling bummed for a couple reasons—the first being that I was leaving for college in a few days and every sort of panic was setting in: that I'd still have trouble making friends, that grandmother and grandfather would struggle without me at home, and I hadn't been able to think of a single suitable gift for her birthday. We go to Arby's every year. They have her favorite coupon—five roast beef sandwiches for the price of two, and you can use the coupon twice. But I was really hoping to do something different, something special for this one.

Grandmother can't stand the thought that I'd willingly hand over money for her sake, so purchasing anything was out of the question, and our walls were already littered with the drawings I'd given her every other year. My coupon book of chores also went unused. Then there was the time I tried to cook for her. She watched so nervously as I wielded the knife that my real gift was giving up so she could finally relax.

I knew she could tell I was feeling down that day. She's always been able to see right through me. Maybe that's why, as she brushed the sesame seeds that had fallen from her bun onto her napkin, she mentioned Meng.

"Meng used to flick sesame seeds at me all the time back in the pencil company." It was the most specific detail I had ever heard about her cousin or the old family business.

I had formed this ghostly image of Meng, someone who had once been like a sister to her, who also grew up in the pencil company and lived through two wars in Shanghai, and here she was suddenly re-appearing, the answer to my predicament. I don't usually press when grandmother speaks about her past. She'll rub the scars on her arm and change the subject to anything other than her cousin, anything other than the pencil company. And grandfather will shake his head, just a little bit. But there's clearly a deep love for Meng hidden there, a tender pain. I thought maybe I could help her resolve it. So this time, I pressed. What if I could find Meng? I asked. What if she's still alive, still in Shanghai, and there's a chance to reconnect?

Normally, I don't think grandmother would have agreed. But grandfather gave her this look, and maybe since it was her birthday she realized she should do something, or she was feeling sentimental, with me leaving for college and all. Whatever it was, she wrote down the characters for Meng's name. That night, I began my search, not expecting it would take me almost a year to find a lead.

Her name was Louise Sun. EMBRS told me this a week ago. Actually, more precisely, it said:

> Sparks are flyin', we've found a match! Your query for "Meng Chen", "陳夢", "Shanghai Pencil Company", "上海鉛筆廠", "Phoenix Pencil Company", "鳳凰鉛筆廠" has sparked a connection with Louise Sun, click to reveal.

I think we've made EMBRS too colloquial, but that's kind of Prof. Logan's cringe style, and since I'm a lowly undergrad researcher and he's a hotshot professor, there isn't much I can say about it.

The matching post was a picture of two women, one old and one young. I zoomed in on the older woman first, searching for traces of grandmother. There were similarities around the mouths and how their hair grayed in specks rather than completely whitening. Behind the women was the waterfront, Shanghai's skyline sparkling. Beneath the picture, a post written by Louise:

> Hello from behind the Great Firewall! Couldn't get my VPN to work until now, but I've been having the time of my life in Shanghai this summer with this absolute BOSS sitting next to me here. She lived through the Japanese occupation of Shanghai and ran the Phoenix Pencil Company, one of the only woman-run companies in the city at the time! They would make custom pencils for people all over. My high standard for writing implements feels justified now! #uniball4eva Two more weeks here, then I'll be back to the Hill. DM if you want to catch up!

I had to stop myself from immediately sending the picture to grandmother, her ninetieth birthday gift finally delivered, more of a ninety-first birthday gift. The other woman had to be Meng. How many women could have run the Phoenix Pencil Company? Only my grandmother and her cousin. But first I had to do my due diligence on this Louise character. Because deepfakes, you know? And it was hard to believe that EMBRS, this new app that ran my code, had worked when all else had failed.

I'm pretty good at knowing what sites and keywords to use to verify information. But I didn't need any of that with Louise. She had so much about herself readily available online for browsing. It was as if she'd never heard of data privacy in her life. She was a Princeton undergrad from Cherry Hill, New Jersey. She had won some first-year award in the economics department and was a starting player on the volleyball team. The article came with pictures—I promise I did not seek them out. But it was hard to look away from her air of concentration, knees bent, arms flat together, eyes up toward the ceiling. She had a strangely captivating jawline.

Satisfied that she was real and thrilled EMBRS was working, I sent grandmother an email with the photo attached.

> Wo gen Louise Sun you 3 mutual friends.
> Yao bu yao connect 😊 ➡️ ⬅️ 😊 ?

Ever since grandmother got a smart phone, this is how we communicate. A third in a thousand-year-old language romanized in the dominant language here, a third in the dominant language when I don't know a word, and a third in the language of the future—emojis—for when I'm afraid she might not understand the English. Grandfather calls it our little cryptography. That was his field, cryptography, but even he says it takes too much effort to read our messages, and so it's become a language of our own.

I expected a quick reply. Grandmother and grandfather are more technically savvy than a lot of my classmates. They always have their phone volume turned way up to hear their notifications. It's woken me a few times—relatives in Taiwan sending memes in the middle of the night—though they can sleep right through it.

When she didn't reply within ten minutes, I started imagining all sorts of scenarios—they had been hit by a car at that bad intersection, one of them was in the hospital with pneumonia, or maybe they were sleeping in after an exciting night of mahjong with new friends.

I hated that it had taken me this long to find Meng, that evasive woman. There was no trace of her on the internet, at least not with the search engines I was using. It made some sense—she would also be in her nineties and had likely never used the internet that much, and then there was China's firewall to contend with. But thanks to grandfather, I have a knack for computers, and halfway through my first semester, I enlisted the computer science lab's servers to help. I configured scrapers that searched the internet every few minutes for any mention of Meng or the Phoenix Pencil Company. I signed up my bots for Chinese social media sites. I researched different search algorithms, spent hours combing through false positives. I wasn't supposed to use the department's servers this way. It's not like anyone told me I couldn't, but I guess the scraping generated enough suspicious traffic tied to my username that Prof. Logan noticed.

I had been skeptical of Prof. Logan, to be honest. He's super young for his seniority in the department, his office hours are always full of fanboys, and computer science fanboys are kind of the worst. But I can only say he's been nice to me and that instead of reprimanding me, he skimmed my code and offered me a summer research opportunity to work on his project called EMBRS.

It stands for something stupid that I can't even remember off the top of my head—okay, I just looked it up—Electronic Memory Bank Enabling Radical Sharing. That's Prof. Logan's thing: radical sharing.

He managed to turn this into an acronym but dropped the second *E* since that's what all the cool companies are doing, and he really went all in on the fire theme. At its core, EMBRS is a souped-up search engine that prioritizes not finding information exactly, but "sparking connections" between people. It doesn't care to index large businesses or medical terms or even news—it only cares about data written by an individual about their own life. Think social media posts, newsletters, blogs, that kind of thing. And because of its status as an academic research project, as well as Prof. Logan's uncanny number of connections, it has access to more social media posts than anything else out there. By then I was desperate for help finding Meng, so I signed on.

Prof. Logan has this dream, which I must admit sounds kind of nice, especially for a shy recluse like me. Right now, EMBRS uses existing stuff people post on social media. But his real goal is to turn it into an all-encompassing journaling app where people write freely about their lives. The journals stay private, just between you and EMBRS. His voice goes all soft when he describes this: he says to imagine you're at a party where you don't know anyone, but EMBRS has already compared your life journal with everyone else's in attendance, and can tell you that you and the guy wearing sunglasses, who you previously thought very rude and standoffish, are actually both huge fans of the same anime, have both written mature fan fiction about the same pairing, which is maybe something that neither of you would have admitted to a stranger at a party. Suddenly you have this shared interest, and just like that, a connection is sparked. Around then is when Prof. Logan gets on his soapbox and says social media posts are enough for EMBRS now, but that they're too short, too performative, and contribute to our perceived isolation, our fractured democracy, whereas a life's journal with only EMBRS as a reader is real and true, and all his fanboys start singing his praises on Reddit.

I guess it's also why I started keeping this journal, even though EMBRS isn't a journaling app quite yet, and that's because Prof. Logan is maybe the only person ever to try to think through content moderation before building a product—we don't want to be in the business of sparking connections between Nazis, after all. While I have to respect him for this, I'm not totally sold on radical sharing yet. I figure maybe one day I will be, though, and I'll feed all this into EMBRS, to let it know some stuff about me, and it'll help me make connections that I haven't really been able to make on my own, on account of the whole recluse thing.

Each minute that passed without a reply from grandmother was killing me. I can't ever repay my grandparents for all they've done for me. They raised me when my parents wouldn't, supported me in every possible way, rejected all attempts to show my gratitude. This was the one thing I could do for them with the skills I have.

I was about to call the landline when she finally texted back.

😈 ➡️ ⬅️ 😈 ☑️ 🙏 xiexie

Relieved, I composed a careful message to Louise Sun. I asked if the woman in her picture was by any chance Chen Meng (陳夢), that if so, she was a cousin of my grandmother's (Wong Yun 王筠). Would she please let me know if it was really her?

With the time difference, I thought Louise wouldn't respond until much later in the day. To my delight, she replied almost immediately.

omg! yes, that's her name! ill ask about your grandmother today! do you have a pic i could share with her?

Something about the casualness of her message, her openness, drew me in, even then. Was it also her face in her photographs, the easy smile, the confident eyes? Okay, maybe. But there were so many questions I wanted to ask her. How had she run into Meng? Was Meng an attendee at economics conferences? Or maybe a volleyball fan? Was Meng a mahjong fiend? Did they play together?

I sent her two pictures. One was me and my grandparents outside the classroom where my grandfather used to teach. The second was from the summer before college, when I'd ransacked the attic and found a bag of used wooden pencils. I brought them down, photographed the pile, even took a few close-ups of the ones that still had their markings. Beautiful etchings that formed the outline of a phoenix. When I asked grandmother about them, she said they were from the pencil company and asked that I put them away. I noticed that a few of them—it's hard to explain exactly—but some were hollow, as if the lead had fallen out, leaving only the wooden casing. Grandmother caught me staring down the barrel of one. She rested her hand over mine. Her hand, all loose, wrinkled skin, should have been soft and familiar. Instead, there was a rigidity to her fingers as she pulled the pencil away. I let her, of course, and we did not talk about them again.

> whoa, awesome! will report back later
> today, your tmrw

I could hardly sleep that night. Summer was ending, which meant I had to wrap up my EMBRS work in the next few days, and the Pennsylvania humidity was awful. It was a tossing-and-turning-and-reimagining-algorithms kind of night. But the end of summer also meant I would be headed home to Cambridge soon, at least for a few weeks, to celebrate another birthday with grandmother, and this time I'd have a proper gift for her.

Louise's message the next morning was all I could have asked for.

> hey! i spent the day with meng. she was
> surprised to say the least! she wants to send
> something to your grandmother and she gave

it to me. i can mail it to you when im back in the
states? ill be back in two days!

I was feeling ridiculously grateful for everything and everyone—
for my grandparents, as always, for EMBRS and Prof. Logan making
this happen, and for this girl, Louise, who would ferry the culmina-
tion of a year's worth of effort to me. I was even grateful for radical
sharing. EMBRS never would have found Louise if she hadn't been
doing her own form of radical sharing. I figured I should try to be more
open, and really it wouldn't do for whatever Meng wanted to give my
grandmother to be lost in the mail, so I asked, contrary to my nature,
if Louise wanted to meet in person. I told her I went to school not far
from Cherry Hill and wanted to thank her properly.

ooh yeah, sounds good! would it be too much
to ask you to come to NJ though? i hate driving
and id make a mess of it with jet lag

I agreed, and it wasn't long before we were setting a date at a frozen
yogurt shop.

Which brings me to today. It wasn't hard to convince Prof. Logan
to lend me his car. I told him the truth: I had been using EMBRS, or
eating our own dog food, as they say in the industry (though Prof.
Logan prefers "drinking our own champagne"), and it had sparked a
connection for me, the potential to reunite my grandmother with
her long-lost cousin, and the only thing stopping me from making
this connection a reality was however would I get to New Jersey? He
practically threw his car keys at me.

"A real-life connection sparked by EMBRS!" he cried. "You must go!"

For better or worse, on the forty-five-minute drive, I was too nervous
about messing up Prof. Logan's car to overthink the upcoming encounter. I relaxed only after I pulled in to the strip mall and saw it had

amazingly wide parking spots. Louise had offered to meet me halfway, said she could get a ride, but I insisted she was the one doing me a favor.

lol you're worse than my parents

I had laughed alone in my dorm room at that.

She was already at the frozen yogurt shop when I arrived, easy to recognize since she was the only other Asian person there. She looked up from her phone when the door opened and broke into a wide smile, standing. She was much taller than I imagined, though really I shouldn't have been surprised, knowing she was on the volleyball team. She had shorter hair than in her profile picture, stopping right above her shoulders. She wore turquoise running shorts and a T-shirt of a band I had never heard of.

We had a good conversation. A really good one, actually, and I'm not sure why that is, given I'm normally not great at conversation. But she was so easy to talk to, open and curious and quick to laugh.

The first thing she insisted on doing was paying for my frozen yogurt.

"You drove all this way," she said. Even when I repeated that she was the one doing me a favor, she ignored me, barreling her way to the register, the teenager manning it happily going along with her demands. As I reluctantly ate my free green tea yogurt, she told me she hated driving, was terrible at it.

"A walking stereotype, I know," she laughed. "Luckily I can walk here. Can't go a mile in Cherry Hill without running into a froyo shop."

Because I was raised by my grandfather, I really could not take her buying my froyo that easily, so I made a fuss that seemed to amuse her, until finally she said:

"Well, there's a favor you can do for me, too. Maybe."

But when I asked her what that might be, she changed the subject.

"Tell me about yourself," she said, eyes bright. "Where do you go to school?"

"A small school outside of Philly," I said, my usual vague answer. Not out of any sense of privacy this time, but because most people had never heard of my school.

"Oh." Her eyes grew real wide. I thought she was about to guess the school. But instead, she said, "Swing state."

"Oh. Yeah."

"Are you registered to vote?"

I told her I had mailed in some form but didn't know what became of it. Which made her face go through all these endearing contortions. Her inner debate was so clear to me: not wanting to come off as pushy but also not willing to relent on something this important.

"I'd encourage you to check," she finally said in a forced light tone.

Amused, I promised her I would. Then I returned her question, asking where she went to school.

"A small school in New Jersey." She winked and I laughed, even though it might've given away that I already knew she went to Princeton, a school everybody has heard of. Grandmother would like her, I thought.

I asked what she studied. Economics, I already knew. But she surprised me.

"I'm thinking of switching majors. I thought econ made sense and was practical and I'd be a big banker or something in New York. Then I changed my mind last semester." When I asked her what she wanted to do now, she clammed up, her eyes wandering.

"I'm not sure how to explain it yet. But I went to Shanghai to get started."

So I asked her what she was doing in Shanghai. Maybe I was too eager, but it was exciting to discover her in real life, this version of herself that did not exist on the internet.

"I wanted to . . ." She shifted again. There was a sudden shyness. "Actually, let me give this to you before I forget."

That was when she gave me the pencil. It was just like the ones I had found in the attic, the wood a striking black. The point wasn't sharp, yet the lead still shone. At the opposite end of the point was a carving of a phoenix, wings raised.

And though the pencil was elegant, I could not help feeling disappointed. I had more tact than to demand if that was it, if really all Meng could think to give grandmother after seventy years apart was a single pencil that was just like the ones she already had in her attic. Instead, I asked if there might've been a note with it. Louise gave me a curious look and said no, it was only the pencil.

I tried to hide my dismay (I'm not totally socially incompetent!), thanked her, and changed the subject, asked how she met Meng in the first place. She said it was through a program that connects older people in Shanghai with those who want to hear and archive their stories. I told her that was amazing. She didn't seem to believe that I meant it, waving her hand and reddening a bit, but I insisted.

I told her about EMBRS. How it was also in the business of connecting people through stories, that it was how I had found her.

"Oh? Is it a dating app?" she asked, which made me flush. I tried to explain that it was a new kind of search engine, a really good one, with more integrations to social media than anything else out there. That one day it would hold our life stories and connect people who did not even know they were looking for connections.

"Oh," she said, and I couldn't tell the emotion behind it at first— skepticism, or wonder? But she continued. "We have quite a bit in common, don't we?"

Thinking back on those words still gives me this silly, fuzzy feeling. I didn't want to linger over this too much, so I made my usual jokes about Prof. Logan, his pitches and cheesy product names, and when she laughed, I felt really, really good. I asked her what Meng was like, and she took her time responding.

"I mean it seems like a cliché to say she's wise, but that's really the best word. And she has a biting wit—she'd always make these snarky comments about what she called my 'elite education.'" She smiled wistfully, and I got the sense that no matter how pleasant our conversation, New Jersey was not where Louise wanted to be right then. She recounted how she and Meng met at a park, how hearing Meng's story made her rethink her own. When she spoke about stories, her eyes glossed over, like she was in a dream.

"Is that what you want to change majors to?" I asked. "Something to do with archiving stories?"

She looked surprised, as if I had unearthed a secret. "Yeah," she admitted. "Which is actually the favor I wanted to ask you. I'd love to interview your grandmother. Do you think she'd be up for it?"

"To archive her story?"

"I guess so." She smiled sheepishly. "Well, I don't really know what I'm doing yet. Let me figure that out first, and then can I reach out to you again?"

"Of course."

I scraped the bottom of my frozen yogurt cup. I regretted not getting more. Not because there was anything special about Cherry Hill frozen yogurt. I just didn't want to leave yet. I wanted to ask her if maybe we could keep in touch even if she didn't figure out her major. Or maybe I could help her figure it out? Even if she didn't want to interview grandmother, she could still come up to Boston before the school year started and meet her and grandfather. In short, I wanted to ask her to be friends, except the lines of our lives were already curving away from each other.

I thanked her again for the yogurt and for the pencil.

"Stop thanking me," she laughed. "It was nothing."

We left the shop, loitering for a bit in the parking lot. I asked if she wanted a ride. She said she'd walk and pointed to the neighborhood across the street, huge houses with two-car garages. All I could do was thank her again for the yogurt.

She laughed again. And when she did, her hand reached out, brushing the inside of my left wrist.

"You'll never forgive me for that, will you?"

My wrist has been tingling ever since.

Back on campus, I've been examining the pencil, hoping it might show me some sort of hidden message. It really is just a pencil, though, from any way I look at it. A nice one, to be sure. But looking at it makes me tired, as if this whole last year of searching is finally catching up to me. Maybe it wasn't worth it.

Grandfather would say to look at the bright side, to think of the journey not the destination, etc. So I guess without the search I never would have gotten the chance to work with Prof. Logan or EMBRS and certainly never would have learned so much about how to build resilient data pipelines. And I met someone new, someone nice, someone I hope I'll see again. And most importantly, in a few days, I'll be going home to see grandmother and grandfather, and to celebrate another year of her life.

So maybe it's a good thing, for it to have ended in this ambiguous way. Part of me feared what I might learn about grandmother, what this rift between her and Meng might reveal. That she might become something other than the unfailingly supportive grandmother who walked me to my bus stop in the worst Boston snowstorms, patiently taught me Chinese even when I was a brat about learning it, and who held me after my father left and said over and over that she was here and she always would be.

So, it's not all disappointment. Still, I was really hoping for more than a pencil.

CHAPTER 2

From the Reforged pencil of Wong Yun

*R*ight now, my words course through your veins.

    I spent a long time this morning looking at your picture. It's been more than seventy years since the last time we saw each other, sixty years since we knew each other's stories. Monica, my granddaughter, found you. To be honest, I did not expect her to succeed. Hoped maybe she wouldn't, even. But she's an awfully determined girl with a knack for bending computers to her will—and while it might be our shared history, I know you and I told ourselves different versions of the same truth, and now that I have a thread back to you, I can no longer delay explaining myself.

    I want to ask for your forgiveness, and I need you to understand how I perceived the world we grew up in, our world of wars and betrayals and pencils.

    In the picture Monica sent, you were small as always, even if your back has not hunched as mine has. Legs dangling off a bench, modern-day Shanghai sprawled out behind you, shining buildings along the waterfront. Not far from where we grew up, no? Remarkable, how you remained in place, while I bounced around the world. I would have thought it impossible that day you and your mother arrived, that I would be the one to leave home while you stayed behind in the city you claimed to hate.

The only memories I have from before you are in swabs of gray. There was the time my father left for war, everything in harsh dark lines, the outline of his shoulders as he tried to embrace Mother and she turned away, back to her machines. There was the smoky haze of my grandmother's room, where I attempted to find comfort and found only the sweet smell of her drugged exhalations—and then there was the pencil company, churning away under the guidance of Mother's ever-steady hand. Her once white smock covered in dark fingerprints, her fingernails always black.

Then you and your mother arrived, in a flash of green, the first color I remember seeing and thinking beautiful. I thought you were the most glamorous people I had ever seen. We lived in the International Settlement in Shanghai, which, in 1937, was still the home of foreigners and expats and some of the wealthiest people in China. Glamour was not new to me, yet it was striking to see it up close on a woman who so resembled Mother. Your mother was younger than mine, always the elegant one. She wore a high-collared emerald qipao with gold threads woven throughout that formed floral patterns around the shoulders, bordering the slit at the bottom that hinted at her long legs. You wore a smaller version made from the same fabric. I stared at your dress longingly, at your hair that was styled after your mother's, thick and upright and voluminous, while mine grew long and limp. The two of you looked like you had walked out of a mahjong game with elite friends. Not like you had fled a war zone into Shanghai's winter.

You glared at me. I imagined you were disappointed with our living arrangements, having heard about the magnificence of the city, only to find yourself living behind a pencil factory. I wanted to disappear into Mother's smock. She pushed me forward and made me introduce myself. You did not meet my eyes when you said your name.

We all sat around the kitchen table that night. You held your chopsticks elegantly, picking the grains of rice into your mouth.

"I want that one," you said when I reached for a tofu puff glistening in a mixture of soy sauce and sugar. Ah-shin, our helper, had only prepared three, not expecting more than my grandmother, mother, and me. I never had to share before. It was the first time you looked into my eyes.

I brought the tofu puff into my bowl. Neither of us broke eye contact as I sank my teeth into it, letting the soy sauce dribble down my chin.

You slammed your chopsticks down on the table.

"I want to go home," you told your mother. There was no mistaking the tears in your eyes.

"That's not an option," your mother said.

"Give the other half to Meng," Mother ordered, pointing with her chopsticks at the half I had left in my bowl. I regretted not eating the whole thing at once.

You did not thank me before shoveling down the rest of your food.

It was like this for what seemed like years at our young age. Each of us prowling around the other, deeply jealous. I wanted your elegance, apparent even at the age of ten, and you wanted my stability, how I had never had to move in my entire life. I knew Shanghai and could without hesitation call it home. We were so absorbed in the war we were waging against each other that we were completely oblivious to the one right outside, dropping bombs around our city.

In Monica's American history textbooks, the war does not begin until 1941, with Pearl Harbor. But for us it began a decade earlier when Japan invaded Manchuria. By the time you came to Shanghai, Japan had been ruthlessly cutting through China for six years. Luckily, we were insulated from much of the violence, thanks to the International Settlement.

Whether the Japanese did not want to anger the English, the French, the Americans who lived there with us, or were simply biding their time for another invasion, we had no idea. But for a few years at least, we lived a relatively normal life.

Your mother insisted we go out and enjoy the safety of the Settlement, that she had heard so much about Shanghai and we had to show her around. My own mother rarely took me anywhere since Japan had taken over the surrounding districts. But that first week, we visited the largest department store in the city.

Inside, the salespeople flocked to your mother, holding pearls to her ears, lengths of silk to her torso, begging her to buy a custom-made qipao. She laughed and, because she could not speak Shanghainese, declined with brisk waves of her hand. She admired the French cloche hats, the Scotch whiskies, the German cameras, the American lipstick. You hated how busy it was, everybody buying and selling with a frenetic air, fueled by the war right across the river, by the knowledge that the Settlement could fall any day.

But as much as you disliked the store, outside was even worse. Nanking Road was the busiest shopping street in the Settlement. Rickshaws mixed with motorcycles mixed with coolies hoisting bamboo poles over their shoulders, buckets of anything from live chickens to vegetables swaying on either end—and everybody had to make way for trucks and automobiles carrying the wealthy foreigners in their silk suits to their mansions along the river. You clung to your mother as I made a show of pretending I was accustomed to this bustling life. Peddlers shoved pastries and tea beneath our noses. One even had your mother halfway into a chair, ready to give her a haircut, before my mother told him off in Shanghainese.

That same day, we visited the Bund, the waterfront lined with foreign buildings, a mix of columns, domes, clock towers, murals.

"Why are these here?" you asked, one of the few things you said all day.

"What do you mean?" That it was unusual for there to be a motley of European architecture in our Chinese city had never even occurred to me. We were in front of the HSBC bank, your mother admiring the columned entranceway, the huge white dome, the glimpses of the murals inside showing all the other cities where the bank operated.

"It doesn't feel like home," you said, and I was peeved at you for rejecting what I thought of as our nicest view.

But you did not notice my annoyance. You were fixated on the two bronze lion statues flanking the bank's entrance. Their paws had been rubbed to a shine by the many visitors wishing for luck, or to be made as rich as the bank owners. You approached one of the lions. It loomed above you on its pedestal. You reached as high as you could to tap its paw. I was close enough to hear you whisper a desperate wish to return home.

Your mother soon registered you for the same elementary school as me, much to my disappointment. But when you sat in the classroom, only a few desks away, I discovered I had a clear advantage over you: you did not speak Shanghainese, whereas I had grown up with it. You stumbled in your responses to our classmates, and we all giggled when you gave a wrong answer.

I doodled a picture of you. This, I am sure, you remember. It started accurate and then I distorted it. Over your lips, I drew slight protrusions of your front teeth. I erased the line where your head started and moved it farther up, almost off the page, elongating your forehead and shading in bushy eyebrows. I gave you a speech bubble with nonsense characters. The girl who sat behind me stifled a laugh and held out her hand. I passed my drawing to her, and before long it had circulated the classroom behind the teacher's back.

When it reached your desk, you did not lift the paper, only cast your eyes downward. Then your eyes found mine, and for a moment it seemed like the classroom disappeared, its giggling students and droning teacher along with it, and it was only me and you and a fury that pulsed.

I thought you would run home right after school and report me to our mothers. Instead, you waited for me by the school entrance. I fell in step with you, maintaining a small distance, wary of your calm.

"You draw well," you said in our mothers' dialect. "What kind of pencil do you use?"

"The eighty:twenty for sketches," I answered slowly. I had never talked to anyone other than Mother about pencil compositions before. But you were from the same line of pencil makers, so I did not shy away from the technical clay-to-graphite ratio.

"Can I see?"

I opened my bag, my box of pencils. I had every type, each for a different purpose. The shortest by far was the 80:20, which I had used for my caricature. I handed it to you.

You twirled it between your fingers. I tried not to admire how you handled it, how it flitted through your fingers, frictionless.

"Do you mind if I try it out?"

"Oh. Sure."

You pocketed my pencil.

That night in our shared room, I crawled through my mosquito net into my bed. The last I had seen of you, you were at the front of the complex, watching Mother guide the machines to press the wood that would encase the pencil hearts.

I was almost asleep when the door slammed open.

"Yun."

I bolted upright. Mother's voice in such a tone always made me do so. Through the mosquito net, she was dark and distorted. You an outline behind her.

"Mother?" I asked tentatively, pulling aside the netting.

She turned on the light and held a piece of paper in front of her like a wanted poster. I was not surprised to see my caricature of you, complete with buckteeth and large forehead and frothing gibberish. But the shape of the drawing unsettled me. My lines had been light, the way only an 80:20 pencil can convey, fleeting and carefree, a thoughtless doodle to stave off boredom in class. In the drawing before me, the lines were dark and thick and *dripping*, as if someone had taken a calligraphy brush and outlined my caricature, then hung it up and let the ink bleed down. Your face became a mess, a facade where teeth dripped into chin and ears I had not distorted drooped.

"What is that?" I asked, only to wince at the click of Mother's tongue.

"Do not act like you do not know."

"That is not my drawing," I said honestly.

"Not the original," you said quietly.

"Maybe someone at school drew it," I tried to reason. "There are always people trying to copy my doodles."

"How about this one?" Mother held up another piece of paper. It unfurled into the doodle I had made the day before, of the math teacher. I had even gone and signed my name at the bottom. Yet this one, too, had nearly the same dripping distortion.

"Yes, but also no—"

"You will defend Meng as if she were your sister," Mother interrupted. "If I learn you have made another one of these drawings, I will disown you and send you straight to the Japanese."

I barely knew about any threat from the Japanese at the time, the war still a rumor to my sheltered mind. But I understood the tremble in her voice. She was angry beyond the point of even physical punishment, and so I knew the threat must be terrible.

"How did you—?" I braved, desperately wanting to know how they could have recreated my drawings in this manner.

Mother turned sharply away, so different from her standard gentle manner. You remained standing in front of your bed, staring at me. I lay back down, pulled the blanket over me in a loud dramatic effort, and turned my back to you. I heard you move, then the unmistakable sound of a pencil rolling.

I peered over the side of my bed and grabbed it.

It was my own, the 80:20 I had lent you hours before. But there was something wrong with it; the weight wasn't right. In the dark, I ran my fingers over it, felt the familiar embellished phoenix logo at the top. When I reached the tip, I realized the point was missing. I pressed my finger against where it should have been and found the beginning of a hole. The heart of the pencil was missing.

I dropped it back on the floor with a clatter.

"Don't mess with me," you whispered in perfect Shanghainese.

I was in awe.

As punishment for my bullying, every night for a month, Mother lit a stick of incense in our room and forced me to hold a chair raised above my head, while you watched to ensure I did not set it down before the incense burned out. You complained it was punishment for you, too, to have to hang around me, though neither of our mothers listened or cared. During this time, I was supposed to speak to you in Shanghainese to help you with your pronunciation.

The problem was that, by then, you did not need help. You picked up the language quickly. You spent this time taunting me.

"You don't know the first thing about pencils, do you?" you asked, dangling your legs off your bed while I stared past you, arms straining against the chair, determined not to show any weakness.

"I know I'm good at using them," I retorted.

Your hands went instinctively to your forehead. I would feel bad about that much later, when you made an effort to always wear hats or grow out your bangs. The buckteeth I had completely made up for the cartoon. The large forehead was only a slight exaggeration of the truth.

"But you don't *really* know about pencils."

I ignored the goading comment.

"Our pencil company was much bigger than yours," you sighed, falling back onto your bed.

I took a chance and lowered the chair slightly when you looked away, hiding the fact that I had not known there was another pencil company. No wonder your mother had been able to step into her role so quickly.

"That's only because there's more room in the countryside. Not like here." Shanghai was becoming more and more crowded every day. The International Settlement especially so. You and I were not allowed to leave each other's sights on the walk to school. Our mothers made us practice bowing, which we had to do anytime we passed a Japanese soldier.

"It was my mother's idea to expand the company to Shanghai," you boasted.

"Then why didn't she do it?"

Your face fell.

"My father didn't want her to. He said Shanghai was full of crime and foreigners who don't let the Chinese even use their own parks. He wanted to stay where we were." You brought your knees to your chest. "I wish we could have stayed there."

"Oh." I lowered the chair a bit more. "What happened to your father?"

"He joined the war."

"Mine too. What was yours like?"

"He was always reading. Especially Russian novels. He wanted China to have a revolution like Russia's."

"My father also wanted a stronger China," I said. "He called the old dynasty a tumor."

You looked at me. I quickly raised the chair back up.

"I won't tell if you put the chair down," you offered.

I dropped it in relief. Before it even hit the floor, you yelled for my mother.

"Yun stopped holding the chair!" you cried, dashing to open the door. I was so shocked I did not think to pick the chair back up. Mother came, and I was still standing there speechless.

Mother lit a new stick of incense and waited for me to raise the chair over my head again. She closed the door behind her without a single word.

"Are we even now?" I snapped as you smiled triumphantly.

"No. You embarrassed me in front of the whole school." You took a moment to inhale and savor the incense. "But we are closer to even now."

As much as you and I disliked each other, we reluctantly found common ground. We were the same age, we both loved pencils, and we both, when suddenly confronted with our aunts—each other's mothers—began to idolize them.

Your mother fit into the decadence of the city in a way I found irresistible. Though she had arrived with only a few belongings, she quickly restocked her wardrobe, her French perfumes, her American cigarettes. She styled her own hair, showing me how she tucked and curled it, so it hugged her neckline perfectly. I helped her clasp her qipao, treating each small nub like a pearl. She found other women from her hometown, who spoke her dialect. It was not hard, in Shanghai, where people from every part of China were fleeing. They formed a mahjong group. She tried to convince Mother to join, but like you, Mother preferred to remain at home.

Despite her extravagant weekends, on the weekdays, your mother rose early and got right to work at the front of the pencil company. It was not until she came that I developed an interest in these operations. She stood at the storefront, directing customers to our samples, laughing with them even if she could not completely communicate with them. I used that as my excuse to sit beside her, to translate as needed, mostly to admire her charm.

Behind us was a wall of pencil hearts, dotted lines against brick. Each heart was made of a different ratio of graphite to clay, lending it a distinct softness and therefore darkness. The wall was arranged from lightest in the top right corner, to darkest in the bottom left, creating a gentle gradient. Your mother would ask the customers what they were looking for in a pencil. The Russian bodyguards wanted dark hearts, the rich students wanted thin tips and lots of them, the gang members wanted the most intricate casings, the Japanese businessmen wanted the logo removed, and your mother's socialite friends wanted light, elegant ones to use for their invitations. Your mother would close her eyes and nod thoughtfully, hand on her chin, subtly showing off a jeweled ring, then turn and delicately select a few pencil hearts. I would slide each one into a temporary casing to mimic the wood that might eventually encase it. The customer would write something, usually their name. They would try a few, make observations, and almost always order a set of their favorite, smiling happily at your mother.

You, meanwhile, took to observing my mother in the room right behind us. With your mother at the front, my mother could finally focus on what she loved—the actual crafting of the pencils. You sat quietly as Mother mixed different graphite and clay mixtures, sent them into the kiln to harden. Only a few days after you came to live with us, she gave you the delicate task of carving the phoenix into the ends of each finished one.

Because most of the complex was used for the company, our rooms were small and there were only three of them. My grandmother had the largest, farthest from the workshop. Our mothers shared the one closest to the workshop, which left the smallest, middle room for us. Sometimes we could hear my grandmother's coughs through the wall, or the crinkle of the newspaper when she flipped a page. On the other side, our mothers kept their voices low, though like you and me, they often clashed.

"Will you keep her in the dark forever, then?" your mother's voice rang.

I could not hear Mother's reply. You shifted in the bed across from mine.

"You have a duty the same way Mother had to us," your mother continued. She wanted us to hear. My mother spoke quickly in hushed tones, clearly trying to end the conversation.

"What are they talking about?" I whispered. You shifted again. I understood it meant for me to be quiet.

"Our power is not one to leave alone," your mother said, her voice rising at the end of the sentence.

"Silence," Mother ordered. I shivered, hugging my blanket closer. I had never heard her raise her voice like that. She was the eldest, but until then, it always seemed like your mother was the one in control.

Your mother quieted down after that. Still, she had succeeded. I could not let the topic go.

"What was that about?" I asked you urgently. It had something to do with the drawings they had shown me, replicas of my own. That you knew and I did not infuriated me more than anything my mother could have done.

To my surprise, you answered my question.

"There is a power in the pencils made by the Phoenix Pencil Company," you said. "And we have the ability to unleash it."

"What's the power?" I asked, desperate to understand.

"I can't tell you."

"Please tell me. I'll draw a better picture of you. You're so pretty, do you know that? That's why I was mean to you. I was jealous. I won't do it again."

"I'm sorry," you said. "I don't understand it, and I'm not allowed to tell you anything about it."

"Why not? Who said that?"

"My mother said if I do, we will get kicked out. And then where would we go?" We frequently walked past the warehouses and movie theaters that had recently been converted to refugee housing, seen more than enough people sleeping on the streets while the foreigners'

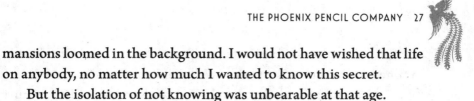

mansions loomed in the background. I would not have wished that life on anybody, no matter how much I wanted to know this secret.

But the isolation of not knowing was unbearable at that age.

"I'll give you a hint," you said. "But then I really can't say more."

You padded over, and I felt your weight on the edge of my mattress. There would come a day when we camped out freely on each other's beds without a second thought, but that was the first time you came so close. In the dark, you guided my hand to your forearm. I felt the lines—long, thin scars—that traveled to the crook of your elbow. They looped and intertwined. I shivered, my body recognizing it before my mind caught up, a buried memory, one from when my father left and I had held Mother's arm, wormed my hand beneath her sleeve, and she let me run my fingers over the strange pattern on her arm—and there it was on you, too.

"How?" I whispered.

My grandmother let out a violent cough. You retreated to your bed, the warmth of your arm against my fingertips gone.

I ran my hand over my own smooth arm. It was a cold night. I pulled the blankets closer, my body curling in on itself, wondering what it was that I was missing, how my exclusion could be branded into my skin.

Like Mother, I have kept the truth of the pencils a secret. Monica does not know. I can see you shaking your head—after how desperately I wanted the truth back then, how can I not tell her, when I have so thoroughly felt the sting of isolation? But Monica is different from me. She has never thought to ask about the pencils. Why would she when her world is digital? And if I don't tell her, the secret might die with us. Would that not be for the best? Or am I just setting myself up for missing a chance for the two of us to understand each other a little better?

There is one more thing I have not told her. She returns home tomorrow, and I cannot be more excited or more anxious to see her. It wasn't that we intended to keep it a secret. The diagnosis came shortly after she left for her summer internship, and it wasn't the sort of thing I wanted to share over the phone. We'll tell her when she gets home, I told Torou, who agreed, perhaps the only person less willing to hurt Monica than me.

The doctor says consistent mental stimulation might help slow the disease's progress—and it turns out a convenient side effect is that your earliest memories become the clearest. So really, my writing this to you isn't only for you. It's for me as well, to cling to something. And maybe, in a way, it can be for her, too.

CHAPTER 3

From the diary of Monica Tsai,
backed up on five servers spanning
three continents

August 18, 2018 (2018-08-18T16:34:08.192273)
loc: Cambridge, Massachusetts. United States of America
(42.3721865,71.1117091)

It's been a difficult day.

When I got off the bus, they were waiting for me. Two slight, hunched-over people, sitting at the food court, sharing a small order of french fries. He was squeezing a packet of ketchup while she wiped her mouth with a napkin. Grandmother was in a neat, collared shirt and long tan pants. Grandfather, despite the heat, wore a formal shirt and vest with a tie, like always. When grandmother saw me, her eyes crinkled and she smiled widely, perfect denture-teeth flashing.

I hugged her first. She barely came to my shoulder and felt so frail in my arms. I told them they didn't have to pick me up, even though I was pleased that they did.

"Grandfather was upset we hadn't used our senior transit passes this month," she explained. While I hugged grandfather, she pushed the fries over to the third empty seat.

I sat down in front of a freshly squeezed mound of ketchup. The familiar sight triggered something in me.

"Oh, 寶貝, why are you crying?" grandmother asked, stroking the hair out of my eyes.

I blinked hard.

"Was the bus ride okay?" grandfather asked.

"It's been a long day for you," grandmother said.

"We made Russian soup. We'll have some when we get home." Though they called it Russian soup, really it was a Shanghainese adaptation of borscht. It was the only way they could get me to eat my vegetables when I was a kid.

I managed to say I was fine and obediently brought a fry to my mouth.

"Let's go home," grandmother said lightly. She poured the rest of the fries back into the bag they had come in. Grandfather threw the extra ketchup packets in too.

We took the train out of Boston and into Cambridge. The sight of the sailboats on the river nearly wrecked me, such a perfect summer sight, a reminder that I wasn't there to take them kayaking for grandfather's birthday or even to upgrade their computer's antivirus. Grandfather noticed my mood. He has this philosophy: the best thing to do when you're sad is to learn something. Or better yet, to teach something.

So he asked me to tell him about my favorite coding pattern that I had used over the summer. I told him about the abstract base class I implemented to work with all the different social media site integrations. He practically purred, and I really did feel better after that.

When we got home, grandfather heated up the soup. Grandmother came with me to my room, insisted on helping me unpack.

I threw my bag onto my bed. The smell of the sheets, that familiar wildflower detergent, the thought of grandmother hauling laundry up and down the stairs just so I would have a freshly made bed to come home to—no, even thinking about it now is going to make me tear up again.

I brought out my carefully bundled hoodie and unwrapped it, handing her the pencil that had traveled so far.

"I guess it's just a pencil," I said, hoping she would not be too disappointed.

To my surprise, she barely reacted. She set it aside, then sat down on my bed. She pulled a shirt out of my bag and began refolding it from its crumpled mess.

"What do you think the pencil means?" I attempted.

She glanced briefly at it.

"I'm not sure yet."

"I'm sorry it isn't anything more."

Then she gave me this surprised look. It took her a moment to reply.

"Oh, no. It means the world to me." She squeezed my hand but would not look me in the eyes. "Really, it does. Thank you."

And so that was the anticlimactic end to my search. It was hard to be totally unsatisfied, since she later did take the pencil, look it over, and bring it to her room. Maybe it means something to her that I don't need to know, and that's okay, I can live with that. It was good to be home, to enjoy a meal with them. The Russian soup had stewed long enough for the tomato flavor to meld with the oxtail, and grandfather had splurged on hand-pulled noodles. It was a perfect dinner.

"Arby's this week, right?" I asked. I started looking through grandmother's coupon pile to find her favorite.

They exchanged a glance, and that's when I should have known something was wrong. But grandmother was so smooth in her response that I totally bought it.

"I think ninety-one might be too old for Arby's," she said. "Too much sodium, and I already had those fries today."

I found the coupon and tacked it onto the refrigerator, right next to the picture of me from second grade Halloween. "We'll have to do something else, then."

"Another dinner of noodles. For longevity," grandfather said, and I could not complain.

That night, full of warm soup, I lay on my childhood bed, staring at my phone. My mind drifted to Louise again, replaying our conversation, wondering what she would think of grandmother's reaction to Meng's pencil. Was there anything I could tell her now? I suddenly remembered to check my voter registration status. I took a breath and texted her.

confirmed voter registration! ✅

Her reply came immediately.

excellent!! how was the trip back to boston?

I smiled. A part of me had worried she'd brush me off, that our lives were done intersecting. Instead she opened the conversation up to talk about not pencils or Shanghai or grandmother or Meng, but me.

not bad! grandparents came to the station to meet me. felt a bit like I was back in elementary school getting picked up from the bus stop. but it was v cute

Again, another quick reply.

ahhh too cute! bet they made you food too

I grinned.

and there were fresh sheets! how's princeton?

so you do know where i go to school!

My cheeks burned. I almost tossed the phone away. I forgot I had feigned not knowing. I tried to salvage my dignity.

I noticed it in your profile today

only today? you didnt research everything
about me before we met?

I could easily lie. Was she upset? Had she somehow figured out I had thoroughly searched her name before meeting her? It shouldn't have been possible—I knew that much about internet privacy. Still, I panicked.

id expect more from a cs major at swat

I managed to relax, even smile. She was teasing. I could not avoid having my name listed on the department website, though I like to think the rest of my internet presence is low.

As I tried to think of a reply, a light knock came from my bedroom door. I stuffed the phone under my pillow. I expected it to be grandmother, the lighter sleeper. I thought maybe I lucked out, that she wanted to talk about Meng and the pencil.

Instead, it was grandfather in his pale cotton pajamas, his hands behind his back. His pure white hair stuck up at the end. He had at least made a show of sleeping.

"I need to tell you something," he said. I sat up on my bed. He came to sit next to me, just as grandmother had earlier in the day.

I did not say anything. A fear had crept into me, one I did not know he could cause. I had heard him roar at my father and be stern with grandmother, but never had his voice reached any level of severity with me. Grandmother scolded me more than he ever did. His grim tone brought back the memory of that time he told me my father was leaving and from then on it would only be me, him, and grandmother.

For a moment we both stared at the opposite wall, the window with its pink shades drawn. The bookshelf's bottom row full of thin Chinese books, the ones grandmother used to read to help me fall asleep. When I was young, she would lie on a cot in my room, holding the book above her, while I curled on my side watching her. Back then I had a small, netted barrier that ran along the side of my bed to prevent me from falling off in the middle of the night. I would watch her through the mesh netting, holding the book close to her face, her glasses lying beside her, telling me stories in the language of her home.

I already knew whatever grandfather would say was about her.

"Grandmother is sick," he said. He cleared his throat. His hands were clasped together over his lap, his back hunched.

"With what?" I asked before even processing the news.

He said something, but I did not understand the phrase. Diseases and illnesses were fortunately not part of the Chinese I had learned while living with them.

"She is losing her memory," he clarified. "It will get worse."

"Since when?"

"We first suspected in the spring. The doctor didn't confirm until the summer, when you were gone. They can't diagnose this kind of thing. They can only tell you what it is not."

"So it's not really a confirmation, then."

He glanced at me with sad eyes.

"Today was a good day for her. Many days are good. Some days are bad. The doctor says the progression varies. I think it was a good day for her today because you were here."

"You could have told me. I would have come home."

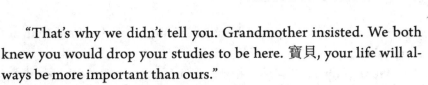

"That's why we didn't tell you. Grandmother insisted. We both knew you would drop your studies to be here. 寶貝, your life will always be more important than ours."

"No it won't." I brought my knees to my chest, hugged them close.

"You should be glad you stayed at school. Otherwise, you wouldn't have found Meng."

My eyes blurred.

"But . . ." I did not have the words. They had been so careful about maintaining their physical health. How unfair that her mind would betray her when it was so quick, so good at learning and adapting.

"How are you feeling?" I asked.

The question surprised him. I was grateful he didn't brush it off and insist he was fine, grateful he seriously considered his own well-being.

"Well. I feel a bit like how you might feel coding. You've felt it, haven't you?" He was hovering somewhere between his grandfather voice and his professor voice. "How desperate you get when you're refactoring and breaking the problem down into smaller pieces and the computer still refuses to understand. How very human and small you feel then."

I knew the feeling well. I grabbed hold of his hand. If I said anything, I knew I'd cry, so I held it together, for both of us.

"Is that why no Arby's?" I asked eventually.

He nodded.

"She says it's too far. She's been getting nervous whenever she is far from home."

"But you went to the train station to get me today."

"She insisted."

And I felt horrible all over again. The things she would do for me, if not for herself.

"You will see her writing," he said. "She is trying to write something for Meng, before she forgets. You've given her something to hold on to."

"But even if we can get her and Meng to meet, she might not remember."

"Her family has always relied more on written words than talk."

I could not think of anything else to say.

"Sleep for now," he said gently. "We can speak more tomorrow. You must be tired."

When I was alone, I turned off the lights and fell back onto my bed, staring up at the ceiling where the glow-in-the-dark stars grandfather had helped me arrange years ago no longer glowed. They were just pale bumps against white paint. I felt like a lost network packet. I'm on my way from one server to another carrying my little bit of precious information, then suddenly the path is severed, perhaps by a bad internet connection, and I'm left floating, my destination once so well defined, gone. No one thinks about these lost network packets because it's easy to replace them, to send another identical packet out until the server on the other end replies, yes, Monica packet received, we've got her information. I never thought about them before either. But that's what I felt like now with the world continuing on as I drifted through cyberspace.

I thought about how difficult their summer must have been. How grandfather had gone through it alone, one small human, and how grandmother—

But I could not let myself think about what grandmother might be thinking, what she must be going through, how her world had become suddenly, irrevocably, disoriented.

The ceiling unblurred as I finally let the tears roll away. I was filled with a sudden aversion for myself, the kid who had spent the past few months blissfully unaware while the most important people in her life suffered.

I pulled out my phone, more out of habit than anything else. I blinked at the messages. I had forgotten I had been midconversation with Louise.

swat isnt far, maybe we can hang out again

And after a break:

hey i didnt mean to be creepy earlier! sorry if i
came off that way

I tried to recall my earlier giddiness and came up empty. In the end,
I went with the only thing on my mind.

sorry for the delay. my grandfather just
told me my grandmother has alzheimer's

Three small circles bubbled—her typing. I imagined the tapping of
her fingers on her phone syncing with the beating of my heart.

oh fuck

I could not think of more appropriate words.

CHAPTER 4

From the Reforged pencil of Wong Yun

Monica has returned home. We prepared all her favorite foods: beef noodle soup, stir-fried peapod stems, soy milk, steamed shrimp, lion's head meatballs, red braised pork with tofu. All food that is too rich for us now. It gave us somewhere to channel our anxiety. After all, she is not coming home to good news. The least we could do was provide her some comfort.

I don't know if you ended up having children. Torou hasn't truly talked to our son, Edward, since he left, which was over a decade ago now. Even when Edward returns, the two of them avoid each other, meeting at the dining table, passing cursory words between them. Torou hated how Edward's leaving impacted Monica, only eight years old at the time. I did too, though not to the same extent. After all, you and I grew up largely without our fathers.

You met my father around what must have been 1939. You had been staying with us for a year by then, and our family had started to adjust to

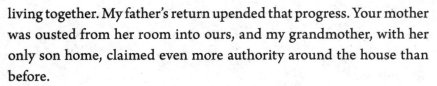

living together. My father's return upended that progress. Your mother was ousted from her room into ours, and my grandmother, with her only son home, claimed even more authority around the house than before.

It was the first time I had seen my father in seven years. More than half my life had passed before he showed up, a stranger. He had been part of the war effort in a nearby province when it was captured by the Japanese. He escaped and snuck back into Shanghai, where he awaited orders from the underground network.

Of my father's job, I understood little. Looking back, I see this was on purpose, for his role had been a dangerous one in the intelligence division. He was to gather as much information as he could on Japanese tactics, using whatever means necessary. In other words, he was a spy.

He hadn't always been a spy. First he was a doctor. He left for the war in the early days, when Japan first marched into China's northeast in 1931. He was part of an aid effort. I remember him hugging me fiercely, smelling of tobacco and pomade, before he hopped onto the back of an ambulance that pushed its way through the crowd.

Where my mother was small and timid, my father was tall and loud. He always wore a Rolex watch, but it was missing when he arrived. He had been forced to pawn it on his way back. He had to sneak past all sorts of Japanese checkpoints, and apparently had been caught at one, only to bribe his way out when the soldier took an interest in his watch. He asked me to buy him a new one. His good luck charm, he called it. It was too dangerous for him to leave the house though. Our area was technically safe from the laws the Japanese imposed on the rest of the city, but we were not immune from the thriving gang scene. Gangsters who had thrown their lot in with the occupiers would have had no qualms crossing the International Settlement border and turning in enemy soldiers.

"How long will you stay?" I asked. He remained in Mother's room all day, the curtains drawn, out of sight of the neighbors.

He was writing a letter at his desk with one of our pencils. He chewed on the end of it, his teeth biting into the phoenix carving.

"Not long," he said, readjusting his new watch. "Ready for your next mission?"

He handed me the letter folded into one long rectangle. I ran to the front of the house where Mother sat working the kiln. She rummaged through her boxes of completed pencils before finding one with the surname Gao printed across it.

She opened the box, lifted the tray inside that held eight custom pencils, then slipped the letter in.

"Mr. Gao lives in the French Concession," she said. "Ask him to send his reply in pencil. Do not ask him any other questions."

Normally, I would have taken my bicycle, which had a basket attached that Mother had made for me. It was perfect for holding boxes of pencils. But my father did not think it proper for girls to ride bicycles. That, and the city was becoming increasingly cramped. More and more, Mother told me to take the tram, sometimes even a rickshaw. I would stare out the window, vaguely aware that each morning corpses were being carted off the streets, out of the city.

Mr. Gao lived on a tree-lined cobblestone street, Rue something or other, in an apartment with beautifully arched windows, typical of the French Concession. His house was larger than ours, and not far from the only other landmark I knew in the area, the former residence of Sun Yat-sen, who overthrew the Qing dynasty two decades earlier.

"Delivery from the Phoenix Pencil Company," I recited when he opened the door, holding out the box of pencils with both hands.

"Thank you," Mr. Gao said. He was young, wore a high-collared suit with his hair carefully slicked back. If he had not had such a serious expression, I would have thought him handsome. Instead, his severity made me straighten, speak clearly and formally.

"How is your mother doing?" he asked.

"Very well, thank you for asking."

"And your grandmother?"

"Very well as well, thank you."

He pulled out an envelope with his payment. I pocketed it quickly.

"My mother says you can reply in pencil," I added, though I did not know what that meant.

He raised an eyebrow.

"Will you wait out here for a minute?"

"Yes, sir."

He closed the door. I planned to read whatever response Mr. Gao sent for my father on the tram ride. I wondered if Mr. Gao was his employer or a colleague. Back then, I still thought my father a doctor, and so I assumed Mr. Gao was one, too. I hoped the letter would say my father did not have to return to the war, that he could stay in Shanghai with us. After all, there were more than enough people in the city who needed medical attention.

But when Mr. Gao opened the door again, he did not hand me a letter. He handed me one of our pencils, a long, barely used one, at that.

"Tell your mother I send her the very best of fortunes," he said with a bow, then closed the door, leaving me with just a pencil.

I puzzled over the pencil on the tram and why he would send Mother one of the pencils I had just delivered. Did it mean he was rejecting whatever my father had asked of him? Or was there something more to my mother's message to reply in pencil? I flicked it a few times, weighing it in my hand, to see if maybe Mr. Gao had removed the heart and slipped a letter inside. But it was a true pencil.

"Mr. Gao sends his very best of fortunes," I told Mother when I returned home.

"Did he give you anything?" she asked, glancing up from where she was overseeing the heart-hardening process.

I handed over his envelope of money. She took it and flipped through, not counting the bills, looking for something.

"Anything else?" she asked.

"I don't think so," I lied. "Did you expect something else?"

"A reply to your father's letter."

"Mr. Gao didn't give me a letter."

"Did he give you a pencil?"

My breath caught. So she did expect a pencil, and there was a secret inside it! I gripped the pencil hidden up my sleeve. Somehow, it would be linked to whatever secret she was keeping from me, the one that you knew, the one that your mother wanted me to know.

"Why would he give me a pencil?" I asked, heart hammering.

Mother frowned.

"Never mind. Go check Meng's accounting."

I ran off as quickly as I could with my secret pencil.

The day after I visited Mr. Gao, a policeman came in for a pencil fitting. Our whole family was wary of the police. Many of them cooperated with the local gangs or, after the turn of the war, aided the Japanese in their control of the city. With my father hidden in the back room, it was an especially dangerous time for a policeman to visit.

Luckily, he was only interested in your mother, who did an awe-inspiring job entertaining him. I handed her different pencil hearts, and she slipped them into their temporary casings. He barely looked at what he wrote, commenting on your mother's beauty in Shanghainese. She either did not understand or pretended not to, continued showing him the pencil hearts until he finally waved at a few and ordered two sets of eight. While dialects could be drastically different, the written language was standardized, and so, after finalizing the purchase, the man took one of the sample pencils and wrote a note to your mother. I craned my head to see it, but she quickly folded the note away, her cheeks flushed. He left with a smirk.

"What did he write?" I asked after the door closed.

"He wrote to say all twelve-year-olds should mind their own business," she replied without missing a beat, then sent me to arrange the samples back on their shelves.

"Are you going to see him again?" I persisted even as I deftly completed my task.

"No, of course not. I am married."

I huffed. I had never met your father and could not imagine any man was good enough for your mother. At least the policeman seemed rich.

When nearly half an hour passed without another customer, I pulled out the pencil I had received from Mr. Gao.

"Is that yours?" she asked skeptically. The pencils that were left for me never looked quite this nice. I was only allowed the battered ones that did not pass quality control.

"No," I said under my breath. "The person I delivered a set of pencils to yesterday gave it to me. I was supposed to give it to my parents."

"And why didn't you?" she asked, her voice steady, eyes penetrating.

"Because I want to know what everyone is keeping from me," I said without breaking eye contact. She had the same eyes as you, and I had stared you down plenty of times. "There's something about this pencil, isn't there? Some sort of message, but I can't figure out how, and Meng won't tell me—"

"It is not for her to say."

"Then would you tell me?"

"It is not for me to say either."

"Why not?" I had viewed her as the one who would enlighten me, the one on my side, and now felt betrayed.

She took the pencil from me and hid it. She glanced at the rear door before turning back to me.

"Your grandmother does not want your mother to tell you."

"My grandmother?" I repeated, startled. It had seemed like a secret between my mother, aunt, and you. It hurt even more that my grandmother was involved.

"Yes. And your mother cannot go against your grandmother." She scoffed. "She can barely go against me. Your grandmother's rules are as good as law here. Meng and I stay here because she allows it. I can't risk that. I'm sorry, Yun. If it were only your mother's choice, you would know everything."

"What will you do with that pencil?" I asked.

"What was the name of the person who gave it to you?"

"Mr. Gao."

"I will say Mr. Gao stopped by and dropped it off." She gave another sigh. "Oh, Yun, I'm sorry. It must be frustrating. But your grandmother is trying to keep you safe. Here." She gave me her handkerchief. "The world is changing in ways we never expected. Maybe your grandmother will change, too."

I took the handkerchief and balled it into my fist.

"Can I at least see your arm?" I asked.

She hesitated. Since the night you had shown me your scars, I had taken to observing our mothers. I had always believed their long sleeves a conservative act, the same way they told us to keep our heads down and move quickly down the street, to be ready to hide should a Japanese soldier pass by—our whole bodies were to be hidden from them. But our mothers were too perfect about it. Even in the damp Shanghai summers, their sleeves remained. They never so much as rolled them up, no matter how close to the fire they worked.

Your mother must have pitied me enough to give me this consolation. She rolled the cuff of her sleeve just once. The scar was clear, much more prominent than yours. It was the head of something larger, something all too familiar.

"A phoenix?" I asked in wonder. The lines were the same as the ones carved onto our pencil. I would have recognized that phoenix head anywhere, even if it was a few minimal lines. I had carved it into our pencils many times.

Your mother pulled down her sleeve and said no more.

A few days later, my father left home again, this time bound for the wartime capital of Chongqing, where Japanese bombs supposedly fell all the time. Whatever message the pencil had carried connected him back to the underground network, and he was ferried away. It was as if he had never been home at all.

Mother took me to the department store that same day to choose a new qipao. She even let me look at the fabrics, offered to pay to have one custom-made. I knew she was trying to cheer me up, since she hated shopping. But none of the materials seemed to shine anymore. I insisted on going home empty-handed.

As we walked through the rooms of the company to the living quarters, Mother stopped me in her workshop. She picked one of the pencil boxes off the shelf and handed it to me. Inside was a single pencil, a few centimeters long, worn down from intense writing.

"Your father's," she explained. "From when he was younger."

"What was he writing?" I asked. I rarely kept a pencil around long enough to wear it down that much.

"Love letters."

"To you?"

"Who else?"

"Can I read them?"

"I think you would find them embarrassing." She laughed. I loved when she laughed.

"Please. I want to remember him."

"Fine. But don't say I didn't warn you."

Instead of a bundle of aging papers, she handed me the pencil. I looked up at her.

"One day you'll find them yourself," she said softly, then left me with his pencil pulsing in my hand.

CHAPTER 5

From the diary of Monica Tsai,
backed up on five servers spanning
three continents

August 20, 2018 (2018-08-20T23: 29:09.208112)
loc: Cambridge, Massachusetts. United States of America
(42.3721865,71.1117091)

*I've been thinking a lot about journals lately and how much Prof. Logan
loves them.* He's read pretty much every article there is on their benefits. Even without radical sharing, he'd be thrilled if the only thing
EMBRS ever did was make people journal more. One of the big ones
he talks about is how it's supposed to help us deal with our trauma since
it's a way of processing on the page, framing the story into something
the writer can begin to understand and share.

That's not the way our family works though. There is an unspoken
understanding that grandfather told me the news. Grandmother and
I won't ever talk about it, and if possible, grandfather and I won't talk
about it again either. It's what we do when faced with an obstacle—let
everyone know so we are all aware. Otherwise, continue as normal. Not
great for processing, I am realizing, but writing this out is helping it feel
more contained. Maybe if I had been keeping a journal when my father
left, things wouldn't have gone so poorly.

I was eight years old. Nobody told me he was leaving. There were only two signs. The first, a furious argument between him and my grandparents that I overheard in the middle of the night. He accused them of being overbearing and driving my mother away. They accused him of being irresponsible, abandoning his daughter in favor of a risky business opportunity in Shanghai. They only stopped shouting when grandmother heard my sniffling on the stairs.

And the second sign: my father gave me a folded piece of paper with an email address on it. The next day, he was gone, all the way on the other side of the world. I cried the whole night.

I'm not sure grandfather will ever stop being angry at my father, but he couldn't refuse when I asked for his help sending my first email. He set me up at his workstation. His chair nearly swallowed me; the bulky computer whirred underneath. He pointed at the monitor and showed me how to compose a message, and because he's grandfather, he taught me how my message would be encoded and passed along cables that lined the ocean floors, connecting Cambridge to Shanghai, and how there were well-established protocols to ensure my email reached my father safely.

I sent my father a message, and when he replied, moments later, saying he missed me, that was it: I was in love with technology. I loved the idea of my little stream of words bouncing around the world's servers, being guided to their destination. I loved the way grandfather described the sending protocols and receiving protocols, like they were little guards hanging out waiting to ferry my note, even though I was just some inconsequential kid missing her dad. Computers can do anything, I thought.

At first, I emailed him every day, and he always replied. As I grew older, I found I had less to say, and slowly not even the magic of technology could mask my growing resentment. He came home only twice—for my elementary and middle school graduations. After my middle school one, I told him he had missed my last five birthdays. The bouquet of flowers trembled in his hands as he cried. He made no promises about future birthdays. Mostly, we never talked about him at all. Grandmother stored her sewing machine in his seat at the dining room table, the three of us eating around her threads and fabrics.

I had not spoken to him since I applied to college and needed his signature on the financial aid forms. Now I needed to send him another email. It felt entirely different than it did when I was eight. There is no magic in email anymore. I asked if he knew about grandmother's illness and hit send.

dude if you want to talk lemme know

I blinked. For a long moment I thought my father had considerably changed his style of writing. Then I smiled when I saw Louise's name there, infinitely preferable.

I started to reply with a no, I was fine, I would figure it out, but that I appreciated her thoughtfulness, when my fingers paused, as if they could sense the lies in the words and refused to type them. I put my phone away.

Instead, I focused on my most immediate problem. Grandmother was sick and grandfather elderly. He would not be able to take care of her by himself. My father was in Shanghai and could not be relied upon. My mother was long gone and had no love for my grandparents. How could I return to school and leave them like this?

The answer was obvious: I couldn't. And in that realization, I found I could suddenly breathe more easily, like the task no longer seemed so insurmountable. I would stay home for the semester, longer if needed. They wouldn't be happy about it. But it was for the best. School was important, though surely not more important than family.

Then I thought of all the progress I had made with EMBRS. How much I had learned about technology, how excited I had been to feel that magic again. To build tech that connected people, no matter how far apart they were.

I told myself it was only a pause. It would not be a larger sacrifice than that. It hardly mattered, really. I had made up my mind.

That morning, I made a list of everything I wanted to learn from grandmother—how to make shaobing, how to cut garlic really thin, that kind of thing. And to ask about the happiest days of her life? The saddest? I had no intention of wasting any of the time we had left together.

Armed with these questions, I went downstairs to the kitchen, where she was in the process of making lion's head meatballs. They've always been my favorite.

"How would you like to spend your days before going back to school?" grandmother asked as she shaped the ball between her hand and a spoon, the pork smothered in a cornstarch and soy sauce mixture.

I jotted down some notes on my phone about how she dipped the meatball in her sauce mixture and lowered it confidently into the oil. "I don't think I'll go back to school this semester," I said carefully.

"What?" Oil lightly splattered. "Why not? Did you have a bad time? Did somebody hurt you?"

I sputtered a no, that wasn't the case at all. I just wanted to stay here with them.

"You can't do that." Her voice continued rising. The meatball was browning quickly in the Dutch oven. "What about your tuition?"

I told her I could defer it. I didn't know how that worked, but the most important thing was winning the argument.

"But why?"

"Because—"

It was impossible to say. We don't talk about that sort of thing, even though she had to know that I now knew, grandfather must have told her, so why could I not say it? That she was losing her memories and needed help, and I wasn't going to let grandfather do that alone, and I wanted to make sure I learned from her before it was too late, and that I had a list—

Grandmother flipped the meatball over. Sizzling renewed. I don't know what changed. Whether she thought about the situation objectively, or felt bad for my inability to speak, or merely forgot what we had been talking about. She continued pan-frying the meatballs, eight total, as I took my silent notes.

Eventually, to restart the conversation, I asked a question from my list: What were the happiest days of her life?

"The years I spent raising you," she said without hesitation.

"Oh, c'mon." I blushed. "That can't be it."

"But it is."

"What about when you were young?"

"You mean when we were being invaded by the Japanese?"

". . . After that, then."

"You mean during the civil war?"

It was clearly my fault for not knowing the history. Or really much at all about grandmother's past.

"After that?" I attempted.

Grandmother shook her head and smiled.

"I am telling you the truth. It is an easy answer for me. You have always been my greatest joy."

I did not know what to say to that, so I fumbled through my phone, looking for another question.

"My turn," grandmother said before I settled on one. She scooped the meatballs out one by one, then filled the pot with napa cabbage, letting the leaves soak in the leftover juice. She pointed her oil-shimmering spatula at me.

"Are you even trying to find a boyfriend?"

"Oh god." I swiveled away from her. I most certainly was not. I could not say that to her though. We had never talked about relationships, or in my case, lack of relationships. "Is that really what is most important to you right now?"

"I want to make sure you have someone once we are gone."

"I'll be fine," I lied. "And you won't be gone for a while," I said, as if saying it out loud would make it true.

"If there's no one you're thinking about, then why do you keep checking your phone?"

I had not realized I'd switched from my list to my messaging app, that I was staring at Louise's offer to talk, my own blinking cursor.

I shoved my phone away.

"Just hoping my professor will reply to me soon," I said, which was not a complete lie. Prof. Logan owed me a code review.

She stared at me, a question in her expression, then her stare continued too long, as if she somehow went from looking at me to looking past me, her eyes widening. She took a step back, bumped into the stove and the handle of the pot, took a step forward again.

"What's wrong?" I asked. "Forget to chop the scallions?"

She had always made the kitchen seem easy, graceful. She worked in a restaurant when she first came to America—that much I knew. But in that moment, she appeared totally lost, and as if looking for something, anything, to do, she opened the lid of the pot. Steam erupted, enveloping her unmoving hand.

She froze there as her hand burned. I stood to say something, to push her out of the way. Before I could, she dropped the lid, the heavy ceramic crashing onto the kitchen tiles.

I ran her to the sink, throwing the cold water open, forcing her pink hand into the stream. I'm sure I said something, or asked her what happened, or demanded why she removed the lid, why it took her so long to move, but she remained silent, not even a whimper of pain. She stared at her hand.

Grandfather was yelling from the stairs, and I yelled back that we were fine. He ran down anyway. I tried to stop him from bending to pick up the lid. He waved me off, stooping low, using the counter as support, grunting as he stood with the lid still miraculously intact.

"Reflexes aren't what they used to be, hm?" grandfather mused. He returned the lid to its pot, lowered the heat.

Grandmother was still looking at her hand. The scars along her arm were especially apparent against her reddened skin. She rubbed at her wrist, as if looking for a pulse.

"Where is it?" grandmother asked, rubbing even harder.

"You don't need to do that anymore," grandfather said. He stepped between me and grandmother, taking her hands in his. "We're safe here."

I had no idea what he was talking about, but his words seemed to mean something to her.

"Let me get a pencil, just in case they come—"

"We're in America," he said. "Look, Monica is here. No one is coming for us."

She turned to face me. Her eyes were wide. As they searched my face, they gradually relaxed. She smiled weakly, and I tried to smile back.

"Monica," she said, in her old familiar tone, without any of the earlier tremble.

I asked if her hand was okay. She nodded slowly.

"I think a nap might help," she decided. I helped her remove her apron. She left the kitchen, heading up the stairs.

"What was that about?" I demanded once she was gone. "Is this . . . Has this been happening all summer?"

Grandfather took his time running a sponge under warm water, wringing it out, wiping the oil splatter on the stove with it. He rubbed carefully, as if it took all his concentration.

"More or less," he said.

"I'm staying home this semester. I'll stay with you and help grandmother."

His wiping became even slower. Then his arms dropped to his sides.

"If you really want to," he said softly, "I won't say no."

I could not speak. That he had not protested, that he had not brought up anything about the importance of an education or making friends—it was as much of an admission of defeat as he would ever give.

Later, in the safety of my room, I texted Louise back.

> thanks, I really appreciate it. I'm planning to take next semester off, so we'll have to delay hanging out

Would we really have spent time together if I had returned to school? It was true that our schools were not far apart. I rarely left the bubble of campus though. Even trips to Philadelphia, advertised as a short twenty-minute train ride away, were unusual. A drive to New Jersey would be at least twice as long, and require a car. And she was not going to drive to me. It was a fantasy that never would have happened. Staying at home was really no loss.

She replied sooner than I would have liked.

> okay I know this isnt really my place to say
>
> but
>
> have you talked to anyone? I might be totally wrong, but it feels like youre processing in a mechanical way. like doing things you can control. even if theyre not in your best interest
>
> tell me to stop and I will!

I felt really small then. I imagined my grandparents in the kitchen, their bent-over figures doing the same thing they had been doing for decades, but slower, less steady, their decline undeniable. I used to be able to ignore their age, their increasing frailty. Now there was a diagnosis—an official label that spelled out our future, our waning time—and when they were gone, who would I have left? A long-gone mother. A father I had talked to more over email than in person. A stab of feeling suddenly so alone and human and with no control.

I could not help but direct these feelings at Louise. I rubbed my eyes to clear my head, steady my breathing. She was just some economics major at a fancy school, a network packet firmly traveling along its well-worn lines. Did that qualify her to be an expert in my life? I regretted telling her about grandmother's condition. It was a family matter and should have remained that way, like how I had never once told any of my friends in school that I didn't live with my parents, that my father had left when I was in elementary and my mother had done the same long before that.

I didn't reply to her that night, or even the next morning. Instead, I biked to Arby's first thing before grandmother and grandfather were awake.

The closest one was miles away. There used to be more, which was how grandmother became such a fan in the first place. But it turns out Massachusetts, especially the area along the shore, is quite passionate about roast beef, with tons of local shops that are admittedly tastier, though none of them have such a good coupon.

I biked all morning, out to the suburbs, along the river and the shaded path. I felt light for the first time since I came home. Like things would be okay as long as I remembered to take moments like this, to feel the wind, to keep moving toward a destination. I received some skeptical looks going through the Arby's drive-through on my bike, but even those felt more amusing than embarrassing.

It was almost noon by the time I made it back to our neighborhood. The early morning chill had faded, and after the long ride, I was sweating and tired. I parked outside the café grandfather used to stop at for coffee on his way to work. I wondered if the café would remember this scene:

this bike, parked temporarily out front, waiting for its owner. I sat on the bench to cool off before going home. Cambridge, without its students, was quiet. I pulled out my phone and read Louise's messages again.

With my head clear, thanks to the ride, I clicked on her name. I mentally gathered a few things to talk about, a few backup points—about the weather and school starting, just in case.

can I call you?

I only had to sit on the bench for a minute before she replied.

of course!

I hit the phone icon.

"Hey!" She picked up on the second ring.

"Hi." I leaned forward, elbows on my knees. "Thanks for taking the time to talk."

"Oh, no problem." In her background, there were faint noises of people chatting and vague thuds. "How are you feeling?"

"Not great," I admitted. I watched an ant crawl around the perimeter of my shoe. "But I'm feeling better. I got out of the house for a bit, and it felt good."

"I'm glad you had that at least."

"I'm sorry I didn't reply to your messages earlier," I said quickly. "I think—I think I was mad that you were trying to tell me what to do. But you were trying to help. So thank you."

She laughed. "Please tell me if I'm being a pain. But I do mean it. Having someone to talk to can really change your perspective on things. That's what I've learned from my therapist."

She was so open in a way that, I now realize, frightened me.

"So you're really not going back to school?" she asked. There was genuine disappointment in her voice.

"No. I want to be here for them." I made more room for the ant by bringing my feet under the bench. "Her condition is going to get worse, and grandfather is the only one around to take care of her, and he's not young either."

"What about your parents?"

I remembered the rows of beautiful houses in her neighborhood. The type of town that needed large houses for large families. Families that weren't fractured into pieces. Cambridge was not much better, if I was being honest with myself. The houses were smaller though, and somehow, I had equated that with more broken families like my own. She must be the type of person who grew up in a place where everyone had their parents shuttling them to all their after-school activities, helping them build up their résumés. How else could she ask about my parents so casually?

"They're not in the picture anymore."

"Oh. I'm sorry I asked." There was a particularly loud thump from her end. I imagined her in a gym, sitting on a bleacher, observing volleyball practice.

"It's alright. I don't really think about them."

"So what are you going to do the rest of your day?"

"It's grandmother's birthday," I said. "So we'll eat roast beef sandwiches. And I'll email the registrar." And hope grandmother doesn't have any lapses like she did the day before. I longed for the birthday I had imagined a week ago—a trip to her favorite restaurant, a reunion with a long-lost cousin. The rest of the day seemed suddenly very bleak in comparison.

"Oh, well, happy birthday to her! You sound a little glum though. Maybe if you had something to look forward to every day, that would help. Oh! Do you want to try something?" she asked, suddenly eager.

"What is it?"

"At the end of each day tell me a story about one thing that made you sad and one that made you happy."

"I don't want to turn you into my therapist."

She laughed again.

"I'll do the same for you. It'll be an experiment in story sharing. And it will help me figure out what my thesis should be about."

"Really?"

"Maybe! Anyway, do we have a deal?"

I fidgeted.

"I want to. But I don't want you to feel like you need to talk to me just because . . ." I could not even say grandmother's condition out loud.

"But I want to talk to you," she said, in such a straightforward way my cheeks warmed.

"Oh." I stumbled. "Okay. I guess that's fine, then."

"Nice! Alright, I gotta run now. See you later!"

Her voice and the sounds of the gym cut off. I let out a breath, then walked grandfather's bike home.

They were thrilled when I slammed the bag of ten roast beef sandwiches onto the kitchen table. Grandmother set out the good plates. I stuck a candle in her sandwich. She declared it her best birthday yet.

In the evening, we revived our tradition of getting ice cream after dinner. Armed with grandmother's coupons, we walked to the local grocery and bought a box of ice cream sandwiches. Grandfather opened it before we were even outside, pulling out one for me and one for him and grandmother to share. We walked along the river that separated Cambridge from Boston, bikers and runners passing us. We were by far the slowest-moving people. I would not have had it any other way. Somebody stopped grandfather in the middle of the sidewalk. It happens often—former students or colleagues. Grandmother and I sat on a bench facing the river, waiting for him.

"There is something I would like to teach you," she said. She bit into her ice cream sandwich delicately. A kayak rowed past us.

"What is it?" I asked. I figured it would be a recipe, maybe for her beef noodle soup, or if I was lucky, her stir-fried rice cakes.

"About pencils," she said. "And the pencil company. It's something I am not proud of. But I would like you to know. Before I forget."

I looked away so she would not see the tears in my eyes. She is the smartest person I know, the most adaptable, the one with the quickest wit, wit so sharp I can feel it even when I can't understand half her language. She survived wars, moved all over the world, learned new languages and customs, how to use a computer when most would have given up. Now her mind is going to betray her, slowly and steadily, and in her words—*before I forget*—she knows. She knows what will happen, that her lucid thoughts are numbered, and yet she wants to spend that time reliving her regrets.

I faked a sneeze as an excuse to blow my nose.

"Hurry up and finish your ice cream," she said gently. "Let's drag grandfather away from his fans."

At night, I composed my message to Louise.

> ☹: the cashier wouldn't take our slightly expired coupon

> 😄: grandmother's lion head meatballs

Louise replied half an hour later.

fuck that cashier!

I grinned, then prompted her:

> what's your ☹ 😄?

The dots animated to show her typing.

☹: didn't make it to the dining hall before it
closed. had stale peanut butter cookies for
dinner instead

😄: talking to you!

    I was lying on my bed, phone hovering a few inches from my face. I brought the phone to my chest. With its light covered, the room darkened. I let it sit there, resting on top of my rapidly beating heart. She was only being nice, I told myself, she was just so impossibly nice, even to someone she barely knew. It couldn't be more than that, could it? I wished the computer could help me like it always had before, when I wanted to contact my father, or find Meng. But there was no technology to help with grandmother's fading memories or that could decipher what Louise's words really meant. I felt suddenly that I owed her something in return. Rather than feeling bad about it, I got a rush of excitement, thinking of what I could do for her.

    I typed a question.

hey, what's your address? can
I send you something?

    She replied with her full address without hesitation. So open, as usual. Maybe there is something to it, after all: sharing your life. Writing all this is helping, I think, if only for myself to look back on, to run through these conversations again, to keep grandmother's memory alive somehow.

CHAPTER 6

From the Reforged pencil of Wong Yun

I'm losing my memories, Meng. It isn't bad yet, but it will only get worse. I need to write everything down, at least in pencil, before I forget entirely. I am not sure I am coherent every time, if you will receive the half-formed thoughts of an addled mind or a seamless narrative. Whatever it is, you will get all of it.

I am afraid of what my mind will be like without my memories. Will it be eternal blankness, a liminal focus on what is in front of me? Eventually, I won't recognize or remember Torou. One day, maybe even Monica. A strange ordering, perhaps, but I am sure you or Monica will be the last person I remember. You were such a fixture of my childhood. The old memories, I've read, are the slowest to fade. And Monica because she is my life. If I forget her, then it is no longer me remembering. Merely the dregs left over, keeping my body moving.

But today is a good day. My mind feels sharp, Monica is home, and she brought me my favorite sandwich. The weather is lovely, and there is soup on the stove.

Now that I am a grandmother, I understand my own grandmother more than I ever thought I would. I've never told Monica about Reforging, or even much about you. Yet back then, I thought it the height of cruelty that my grandmother would not let me learn whatever secret there was to the pencils. I thought she purposefully isolated me.

Though we all lived in the same complex, I barely saw her. She remained confined to her room, or if the weather was nice, she ventured into the garden to meditate. She could not move much farther than that by herself because of the pain in her feet, part of the last generation of women in our family who had their feet bound, broken, and rebroken since a young age.

If I had been a good granddaughter, I would have spent more time with her in her room. Especially in those months after my father left, when she clearly missed him. But I hated the smell of the smoke and the chance she would ask me to help load her pipe.

She was also obsessed with reading the news, always looking for hints of wherever my father might be, the danger he could be in. You had already been living with us for two years by then. You were the more considerate one, but she only ever called me in to read her news. I was thirteen and impatient to be away from her.

"Another British newspaper office bombed," she'd say for what felt like the fifth time in a matter of months. At first, I thought she was happy about it. She had no love for the foreigners, complained about how they spent all their time in Shanghai gambling and throwing parties, brawling in barrooms. But when the Japanese continued their bombing, targeting American and French newspaper offices as well, her tone changed.

"They won't know what is happening to us here," she said solemnly.

One day we read that a famous Chinese newspaper editor was decapitated. The Japanese had displayed his head on top of a lamppost in front of the French Concession's police station. She gestured for her bamboo pipe. I protested, but she insisted, so I had to go to Mother, who gave me the key to the opium drawer.

I didn't really know what it was at the time, only that my grandmother and Mother would get into terrible arguments over it—that apparently my father did not want her smoking it, and when he was around, he regulated her intake, since she could never quit completely. During her withdrawal periods, she wailed that it wasn't her fault, that everything hurt—her back, her mind, her feet—and it was the fault of those white devils, the British, for forcing the drug into our country even after they had banned it in their own, before they then carved up our land for their own pleasure and wealth. The only thing that seemed to work was this arrangement: Mother keeping track of her usage and me assisting with the task. My grandmother miraculously cooperated.

If only I could pick and choose which memories to keep! I'd certainly part with these—rolling the tiniest bit of drug between my fingers, heating the needle, dropping the smoking pellet into her pipe. How her whole body would relax, and I'd stash the drug away, leaving her in temporary bliss as I scrubbed my hands clean and she counted down the days until we could do it all again.

After my father's visit, she took a long break from smoking. A few days after he left, she called me into her room. She was sitting upright, her eyes remarkably clear.

"It has come to my attention that you have learned of a sorcery your mother possesses." That was the word she used: *sorcery*.

"Yes, Father told me," I lied. I had not planned to lie. I had no idea she would bring up such a topic. But it seemed like I spent my whole childhood spewing lies.

She glared at me, long and hard. I met her gaze.

"Your father told you?" she repeated.

"Yes. He had to use Mother's power to receive a message so he would know where to go next." I held my breath, hoping I guessed right. "He sent me to deliver the pencils."

"Hm." Her eyesight was not good, so I hoped she could not see my trembling hands. "Did you see your mother do it? Or was it that frivolous aunt of yours?"

"Mother," I invented with eyes lowered.

"Horrible, isn't it?"

"When did you first see her do it?"

"The first time your father needed to receive a message. She didn't mean for me to see. Something went wrong. Blood everywhere. Ah-shin was out at the market, your father at work, and only I was here to hobble around and save her from losing all her blood."

"What went wrong?"

"How should I know?" she snapped.

"Is that why you don't want me to learn?" I asked quietly.

"Only partly." She reached over and smoothed my hair with her skeletal hand. "I understand the utility. But I have lived longer than all of you and have seen how the world can use your abilities for its own purposes. Sometimes it is best to forget and move on. Do you understand?"

"Yes, Grandmother," I said. I knew if I was disagreeable, she would want her pipe.

"Good," she said, and opened her newspaper to drown herself in news of all the battles China was losing.

I have not yet done anything with your pencil. I am glad to have it though. I would have been surprised if you gave me anything other than a pencil. Hurt, even. After all, if I boarded a plane (though I do believe those days are over for me) and showed up in Shanghai, on the doorstep of wherever it is you live now, would we even be able to understand each other? We'd probably spend too much time being polite. You would offer me tea. I would have a box of chocolates from Boston for you. We would nibble and sip, and I'd say, "My, how Shanghai has changed!" And you would either go along, and tell me exactly how Shanghai has changed, or you would slam down your teacup and order us to move on to what we really needed to talk about.

But the problem is, there isn't really anything specific we need to talk about, is there? Nothing that can be said in an afternoon visit, or even a yearlong one. Written words are incredible in this way—they take a whole idea and condense it down with the help of the writer's mind. The writer pulls in only the important parts. Each word is efficient, each tells the reader something. No, a trip to see each other would not do us much good now, not when I have so few good days left.

I will get to your pencil, though, I promise. I would like to explain myself to you first, independent of whatever it is you have to say to me. My time is short, and so I must hurry—to when I finally learned the secret of our pencils.

We stopped going to school once we reached middle school. There didn't seem to be a point when the world was falling apart—and not only China, either. My grandmother reported every gruesome detail she learned of the bombs tearing through England, the massive German armies invading the Soviet Union.

Fewer people were buying custom pencils, not when they could use their money at the amusement centers instead, or in the Badlands, the surrounding area where the Japanese made sure the opium usage was high and morale low. Our mothers began to make batch pencils almost exclusively, most popular among the students of Shanghai's elite who continued their schooling at the foreign missionary schools, and who burned through pencils faster than any other type of customer. We could do math and speak Mandarin, Shanghainese, and a smattering of English. We were about as well-off as one could be for inheriting the Phoenix Pencil Company. However, business was slow.

As our customers dwindled, for the first time, Mother wandered around the complex with nothing to do. Your mother practically pounced on her.

"It is time to enjoy yourself," your mother said with a wicked smile.

She forced herself into Mother's room and let us watch as she brushed out my mother's hair and carefully applied lipstick. It was late in the night—my grandmother was already asleep—which lent the moment an unfamiliar electricity.

"Doesn't she look beautiful, Yun?" your mother asked, fluffing Mother's hair. With a discerning eye, she chose earrings to match the qipao she had loaned—deep blue with pink orchid embroidery. Your mother put me in charge of choosing a perfume and purse. With her free hand, she held out a cigarette. You jumped at the chance to light it for her.

Mother sighed, though she went along with it. By then, it had been two years since my father's departure, and we rarely heard from him. She was not the type to show her worry, but as your mother brushed her hair, she seemed to shed an incredible weight, leaning into her sister.

"I suppose it is nice to relax a bit."

They would go out to play mahjong. Supposedly it helped them form connections, draw more potential customers to the company. But it was also a source of important information—rumors floating around the city, speculations on which way the war would turn, horror stories of what was happening outside the International Settlement.

Looking back now, I think it was also an important time for our mothers. Hours my mother could spend free from her mother-in-law, enjoying her sister's company instead. And for your mother, it was how she integrated herself in her new home, formed the connections she so missed from the home she had to flee. A reprieve from a war and a failing economy.

As we became more adept at running each aspect of the company, our mothers ventured out more and more. They would return late at night, gossiping about the rumors they had collected—which families planned to test their luck in the countryside, which husbands had been seen negotiating with Japanese officials, eager for a better life by supporting their government. They brought home other news, too: battles won by the Chinese army, the Japanese allying with Nazi Germany. Our grandmother only condoned their nighttime ritual since the information they brought back was, indeed, valuable.

The Settlement was changing, though it remained preciously unoccupied. My grandmother read out the headlines from abroad—the war in Europe was taking a turn, France fell to Germany, and just like that, the French Concession was under new leadership. The French troops were leaving, followed quickly by the British, shipped off to Australia to train for their war. Only the Americans and Japanese remained— the former determined to stay out of it, the latter waiting to strike and accepting our bows in the meantime. But the Settlement was more crowded than ever, and not only with Chinese refugees. There were Jewish ones, too, fleeing the Nazis. Shanghai was now the only place in the world providing unconditional refuge for Jews. We rarely saw them, since they settled in the Chinese district, but we heard the stories of cramped spaces, starvation, disease.

At the same time many fled to Shanghai, others needed to flee.

One night, you and I were at the front of the store, boxing pencils. As always, we competed. Eight to a box, all facing the same direction. We had to read off your mother's notes carefully to ensure each had the proper breakdown. The composition of a pencil was indicated by the phoenix logo—the more strokes on the logo, the more graphite the pencil had, the darker it was. The darkest pencil had a phoenix with a bushy tail, while the lightest pencil had a minimalist phoenix of a few strokes. I was behind, and so I was relieved when a knock on the door interrupted our contest.

We both peered out the window. It was raining. I could just make out a woman huddled as close to the door as possible. We glanced at each other.

"Maybe we should ask your grandmother," you suggested.

But I was too curious and did not want to waste time going to my grandmother's room, escorting her out at her slow pace. I raised my head higher, trying to get a better look.

"Hui-ling?" the woman called.

We exchanged another glance.

"She knows Mother," I said.

"Then I guess we should let her in?"

We had received all sorts of warnings about letting people inside, especially men, especially police, especially anyone who could remotely be Japanese. But she did not seem to fall under any of these categories, so I opened the door.

We both stepped aside as the woman entered. She carried a thin coat over her head, shielding her from the rain. She dropped her arms with a sigh of relief, taking in the scene around her. Then she looked at us.

"Is your mother here?"

She was a mousy woman, her thin hair wet and sticking to her cheeks. Her eyes were sunken, her voice hoarse. Unlike our mothers, who wore their qipaos when going out, this woman wore loose clothing and drowned in it.

"Not right now," I said. "She won't be back until late. Who are you?"

"A friend of your mother's," she said, fumbling with her purse. Then she pulled out a wooden box, much like the ones we had been packing earlier. "Or rather, my husband is friends with your father." She swallowed. "Well, until . . ." She glanced between us. It seemed like she was going to make some sort of comment, maybe about our age, or how we shouldn't let strangers in the house, but then she started crying, a curled-up, violent sob.

"Sit down," you offered, pulling over a chair. She dropped into it, burying her head in her hands, still sobbing uncontrollably.

You jerked your head toward the back of the house. I sighed. You were right. It was time to get my grandmother.

She was already on her way. We ran into each other in the courtyard. "What is that noise? Is somebody here?"

"Apparently she's the wife of father's friend," I said. I lent her an arm, and we walked to the front of the company, where you sat awkwardly across from the woman.

She straightened when she saw my grandmother, and stood suddenly, sending her chair teetering before bowing her head a few times, mumbling all the honorifics. You passed her another handkerchief.

"Do you . . . ?" the woman began. "Can you also . . . ?" She held out the box of pencils in front of my grandmother; her shaking hands made it tremble.

Any sympathy my grandmother had for her evaporated. She scowled.

"Come back tomorrow if you must," she barked. "Can't you see it is late?"

"I know. I'm sorry. But I must leave Shanghai tonight. It isn't safe for me or my son here anymore. I need to get these pencils—"

"We can't help you."

"Please. They were my husband's pencils. He wrote poems with them. When we fled here, we lost them all. And now he's—" Her throat caught. "Please. I want to remember him. I want something so our son can remember him."

I expected my grandmother to be untouched. But she softened. Still, she scowled and took her time replying.

"Your husband . . . was a friend of Kangshen's?" She said my father's name softly, gently.

The woman nodded, vigorously at first, before turning timid.

"Same intelligence division. We got word today that my husband was caught. He . . ." Her words trailed off yet again. My grandmother paled.

"What about my father?" I asked.

"Oh," the woman said. For the first time, she seemed to really see me. "I'm sorry, he is . . . he is probably fine if you haven't heard anything."

"I'm sorry," my grandmother said. "But we can't help you. Not unless you wait for Hui-ling to return home. That will not be for a while."

"We have to leave. I've already wasted too much time coming here." She gave a trembling sigh. "I hope you hear from your father soon." She picked up her thin coat.

"I can help you," you said, suddenly and clearly.

We all looked at you. You shifted, unaccustomed to being the center of attention.

"I know how," you said quietly.

"Please," the woman breathed. She handed you the box.

"I'll do it in the back," you murmured, casting my grandmother a wary glance. And then you took the box of pencils and retreated to the workshop.

The three of us sat at the storefront. My grandmother still scowling, lost in thought, perhaps thinking about my father. The new woman fidgeted with her coat, brushing away droplets of water, perhaps from the rain, perhaps from her tears.

Meanwhile, I tried to remain calm. A great distance had formed between us in the moment you volunteered to help. We had started getting along, even liking each other, but there would always be this imbalance—you knew something that I didn't, you had access to our family's power, and I did not. A power that was proving useful now, even critical, to this woman's life. I realized then that even if I could make pencils as well as you, or pack them away just as fast, I would never match you in this, this secret you all collectively decided to keep from me.

At some point, I gripped the sides of my chair, the wood indenting my skin. I was barely holding back my tears. The chair creaked beneath me. My grandmother looked over.

"I'm sure your father is fine," she said.

"I'm not thinking about him," I snapped. I knew it was the wrong thing to say, cruel, even, but I said it anyway. She was the reason I was so disconnected from the rest of you. "I want to do what Meng can do. What my mother can do."

I prepared myself for her admonishment, even for a slap. For her to remind me that there was a whole war going on outside, where people were dying, where my father might be dying, and all I could think about were pencils.

Instead, she looked away from me, silent.

You returned from the workshop, pale but triumphant. You handed the woman a notebook. Your left arm was sloppily bandaged.

"They're beautiful poems," you said shyly.

The woman took the notebook with both hands, as if it were a sacred object.

"Thank you," she said breathlessly. She ran her finger down the page, where the characters lined up in neat columns. "Oh, thank you, thank you."

You smiled. You rarely smiled. That night you did, though, as this woman thanked you profusely, as she took your hands in hers and shook them, practically crying into them.

"He will live on, thanks to you." She bowed deeply.

She had to leave in a hurry, thanking you even as she bundled up the notebook, even as she closed the door behind her and left the three of us in the pencil company.

You looked at my grandmother again, that same wary look. You flinched when she spoke, as if she would kick you out of the house, right then and there. She sounded so tired.

"We are going to wait for your mothers to return," she said. "We will need to explain what has happened."

We nodded. Neither of us wanted to anger her any further than we already had. We resumed our pencil boxing. By the time we were finished, our mothers still had not returned.

At some point, we both dozed off at the counter, graphite on our fingertips. When we woke, it was to the sound of the door opening, and my grandmother's gruff "Finally."

"What is going on?" Mother asked, looking around the room, her hair in its neat updo. She and your mother seemed out of place, their Shanghai elegance against a backdrop of graphite and your bandaged arm. "Is everyone okay?"

Your mother rushed to your side, examining your arm even as you rubbed the sleep from your eyes.

My grandmother gave a spare account of the evening's events—a desperate woman showed up, asking for Mother, begging us to take her late husband's pencils, how we couldn't get her to leave, how you stepped in and granted her wish, and she finally went away.

"Meng," your mother said, slowly. She had looked radiant when they came through the door, probably high off a mahjong win. Now she paled. She was eyeing my grandmother. "I told you that you couldn't—"

My grandmother waved a hand in dismissal.

"The woman said her husband was a friend of Kangshen's," she said. Her voice shook when she said my father's name. "She said they worked in the same division. She said her husband was caught and killed."

Mother frowned.

"That doesn't necessarily mean anything for Kangshen," she said, always the rational one. "His division is sent all over the place, mostly on individual assignments."

"I know."

Mother's frown deepened. I glanced between them. My grandmother was not angry that Meng had used whatever power she had to help the woman. Nor was she worried about my father's safety. Then what could she be pressing on about?

She took a deep breath. We could hear all her subsequent ones too. She took her time. Her hands gripped her knees. Instead of giving us her normal piercing look, she stared at the floor.

"He is my only son. My only child." She took a shaking breath. "And he is out in a war where so many have already fallen. He hasn't been around for half of his daughter's life. I want . . ."

She raised her head. For once, she was the one looking up at Mother, asking something of her.

"I want her to know him. Your power—it would allow this, correct? Even if . . . even if he didn't come back."

Mother gave a slow, single nod.

"Teach her, then," my grandmother sighed in defeat. "Teach her so she can know where she comes from, and what she can do."

Mother bowed deeply.

"I will," she promised.

As grandmother started to hobble out of the room, I went to her side, offering my arm. She held on to it tightly.

"Thank you," I whispered.

She did not reply until we were in the courtyard. The bamboo lattice of the fence cast a web of shadows over her face in the moonlight.

"I can't protect you forever," she said. Her tone once again stern. "But I also cannot keep you isolated from your family forever. Be careful and use the power to survive."

Decades later, I understand why grandmother did not want me to learn and why Mother went along with it. How much pain the pencils have brought to the both of us! But it cannot be denied that you helped that woman and her son. You helped restore a story otherwise lost and reconnected a family through it. That is the moment I always returned to when the world went dark, and our power really became the only way I survived.

It would be easy to keep all this from Monica. To not let her see the pain we once caused. But then I think back to that woman, who desperately wanted a way for her son to connect to his father, so much so that as she fled for her life, she stopped first for his pencils. I think back to my grandmother, who wanted me to be able to connect to my father. And of course, I think of myself and Monica, and here I am, with such little memory left, and I've come to realize I want us to connect in the way only Reforging can allow. I want her to know you, and our mothers, and all those who came before her, so she knows she is not alone. How she might use a pencil or our power in her technology-filled life, I do not know. But the cruel lessons we learned from the pencils transcend the wood and graphite. Who is to say she won't find a bit of pencil within her pixels?

CHAPTER 7

From the diary of Monica Tsai,
backed up on five servers spanning
three continents

_____

August 24, 2018 (2018-08-24T14:50:05.327700)
loc: Cambridge, Massachusetts. United States of America
(42.3721865,71.1117091)

Lots to process today. Pencils, EMBRS, Louise. All things that were not in my life a year ago, and which bombard me now.

It all started a few days ago when grandmother forgot she'd already prepared a batch of lion's head meatballs and so we ended up with eight extras.

"Some perks to your forgetfulness," grandfather said cheerily. Grandmother frowned the whole meal.

I asked if I could send some to a friend. I had planned to make them myself, but the ones grandmother prepared would be even better. I had already looked into the frozen packaging options.

"Sending to Stacy? Or Alex?" grandfather asked. Once again, he showed off his perfect memory for the names of any friends, even if they were people I had mentioned only once. I think he wanted to support the endeavor in any way he could. It was sweet, even if it made me wince. Stacy had been a high school acquaintance. We lost touch after

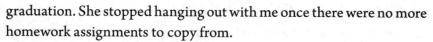

graduation. She stopped hanging out with me once there were no more homework assignments to copy from.

"Louise," I clarified. "The one who posted that picture of Meng."

Grandmother looked at me thoughtfully. Then she put down her chopsticks and asked if I was ready to learn.

We went to grandfather's office and sat at opposite sides of his desk, which was really an outdoor table they had found on the curb decades ago. Grandmother had two pencils with her. The first was a familiar yellow, the type I had grown up with, simple and topped with a pink eraser. The second was the black of the Phoenix Pencil Company, dark and alluring.

She had me sharpen them both and write with them. The difference was clear. While the yellow one was easy and comfortable, the black one was more than comfortable; it made my hand glide. Still, it didn't seem that special, more like a nice-to-have. The yellow one had served me perfectly well all through school. The black might be ideal for an artist like grandmother, but for me it didn't seem necessary, not when pens and computers exist.

Then she hit both pencils against the table and asked me to sharpen them again. The black one sharpened beautifully. But as I sharpened the yellow, a segment of the lead slipped out. I looked down the pencil point into the dark hollow.

"It's a bad heart inside," she explained. The bit of lead had rolled out on the desk. She flicked it away. "Shatters inside as soon as it drops. That doesn't happen to our pencils."

She went on like this for a while, pointing out the perfect angles of the wood, the simple phoenix carving, the sharpness of the point. How well it could make both broad strokes and precise stipples. It was nice, and undoubtedly a good pencil, but I quickly lost interest in these intricacies.

"Take this pencil for a few days. Write with it. Or draw with it. Whatever you want. Don't lose it."

"Alright."

Back in my room, determined to use the pencil in some way, I made a card to go along with the frozen food. I had to dig through my desk drawers to find an eraser. Once I did, I was able to draw freely in a way I had not since I was a child. I drew a picture of a lion, curled on top of a bed of cabbage. As I drew, I wondered what there could be to teach about these pencils. A form of meditation, maybe? The pencil glided perfectly. I was almost disappointed when I finished. I added a message inside the card.

Hope this makes up for your dinner of stale cookies!

I tapped the pencil against my chin. It smelled comfortingly of incense. I wrote one more line.

Thanks for looking out for me.

Yesterday, something really good happened. I was biking back from the grocery store when Prof. Logan called me. I was horrified at first. But quickly composed myself enough to answer. It turned out he had been in the registrar's office and happened to overhear that I was taking next semester off. I cursed the small school.

"I am sorry to hear about your grandmother," he said, voice softening. "My uncle also had dementia. God, it's a hard disease. I am so sorry, Monica."

I swallowed the lump in my throat. Then I started babbling about how I had really been looking forward to returning to school, taking his classes, working on EMBRS.

"But, Monica." His voice changed. "What if you did keep working on EMBRS?"

Then he said he could pay me to work on it from home and that without a class load, I could probably contribute even more than I'd otherwise be able to.

"I understand if you have too much going on right now," he added. "But for this sort of thing, it might be nice to have something steady to work on."

"You would offer that?" I asked in disbelief.

"You're a very talented engineer. And you've got a personal connection to EMBRS. So of course I'd want you on my team in any way possible."

He said he'd send over the paperwork, to take some time to think about it, but it was the easiest decision of my life. For the first time, I imagined doing something with my semester other than languishing. That maybe I could keep one foot on my original path.

At the end of the day, I sent Louise my summary.

> 😊: my professor offered to have me keep working on our summer research project! and will continue to be paid 🤑

> 🙁: grandmother misplaced her dentures and we spent all afternoon looking for them. it turned out they were in the basil plant

It was taking her longer to reply these days. Her semester was starting, and she had volleyball. I wondered if she would make time for me once the season really got going and she had to travel for games. After all, there was less reason for her to talk to me now.

She always got back to me eventually with her summary.

> 🙁: congrats about the summer research and the $$!! but sorry about the denture hunt, that sounds really hard

> 😊: im finally feeling good about changing my major

I'm starting to notice a trend with our summaries. Most of the time, she uses hers as an opportunity to ask me about mine, avoiding answering any questions regarding her own life. I always thought of her as open because she has so much data out on the internet and she's so easy to talk to, so enthusiastic. But if I were a machine learning model meant to give a rating to each message on how much information it offered the other person, my score would be much higher than hers. Even though I consider myself private, as I scrolled through our earlier comments, I was surprised to see how much I shared. The one where I told her that grandmother had Alzheimer's was enough to rate higher than all of her messages combined.

What did I really know about Louise? My thumb flicked through the screen again. I knew she played volleyball and that she was working on changing majors. But I did not even know the new major she was considering. No more than I knew after meeting with her in person. I decided to change that.

> congrats to you, too! what's the new
> major called?

I don't have a name for it yet . . . will let you know
when I do!

Another dodgy answer. I guess all this journaling and Prof. Loganisms have started to change the way I think, since I suddenly wondered—why not be honest more often, especially with those I cared about? Why dodge and hide when we're all just people trying to reach one another? Shouldn't I, once again an EMBRS engineer, embrace radical sharing in real life? If I shared more openly, maybe she would too. So I texted.

> I really enjoy talking to you

I have forced myself to reckon with an uncomfortable truth—and I can't believe I'm writing this down. I guess this journal is really proving to be a safe space—that I spend an awfully high percentage of my time thinking about Louise. Like, two-thirds. Or maybe, five-sevenths. Which doesn't make any sense! I barely know her. Yet my arm still tingles where her hand brushed, and I can't help wonder what she meant in that touch. Was it something she did often, or an attempt to connect with me specifically? It had been brief, soft, questioning. Like the first time I sent an email to my father across the world.

Maybe she's just a certain kind of intriguing I've never encountered before. Like a coding puzzle that keeps me up at night. A coding puzzle that's thoughtful and clever and magnetic and tall and athletic and whose messages I look forward to every day.

Ah, who am I kidding? I grabbed grandmother's pencil.

I wanted to draw again, to feel the smoothness of making a mark on paper, to take my eyes away from my phone and the lack of communication it promised. I didn't know what to draw. Instead, I let the pencil carry my hand, the strokes clear my mind.

In the end, it was not anything concrete, merely an abstract series of tangled lines. There was too much confusion all around—not only how grandmother's memory would be the next day, or what I was doing with this pencil, but also what was developing between me and Louise, what did I want it to be, what did she want it to be, and how could I even be thinking about this, in the face of grandmother's illness?

I would discard this paper, I decided. Knowing this gave me a freedom I would not otherwise have had. I glanced at my phone again, another sinking feeling when I saw there was still no notification. I added a caption to my scribble, a line that fit my mood, right below the tangle of lines.

How can you make me feel this way?

I tore the paper into shreds, then crumpled the pieces into a ball. I brought it to the kitchen to toss.

When I returned to my room, there was a response from her.

♥

I resumed my tangle of lines.

CHAPTER 8

From the Reforged pencil of Wong Yun

The first words I Reforged were *hello, hello, hello!* It was from a sample pencil, one your mother brought down from the wall that customers used to decide which pencil heart suited them best. It was a heart without its wooden body, which made it all the easier to Reforge.

Mother demonstrated with a real pencil first, while you and your mother observed. Mother closed the company early that day, drawing all the curtains. We did not have many customers during that time.

On the table between us, she laid a pencil, a small knife for sharpening, and a longer knife for something more sinister. Your mother contributed a roll of bandages. The last item on the table was a blank notebook.

"Have you been working on your sharpening?" Mother asked me.

I nodded eagerly. Because I ran through so many pencils in my sketches, I sharpened often and thought myself very good at it. When she nodded at the pencil, I took the sharpening knife and began to show off my skill.

"Sharpen the heart as much as you can," she said.

I carved carefully, my thumb guiding the knife, shaving thin strips of wood onto the table. It was the most patiently I had ever sharpened a pencil. I handed it to Mother.

She held it up to the light.

"The thing you need to know about pencils," she said as she rotated it in her hands, "is that their hearts remember."

She held out her hand. I gave her the knife. She somehow sharpened the pencil even further.

"Each time you make a stroke, what is left of its heart remembers that stroke. Like when you scrape your knee, your body remembers through a scar. Your own heart remembers too—the next time you are close to falling, you will think of the other times you have fallen."

The way she held the pencil, the way she looked at it—it could only be described as love.

"And our family can Reforge those memories."

At last, she rolled up her sleeve. The scars, visible at last. The phoenix in its entirety revealed, pale wings curving along the sides of her arm, tail weaving to her elbow, head held high at her wrist. My own arm ached at the sight, as if in recognition, in longing.

She tapped the sharpened pencil heart on her wrist a few times, right at the phoenix's head, the point where all the scars on her arm met, at one of her blood vessels.

Then she stabbed the heart into her wrist.

I bolted upright, knocking back my chair. Your mother grabbed my arm. Mother winced from the pain but still held the pencil to her wrist. The heart melted, pooling into ink before being absorbed into her vein. The pale scars that formed the phoenix filled out and darkened, climbed up her elbow. The heart melted entirely into her wrist, and the phoenix glistened, dark and pulsing.

She shuddered. I sat slowly back in my chair. She handed me what was left of the pencil, just the hollow wood, its heart sucked out. Then she picked up the longer knife. She pressed the blade to the phoenix's neck and sliced.

I flinched. She brought her sliced-open wrist on top of the notebook, pressing her wound into the pale-yellow paper. Yet instead of coloring the paper red, the paper turned the black of a pencil heart as she bled.

"She's not actually bleeding," your mother assured me. "It's the heart coming out."

Mother lifted her wrist carefully, then pressed it into the next page. During the brief instant her wrist was raised, black dripped from the gash.

At last, a bit of red crept into the ink. Mother stopped, and your mother bandaged her wrist. I continued staring at the notebook, already knowing what was going to happen and not wanting to miss a moment of it. Something would appear, fresh and dripping, like my drawings from the pencil I had given you when you first came to Shanghai.

The wet mass of ink shifted right before our eyes, moving across each page, drawn to different corners. It was not long before the shapes turned into columns of characters falling down each page, the single mass separating into thin, elegant strokes.

"That's what the pencil wrote before?" I asked.

"Before you are its memories, Reforged."

"Can I try?" I asked Mother eagerly. That was when your mother brought over one of the sample pencils. Mother sharpened it for me.

"Be careful," she said softly before handing it to me. With the pencil heart gone, her phoenix had faded to pale scars.

I hovered the pencil over my wrist. I refused to let my nervousness show. But I also could not watch the heart break into my skin. So I found your eyes instead. You held my gaze as I pierced my wrist.

It stung only briefly when the skin tore. Then a numbing sensation as I pushed the heart into my bloodstream, all the while never looking away from you. But something strange happened as I pushed it into my wrist. Your face faded, as if I was seeing you through fog, and another image appeared, students milling around the front of the pencil company. One of them grabbing a sample heart and writing on a scrap of paper, a quick message to test it out, as he scratched the heart against the paper—*hello, hello, hello!* Only when the heart had melted completely into my wrist did the image fade. I looked down. The same phoenix pattern that adorned all of your wrists finally adorned mine.

Mother handed me the knife.

I tapped the blade to my phoenix. Its dark lines gleamed, daring. I sliced.

Again, it only hurt for a moment. Black seeped out of my cut, and I pressed it to the blank notebook as Mother had. It had barely been used, and so the ink covered the center of one page before it turned into my blood. Your mother was ready with the bandages again.

hello, hello, hello! slowly formed on the page. More came afterward, words I had only caught glimpses of earlier—*today is Tuesday, wow, this is smooth,* and *when will this war end?*

"How do you feel?" Mother asked gently.

"I saw them," I said. "The people who wrote with the pencil before."

All three of you nodded.

"Their heart joins with yours, for a moment, when the heart goes into your wrist," Mother said. "Everyone can read what they wrote if you Reforge into a notebook." She nodded at the dripping words. "But as the Reforger, you are the only one who gets this connection with the writer."

For one full day, I was happy. Even after I bled out the words, my arm still bore the ghost of a phoenix, not nearly as solidified as our mothers', or even yours, which was barely visible. But I was thrilled. Your mother declared it a day for celebration. Mother showed me how best to bandage my arm after a Reforging, while you and your mother and Ah-shin went to the market to splurge. You brought back five-spiced beef and hot soy milk. Ah-shin cut the beef thinly and made shaobing. We flicked fallen sesame seeds at each other, and nobody reprimanded us. We ate so well that night even my grandmother seemed pleased.

That was the winter of 1941. We were fourteen years old. Most years are fuzzy, but that one is clear. A few days after our feast, Japan attacked many places, all at once. The Philippines, Hong Kong, Thailand, Pearl Harbor—and finally, the International Settlement of Shanghai.

We hardly knew when it happened. A few British boats, or maybe they were American, were rumored to have tried to defend the city. But most of the foreign navy had withdrawn long ago. The Japanese tanks rolled in, their red-on-white flags flying.

"It's over," my grandmother whispered, before Mother drew the curtains firmly shut.

By the end of the week, the foreigners were rounded up. The untouchable Americans and British were placed under house arrest, limits established on how much they could withdraw from their foreign banks, ending their lives of luxury. The Japanese registered each one and made them wear armbands indicating their nationalities.

We overheard these pieces of news from the few customers who still came into the shop. We listened with a dulled numbness, as if everything was happening in an alternate universe and if we stayed inside the pencil company, we would be preserved in our little bubble of peace.

But not even a week later, Ah-shin reported that bronze statues throughout the city had disappeared, taken by the Japanese to be melted for their metal. You asked about the bronze lions outside the bank, the ones with the shining paws you had reached for that first month and wished for home. Ah-shin did not know, but she could not imagine they would be spared. Somehow, it was the doomed fate of the lions that broke us, and we finally let ourselves cry.

Our mothers were now poring over the accounting books that you and I had taken charge of the last few years. They had trusted us with it, and we were lucky the company had done well enough that our mothers had not needed to fuss over the finances. But now they were always whispering to each other, falling suddenly silent when you or I entered the room.

"You aren't thinking about leaving, are you?" you asked darkly.

Our mothers exchanged a look.

"We'll see how things go," your mother said carefully.

"I'm not leaving again," you warned.

"We might not have a choice," Mother said.

"There's nowhere else to go," you said, voice rising. "They've taken over everywhere."

"Not everywhere—"

You had already stormed out, and I followed close behind.

We ended up in our bedroom, sitting together on your bed.

"I wish this war would end," you said miserably.

I understood, and not only from my own experience. It was an echo of the words I had Reforged, the writer who asked that same question.

"Maybe it will soon," I said, trying to be optimistic. "They say the Americans are getting involved."

"But why do we need to rely on them? Why can't *we* do anything?"

I nodded, resonating deeply with the sentiment.

"I feel like I finally got what I wanted." I admired my arm, which was starting to look like yours. "And I'm glad I know about the pencils. Really, I am. But it's like I wished for one thing all this time only to find out it can't help us. Not now." Not when our home was no longer safe.

I thought we had, for once, agreed on something. But you shook your head vigorously.

"The pencils are important. If you had Reforged those poems, you'd understand. I felt that writer's hope, his love for his family, his love for his country. And we both saw how much it meant to that woman to have her husband's words again. These stories the pencils can revive—that's important, especially now."

I was peeved you were so eager to disagree with me.

"It's not useful," I argued. "If a soldier were to come in right now, point his bayonet at our mothers, what could we do? Show him *hello, hello, hello?*"

"Maybe in immediate situations it's not useful," you conceded. "But in the long run, being able to bring somebody's words back to life, being able to tell their story after they have lived it, written it—"

"That's what books are for."

"But not everybody gets a book! Especially not the people who are going to die now that we're occupied."

"*We* might die, even with our power."

You stood up from your bed and crossed the room, rummaging through your backpack. When you did not find what you were looking for, you tore through mine, the one I had not used since we stopped going to school.

"What are you—"

You took out my notebook, the one I mostly used for doodles, and my bag of pencils. The misshapen ones from the company.

"I'll show you what stories can do," you said fervently. "How they can bring hope. Write this down." You pushed my notebook and pencil into my hands.

"In an old building in Shanghai lived two girls," you recited.

I reluctantly wrote down your words.

"They didn't like each other very much," you continued, "and in many ways they were very different. But they both had a special ability, and they were going to use it to change the world."

I managed to smile.

"What comes next?" I asked.

"I don't know," you said. You sat next to me. "It's your turn."

And so I wrote another line, and then you wrote a line, and together we began piecing together our story, our only weapon against the invasion of our home.

CHAPTER 9

From the diary of Monica Tsai,
backed up on three servers spanning
two continents

September 4, 2018 (2018-09-04T20:13:29.681998)
loc: Cambridge, Massachusetts. United States of America
(42.3721865,71.1117091)

It's September in Cambridge now, which means the students have returned.
The curbs are littered with furniture looking for a new home, the shuttles
ferry students to campus and to the store, everyone wearing a backpack. It's weird seeing them ease back into their lives while mine has
stalled—it's like I've gone from being a character in my own movie to
being a member of the audience, watching as something more exciting
plays out before me.

I try not to think about it too much and channel my energy into
EMBRS instead. I've learned a ton and developed a good routine.
Somehow, Prof. Logan always finds time to review my code, leaving
insightful comments around 3 a.m.

As I work, grandmother sits across from me at the dining table,
writing. She pauses and crosses out words or a line often, murmuring under her breath. Sometimes she only writes a few characters and
then stops, distracted, forgetting what she's doing. Other times she

writes without pause, the sound of the pencil scratching on paper the perfect white noise as I code. Sitting with her, both of us working independently, her with pencil and paper, me at my computer—it almost makes me feel like I'm back at school.

When I'm not coding, I run whatever errands my grandparents need done: packages returned, medicine picked up, groceries bought. The bike has been amazing for getting around, for getting out of the house, for letting me feel like I'm still moving forward in some way.

let me guess. your 😄 is biking again

Dinner is always prepared by grandmother and grandfather, with me observing. Then it's the postmeal walk through the neighborhood, and finally, returning home, where I message Louise my 😔 😄 and hope our conversation might last late into the night. And if there's something I need to process, I turn back to this journal.

Which brings me to yesterday, when, after our postmeal walk, grandmother called me into grandfather's office again.

"How did you enjoy your time with the pencil?"

It was really a strange thing to ask about a pencil. I tried to reply enthusiastically.

"It was great. Do you have more?"

"Not a lot. I lost most of them after I came to America."

"What happened?"

"There was a fire at home."

I had never heard her mention such a thing before.

"What? Here?"

"No, when I was in California."

"You were in California?"

"For a little bit. It was not a good time. Can I have the pencil back?"

"Oh. Yes, of course." I was sad to part with the pencil. I thought it was a gift.

She held the pencil with her left hand. Her scars snaked from her palm down her wrist and into her sleeve.

"You will have to forgive me, Monica," she said. "I have kept a secret from you, one that you had every right to. Of course you wouldn't know to ask for it. But you know our family used to run a pencil company in Shanghai."

She held the pencil tenderly, almost with a sense of wonder, though it was just a pencil. Was it possible her eyes were wide from fear?

"In Taiwan too," she continued, "and even a little bit in America. Crafting the pencils was one part of it. We were very good at it, of course. But we could not have survived the wars with only that."

She rolled up her sleeve. I used to trace my hand along her scars when I was little. They must have been more prominent then. Now they sag with her skin, pale and unnoticeable if you aren't looking for them. She used her other fingers to splay her skin flat. The scars ran down her arm, curving, familiar.

I suddenly recognized the pattern. I found the carving on her pencil. It was the same—the tail of the phoenix flowed and curved in a shape that matched her scars.

She noticed my realization.

"These scars are remnants of that power. We called the power Reforging."

"And what is Reforging?"

"The power to bring a story back to life. The power to understand a writer's words, exactly as they intended them. The power of perfect connection."

I shivered.

"And what did you use this power for?" I asked.

She made a strange sound then, somewhere between a groan and a sigh.

"Too many things," she said, barely above a whisper.

I changed the subject for her.

"And you could all do this? You and Meng? You both have these scars?"

"And your great-grandmother. Your great-grandaunt. And so many before you."

I was not used to thinking of myself as part of a long line. I had grown up in a totally different country than grandmother and did not have much of a connection to my parents. But for the first time I thought of the chain of people who came before me, who survived wars and more, and I felt a bit braver, a bit surer of myself.

I still did not completely believe what she was saying, thought it perhaps a side effect of her illness. Except then, in an unforgiving stabbing motion, she stuck the pencil into her wrist.

I was beside her in an instant. I tried pulling her hand away. She was surprisingly strong, and I didn't want to hurt her. I screamed for grandfather to come help, and grandmother told me to quiet down, as if I were throwing a tantrum in a supermarket.

I looked at her wrist. The pencil heart had—I can't believe I'm writing this—*melted* into her wrist. And her eyes rolled back, in pleasure or pain I could not tell. She breathed hard, closing her eyes. The scars on her arm pulsed, and for a moment, I saw the phoenix so clearly, dark and swollen. Eventually, the pencil heart emptied, and the wood casing fell to the floor, a husk.

When she opened her eyes, she was looking at me in a way I had never seen before, as if she was seeing past me or through me or maybe into me. And I froze because I could sense it—the pencil had marked my words and, somehow, they were in her body and she knew, she knew everything I had put into that pencil, all my questions and uncertainties, all the unsure feelings toward Louise, the jumble of thoughts I had tossed away thinking nobody would ever see. My story brought back to life. Understood perfectly by the Reforger.

I stepped back slowly. Then I slumped into my chair.

It's just—it wasn't how I envisioned coming out to her. In truth, I didn't envision it happening at all. It's a terrible reality that neither she nor grandfather will live much longer, and I figured I'd rather let them go happy than risk their potential disapproval. I didn't know how they felt about any sort of sexuality, and I was content to remain in blissful ignorance, or maybe for them to remain in blissful ignorance. I mean, they're old, they grew up in a different world, so I wasn't expecting them to be super open-minded. It's not something we've ever talked about. I haven't been in any real relationships, much less with a girl, so it was easy to avoid—and it's not like I wrote anything as direct as *I think I'm really starting to like this girl.* But grandmother knows me in a way nobody else does—and I sensed the pencil had told her all she needed to know as it melted into her. She'd seen right through my unsure scribbles to my state of mind, to the pining that I tried to hide, that I had not even fully admitted to myself.

All of that was going through my head, my self-doubt and paranoia so all-consuming, I barely even registered when she sliced into her wrist.

She bled black ink out onto a notebook. I watched everything I wrote and drew with the pencil recreate itself on the page before her. The drawing of the lion on the bed of cabbage, the note, the scribbles, and the message: *How can you make me feel this way?*

Grandmother looked at the wet scribbles for what felt like hours.

"Does father know how to do this too?" I asked in a desperate attempt to get her to look away from my words. It should have been easy enough. She had just done something absurd, after all, yet neither of us seemed to be able to stop staring at my scribbles.

She shook her head slowly.

"I never taught him," she said. "Or even told him about it."

"Why not?"

"The skill seems to pass to women. And I don't think your father would have been interested."

"To women? Why's that?" I really thought I was succeeding in changing the topic.

"I don't know. Maybe because we are more used to bleeding."

Then she touched my still-wet words with the tips of her fingers. I swallowed.

"What does this mean?" she asked, looking so small with eyes so wide.

"It's nothing," I said immediately. I could only hope what she said earlier about understanding a writer's words, about perfect connection, was an exaggeration. "Really."

"This is about the girl you wanted to send food." Her voice revealed nothing. "What was her name?"

"Louise," I said weakly. "But really, it's nothing—"

Her hand ran over the scribbles again. I wanted to grab the notebook, to run out of the house, hop on my bike, and ride out of Cambridge, over the river, past Boston, to be anywhere except here.

But then she said:

"Maybe you can invite Louise over sometime."

We looked at each other. Grandfather's clock ticked on the wall. Outside, a truck rattled by, and a dog barked. Grandmother's hand brushed my Reforged words again, the lead from my pencil heart staining her fingertips. She understood.

And I fell apart. I can't remember what happened after that. I must have crossed the room, seeking her embrace the way I had since I could first walk, her arms always open and ready to accept me. Even when my parents were still around, it was her arms I sought, as if I knew even then, she would be the one to love me unconditionally. I ended up in her embrace, and she stroked my hair, that familiar pattern of her strokes, the same after all these years. She hummed a lullaby I had not heard before, or maybe I was too young the last time I had, but the tune went straight into my ear, a soothing buzz until my eyes were swollen, my head hurt, and my throat stung.

"You won't . . ." And I had to pause because I was breathing too hard. "You won't forget this, will you?"

She held me tighter.

"There is not a single moment with you that I will ever forget." She kissed the top of my head. "Every part of you is precious to me and marked on my heart." But then I felt her warm tears on my scalp. "I won't forget." She took a handful of my hair. "I won't . . . I won't."

By then it had become more of a plea than a promise. But I believed her anyway.

CHAPTER 10

From the Reforged pencil of Wong Yun

1 fear I have done something wrong, and you are the only person who may understand. It always comes back to our pencils and the stories we force out of them.

I didn't think Monica would write anything so personal with the pencil. She is always on her computer. I thought the pencil would be like a toy for her, a novelty. Maybe she would doodle and write her name. She only had it for a week. And yet she opened her heart to it in a way she never has for me.

And then I Reforged it, without first telling her what would happen. Or maybe I did? I can't remember. Regardless, it was not a story she had wanted to share with me, and there I was, wrenching it out of her pencil, and all she could do was watch.

It was all too familiar. All too much like what I did to you.

Luckily, there is no rift between me and Monica. It may even have brought us closer, now that I understand her. What's done is done, yet it feels as if I have not learned anything at all after all these decades. How the pencil can hurt as much as it can heal.

This is the first time I wish you had given me more than your pencil. How about a phone number, Meng? Do we not live in the twenty-first century? I am very good with a computer; an email address would have been fine as well. A few days ago, I would have agreed with you that this way of sharing our feelings is better, more accurate, more intimate. But when the news is urgent, this hardly suffices.

There is something circular about this, that you should be the only person I know other than Monica who has met this girl, Louise. And if I had an immediate way to contact you, I would grill you—is she nice, is she caring, is she going places in life? Monica likes her in a way I would not have fully comprehended had I not Reforged her pencil. And I need to know that this person would treat her well, because I won't be around much longer. I need to know she will be happy and safe.

I want everything in the world for her. I want her happiness so much that sometimes I wake at night, gripping my blankets so tightly my fingers cannot unclench. I don't deserve any wishes granted—you know that better than anyone—but every one of my memories would be a trivial sacrifice to ensure this future for her.

Have I said this before? It runs through my mind all the time. I've been tossing pages I wrote, pages I realized were repeats or not about our lives at all. It will be a tremendous task to piece together all this nonsense I've written. But I believe you'll understand me because we have been through too much together—and it all started when you had to change your name, when we became sisters.

It was an attempt to distance us from our fathers, who at the time were fighting against the Japanese. It would have been impossible to account for two missing men, so your mother became childless, a woman staying with her sister, and Mother became a widow whose husband died years ago, before the Japanese had ever come to China, and you became my sister.

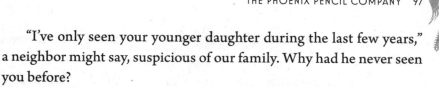

"I've only seen your younger daughter during the last few years," a neighbor might say, suspicious of our family. Why had he never seen you before?

"She was sickly, and it was difficult to care for two children without my husband," Mother explained carefully. "I had to send her to my sister."

The lie managed to explain away your sometimes shaky Shanghainese and the way you gravitated toward your mother, even unconsciously. The neighbors left us alone, at least for a while, and Mother holed up in her workshop.

Our mothers never wore qipaos out anymore. They swapped their dresses for drab blue clothing, doing their best to go unnoticed. The few times I had to run an errand, even Grandmother told me to ride my bicycle, no matter how improper. Gasoline was far too expensive, and they wanted me home as quickly as possible. I'd bike past the old cabarets and restaurants that once teemed with Americans. They were still popular, thriving even, but now with a new set of patrons: the Germans, the Italians, and of course, the Japanese.

At the beginning, the police came often, collaborationists of the puppet government. Your mother tried to charm them in her usual way. They were gruff and uninterested. If they brought a Japanese official with them—tan uniform, bayonet at his side—our mothers made us hide behind carefully placed boxes of graphite. One time, the policeman threw a pile of pencils at Mother. Even contorted behind those boxes, I could see them roll toward her, all of different lengths.

"These were found in the homes of Nationalist spies," the policeman said. "These pencils were made here, yes?"

Mother picked one up and pretended to take her time inspecting it, as if there were any way she would not recognize her own pencil.

"Yes, sir," Mother answered smoothly. Your mother sat very still at the counter, eyes determinedly looking away from our hiding spot.

"So you admit to selling to Nationalist spies?" the policeman pressed.

"Our pencils are often passed around. We are unfortunately unable to track what happens to them after they are sold."

"One of the spies told us they bought straight from you."

"I have never knowingly sold to a spy."

"You should interrogate all of your customers."

"Yes, sir."

"Now you have supplied the enemy with the means through which they communicate. How they spread their propaganda and how they plan to bring down China."

"We will be more careful, sir."

"Where is your husband?"

"He died many years ago."

"Do you have proof?"

"No. But my mother-in-law still lives here. Would you like to ask her?"

The policeman turned away.

"No. We will be keeping an eye on who you are selling your pencils to."

"Of course."

After they left, you pushed me out of our hiding spot. My arm had fallen asleep, and you were rubbing your back. We hated hiding, but we did not argue about it. We had heard too many rumors of what they did to young girls.

"What are we going to do?" I asked.

Our mothers exchanged a look.

"It's impossible for us to prevent our pencils from being borrowed or taken," I continued when nobody replied. "There's no way to ensure who is using one, even if we interrogated them."

"We could stop selling pencils," Mother said quietly. Nobody spoke after that.

When our mothers were not looking, you picked up one of the pencils the policeman had thrown. Our eyes met. You nodded and slipped it up your sleeve.

At night, when I heard the rustling from your bed, intentionally loud, I followed you. It would be too easy for our mothers to hear us from their bedroom next door. We ran through the courtyard to the front of the complex, to the workshop. I turned on a light, and you sat at the table where Mother normally sat, pulling a blank notebook off her shelf.

"You do it," you whispered.

I took the longest pencil. It would have written the least. Up until then, I had only Reforged the samples, never anybody's real words or stories. I sharpened the point.

I took a breath and pushed the pencil into my wrist.

It was immediately different. Whereas the samples were typically light memories of a day out shopping, this was all darkness. I could see the inside of somebody's house, a grand desk with a scholar's rock on the side and art hanging on the walls. The smell of cigarettes and wet calligraphy ink. I could feel the writer's pulse and the words they scrawled against my skin, as if someone was writing directly on my arm, each stroke carving, each sentence ending with a period on my wrist, drilling through it.

The characters formed something about a daughter, a girl, not so different from us, who was tired of being told to hide in closets when the soldiers came, tired of only being defined by her body, unable to do anything for the war. Who left the house one night, dressed in her brother's clothing, leaving a note to her parents that she had to do something other than hide, was going to fight in any way she could. Whose body was brought back the following week, bayoneted, raped, white and bloated from the river, larger than it had ever been in life.

I don't remember more. Is it the illness, or did I block it out long before that? I remember my own body convulsed—the floor crashing into my knees and you wrapping your arms around me, shoving a bundle of bandages into my mouth to stop my screaming. I could only rock back and forth, holding on to myself, mind racing between pain and bodies and women, and what it meant to have to be all of those things during a war, wondering if the pain was inescapable.

We did not Reforge any of the other pencils. All I remember taking away from that night was a deep unease and a flinching terror whenever I saw a police uniform. I became all too eager to hide behind the graphite boxes.

It was also the first night we experienced a story that did not connect, that hurt us instead. The story told a truth I could not face, a truth that showed us a brutality we had been sheltered from.

We did not tell our mothers about that night. I think they might have known somehow, noticed our trepidation. I was sure Mother Reforged the rest of the pencils the policemen had thrown at us, hiding their darkness within herself.

Then, two months after our occupation, in the early months of 1942, Mr. Gao showed up at the pencil company. It was three years since I had last seen him, when I had delivered a box of pencils to him and he sent my father away. He looked largely the same, young and severe, though a bit gaunter in the face. Mother immediately let him inside, not wanting anybody to see him at our door, then promptly told him to leave.

"We need your help," he said. He took off his hat. He stood tall and imposing. Though he was younger than our mothers, he showed no deference.

"We are already under suspicion."

"We can help divert their attention from you."

Our mothers looked at each other.

"Is it messages you want?" Mother asked quietly.

"Yes. Messages keep getting intercepted, and we lose people, plans get foiled. But if the message could be passed by pencil—"

"I understand," Mother cut in. I wondered how it was Mr. Gao knew of our abilities, if my father had told him. "And if I don't agree to your proposal?"

Mr. Gao took out a cigarette. He had to have been very rich to still buy cigarettes. His voice was slow and calm, completely in control.

"I can easily let slip who your husband is and where his loyalties lie."

"I can turn you in at the same time."

"I am well protected. Don't do this to your girls." He cast a pitying glance at us. "Help us, and you will have my protection. Surely you believe in our cause? Of a free China?" He exhaled smoke, cloudy and wavering.

Mother did not take long to respond. I think she may have known this was always what was going to happen.

"Yun," she said eventually. "Please bring some tea for Mr. Gao."

I slipped out of the storefront. You followed me. We did not say a word to each other as we pattered through the courtyard. No words were safe.

We no longer left the pencil company. Only Ah-shin did anymore, taking our identification cards to retrieve our rations. The police came nearly every day, but your mother had learned how to handle them. You and I triple-checked our accounting. They wanted records of who we were selling to and how often.

"They fear the pencil," Mother said quietly when it was only us around the dinner table. "None of the other stores are receiving as much scrutiny."

"Stop talking," my grandmother ordered, and we would eat our meager meal in silence.

My grandmother was right to monitor our talking. We often saw neighbors lurking close to the complex. Because we were grouped together, if one of us went out of line, the whole group could be punished. And we were such a strange family—the men gone, the women running the business—that it felt like all the neighbors watched us, waiting for a moment when we would slip and they might earn their reward.

Without anywhere to go, you and I took turns writing our little story. Though it quickly became depressing, to see our characters go through the same fears that we faced.

"It would be better if they could actually fight with their pencils," I said as we tried and failed to think of what should happen next.

"Fight?" you repeated, amused. "Like if someone ran at us with a bayonet, we could parry them with a pencil?"

"No," I said. I was excited by the idea forming. "What if they could still Reforge the pencil, same as us, but instead of bleeding it out, the pencil became armor over their hands! Like a layer of pencil heart, hard and strong, protecting their skin."

You perked up and continued the fantasy.

"And if someone tried to kidnap them, they could just go, bam!" You clenched your first, then released dramatically. I could almost see it, armor snaking over your skin, erupting from your phoenix, a hardened shell, molded perfectly to your hand.

"Then they could sneak into those Japanese buildings," I said, practically bouncing. "Nobody would suspect them because they're just two young girls. But really, they're powerful spies. And then they'd be behind the guy in charge, their armored hands at his neck, and he'd have no choice but to surrender, and the Japanese would leave, and we'd have our home back, and we wouldn't have to worry about food or if our fathers will make it back or the people flocking the streets, or the buildings being bombed and tumbling down."

You smiled. I smiled back. We spent the afternoon writing this new superpower into our characters, sending them on missions we never would have dreamed of before.

"Wait," you said when the sun was setting. You had taken the pencil, stopped writing midsentence, the tip hovering over the paper. Then you crumpled the paper.

"What are you doing?"

You took the previous page and crumpled that one too.

"Stop. Why are you—"

You did the same to each successive page, each more violently, the paper crunching in your fist, even as I begged for you to stop, as I tried to pull what remained of our story from you.

"We can't write this," you said, shoving me away. "Don't you remember the police who came by? They're looking for people who are against the Japanese, and here we are, writing about infiltrating their buildings and spying on them. As if they weren't already watching us, as if our mothers weren't under enough suspicion." You slumped against your bed. "We can't have even this made-up story."

"Yes, we can," I argued, and took the pages you crumpled and gathered them into my shirt. I left you in our room while I took the pages to the front of the complex, to the workshop. I started the kiln. As soon as the fire was substantial enough, I tossed our story in. I knew you were right. But I also knew there was a way around this.

I came back to our room with an old newspaper and a handful of pencils that Mother had tossed for not passing her discerning eye. You looked up questioningly.

I ignored your curious gaze and continued our story where we left off, writing over the article in the newspaper. It was illegible, my characters tangling with those of the article. I kept writing, allowing my words to stack on top of one another. Somewhere along the way, as I wrote about our characters using the money they had pilfered on their last infiltration to buy two freshly steamed fish, garnished with scallion and ginger, the aroma making their stomachs growl, you peered over my shoulder. Only when I finished the chapter did I put the pencil down.

You took the newspaper, trying to decipher my words, flipping the page, rotating it. It was practically one solid black rectangle where I had written. The side of my hand was stained in graphite.

"It's unreadable," you said. I tossed the pencil to you.

"We can still share our story with each other though," I said. "When you're done with a chapter, give me the pencil, and I'll do the same for you. Reforge it so you can experience the story but toss the Reforging immediately afterward or bleed it out over water." I crumpled the newspaper. "We'll burn these too, just in case. The story will exist only between me and you."

You took my pencil with great care.

"That's clever of you," you admitted, which pleased me to no end. "We don't have much, but we have this power, and we have this story."

"And we have each other," I added.

You stared at me. I was embarrassed to have said it, but it was the truth. I could no longer imagine a world where you were not by my side, eating rationed meals, quarantined in our home, writing a story just to make the days pass.

Eventually, you nodded.

"We'll have to stick together, then," you said quietly.

I watched you prepare my pencil for Reforging, your hands quick and precise, holding my words.

"Always," I promised.

CHAPTER 11

From the diary of Monica Tsai,
backed up on three servers spanning
two continents

September 13, 2018 (2018-09-13T23:48:00.098929)
loc: Cambridge, Massachusetts. United States of America
(42.3721865,71.1117091)

I've been doing a lot of reflecting this week about how grandmother Reforged my pencil. I don't think I really believed her until I saw the heart melt into her wrist. That's why I didn't try to stop her, even though I knew what it might betray about me. Looking back, I'm glad I didn't. Though it does make me uneasy, how she managed to resurface words I thought I had destroyed all evidence of—and how she could have done it without my ever knowing.

It has me in a bit of a funk, to be honest. I trust grandmother and cannot imagine her ever using my words against me. They're mostly typed anyway, and I'm pretty sure she can't Reforge bits on https connections. But I can't push the image out of my mind, how her body seemed to shrink when I asked her how she'd used this power in the past. I can't bear the thought that maybe she used it against someone. Could that be how she and Meng lost touch?

Of course, this changes the significance of Meng's gift. There is something written inside that pencil, some sort of letter, no, maybe more than a letter, something grandmother can experience. So why does she leave it untouched?

I asked grandmother if she would Reforge Meng's pencil soon. She tapped her own pencil against her paper, looked at me, and said *not yet*. I asked when the right time would be. She stuttered and shook her head so vigorously I backed off right away. Since then, instead of working beside her at the kitchen table, I have stayed in my room, on my bed, with the door closed.

Now that grandfather is retired, he's always a bit restless in the fall. He used to be so busy this time of year. Grandmother told us we should get out of the house, go enjoy the beautiful weather. Me and grandfather exchanged a guilty look at the prospect of leaving her alone. But she insisted she'd be fine, needed a nap anyway, and he was excited to use his senior pass.

We took the train into Chinatown. Grandfather likes to point out how everything has changed since he was young, how the neighborhood was cleaved in two by the highway, one building literally truncated, all its feng shui ruined. We decided to buy one egg tart at each bakery we came across and rank them with grandmother when we got home.

As we waited for a fresh batch that would be ready in a few minutes, I asked grandfather how long he had known about the pencils.

"For years," he said. "Decades. Seven decades, perhaps."

"And what do you think of it?" I pressed. I wanted to hear the opinion of the smartest man I knew.

"It is nothing short of a brilliant power," he said.

"Really? Even if no one uses pencils anymore?"

"Even so." He was looking at the zongzi, but grandmother is picky about her zongzi, preferring the Shanghai style of marinated pork belly wrapped in glutinous rice, no peanuts, no eggs. "I think it's about understanding, and about sharing."

I considered his response.

"How did she share with you?" I asked.

He chuckled. "You don't want to know. Oh, don't pout. Tell me about your latest algorithm."

He said it the same way he used to when I was a kid waiting at the bus stop. He'd always have me recite the multiplication table until the bus arrived. As the baker emerged with a tray full of tarts, their warm buttery flakiness filling the air, I told him about my latest effort for EMBRS. The tricky data transformations to convert a news site into something EMBRS could use to improve its understanding. After all, EMBRS will need to have some base knowledge of the world to understand what's most significant in a blog or journal entry. As we paid, grandfather poked at my logic, asking about the size of the payload, the storage options, the efficiency, and I proudly countered until he was satisfied. He did give me an idea for an optimization that I admitted was a good one, and he remained smug all the way home until grandmother asked what had made him so happy.

"Education." He beamed, and I rolled my eyes.

I met Prof. Logan for our weekly 1:1 meeting after that. Ever since I've gone full-time, he's taken me more seriously, almost like a partner in the development of EMBRS. Maybe because I'm churning out an absurd amount of code. There's a comforting normalcy to writing code, and I find myself working on EMBRS constantly.

"I have two requests," he said as soon as our meeting began. Now that the semester has started, his time is short. "First thing, I'd like to use your story of how you connected with that person in New Jersey and reconnected your grandmother to her cousin. If that's alright, could you send me the keywords that matched, whatever EMBRS turned up, and some info on what happened afterward?"

I readily agreed. It would be easy to pull from the EMBRS logs.

"Second thing. Since I'll be away pitching, I won't be able to make one of my lectures. Can you pull together a live coding demo? I've got freshmen this semester. I want them to see a real-use case of good version control hygiene, and you're excellent at it. Throw together a sample project and show how you make commits, what messages you write, how you chunk out your work. If you're feeling frisky, maybe show them some rebasing. We can arrange to call you in over video."

So I guess I'm putting together a presentation for next week. I was just about to start brainstorming a sample project to use when Louise texted.

dude!!! did you make these? how do I heat it up?

It took me a moment to remember what she was talking about. It felt like a lifetime ago, when I carefully packaged the frozen meatballs and biked them to the post office.

no my grandmother did! I'm still apprenticing. do you have a steamer?

uh no I live in a dorm

just microwave it for a minute then

ill heat it up now!!!

Before long, my phone rang. I took a breath and picked up.

"Monica!" There was something sharp and unfamiliar about her voice.

"Are you alright?" I turned away from my computer. I imagined her at an urgent care, some sort of tear in her leg, ending her volleyball career.

"Yes, I'm fine." She sounded on the verge of tears.

"Are you sure?"

"I'm just overwhelmed." There was an unmistakable sniff. "They're so good! I've only got one left now. I was starving, and this was . . . It was perfect."

"I'm glad you liked them." I couldn't stop smiling; it was kind of stupid.

"Please thank your grandmother for me too."

"I will."

"It was so sweet of you. Really." She paused. "I think this is one of the nicest things anyone has done for me."

I gripped my elbow, the hand next to my ear trembling.

"It's nothing," I mumbled, running out of ways to fend off her gratitude.

"And the card! I'm going to hang it up on my wall. I didn't know you could draw."

"I haven't in years. But grandmother gave me this really nice pencil, and I ended up drawing."

"A pencil? Like the one Meng gave her?"

"Yes." I wanted to say more. But to explain Reforging would require revealing too much. At least, that was my instinct. It's always my instinct to default to secrets and handle everything on my own. Yet with her on the phone, gushing about grandmother's cooking, asking about a pencil, about grandmother, I was overcome by a thought, that if I could not share with her, who could I share with? Only this journal, and that's starting to not feel like enough.

"I have something to tell you," I blurted out before I could change my mind. "Do you have time now?"

"Of course! Is everything alright?"

"It's about the pencils that grandmother and Meng used to make."

"What about them?"

Now that I reflect on our conversation, I am struck by the careful evenness of her tone right then. That despite her openness, she was a master of giving little away when it counted.

"This is going to sound off-the-wall, but don't hang up on me, okay?" I said.

"I would never." The assured validations.

I closed my bedroom door, the downstairs television fading.

Then I told her about Reforging. How grandmother stabbed a pencil into her wrist, how the lead melted into her skin. Louise kept trying to interrupt me. But I kept going. I needed to finish, no matter how unlikely the story. Needed to tell her how the ink filled grandmother's scars, to describe how grandmother cut her wrist and then—

"And then the words the pencil once wrote came out with her blood," Louise finished.

I sank to the ground, the room blurring around me. I calculated and recalculated, nothing was adding up. It did not make sense that she would know this. Or rather, that she would know this and not tell me. Like I should have gotten an alert that we both knew this strange secret. It should not have been possible for us to talk every day and miss this commonality.

"How did you know that?" I asked weakly.

I could hear her moving past a crowd.

"Meng told me. I didn't—I didn't really believe her though."

"Why didn't you tell me?"

"I never saw her do it. It's hard to believe, you said so yourself. I didn't fully believe her, and when I gave you Meng's pencil, you seemed so disappointed, even asked if there wasn't a note that came with it. So yes, I knew, but I didn't believe, and I wasn't going to ask and make you doubt your grandmother."

I bit my lip. It made too much sense, like it was well practiced.

"Do you believe me?" I asked.

"Of course I believe you. Even if Meng hadn't told me the same thing, I'd still believe you. There's something about you."

"What about me?"

She gave a light laugh.

"Like you can't lie."

"I can lie!"

"Tell me the last time you lied."

"I told grandmother the cashier did take the expired coupon."
She laughed again.

"Alright, you've proven me wrong yet again. But I don't think you could lie for nefarious purposes. In any case, how do you feel?"

"I don't know," I sighed. Something still sat uneasy with me. Grandmother had kept these pencils a secret despite how much they've haunted her, and she's only sharing with me now because she's sick. Yet Louise, a random girl on the internet, already knew. What kind of person was Meng to share this family secret with a stranger? There was no time to process, though, and so I responded to her with my barely formed thoughts on Reforging. "It's such a mysterious thing, and I had no idea she could do anything like it, but also, I wonder about its purpose? Did I just find out my grandmother has this magical ability, but one that is not at all useful? Like if I found out she can make rocks dance, or something?"

"It's very useful," Louise said sharply.

"Is it? Do you still use a pencil? The only time I use one is for standardized tests, and a bunch of filled-in bubbles isn't going to reveal anything—and once I'm done with school, what use will a pencil be? I will be at my computer all day. And there are already lots of ways to preserve computer data."

"I'm sure you would know all about that."

Her tone stung.

"What do you mean?" I asked.

"A computer may be good enough for you. But not everyone has a computer. And if you include the people of the past, the overwhelming majority of people have never used a computer."

"But that's absurd, why would you include the people of the past?" I asked. "If you include the people of the future, eventually the majority of people will never have used a pencil."

"Fine. They will have computers, and we can get their stories via whatever it is they type. But how do you get stories from the past when you are no longer living in the moment? How do you get stories about a time period that is quickly aging out? What do you do when the people who have lived through a significant experience are dying or losing their memories? Computers can't do anything about that. And pencils shouldn't be able to either. But they can, with your grandmother's ability."

"Oh." A fear gripped me then, one that held too tightly for me to be able to say more than the one word to her.

"What's wrong?" Her voice became gentle. It was almost annoying, how perceptive she was.

"It's nothing," I said automatically.

"Take your time. I'm here."

For a moment we did nothing except listen to each other breathe, me, frozen by indecision, and her, waiting for me.

I swallowed. If I did not ask, it would gnaw at me until I spoke to her again. It would be a stabbing pain whenever I thought of her, maybe even whenever I thought of grandmother, and I did not want what was normally a source of comfort tainted. I finally voiced my fear.

"Did you only start talking to me because you knew about my grandmother's ability?"

She took her time replying. I fidgeted in her silence. It had only been a month, I had to remind myself. A month of potential delusion, when I had really needed someone to talk to, when it seemed she was interested in me and I thought—No, I can't write it.

"I can't say no," she said finally. "You and I only met because of your grandmother. And who wouldn't be curious about whether the power Meng told me about was real? And you know I had an interest in archiving. But maybe I can answer the question I think you are really trying to ask. Do I still talk to you only because of your grandmother's ability? No, not at all. I *like* talking to you. I like *you*."

I gave in then, mumbling something. When she asked me to repeat myself I couldn't, because it was unintelligible even to me. She had said all I wanted to hear. Still, my view of her had shifted—from seeing her as open and eager to someone who was careful and calculated, who of course knew exactly what to say. Somehow, she had become both the only person I could talk to about grandmother's illness and the only other person who knew about the pencils.

"This must be wild for you," she said. "Maybe take some time to process? And if there's anything that comes up later, just call me, okay? Let's—" The genuine concern in her voice melted me further. "Let's talk about your project. EMBRS, right?"

I had buried myself in EMBRS to distract from everything else going on, and it was easy to return to that now, the architecture I knew so well. I could lean against it with confidence and know it would never change unless I changed it myself.

I told her about our latest effort, to break ground on the journaling component of EMBRS. It meant not only building a slick website, but also processes that could operate on longform text instead of short social media posts. Different algorithms, brainstorming how best to store such data. It was silly, how much my body relaxed, talking about data and code. I told her about how Prof. Logan wanted me to prepare a presentation—and I probably went into too much detail about one of the natural language processing papers I was reading.

She began to laugh.

"What?" I asked, suddenly self-conscious.

"I don't think I've heard you this excited before."

"Oh. It's interesting, I guess."

"It is," she agreed quickly. "But I would never have guessed my post would be scraped by a college student's bot."

"It's in the terms of service."

"Do you read those?"

"No, of course not."

"Even you don't read them!" she laughed.

"Do I seem like the type to?"

"I think out of everyone I know, you would be most likely."

"I—I have better things to do—"

"It's fine! I think it's cute."

"Well, I don't do it," I said, stupidly adamant.

"Cool."

"Your turn to tell me what you're working on," I said.

"Ah!" It was a sound somewhere between surprise and a groan. "You and my advisor would both like to know. Tell you what. Let's trade. I'm supposed to send a proposal by the end of the week. I'll BCC you on the email, and you can get the official version."

"And what do you want in return?"

"A video of your presentation for your professor. I like listening to you."

That jumbled everything in my mind. Even now I don't remember what I said to end the call or if I was coherent at all. I sat there on my floor for a while, just thinking, until grandmother knocked on my door.

She carried with her a plate of freshly cut mango, my favorite fruit. It's impossible to find mangoes as good as the ones in Taiwan here, but that doesn't stop grandmother from trying.

"What's wrong?" she asked.

We sat on my bed, taking turns forking mango chunks. A few weeks ago I would have brushed her off, told her everything was fine. Even now I wanted to, but something's changed between us, a simultaneous opening and closing, and I recognized the mangoes as an apology of sorts. Slowly, I opened up to her. I told her Louise knew, that Meng had told her about Reforging, and I was feeling betrayed, though maybe that was too dramatic, and how, really, I didn't know what to think.

Grandmother chewed her mango thoughtfully.

"But, Monica," she said, "why do you frame this like a bad thing? To have somebody you can share all this with. Isn't that a great fortune? That I had Meng to share my childhood with made all the difference."

"Then why don't you Reforge her pencil?" I braved. "To see what she has to share with you?"

She pushed the remaining mango to my side of the plate.

"I will," she said unsteadily, and then her voice became sly, a return to form so strong it made me realize how much she had faded this summer. How much more she used to tease. "How about a trade?"

"A trade?" I asked warily. It was too close to what Louise had said. And it's rarely a good thing for me when grandmother gets into one of her trickster moods.

"Yes. I will Reforge Meng's pencil once you invite Louise over."

I sputtered and could not think of a single reason to turn her down. After all, they were both things I wanted. I agreed.

Then there was another glint in her eye, and I was sure she was about to say something super embarrassing, like how she was excited to meet her future granddaughter-in-law. She said, "If Meng told Louise about Reforging, she must have seen something remarkable in her. I'm looking forward to meeting her."

After that, I was smiling too much, and grandmother rolled her eyes, gathered our forks onto the empty plate, and left.

So now I'm caught between feelings. I keep looking at my calendar and at the Princeton academic calendar. Replaying our conversations, wondering how I can ask her to visit. Wondering if I've been making life harder for myself this whole time because I've been too unwilling to share my feelings with the people around me—and what it might feel like to be pried open, to have my heart in the hands of another.

CHAPTER 12

From the Reforged pencil of Wong Yun

There are things they say you never forget, even with a disease like mine. The motions you went through the most can become ingrained. It is a terrifying thought that once all my other memories are gone, I might still Reforge a pencil, another person's memories playing out before me, long after my own have left. I'll have to ask Torou to keep all pencils away from me, the way others must hide their knives. I could never forget how to Reforge, not after all the years we spent working for Mr. Gao.

Mother insisted he not know that you and I could Reforge. She told him she was the only one so he would not assume it was genetic. But when there were too many messages, she recruited us. Mr. Gao, or someone posing as a customer with his seal, came almost every night to retrieve our work.

For three years, all we did was Reforge. I came to understand the rhythm of these messages. They were never obvious, never even interesting. Reports of names I did not know being sent to different cities, requests to move family members, some that didn't make sense at all, probably part of a code. The outline of the phoenix on my arm, which used to nearly disappear after I had bled out the heart, was becoming a scar. You and I would compare, pressing our arms together, competing on who was giving more of themselves to the war effort and to the pencil company.

There was a risk to the process though. Our mothers, or maybe their mother before them, had designed the Phoenix Pencil Company pencils not only for their quality in writing, but also so they were safe and easy to Reforge. Mr. Gao paid for pencils he sent into the field, but the soldiers often wrote with whatever they had nearby.

"I should never have told him I can Reforge those as well," Mother sighed every time your mother helped bandage her wrist.

She never let either of us touch the pencils that were not from the company. Their hearts were impure, she would say. She Reforged those herself.

One time, it left her incapacitated for a week. She remained in bed, shivering despite both you and me bringing all of our blankets to drape over her. We slept in the same bed to keep each other warm. Your mother redressed her arm every night, bandaging over cuts that refused to heal. Even my grandmother went into her room to check on her.

That was the week I Reforged most of the messages. When I finished all our pencils, I tried to sneak one from the impure pile. Your mother clamped my wrist. I had not even known she was there. She knew me too well. Before I could argue, she swept them into a bag, knotted it, and brought it with her to the back of the complex, back to the room she shared with my mother.

The next time Mr. Gao came, Mother managed to sit upright at the front of the store. She handed him each paper I had Reforged, and more. She had somehow completed all the others.

I will never forget that image, even now—Mother barely able to remain sitting, her left arm limp, her right trembling as she passed everything over, a pencil clattering to the floor, nobody picking it up. Mr. Gao, tall and strong and young, flipping through the pages while Mother fell apart in front of him.

He must have pitied us, for when next he came, he brought a small bag of white rice, a luxury during that time. Ah-shin portioned most of it out to Mother, who was still recovering. Mother scraped it into my bowl, saying the young were more in need of good food. I scraped it into your bowl, saying the same thing, for you were a few months younger. Then you passed your whole bowl to your mother, saying we had to respect our elders, and your mother huffed and passed it to Ah-shin, who she said we did not appreciate enough. Tears came to Ah-shin's eyes before she split the small lump of rice into five, giving the smallest chunk to herself. Only then did we eat.

"If your pencils were the monopoly, your sister would not hurt like this," Mr. Gao said to your mother when my mother was still confined to her bed.

"Is that something you can help with?" your mother asked.

He eyed her. We both noticed. I saw your hands clench, as if you wanted to call upon the armor we had given our characters.

"I can help you with anything you like," he said smoothly.

"Buy more pencils, then," your mother said. "My sister cannot process all the messages you need if you keep giving her trash pencils."

"I will do my best," he said with a bow. Then he took your mother's hand and kissed it. She let him. She even smiled.

You refused to speak to her for a while after that. You told me your mother only let him kiss her because of the power difference. You told me your father was going to come home soon. Both of our fathers. That the war could not last forever. That once our fathers were back, we would not need Mr. Gao's protection.

You insisted all of this and more, even when I did not argue against you. Each time he came and made your mother laugh, you shot me a dark look, as if daring me to say something. Looking back, there was, indeed, a power imbalance, and your mother likely wanted to please him for our safety. But also, and I hope enough years have passed that I can say this without stirring anger in you, there was desire from your mother. She was so social, elegant, and charming, a woman made for flirting her way through the Shanghai elite, the kind of woman I wanted to be. And Mr. Gao could be handsome when his mood was light, when your mother made him smile. Instead, she was trapped inside with only us for company, your father missing, and no way to socialize without risking someone discovering that our fathers fought against our occupiers in provinces far away.

Mr. Gao kept his promise and bought more of our pencils, pencils that eventually made their way back to us to be Reforged. Compared to our neighbors, we became very well-off, though Mother hid our money, and we lived the same as always to not attract attention. Whenever Mr. Gao brought over a small bag of white rice, he would stay for dinner and sit beside your mother, who would touch his shoulder lightly whenever she rose from the table. He even gave my grandmother a shortwave radio to receive the news. She stopped complaining about his visits after that.

Meanwhile, the world was changing all around us, but we were too focused on Reforging to grasp everything that was happening. What should have been a remarkable event—the British, American, and French renouncing their rights to Shanghai, where they had partied and gambled and prospered for one hundred and one years—became another piece of background noise. The Westerners had finally been expelled, as my father and the Nationalists wanted all along, except it was the Japanese who had done it and whose occupation remained ever present.

When we were seventeen, we received word that your father had died in a battle defending a railroad down south in Hunan, so far away from us. Mother told me to give you space to process.

By then I understood that your father and my father had joined different factions of the Chinese army. My father fought with the Nationalists. More than anything he wanted a strong China. The Nationalists were the stronger party at the time with a pipeline from the military academy straight into their ranks. Your father joined the Communists, who were propped up by the USSR. He also wanted a strong China, as your mother said, but believed we should follow the model of the Bolsheviks, the common people first. The two parties had once fought each other over China's future. Now they were united against Japan.

"Are you alright?" I whispered, ignoring Mother's request.

You nodded.

"I really didn't know him. Even before the war, he wasn't around much. My mother, though . . ."

Your mother continued her tasks, maintained her usual demeanor for the few customers who came to the store. For the first time, though, I saw her stumble over her words, select the wrong sample pencil hearts, speak brusquely instead of with her usual soft charm. It was as if I was watching her fade before my eyes.

The next time Mr. Gao came for dinner, your mother burst into tears. My mother reached for her, but she had already latched on to him, crying into his chest as he wrapped his arms around her. Mother ushered us to our room. Even my grandmother left the table, clicking her tongue, but leaving them alone all the same. Mother joined us in our room that night, sharing my small bed. You rolled yourself up into your blanket, your back to us, as close to the wall as you could get, as if you wanted to become a part of it. Mr. Gao stayed the night.

Mostly I remember the next morning, when your mother hugged you and promised she would never leave you, scattered your head with kisses and gripped the back of your shirt so tight the wrinkles stayed long after she released you. There was a light in her eyes I had not seen in years.

You and I did not fully comprehend the danger of our work then. There were rumors about a former Chinese hotel that had been converted into holding cells and torture chambers, right in the International Settlement. I didn't learn about that until much later—our mothers shielded us from the worst. The Japanese imprisoned Chinese and foreigners there. They wanted information on Chinese patriots, anybody related to them, and that was us—my father was still fighting in the war, and perhaps even worse, we were Reforging messages to aid his cause. But Mr. Gao kept his promise. He protected us and our operation. None of us came close to ending up in that building. Still, we were always on edge. Your mother, normally so calm and collected, startled violently whenever there was an unexpected knock on the door. Once, she even screamed at us for wearing short sleeves, our phoenixes exposed, though we were in the house, the black curtains drawn.

In the last year of the war, the two of us Reforged the majority of the pencils. Our mothers insisted on handling the impure ones, and so we did the rest. We became very good at it, discovering tricks like how to bleed out Mr. Gao's pencils but not each other's stories. Our days became routine. Wake up, Reforge, see what Ah-shin could scrape together for us, Reforge, eat any leftovers, and end the night by working on our story. Sometimes we were too tired to write and just lay there whispering about what we would do if there was no war. The shops we would visit, the boys we would meet, the places we would take our mothers. Those memories are hard for me to reach, each day blurring into the same.

My grandmother listened to the radio constantly. It received the best signal in the workshop. While we Reforged, she would relay snippets of news to us. That the Japanese were losing ground and there was a new curfew, that the Americans had invaded and opened a military base in Okinawa, not far from us.

Even without the radio, we could tell things were changing. The Japanese soldiers in Shanghai were increasingly old and injured, the young, healthy men sent to the front lines where they were needed. We heard the drone of American planes overhead. One day, hundreds of them flew past, and the street outside the company erupted in cheers. The Japanese soldiers did not even attempt to punish us.

Soon after that, we heard the emperor of Japan's voice over the radio. We all froze, pencils in hand, waiting for the translation, and then the news, a blur drowned out by a gasp from our mothers, a single sob from my grandmother. A terrible bomb in Japan. The empire's unconditional surrender.

We took to the street, supporting my grandmother between us so she, too, could witness this moment. Hastily made bamboo victory banners thrust in the air, more and more firecrackers launched with every step we took. When we passed the racetrack, the speakers were broadcasting the emperor's surrender, crowds cheering with each replay. And when the Americans rolled in on their tanks—my goodness. How they were applauded, their white teeth shining, soldiers handing out chocolate and gum to children with barely any clothing. Some of the Americans hoisted a rickshaw puller into his own rickshaw, then pulled him around, delighting in their strength to spare, hooting at their vitality, their ability to end a world war.

At home, we were finally able to draw back our heavy black curtains. They had remained closed to prevent bombers from seeing the light in our homes. Sunlight fell into the pencil company for the first time in years, illuminating the swirling dust, graphite mixed with isolation.

The Nationalists were to return to power, and the members of the puppet government were fleeing. Mr. Gao came by with a huge bag of white rice, only to be topped by Ah-shin who returned with meat and vegetables taken straight from the homes of those who had fled. We ran to our old school. Many of our classmates were there. We laughed and hugged and dreamed of what might come next.

We were eighteen years old. The last eight years of our lives had been spent in constant fear of the Japanese, and the past four, under actual occupation.

"Do you think you'll leave Shanghai?" I asked.

"No," you said. "Shanghai is my home now."

We spent the afternoon with our former classmates, learning who had fled, who had stayed, and who had cooperated with the puppet government only to be punished now. It made me appreciate what our mothers had accomplished. Our family and the company were intact. It had been so long since we had seen the boys in our school. All of them had grown tall, if skinny from lack of nutrition. They laughed loudly and attempted to charm you.

One of them asked you out that very day. I was jealous at first—I was always jealous of you, you must know that—but that feeling quickly gave way to mirth. I saw you redden as the boy stared at you so eagerly, watched you glance away, glance at me, then focus only on the ground.

"She'll go on a date with you if you buy a pencil," I said. I took an unsharpened one from my bag. I had nothing in mind at that point, only an urge to tease him, and to embarrass you, and to bring back the story of a business transaction I was sure your mother would enjoy.

"How much?" he asked. I made up a number—it had been so long since I had sold a single pencil. He offered a packet of just-pilfered white rice instead. It was a great deal.

"I never agreed to this," you cut in as the boy took the pencil with a smile.

"Come by the pencil company tomorrow," I said. "She'll be ready." And then I ran, you trailing close behind, yelling my name until I stopped, halfway home, both of us breathless and doubled over. I could tell you were about to start in on me, so I grabbed your shoulders and shook.

"Look," I demanded. It was just you and me in an alleyway in Shanghai, our home, on a beautiful day without war. The air was delicious, and I took huge gulps of it. "Live," I said, then laughed. "It's finally time to live."

Somehow that got through your war-hardened exterior, and you smiled, shaking your head.

"What will I even wear?" you asked. I grabbed your hand, and we ran the rest of the way together.

At home, our mothers watched us search through their closet for something suitable. They were in a good mood. Your mother reclined on her bed, passing a cigarette to my mother, who sat on the same bed, legs crossed, leaning back. For once, they were relaxing instead of Reforging.

"Now that Meng is dating, should we tell her?" your mother asked mine, a spark in her eyes.

Mother tapped her foot, pondering the question.

"You two can't possibly have more secrets," I said, holding one of your mother's dresses up to you. The dresses had not left the closet since the Settlement was occupied. Now they could live a new life.

"Of course we can," your mother scoffed.

"But how to say it?" Mother asked.

"Not the way our mother told us, that's for sure," your mother said. "I was traumatized after that talk."

"What are you two going on about?" you demanded. Even you were growing impatient.

"Well, when you're with a boy—" your mother began.

"Maybe I don't want to hear this," you said quickly.

"—you might find yourself Reforging," your mother finished.

We both perked up, the search for an outfit forgotten.

"So make sure your arm is clear before you meet with this boy," Mother said. She tapped at her own bare arm, at her phoenix. It had darkened during the war.

"He won't notice it. Your dresses all have long sleeves."

"It's not about what he sees. It's that we can't go losing any Reforgings."

"But why would I be Reforging?" you asked.

"And how do you lose a Reforging?" I added.

"It's . . ." Mother began. "It's another way of Reforging that you might stumble upon. A way that is much less painful than bleeding. Pleasurable, even."

"Well then, why didn't you teach us that way?" I demanded.

They both shifted.

"You'll understand one day," Mother said lamely.

"You're not going to tell us what it is?" you asked, as incredulous as I was.

"Just make sure your arm is clear before you see him," your mother said. She got up from her bed and pulled out another dress that was buried deep in the closet. "I think this one would look perfect on you."

They clammed up after that, revealing nothing about this other way of Reforging, no matter how many questions we asked. Our only solace was that we were each as clueless as the other.

Of course, now we both know what they were talking about. I want Monica to be able to Reforge this way, to know only pleasure, not pain, and so I have the unenviable task our mothers once had. Though I like to think I'm bolder than they were and that I'll feel comfortable coming right out and saying it. But Monica. Well, she's . . . she's going to hate this conversation. I can already see the red in her face. My little tomato.

CHAPTER 13

From the diary of Monica Tsai,
backed up on three servers spanning
two continents

September 22, 2018 (2018-09-22T22:34:29.442041)
loc: Cambridge, Massachusetts. United States of America
(42.3721865,71.1117091)

Grandmother is getting worse. The other day she came into my room and
looked at me curiously, almost like a child. Her hand wavered as she
pointed at me, an overlarge tremble. When her lip began to quiver, too,
I stood up from my desk and asked what was wrong.

She stopped pointing at me and shook her head.

"I think I have done something terribly wrong," she said.

Words you never really want to hear from anyone, least of all from
your grandmother. I thought her memory might be playing tricks on
her and so I asked what she meant.

"Never mind. I should not be bothering you at work."

I insisted it was fine and waited. She remained at the door, holding
her wrist, running her thumb over what I now know are her scars from
Reforging.

"I should not have Reforged your pencil," she said finally. "They
were your private thoughts."

I shrugged. I had already gotten over it.

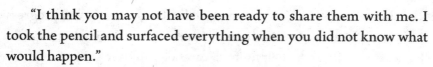

"I think you may not have been ready to share them with me. I took the pencil and surfaced everything when you did not know what would happen."

"It's fine," I insisted. "I'm glad you did it."

She fidgeted and remained at my door.

"All those pencils . . ." she said, more to herself than to me.

"It was only the one pencil." I tried to sound lighthearted.

She shook her head, vigorously this time. "If you don't want to learn more about Reforging, I would understand."

"I do want to learn more," I said. It had not even occurred to me that I had the option. But once she offered, I admit I hesitated. It would indeed be no small relief for grandmother's past to remain hidden. I could go on seeing her as my hero—and this power I had inherited, while remarkable, would stay dormant. After all, I had experienced firsthand what it could unearth.

"Maybe after I think about it some more," I backtracked.

She nodded.

"Let me know when you are ready."

She looked like she was about to say something else, then her eyes lost focus. A look that is becoming more common. Her eyes either cloud over or look at me without seeing, then she panics. I brought her to her room, sat her down in her rocking chair. She keeps a sack of knitting supplies there. I dug through for a half-started project, placed the needles in her hands. Even though her eyes were still lost, she picked up the needles, looped the yarn around her pinkie, and began to knit. The panic on her face ebbed as she returned to this familiar task.

It's happening more frequently, these moments of disconnect. Grandfather and I have tried our best to reassure and reestablish her routine and she always regains herself within a few minutes. But the episodes are longer, and this time, when I checked on her half an hour later, she was still knitting, lost in thought, or maybe lack of thought.

The forums say it's an uncontrollable disease, that it will progress differently for everyone and there is nothing you can do except watch. They also say it can be helpful for a caretaker to have something they can control. So, when I'm not working on EMBRS, I clean.

Every day after work, I attack one thing. First the rice cooker, then the air filter, the toilets, the bookshelves, the stove, the kitchen sink. With my first paycheck, I bought the best vacuum cleaner I could find. I listed it as my 😄 for the day, and Louise laughed.

The next day I stumbled upon a sale for the same vacuum that included extra filters, and I cursed my luck.

Grandfather's coping mechanism is his computer. He claims he's replying to correspondence from former students, when really I know he's taken to answering people's math questions online. I found his profile. His avatar was a doodle I'd drawn of him when I was in middle school—a stick figure wearing a tie, with square glasses and an inexplicably rectangular mouth. He had thousands of reputation points, and his username was "mango_grandpa." I swelled with pride, reading his clear answers to their algebra questions and even the occasional chemistry one, nobody knowing that mango_grandpa was a former MIT professor desperate for a distraction, attempting to cope with his wife's decline.

"You don't need to clean this much," he said as I disinfected his desk for the second time that week.

"And you don't need to help the mango grandchildren all the time," I countered.

He chuckled.

"There can never be too much math education," he said. In that moment I agreed with him, found myself thinking of the multivariable calculus class I should have been taking that semester. I dismissed the thought before I could linger on it too long.

On the other hand, all things EMBRS have been going super well. I did that presentation Prof. Logan asked me to do for the freshmen. It was weird doing it over a video call, but at some point, I got into it, murmuring to myself as I worked as usual. It's a habit I picked up from grandfather. In any case, Prof. Logan gave me loads of compliments afterward.

"You made it very accessible," he said from his office, during our weekly 1:1. "The students loved it. That self-deprecating humor really works for you." Then he paused. "Of course, you don't actually feel that way about yourself, do you?"

"Of course not," I lied. Perhaps I had referred to my work as "trash code" one too many times.

He raised an eyebrow. The delay in the video connection pixelated his eyebrow, making it appear fractured.

"I'm only going to say this once, Monica. You are likely the most talented sophomore I've ever worked with. Not only in your code, which is clean and beautiful, but also in your communication, which is transparent and accessible. Those are really the most important things about being an engineer. When EMBRS succeeds, it will be in large part thanks to you."

I'm going to be riding this high for a while.

When I mentioned his compliments as my 😄 for the day to Louise, she demanded the presentation recording. I was nervous, waiting for her reply, wishing the video wasn't so long, suddenly fearing she would contradict everything he had praised about me.

But she didn't. As soon as twenty-seven minutes passed, she replied:

wow, that was really great! even I understood

And a few seconds later:

and damn, youre cute

I melted into my bed and couldn't move for a while. I lay there staring at the ceiling, at those stars that don't light up anymore, grinning uncontrollably. First Prof. Logan's compliments, then this. It was too much. I felt like an electron when it's given too much energy and all it can do is vibrate over to the next orbital. And somehow, the only thing I could think to send back was:

> and you're late with your email about
> your major!

Which totally killed the vibe. But she took it in stride.

lol I know. im terrible with deadlines. gimme a
few more days

Her email came three days later. She BCC'd me on her message to her advisor, as she promised.

ugh stayed up all night working on it . . . and it
was still late! but lemme know what you think!!

I had been in the zone, debugging something in the EMBRS logs— and even though I needed to complete my work before the logs rotated, I was so curious I ended up just scp'ing the logs to my own machine so I could look at them later.

Her thesis proposal was good: well laid out and convincing, with strategically placed graphics and pictures from Shanghai. She's a talented photographer, and I told her so.

d'aw, thanks!

It turned out her project was not archival exactly. It had a digital spin to it, and there was a field for it out there called—what do you know—digital archiving. But she went a little further, cited other works, and said the version she wanted to focus on was called—and I got chills when I read it—memory work. I didn't really understand what it meant from her proposal. Her advisor likely knew definitions I didn't. So I looked up some of the works she had cited; even those had a number of technical terms.

She texted again.

well??

I prepared a list of questions and texted her, warning that I was about to call.

finally!

The phone did not even finish its first ring before she picked up.

"Was it okay?" she asked, breathless.

"It looks great. I didn't understand a lot of it—"

"Oh no . . ."

"But it's not my background! I only know about computers."

"You know more than computers."

"Not really." I held up my first question. Suddenly, I felt like a journalist, and so I played into it, lowering my voice and articulating clearly. "Memory work. That's a very striking term."

"Isn't it?" There was a smile in her voice. "Archiving has been a thing for ages now. Digital archiving, too. But memory work takes a different approach."

"By trying to be more ethical?" It was what one of the sources had claimed, though I couldn't discern what made it any better.

"Maybe. The idea is that one person's memory is never the whole source of truth. Everyone interprets what happens around them based on their own circumstances. Historians and archivists are most at fault here, since they get to decide what lives on and what doesn't, and this also goes through the filter of their own experiences. So if you're in archiving, you have to acknowledge the importance of your role and the impact you have for future generations referring to your work.

"Let's say you're an archivist for Cambridge," she continued without pause. I wondered if this was what I sounded like when I was explaining EMBRS to her. "And let's say there's a march demanding better roads for bikers. There are some articles about it, and some photos, which you save to the archives. Because they are there, Cambridge suddenly has this history of having fought for biker rights. And that helps shape the community—there's proof this has been done before, a rung on the ladder, so let's build the next rung and have an even bigger march. Bike lanes show up, and the city invests in a widespread bike share system. Now you're a city known for biking, and it's a source of pride. Everyone in Cambridge has different experiences but in some way, you are all shaped by its good biking system."

"Biking's not *that* great in Cambridge," I muttered. She ignored me.

"But now let's say you find out about this elderly couple who was bought out of their home in favor of installing a hub for electric bikes. The couple doesn't speak English, and so they were never able to advocate for themselves. How do you reconcile that with the narrative of Cambridge as a great city for biking?"

"Did you have to make it an elderly couple with bad English?" I asked miserably.

"Sorry," she said gently. "But this is where memory work fits in. Now let's say you decide you need to advocate for people like this elderly couple. You want to go back and look at this narrative from a different lens, from the perspective of a less privileged group. The great biking city narrative already exists though. And so you have to operate on the memory which the city already has of itself. If you don't surface their voices, you're giving tacit approval for displacing the elderly in favor of bikes. It's about no longer excluding those who are always excluded. Not only that—it's about actively working against it. So that the next time you're archiving something, you automatically look for the narrative of the older population and work that into your community's collective memory."

I closed my eyes. I pictured her with Meng, the picture that started it all, the one that triggered the EMBRS alert and brought her and Meng into our lives. Shanghai's skyline in the background. Someone Meng found remarkable.

"But you're not looking at biking in Cambridge, are you?" I said.

"I know nothing about biking in Cambridge," she agreed.

"You're looking at Shanghai. At Meng's generation. At my grandmother's generation."

"Women who survived both wars," she confirmed. "Especially the ones who made their way here, whose stories were never added to the nation's memory. Not to China's, or Taiwan's, or America's."

"My grandmother, then."

"There aren't many who are still alive. And people really care about recovering these stories. There's this huge grant that my professor wants me to go for that's all about surfacing underheard stories like that. And your family's story—the wars, the pencils. It's incredible." She paused and seemed to swallow hard. "If you and your family are open to that, of course."

It was just my luck to start falling for someone who was interested in me for an entirely different reason. I couldn't reply, choked up on the feeling that I was only a stepping-stone for her and that when she was through with me, she'd move on and not look back. And who was I, a mere stone, to ask her to linger, to squash me a little more gently?

"Hey," she said, interrupting my thoughts. "I'm being rude, aren't I? Throwing my goals at you and pressuring you to help me. Do you remember what I said last time? I really meant it. I like talking to you in a way that has nothing to do with pencils or archiving or memory work. In fact, let's not talk about this anymore. Let's talk about something else."

I wondered if this was how it would always be, a last-minute change of the subject to avoid my insecurities.

"Like what?" I managed to say.

"Hm, what do girls talk about? Tell me about your first kiss."

The question made me flush.

"It wasn't a good one," I said.

"What made it bad?"

"It was with a boy," I said before I could hesitate.

"Ah," she said, and I wondered what that meant, what exactly it was she understood with that one syllable.

"Your turn," I said.

"It was in one of the staircases in my high school, after volleyball practice. And it was electrifying."

She did not elaborate, and I had so many questions.

"I'm glad yours was good, then," I said to draw out more information. It worked.

"Well, I didn't make the mistake of being with a boy."

"Ah."

"Ah," she agreed.

We didn't talk much longer after that. I was going through various highs and lows, and they were all conflicting, and she had to go meet with her study group.

After hanging up, I came to this conclusion: There's a power that my grandmother possesses, which she says she is willing to teach me, and Louise is particularly interested in this power, and I am particularly interested in Louise. Which results in a weird dynamic that can go wrong in so many ways it is best that I don't tempt it.

I decided I would try to distance myself from her. I had a hopeless plan—I'd send vague end-of-day updates and eventually phase it out completely. I'd focus on EMBRS and my grandparents. I'd still invite her to visit, if only to satisfy grandmother's end of the deal, and she could interview grandmother if she wanted, but I'd stay out of it.

The plan felt achievable until a package arrived for me. Both grandfather and grandmother eyed it curiously. I opened it in front of them. Inside were two vacuum filters and a note.

don't worry, I found a coupon ♥ *L*

I could not stop smiling. Grandmother noticed. It was a good day for her.

"I miss playing mahjong," she said suddenly. "Why don't you find us a fourth player, Monica?"

"Oh yes," grandfather agreed. "Nothing would make me happier."

The image of the four of us playing mahjong thrilled me, a world where Louise met my grandparents and we all happily spent time together. A world where grandmother's mind worked effortlessly in pursuit of a winning hand.

And so my short-lived resolve broke entirely, crushed by vacuum filters and mahjong, of all things.

do you want to come visit some time?

Her reply was exhilaratingly immediate.

id love to! my fall break is coming up and we
have a game at harvard. would that work?

that's perfect! we can try out the new
vacuum filters!

how electrifying

I told grandmother that I did it, that I invited her over, and so she needed to Reforge Meng's pencil.

"What?" she exclaimed. "Surely I said only after she came."

I told her she definitely did not.

"Monica," she said sternly. "Don't trick the elderly."

I even showed her my journal entry where I had written it down, that all I had to do was invite Louise over.

She waved her hand.

"Words on a computer," she said dismissively. "The easiest thing to forge."

I couldn't bring myself to pout over it though. I was too excited and eager and busy cleaning every inch of the house. But there are times when I pause and try to brush away this feeling that I'm standing on the precipice of something. As if holding a pencil to my wrist, and I can either continue using it like a regular pencil or I can stab it into me and see if some beautiful truth will come pouring out. Lately, I feel like I'm just sharpening the pencil, honing the tip, and waiting to see where the impulse will take me.

CHAPTER 14

From the Reforged pencil of Wong Yun

Monica has been flitting around the house. Half the time she is excited, using her new vacuum, biking to the store for supplies, watching videos on cleaning techniques. The rest of the time she is all nerves, fiddling with the art hangings on the wall, using her phone to determine if they are straight. You see, she finally worked up the courage to invite Louise to visit. It's not even happening until the end of October, still a month away—and yet she's frantic. Her restless energy has infected me and Torou. We've resumed our early morning walks, and Torou spends a lot of time at his computer, responding to messages from his former students. As for me, I write. Sometimes I get lost while I'm writing and end up wandering the house and find myself back in my rocking chair, knitting needles in hand.

There are some things I can't remember at all. I don't know if this is because of the disease or if I would have forgotten them anyway. For instance, I cannot, no matter how hard I try, recall the name of that boy you were seeing, or even much of what he looked like. You would say it's because I didn't like him. That's not true though. I had nothing against him. I only hated what he did to us, even if it was my own fault.

Shortly after Japan's surrender, you went on your date, and then another, and another. At first you told me everything. When the two of you went to that store that sold American ice cream sodas, and you thought it was too sweet and forced yourself to finish to not appear rude. Or when he took you to the silk shop and offered to have a dress made for you, but you were never into silk or fashion, and so you fumbled out an excuse and left empty-handed. Or how he learned from those not-so-successful outings and brought you to the river and you both sat in silence, watching the ocean liners and barges drift, admiring the American warships that now occupied the port.

As the year progressed, you would be gone for entire afternoons with him. It was startling, to be suddenly without you, when we had been trapped in the same house, the same room, for so long. You even missed the day Mr. Gao came with news of my father.

Mr. Gao was dressed in a crisp western suit, his hair combed neatly to the side. He looked impressive, even more so once your mother took his arm, wearing a beautiful floral qipao.

"I have good news," Mr. Gao said to my mother. "Your husband is on his way home."

"He is?" I blurted. We had not heard from my father in months.

"Yes. I suspect he will be here by the end of the week. His passage should be smooth, thanks to his devoted service."

"Thank you for the news." Mother bowed.

Something passed between our mothers then. A look I only recognized because I had cast the very same look at you, a jolt of jealousy that hit when I learned you had something I wanted. One of our mothers had a husband who was coming home alive. The other had a new man in her life who took her out in the city at night to enjoy herself, the way our mothers used to together. So who was jealous of who? I think it most likely they both were, though I did not reach that conclusion at the time. This exercise of looking back has proven useful. It helps me untangle these memories, apply the wisdom of my years to our mothers who seem so young in comparison to how old we are now.

Mr. Gao also brought more pencils he needed Mother to Reforge, even though he had assured us that with the war over, she would no longer need to do this—and yet more and more pencils came, the same as before, the Nationalists paranoid of their old enemy, the Communists. They preferred to pass their messages the way he had established; none of the messages he had ferried during the war had ever been compromised.

Because you were out most afternoons, you worked on your allotment that evening. While you Reforged, I sat beside you, happy to be finished, and told you my father was returning any day now.

"Oh," you said softly. You claimed not to miss your father, but in that moment your voice was far away. Not long after, you reverted to your father's last name, casting mine away, no longer needed now that the Japanese were gone. You spent even less time at home.

The more I tried to reconnect with you, the more you pushed me away. Whether it was intentional or not, I did not know. You stopped telling me about your dates, only gave me vague summaries when you used to give me every detail. I was no longer more knowledgeable of the city, the one advantage I used to have over you. You were always out exploring, learning about Shanghai as it was now, no longer under foreign control, a city finding its place in the world like you were. You would return from your dates bright-eyed, cheeks flushed, as if you had learned some great secret, and even if it had nothing to do with pencils or Reforging, it turned out my heart could writhe with as much envy at nineteen as it had when I was ten.

One night, I confronted you directly.

"What are you keeping from me?" I asked the shadow you cast through the mosquito net. We were lying in bed. I knew from your breathing you were still awake.

Your shadow shifted. You asked, in a small voice, "Why do you think we bleed pencil hearts?"

"What do you mean?" I had not expected a philosophical question.

"I just mean, we already feel the writer's words when we Reforge the pencil. So why do we bleed out the story too?"

"Maybe because it's not ours," I said. It was nice, to speak this way with you again. "Because it doesn't belong in our body, as part of us?"

"It seems like things might be easier, safer, if we could only Reforge, and not bleed it back out."

"But then we wouldn't be nearly as useful to Mr. Gao," I said. "The company would've fallen during the war. And we have to bleed it out, there's no way around it."

"There is," you said eventually. "You can lose a Reforging."

You had discovered the secret our mothers had alluded to.

"How?" I asked. "How can you lose a Reforging?"

"It's not that you lose it," you said. "It's that the world loses it."

The words made me shiver, even under my blanket.

"But how does that happen?" I asked.

"It's—" You stopped. I watched your unmoving shadow. Finally, you said, "I can't say."

I tore my eyes away from you. In that moment, I was thrust back to those nagging feelings I had experienced when we first met, begrudging the elegance of your clothes, your pretty face, but most of all how you knew something that our mothers knew and only I didn't, and nobody would say why. When I was welcomed into that circle, I thought we were equals. I thought nothing could separate us after that, not after we had lived through a war, cut our arms over and over, bled out onto the page together. Now it was as if the war was the reason for our closeness—the only reason you came to Shanghai, the only reason we found anything in common, both our fathers off fighting, and now that it was over, our natural differences reemerged and the resentment that came so easily to me blossomed once again.

"Why not?" I asked, not daring to raise my voice for fear of what it might betray.

You took another long pause before replying.

"Because it's something—it's something between me and him."

I flipped over in bed, turning away from you. I closed my eyes, willed myself to sleep. You called my name. I ignored you. I slept fitfully, waking every few hours, convinced you were no longer in the room, that I was alone.

In the morning, we ate breakfast together while our mothers chatted. We had a rare day off. Mother was heading out to buy supplies in preparation for my father's return. And your mother was going to the department store with Mr. Gao. They asked about our plans.

"We are going to a movie," you said, picking at your congee grain by grain.

"Oh, lovely," your mother said. "Yun kept talking about wanting to see that new one, the American one—"

"I'm not going," I said. "She's going with her boy."

"Oh," your mother said, looking between us. "Then what will you do, Yun?"

"Stay home and Reforge, I suppose," I said. Before they could cut in with some compromise or attempt at solace, I shoveled the rest of my breakfast into my mouth and went to the front of the store, intent on drowning my self-pity in pencil work.

When I reached the front, your boy was already there waiting to pick you up, standing outside the locked door. I let him in.

"I know I'm early," he said. "I can wait here if Meng isn't ready."

The first thing I noticed about him was the pencil tucked behind his ear. It was the one I had given him, back when I still thought it a fun way to tease you.

"How is that pencil treating you?" I asked, an idea slowly forming.

"It's wonderful," he said, lifting it from behind his ear.

"Let me see how it's doing."

He handed it over without a second thought. I brought it to the counter where your mother normally worked. I took out a notebook and made a show of drawing lines of various darkness. I flicked it a few times, held it up to the light, then stooped below the counter and came back up with your mother's glasses, as if to examine it more closely. It had been the easiest thing in the world, while I was out of sight, to swap his pencil for another.

"It's flawless." I smiled, handing him the new one.

He tucked it behind his ear. Somebody like him, who had not grown up in a pencil factory, would never notice the difference.

"I'll go get Meng for you," I said.

You left with him shortly afterward. Mother left too, then Mr. Gao came for your mother, and finally I was alone. I wasted no time Reforging your boy's pencil.

As his heart melted into my wrist, the overwhelming emotion I experienced was sincerity. He wrote poems, like the husband of that woman whose words you had Reforged all those years ago. Did you have a soft spot for poets? His poems kept coming. The early ones slow and elegant, dwelling on the landscape, the rivers, the ocean around Shanghai. But soon they morphed, became fast and feverish, focused on bodies and desire. They brought a heat to my cheeks. His sincerity multiplied my guilt. I had forced open a curtain I should not have, witnessed something intimate and special and private. Yet I could not stop, not while there was still pencil to Reforge. It was like I had stuck my hand in a fire. I couldn't take it out now. I forced myself to feel every lick of the flame.

As soon as I had absorbed it all, I cut my skin and bled out his words. The cool knife a relief. By the time I was done, I was out of breath.

I gathered my thoughts and cleaned up any evidence of my Reforging. I hesitated to burn the notebook, though. I opened it and read one of the early poems again. It was well written. I read the others, taking my time, even when I knew he was describing you in a way that was never meant for me to see. Mother came home earlier than expected, and I had to shove the notebook away, no time to burn it, only enough time to make sure it did not go in the pile of Reforged papers Mr. Gao would come to take away.

You did not return until after dinner. I found myself observing you more closely, convinced you had changed. Before you had hunched, as if to protect yourself. Now you sat up straight, leaning back comfortably in your chair, letting your phoenix's head peek out from your sleeve when our mothers were not looking. I wondered if you had shown it to your boy, if you told him about our ability, if he kissed your scars, pressed his lips to the stories within you. The thought made my own body stir in an unfamiliar way—different from the point of the knife or the fear of the soldier.

We passed each other in the hallway, when I was returning to our room and you were heading to the workshop to Reforge your allotment.

"Hi." I tried to act normal.

You continued walking without acknowledging me. I was sure you had found the notebook in our room. Why had I not hidden it somewhere better than under my pillow? I should have ripped it to shreds, even if I could not make it to the kiln. Why had I Reforged it in the first place, why had I tricked your boy, why could I not stop lying and deceiving?

Your shoulder brushed mine and your hand slipped what could only be a pencil into mine. We moved past each other, not a single word exchanged, your pencil hot in my hand.

Back in our room, I trembled, holding your pencil. I feared what you might say, what you might have figured out about me. I feared I had done something so unforgivable that it could not be addressed via conversation, only pencil.

To be honest, it was not so different than what I feel now, looking at your pencil.

But unlike now, I did not hesitate. I held my breath and pushed your pencil into my wrist.

I almost laughed when I was finished, a laugh that was a mixture of relief, guilt, and sorrow. It was nothing more than the next chapter of our story. I did not know when you had written it—you had been out all day. Had you written it while you were with the boy? Were you thinking of our story even then? It was a brilliant chapter, filled with our usual espionage and the dash of fun that had become prevalent since the war's end. Our characters used their new ability to armor themselves to great effect—a shock to the soldiers who preyed on them because they were young women—and as they worked on their plan to infiltrate some important government official's house, disguised as housekeepers, they passed each other messages through pencils. They pretended not to know each other, walked right past each other, and slipped the other a note without a word.

I went to the workshop. You were bleeding into a notebook, surprised when I sat beside you and grabbed a handful of pencils.

"But you've already done yours," you said.

I pushed a heart into my wrist anyway.

I didn't apologize to you, not then. But as we quietly sat, Reforging, I once again felt close to you. Not in the same way as before—it would never be the same. It was the first time I understood that I did not need to know everything about you, that it would be better, in fact, if I did not, and that not all stories are meant to be shared. The beauty was in the ones that we shared willingly and those were to be cherished.

Neither of us knew then that another war was right around the corner, or that we'd soon be separated. In many ways, that was the last peaceful moment we spent together.

CHAPTER 15

From the diary of Monica Tsai,
backed up on three servers spanning
two continents

October 10, 2018 (2018-10-10T20:11:53.740456)
loc: Cambridge, Massachusetts. United States of America
(42.3721865,71.1117091)

It has been a difficult few weeks, I'm not going to lie. I took some time off work to accompany grandmother to the doctor. At first, she was in good spirits as we helped her with her shoes, insisting we all wear the scarves she'd knitted us last year, now that it's getting colder. It was only when we stepped outside that things started to turn. Grandfather tripped over our porch step, and I barely caught him in time. His palm scraped against the pavement, and he was struggling to breathe. I sat him down, holding on to his thin torso. But when I tried to help him to his feet, grandmother on his other side, also fruitlessly trying to hoist him up, he kept shaking his head.

"Just give me a moment to catch my breath," he said.

Something changed in grandmother. She began to panic over him, speaking rapidly, except the words coming out of her mouth were neither English nor Mandarin nor Shanghainese. I clung to a hope they were Japanese or Taiwanese, languages she might have picked up years ago, though deep down I knew that they were gibberish, as she patted grandfather's coat down and pleaded with him.

Grandfather nodded placatingly. It clearly was not his first time hearing her speak this way. I ran back into the house for something to clean his hand. When I reached the bathroom, I gripped the sink, and all I could do was stand there telling myself to stay calm. Grandfather was allowed to falter. He was not young. Yet until right then, I had not even considered it a possibility. He was the stable one, the one with the successful career that allowed us to never worry about money, the one who delayed his retirement after my mother and father left, the one who was supposed to be around to help with grandmother as she faded. I shrank into myself, wanting nothing more than to remain in place, to freeze time before things got any worse. But we had a doctor appointment to get to. I reminded myself that grandfather was barely hurt and grandmother would snap out of it soon.

When I returned, grandfather was standing again. I helped him clean his scraped hand. Grandmother was still panicking. We reassured her that we were just going to see the doctor for a routine visit, and that we would be home soon. Her Chinese returned. I almost wished it hadn't because she begged and begged:

"Don't take me away from home."

"You love Dr. Wu," grandfather said in his most soothing voice. "You offered to send Monica to her office to fix her computer, remember? And she asked you all about Monica and the two of you talked forever and you didn't even notice all the tests she was doing on you. Afterward you said you couldn't wait to see her again. And she is a very busy person. It is difficult to reschedule an appointment with—"

"I don't know who you're talking about." Grandmother was trembling, holding her head in her hands, trying to turn back toward the house. I held her arm, enough to keep her in place. With my free hand, I called a ride share since we had missed the bus.

I attempted to reason with her, but I was even less successful than grandfather. In the end, she fell against him and pounded weakly at his chest, crying.

"They'll find us. Even here. Torou . . ."

Grandfather held her until she went limp in his arms. I stood there, useless, not knowing how to help and too scared to even try. To our relief, by the time the ride share pulled up, grandmother had worn herself out.

At the clinic, Dr. Wu greeted grandmother enthusiastically and received wide, uncertain eyes in response. The doctor ran her tests and talked mostly with me. She tried to engage grandfather, too, but he was too spent. The tie he always wore was a little crooked, his bandaged hand resting in his lap.

When we left, Dr. Wu pulled me aside while grandmother and grandfather walked ahead.

"Hey," she said. She was like me, Asian American, maybe even with a grandmother who lived with this same disease, and who had inspired her to go into this field. The similarities made me shy away from her, not wanting her to map onto me so cleanly, to be able to perceive me so clearly.

She handed me a pamphlet of resources for caretakers.

"Make sure you take care of yourself, too," she said. I mumbled a thanks before leaving as quickly as I could.

The journey home was smooth, and the bus lulled both grandmother and grandfather to sleep. I had to pat them awake when we reached our stop. The bus driver lowered the landing so they could get off without having to take such a large step. The bus was running late, and a younger man holding on to a strap hanger let out a huge sigh as we went through the slow process, grandmother and grandfather carefully stepping down. I wanted to yell at him to please be patient with us, that we were trying our best, to stuff his sigh back in his mouth so he'd choke on it. Instead, I said nothing, hurried off the bus, down the sidewalk, and back into the house.

Louise texted me at the end of the day, asking for my 😄 and 😔. I told her it had been hard, and she offered to call. I did not have the energy. I buried myself in EMBRS. As my world fell apart around me, I wrote my code. If I could enforce enough logic there, maybe the rest would follow suit. I coded until midnight. When I left my room to use the bathroom, I saw grandfather at his computer, answering another math question, and another, and another.

There are still some days when grandmother is mostly fine. Typically, when she has a bad episode, we don't have to leave the house for any reason, so she passes them in relative comfort. I almost wish there was a recognizable pattern to it, even if that meant a steady decline. Some mornings I wake up and stare at my ceiling, fearing which grandmother she will be that day—and then I feel guilty because every moment I'm in bed is another when only grandfather is looking after her. And so I haul myself out of bed and face the day.

it sounds like things are rough up there. if it's too
much trouble, i don't have to visit. or we could
just meet for a quick lunch or something

I grabbed my phone and typed the quickest reply of my life.

no. please come. I really want to see you

i'll be there

I began counting down the days.

A few nights later, when usually only I am awake, I heard grandfather's voice coming from the spare bedroom. When I went to check on him, I recognized his tone, the mix of English and Chinese, and knew the only person he could be speaking to was my father.

"You're selfish," grandfather hissed. I flinched away from the door. He never spoke like that to me, only to my father. And even then, as far as I was aware, he had not spoken to my father in years, had only done so through me or grandmother. "What can be taking so long? You're delaying on purpose. I know you. Making Monica do what you should be doing." His voice broke when he said my name. "She should be in college learning, making friends and falling in love. Instead, she's here because you are not and I can't do this by myself." He paused to catch his breath. "I can't do this by myself," he repeated, as if realizing the truth of his words.

I leaned against the wall and slid down until I was sitting, holding my knees to my chest. I did not even have my phone with me. I just waited there in the dark, listening to grandfather reply in monosyllables and grunts to whatever my father was saying. They ended their call. It was a while before grandfather came out.

He saw me immediately, even in the dark, as if he was looking for me.

"I can ask Louise not to come," I said. I stared straight ahead as I spoke. "I can also just work part-time."

"No." He looked like he was trying to sit down so I stood up. He placed a hand on my shoulder.

"I want to meet her," he said, then squeezed my shoulder. "And no part-time. You'll never properly learn computer science that way."

I rolled my eyes and sniffed.

"Tell me about your latest algorithm?" he asked, his voice small. We stood together in the dark hallway.

"I had to implement a pipeline for a library's archive today," I said.

"That's a lot of data," he said. "How did you store it?"

"Gzipped. Timestamps for filenames."

"And how will you query it?"

We passed each other questions and answers in the dark, each offering the other a little ledge of a foothold, something to keep the other moving forward.

Soon after, the new medication that Dr. Wu prescribed started having an effect. Grandmother was more present, less paranoid, and even began writing again.

how do you record the stories of someone who is losing their memory? I asked Louise. I wondered how coherent whatever grandmother was writing could be.

i'm not sure, she admitted. very carefully

I tapped at my computer. I had spent so long searching for Meng, but I had never thought to search for grandmother. I tried all the tricks I had learned, and the results came up similarly blank. It was as if the world had accepted she was fading and was prepared to let her fully disappear.

For the first time since I connected with Louise, I dove directly into the EMBRS data. There's a lot more now, not only social media posts. We've been building up its knowledge base as we prepare the program to better understand journal entries. Prof. Logan has assembled a moderation team of minimum-wage undergrad students. They don't have access to the journal entries themselves, but they can approve connection topics—yes, connect mothers returning to the workforce; no, do not connect those scheming violent insurrectionists.

Prof. Logan's latest pitch had been in San Francisco, and we'd recently received an influx of users from California, really the first to use EMBRS as a journal. Unfortunately, there had been a lot of false positives, so he had me work on ingesting local newspaper articles and historical archives and such. The data was meant to inform EMBRS about the region so it could better determine a unique connection point between users. I decided to do something I had never done before: I fed all of my previous journal entries into the system.

I made sure it wouldn't reach out to random test users and tell them about me. But it would parse my entries and try to find connections for me among its data. I didn't think it would actually surface anything, just that my journal entries would be realistic test data.

After running for eight minutes (I know, we need to optimize), EMBRS returned a single result, from the archives of one of the local newspapers.

The fire appears to have been a grease fire, though officials were unable to find an occupant of the house. The fire spread unusually quickly due to the amount of flammable material near the kitchen including paper, cardboard boxes, and, most peculiarly, pencils. Most of the wood of the pencils burned, leaving strips of lead at times, piles of ashes, others. Neighbors varied widely in their statements on who lived in the house. Some said it was unoccupied, while others insisted a large family lived there, and one even thought it was a restaurant.

I almost dismissed the article as another false positive. But then EMBRS showed my journal entry that matched. It was the conversation between me and grandmother, when she said she'd lost most of her pencils in a fire in California. I nearly slammed my laptop shut.

How had I forgotten? Was memory that fallible? EMBRS provided a link to the source article. It was from 1954. I calculated. Grandmother would have been twenty-seven. She would have just gotten to America. I was finding her ghost in these pixels. The article included an exact address, which I searched.

It did not take long to find a city record for the property. It included a name, a Chinese one, definitely not grandmother's. I searched the name separately. This was the kind of thing grandmother wouldn't understand, and neither would Louise. Even if pencils had great power, they could not compare to the power, the widespread usage, the sheer amount of data, of the computer.

The name was that of a military man, high-ranking in the Nationalist forces. I did not know much about the Nationalists other than that they were a political party in Taiwan. Did he know grandmother?

There wasn't much detail about him available—in English, at least. Though he was not well known, the division of the government he served in was, and so I searched for that. The results returned with too many articles, all on the same topic.

An extensive intelligence network designed to purge dissidents.

I skimmed the articles and quickly shut EMBRS down, purged the data I had fed it, and closed my laptop. I was left with the laptop fan slowly whirring and the eventual silence of my bedroom. I could hear, beyond my closed door, the Taiwan news grandfather always watched, passionate voices debating one matter or another, grandfather yelling his opinion, while grandmother stayed out of it, cooking or knitting in the background.

There are a lot of things I don't know about history, about politics, especially when my public school only covered American history for the most part. I knew America had a strong anti-Communist movement, that there had been spies, and it seemed like Taiwan had spies, too. But it all felt so foreign to me, so different from the Taiwan I knew, where I went every other summer to visit family in their air-conditioned skyscrapers. Even grandmother felt it was safe for me to explore the city on my own, take the subway and buses, decide for myself that yes, I did want to drink three bubble teas in one afternoon and be too full to eat dinner, and venture out to the night market for a midnight snack.

I couldn't reconcile the Taiwan I knew with the Taiwan that EMBRS was trying to show me, a history of martial law and terror, its citizens disappeared or mysteriously killed for protesting, or simply for attending one wrong gathering. And of course, I could not reconcile the grandmother I knew with someone who might have had any part in that history.

For the first time, I thought, Why not let her be forgotten as she wants to be?

But I had promised Louise I would ask about grandmother's story. I waited for one of her good days.

"Louise is interested in archival." I had to use the English word because I did not know the one in Chinese. We were watching television in the living room, one of the Chinese singing competitions we had recently gotten into. It was a commercial break, and grandfather was in the bathroom. "She's interested in preserving stories. I think she'll want to interview you while she's here. Is that alright?"

I hoped she would immediately agree, that she had nothing to hide. But she remained silent, staring at the television. I repeated my question.

"I heard," she said, voice distant. There was a rapid ad for peanut oil. It was louder than her voice.

"Is that not okay?" I suddenly felt very small.

Grandmother sighed.

"I have mixed feelings on recording stories," she said finally.

"Oh," I said quickly. "That's fine. I'll just tell Louise—"

Grandmother patted my knee.

"If you trust her, then I can too. Let me think about it," she said.

We watched the peanut oil perfectly fry a pork chop. Only once we could hear grandfather's footsteps coming our way did grandmother add:

"Preserving stories is not always a good thing."

Grandfather sat down, draping the couch throw across the three of us, and we continued watching the show. I texted Louise.

> do you think there are any downsides to archiving stories?

She began typing immediately.

if the person doesn't want their story preserved.
or if the story lies. or like a story perpetuating
racism, bigotry, etc. . . . . so yes

> so it's not about collecting all stories.
> there's some curation involved

Her thinking echoed Prof. Logan's content moderation policy, and yet it was so different from the tech world. Prof. Logan had me reading blog posts, watching talks on best practices in dealing with large amounts of data. The first rule as soon as any data is received is to save it before processing any of it. Even if it's not used, it must be saved, in case it's needed in the future. Storage is cheap, and data is king. Most computers in the world are holding gigabyte after gigabyte of data that's never looked at again. But at least it is saved.

arguable! we don't need more of the same
stories, or at least not as urgently. we need to find
the parts history omitted and fill those back in.
and sometimes I think we are running out of time

Halfway through the episode, grandfather began snoring. I looked over and found they were both asleep, their hands clasped together.

I took a picture, wanting to remember them like this, relaxed and content. I was about to send it to Louise because I knew she would like it, then I deleted the message and put my phone away. I decided to keep the picture as a memory just for myself, at least for now.

CHAPTER 16

From the Reforged pencil of Wong Yun

A year after the Japanese left, my father finally made it home. Mother was chipper, spending less time in her workshop, and even my grandmother left her room to enjoy the company of her only son. Mr. Gao came as often as usual, though now, instead of whisking your mother away for the night, he would stay, laughing with my father. The four of them would be up late, playing mahjong, our mothers getting dressed up to go out, this time with their men, enjoying the jazz clubs, the swing dancing, all the entertainment Shanghai had to offer. For a brief period, the world seemed bright. The city was finally under Chinese control, there were grand plans to fix its port, improve transportation, maybe even build a transit system. To develop the outer regions to create more space for the crowds. Mr. Gao wanted to publicize what the Phoenix Pencil Company had done for the war, to advertise our part in helping China. Our mothers refused. They did not want our powers known. And my father agreed, adding:

"After all, we may need those powers again soon."

The first sign of the civil war was inflation. I remember the day your mother gave you money to buy rice while you were out with your boy. But you returned empty-handed. The amount she had given you wasn't enough.

"That should have been more than enough for a bag of rice," my father said. "I passed the stand last night."

"That was last night," you said evenly. "It changed by this afternoon. It's over a million yuan now."

"This afternoon?" my father countered. There was something so militant about him. I did not know if that was how he always was, or if the war had made him this way. "Then you should have gone first thing."

"I couldn't," you said, voice clipped. "The stalls were closed. They close in the middle of the day now because they know prices will be higher in a few hours."

My father was ready to retaliate, to at least scold you for talking back to him. You were saved by Ah-shin, who returned with a limp bag of food scraps, complaining the stalls had changed their prices right in front of her, that they were setting themselves up outside the banks so that customers could use their money as soon as possible, before it devalued even more.

The adults argued over the cause. My father blamed the Communists for trying to force radical ideology onto a country that needed stability. Your mother argued the Nationalists were to blame, that they were keeping an army as large as the one they had during the war against the Japanese and spent all their money on the military rather than using it for the aid the country so desperately needed.

My father scoffed and shook his head at Mr. Gao. He clearly thought Mr. Gao could do better than your mother. Mr. Gao gave a helpless shrug. Behind this exchange, you fumed. That was before my father suggested the worst.

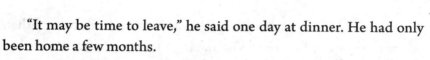

"It may be time to leave," he said one day at dinner. He had only been home a few months.

You flinched. It was the first time anyone had mentioned leaving Shanghai.

"We'll be fine," my grandmother insisted. My father and Mr. Gao exchanged dark looks.

"If the Communists win, we won't be able to stay here," my father said.

"They won't win," my grandmother said firmly.

"Why wouldn't we be able to stay?" I asked.

"We fought with the Nationalists," he said. "We own land. We run a capitalist business. They blame everything on landowners. Their peasant armies are rampaging through the countryside, killing anyone they want. They would take everything from us."

"We don't need everything," you said quietly.

My father looked at you, tilting his head. He had never paid much attention to you.

"You have never had nothing." His voice was cold. "We worked for the life of comfort you live now."

"We could afford to give some of this up," you continued even as your mother shot you a glare. "And you didn't work for this life. Our mothers did."

"Meng!" your mother exclaimed.

"I didn't work for this life?" His eyes flashed. I shrank into my seat. His anger was one of the few things I remembered from the days before he left. "I fought for it with my life! Was it your mother at the end of a Japanese gun, spared only because he thought I was already dead? Was it you who could never sleep, because if it wasn't the Japanese, it was the Communists who were going to stab you in the back even as we fought the same war? You think the war ended because your mother was making pencils? We ended the war—"

"The Americans ended the war," you corrected.

"Be quiet," your mother ordered. If you wouldn't listen to my father, you at least listened to her. "Who made you think you are allowed to talk this way to your uncle? Was it that boy? Answer me."

The others couldn't tell, but I knew you. I knew when you were upset, you lashed out, then went quiet. Any further speaking might cause the tears to fall, and you would not let that happen, not in front of this many people.

"There are far worse things than leaving a home." My father's voice was low.

"Calm down and eat," my grandmother ordered. She was the only one who could speak like that to my father. We ate the rest of our meal in silence.

At night, you paced our room.

"He was going to hit me," you said.

"I don't think he was—"

"He was. I could sense it. He would never hit you, but he would hit me, without a second thought."

"I'm sorry." I wasn't only sorry for the way my father had treated you. I was sorry that my father returned and yours didn't. That yours had been replaced with Mr. Gao, a man you refused to trust, who never showed you any love, only your mother.

Refugees had poured into Shanghai during the war against the Japanese. Now the opposite happened. People began to leave out of fear of the Communists. The Nationalists lost battle after battle. Not even scrappy Ah-shin could find enough food to buy. There was no more hope of meat. The only vegetables we had were pickled, and every bit of rice was watered down. We once thought we had a good amount of money saved. It seemed we would blow right through it. Our mothers skipped dinner often.

"We spend all this money on the military, and they can't even win these battles against a bunch of peasants," my father complained. He read the news even more than my grandmother. Those days, she normally contented herself sitting beside my father and nodding off.

"The Communists have infinite peasants to throw around as they please," Mr. Gao scoffed.

It was a soggy summer day a year into the civil war, as we ate our dinner of watery gruel, that you told us your boy and his family were fleeing to Hong Kong. His father, alarmed by the Communists' crossing of the Yellow River into central China, had already arranged their travel. Your boy had offered to bring you, even to marry you if it would help get you out of Shanghai.

"I'm not going to, of course," you said as you stared my father down, as if winning this argument with him was more important than your life.

For all the resolve you showed our parents, you broke down in our room. You wondered out loud if you were making a mistake, sighed that you would miss him, but it would be too much to marry him, to move to a place like Hong Kong, wouldn't it? No, you would not leave home again, would not leave us, would not upend your life all over again, even if it meant living through another war. No, it was not possible, even if you already missed him.

You were depressed for days. It was your turn to write our story. You wrote nothing. Sometimes you made an effort to pick up a pencil, to tap at a newspaper article. Most often you were distracted by the contents of the articles—tales of savings suddenly meaning nothing, reports that there were now seven hundred trillion yuan in circulation, compared to only a few trillion a year ago, the never-ending string of suicides, businessmen found dead at the feet of Shanghai skyscrapers.

Your boy and his family, like many other families, left suddenly. Only a day passed between when he asked you to go with him and when his family fled. They owned significant land throughout Shanghai. We had all heard the horrifying stories of what had been done to landowners in the countryside.

"I wish," you told me one day, "that he had left me something to remember him by."

How could I deny you after such a direct wish? Every day I wanted to burn his notebook, but every day there were people at home, whether it was our mothers, my father, or you. You were so miserable, I reasoned, that even if I had wronged you by stealing the boy's pencil, perhaps I could start making up for it by admitting what I had done and sharing the Reforging.

And so I willingly gave the notebook to you. You read it slowly while I waited on my bed, wishing I could disappear from the room.

"How did you get this?" you asked, your voice betraying nothing.

I explained the trick.

"I wish I hadn't done it," I said honestly. "I was so angry. I felt so left out, like you had abandoned me for this boy you barely knew. But after I Reforged it, I understood. It was between you and him, and I shouldn't have tried to meddle. I did it because I loved you, really."

You closed the notebook, gripping it tightly. His words, gone through my body, into your hands.

"You know what your most outstanding trait is?" you said, your voice eerily even. Then your eyes, dark and unreadable, locked on mine. Like it was only ever you and me.

"Your ability to lie."

You walked out of our bedroom, slamming the door shut behind you.

I curled up into my bed, hugging my pillow. I told myself I deserved it. Even so, I cried. I could have lived through any war as long as you were there with me. But for you to bury a knife so deeply into my heart with your words? That was unbearable.

Two major events prevented you from cutting me off completely.

The first, at the start of the new year, my grandmother died. She did so peacefully, in her sleep. It was a small blessing, really, that she died before the civil war took a turn for the worse.

We burned folded paper for her, sent her messages that she had left the world at a good time, as one war ended and before the next had displaced us. It was the five of us—me and my parents, you, and your mother, all circled around the little metal cylinder where our fire roared. I folded a paper car for her. I thought she would have liked having a car so she would not have to burden her feet so much. The fire ate it hungrily.

"She likes it," my father said, placing a hand on my shoulder.

Mother tossed a whole pencil into the flame. The flame chewed through it slowly. I wondered what she had written with it, what sorts of things she wanted to say to the mother-in-law who had been a controlling force all her married life. But that was a secret the pencil carried into the flame.

You and your mother burned paper, too, though you did not have to. She was not your grandmother, and she had not been particularly kind to either of you. All the same, you went through the motions, bowed when appropriate, helped us light incense and wash the fruit.

"Thank you." My father bowed to you both, a small smoothing over of tensions.

I caught your eye, and you gave me a small nod.

Without my grandmother around, my father gained full control of the house. I like to think for the most part he was kind. Your mother, who had, since my father's return, either been staying with us in our room or with Mr. Gao, took my grandmother's old room. Our mothers continued running the pencil company. Even the Americans enjoyed our pencils, though business faltered. Our main source of income was the Nationalists who continued using them for their messages. My father met with Mr. Gao often, smoking in the courtyard, talking

Nationalist strategy. By then, Mr. Gao knew all the women in the family could Reforge. We would work in the factory, bleeding out our arms, while they talked in low voices and hypotheticals.

And the second event, at the end of that same year, was when my father announced over dinner that we would be leaving for Taiwan.

"Taiwan?" you and I blurted at the same time.

"It is safe there."

The year 1948 had not been a good one for the Nationalists. I could feel it in the energy of the pencils, the desperation of the messages, even though they were encoded. They suffered defeat after defeat in the northeast, their best armies losing to the peasants, who subsequently took their tanks and turned their own weapons against them. The words they wrote were of strategy and loyalty, a rebuilt China, but I could feel their fear when their hearts met mine—how their soldier salaries amounted to nothing, not with this inflation, how much easier it would be to defect. My father was sure that if the Nationalists did not fall to the Communists, they would fall to inflation. The paper that our money was printed on had become worth more than the money itself.

Your mother frowned.

"Taiwan is . . . far from Shanghai." She was looking at Mr. Gao.

"That's why it is safe," he answered simply.

"I don't mean physically. It's the farthest thing from Shanghai. It's not developed. There aren't toilets. They think they're Japanese." She said this last with a particular vehemence.

"The Japanese have left Taiwan," my father cut in. "Many of our friends are already there. The Nationalists have a hold. In any case, it is up to you and Meng if you want to join us."

"Come with me to Taiwan," Mr. Gao said gently. He took your mother's hand. "It won't be for long. Only a few months. Until the Nationalists win the war."

"I could wait here for you to come back," your mother said.

"It won't be safe here! The Communists will not spare you."

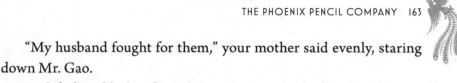

"My husband fought for them," your mother said evenly, staring down Mr. Gao.

He left the table, his chair almost teetering to the floor. On his way to the courtyard, he slammed the door so hard behind him it jumped back open. I could hear him light a cigarette.

"He wouldn't have this problem if he would hurry up and marry you," my father huffed.

"That is not a decision for only him to make," your mother said.

"Regardless." My father shook his head. "We need to be ready to leave for Taiwan, whether or not you decide to come with us."

Your mother began eating again, picking at the watery grains. You glanced at me before quickly looking away.

"We still have time to think," Mother assured us.

For so long, we had thought of the Japanese as our sole enemy. In every one of our stories, as long as we defeated them, our homes would be safe. Yet what was forcing us to leave now was not any foreign power, Japanese or Western, but our own people.

Around us, it seemed all our former classmates were fleeing, many to Hong Kong, many to Taiwan, and the lucky ones, to America. My father pulled all the strings he could and had a lead on plane tickets to Taiwan. The only question was how many he would need.

Mr. Gao hounded your mother, trying to convince her to leave with the rest of us. He was too involved with the Nationalists, even more than my father, to have any hope of surviving a Communist takeover. He showed up every day, telling your mother how much he loved her, how much he wanted both of you by his side in Taiwan, how yes, it was an underdeveloped island, but it was beautiful, like her, and the fruit so sweet, and how he'd wipe the overflowing juice of a mango clean from her chin.

You and your mother would converse by yourselves in the courtyard. I tried not to imagine what those conversations were like, if you told her what I had done. We still had not spoken since our fight. At night, you would remain in the workshop for as long as possible, only returning to our room when you could go straight to bed. I imagined your mother asking you seriously if there was any part of you that wanted to go to Taiwan with us, if you would at least want to be with me. After all, weren't we close, weren't we like sisters, weren't we inseparable? More than any city, hadn't we buried our roots in each other? And you would reply—maybe that was the case once, but not anymore, I will not go with her, no, I will stay in Shanghai.

And so, not even a week after my father's initial announcement, your mother and Mr. Gao separated. You and your mother would stay in Shanghai, while the rest of us went to Taiwan. Your mother tossed everything that had to do with Mr. Gao into the kiln and spread what she had left of your father's belongings through the complex. The few letters he had sent, some of his books with his notes scrawled inside, his favorite Russian classics. Most importantly, a medal he had received from the Communist party. Anything that would help protect the two of you once the Communists took over.

"I hope in your lifetime, you will not be forced to let politics dictate your love," she said as she tossed the last of Mr. Gao's work orders into the kiln. There was no evidence of their relationship, not even anything a pencil could bring back.

The next day, my father came home with three airplane tickets. Only then did you speak to me again.

"We need to finish the story," you said. It was the last thing I expected you to say. I had assumed our story abandoned.

"Okay," I agreed, and followed you into our room.

We couldn't agree on what had happened last, and there was no paper trail to refer to. You were convinced your character had Reforged some critical piece of evidence that revealed my character was walking right into a trap. I accepted your version, even though I did not think my character would be so dumb.

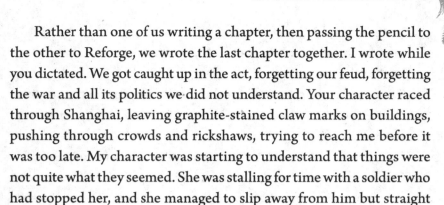

Rather than one of us writing a chapter, then passing the pencil to the other to Reforge, we wrote the last chapter together. I wrote while you dictated. We got caught up in the act, forgetting our feud, forgetting the war and all its politics we did not understand. Your character raced through Shanghai, leaving graphite-stained claw marks on buildings, pushing through crowds and rickshaws, trying to reach me before it was too late. My character was starting to understand that things were not quite what they seemed. She was stalling for time with a soldier who had stopped her, and she managed to slip away from him but straight into the lair of his boss.

At the last possible minute, your character made it to the lair and screamed her name. My character armored up—by then she could call the graphite around her hand in the blink of an eye—and she caught the blade of a bayonet as it swung down at her.

The blade clashed with her armored hand, metal against graphite. For a moment, it looked like my character's arm would give out. But then, slowly, the blade began to bend, at the same time as my character's mouth bent into a smile.

"There," you said. "That's how it should end."

"Really?" I did not feel it wrapped up the loose ends we had left behind.

"Yes. It should end with a smile. Because that's what this story has done for us."

"It doesn't feel complete though," I said.

"Well, that's because you're coming back, right?"

I should have gotten on my knees and apologized then, should have begged for you to come with me. Even now, I don't know what would have happened if we had never fought. Would you have left Shanghai? You didn't want to leave another home, I knew that, but would our connection have been strong enough to convince you otherwise, to let you avoid the years of famine and persecution China was about to go through?

Instead, I nodded.

"Yes, of course I'll come back."

We left the rest unsaid.

The next day, we stood outside the pencil company for the last time.

"I'll see you in a few months," I told you as you and your mother came to see us off.

You gave me the pencil, the one that contained our story.

Our mothers embraced, also exchanging a pencil. My father went into the courtyard where he bowed before my grandmother's favorite bush, which was beginning to flower. Then we gathered our belongings.

I turned away from you, following my parents.

It was my last time in Shanghai, and the last time I saw you.

CHAPTER 17

From the diary of Monica Tsai,
backed up on three servers spanning
two continents

October 28, 2018 (2018-10-28T23:33:40.720614)
loc: Cambridge, Massachusetts. United States of America
(42.3721865,71.1117091)

This whole semester has passed so slowly until today. When Louise arrived at the train station like a burst of color and jumbled my thoughts more than ever. Maybe I'll save this entry as a particular challenge for EMBRS, to see if it, with its state-of-the-art natural language processing, can even sort me out. Because I am so confused.

She was easy to spot among the crowd, a head above most people, her smile already wide. She had cut her hair even shorter than the last time we met. I counted the number of steps it took her to reach me. We should probably hug, I was thinking, even as she wrapped her arms around me and squeezed tight.

"Wow, what service!" she exclaimed. "Picking me up from the station."

"My grandparents would have kicked me out if I didn't." We sat down at one of the rickety tables where I had french fries laid out. She dropped her duffel bag on the ground. I handed her a bus pass.

She took it and flipped it between her fingers.

"Is this your grandfather?"

I told her how grandfather had insisted she use his discounted pass. She studied the picture.

"He looks like a nobleman. Full pure white hair. Neat tie. Very dashing. It's my honor to impersonate him." She devoured the fries.

As we took the bus home, I pointed out the various sights: my high school, the tennis court where grandmother taught me how to bike, the corner where I last saw the busker dressed as a bear playing the keyboard. Louise's game is tomorrow, and she's staying with us for two nights. When I tried to tell my grandparents that she said she had friends whose couches she could sleep on, they became furious and insisted she use our empty bedroom. It was the room we saved for my father, those in-between years when he'd return for a few weeks.

"This is it," I said after walking the block from the bus stop to the home where I had grown up. It was smaller than the houses in Cherry Hill, and, like many in the Boston area, much older. I found myself nervous, wondering what she would think of it. I could hardly believe she was here.

"Amazing." She looked up at the house. "This is always what I imagined New England to be like." She bounded up the porch steps, and I unlocked the door for her.

"Oh!" grandmother exclaimed when we came into the kitchen. The overhead fan was whirring and the pork sizzling. "So tall!"

"Hi, Tsai nainai," Louise said happily. She towered over grandmother. Her Chinese was better than mine, smooth and accentless, at least to my ears. "Thank you so much for having me."

"Of course. Have you eaten?"

"Monica bought me some fries."

"Sit down, sit down. Monica, come help me. Torou! Torou!"

Grandfather had not heard the doorbell, but he did hear grandmother's call. The television switched off, and he hobbled into the kitchen.

"Oh!" He straightened. "So tall!"

"Hi, Tsai yeye." Louise grinned, with a small bow. "Thank you so much for letting me stay here."

"It's the least we can do."

"And for letting me use your senior card."

"Of course! Monica always complains that it's not the right thing to do. It is good you see the value in these sorts of decisions."

"I do."

While taking over stir-frying from grandmother, I protested that public transportation was underfunded.

"We already pay more for those cards than we get out of them," grandfather huffed. "In Taiwan, the government would be paying *me* to take the train. And when I turn one hundred, they'd hand me money. Here though—"

"No need to rant about Taiwan right now, Torou," grandmother interrupted. "Please, sit down, Louise."

"Can I help?" she asked. "I could set the table? Wash some dishes?"

"No!" grandmother cried as if Louise had insulted her. "Torou, take her suitcase to her room."

"I'll take it—"

"Give it to me, I need the exercise."

"So do I! I've got a big game tomorrow . . ."

They continued to argue their way up to my father's room. Grandmother returned to my side, turning off the heat and ladling out the rice cakes.

"I can see why you and Meng took to her," she said. "She is very charming. What a wide smile. And so tall!"

I smiled, wondering if they would ever stop commenting on her height. I hoped they wouldn't, if only so we could continue talking about her.

Once we were stuffed full of rice cakes stir-fried with pork, cabbage, and shiitake mushrooms, Louise took out a brown bag from under the table. She must have stowed it there before grandfather helped bring her luggage up to her room.

Grandmother gasped when she saw the familiar brown bag.

"Arby's?" she exclaimed.

Even I was shocked. Louise winked at me.

"There's one really close to my house, so I got some before heading over. Much easier than Monica biking for hours. Don't worry, I kept them in a cooler." She unfurled the bag and pulled out sandwich after sandwich, stacking them into a pyramid in front of grandmother.

"I can't believe you'd do that," I mumbled. I'd forgotten we even talked about Arby's.

"Well, I checked on the map how far it was from your place, and it's *far*. You must have calves of steel. Really, it was very easy for me. Though I did have to get my brother to drive me," she added sheepishly.

I could only see grandmother's forehead over the pyramid of roast beef sandwiches. She took the top one, patting the foil in satisfaction. Then she looked around the table, first at me, then grandfather, then Louise.

"Hannah?"

I opened my mouth to say something, to apologize. Grandfather spoke first.

"Like Hannah was ever so nice. This is Monica's friend Louise. Remember?"

"Oh. Of course." Grandmother smiled, but I could tell she did not remember.

"I'll clean up," I said.

"Time for us to watch television, then," grandfather said cheerily. Grandmother followed him, steps hesitant, still unsure.

"My mother's name," I explained once they left. Louise helped me gather the sandwiches to bring to the refrigerator.

"I thought that might be it. Do I look like her?"

"I don't think so." I handed her a container for the leftovers. "I haven't seen her in a very long time though. The last time grandmother

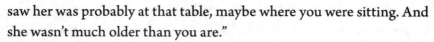

saw her was probably at that table, maybe where you were sitting. And she wasn't much older than you are."

"Can I ask where she is now?"

"I think in Kansas. We don't talk. But I guess grandmother still remembers her. I think they had a falling-out."

"Ah."

That she did not ask more pleased me. As I loaded the dishwasher, I wondered if it was because we had dodged so many of each other's questions in the past, or if it was our shared heritage, both from families of immigrants, families used to holding their shames close so to fit in.

After cleaning, I showed her around the guest bedroom. It was a sterile space, devoid of any character my father might have given it. Most of his belongings had been shipped to Shanghai or donated. I had cleaned it recently, washing the sheets, vacuuming, even swapping HVAC filters.

She fell onto the bed, spreading her arms. I asked if she wanted to rest. She shot back up and insisted we go do something. I was delighted, as I had a whole list of things planned out. I had been thinking a lot about her thesis proposal and digital archiving, thought she'd probably love the Cambridge Public Library, or we could cross the river into Boston and check out one of the many museums there. As I pieced together my plan, though, I realized there was only one place that felt right.

I said we would bike there.

"Of course you want to bike," she said as she followed me outside.

I paid for her bike share rental on my app before she even finished reading the instructions on how the system worked. That was the best part—her face when she realized.

"You don't want to start this war with me," she warned. I reminded her of the froyo incident and biked away before she could escalate.

She followed me through Cambridge. Luckily, it's the time of year when the weather here is amazing—no longer humid from summer, the bitter cold still weeks away, like the city was showing off. The leaves were just beginning to turn, deep yellows and oranges against the freshly painted green of the bike lane. We even got to see some turkeys halting traffic; it was never better to be a biker.

For the first time since I came home, I could pretend my life was on track. Like I was a student back for fall break, blazing along the same well-worn path as everyone else, maybe even a better one because she was there with me. Her flannel billowed behind her, a trail of cozy colors that warmed me whenever I looked at her. She would squeal each time she saw a dog in a sweater, and her bike would teeter dangerously. I smiled down at my handlebars, just really, truly grateful.

"Where are we?" she asked skeptically when I stopped at the building where grandfather used to teach. I could understand her skepticism—the MIT buildings are not quite as New England grand as Harvard's or (I imagine) Princeton's. They're quite a bit weirder-looking. Grandfather's has a particularly lopsided structure, a near-collapsing quality to it, in an endearing way.

I locked my bike and told her we were going to class. That I was going to teach her.

"But I'm on fall break!" she complained.

"Humor me," I said. "I haven't been to school all semester. I miss it."

"What a nerd," she laughed.

"Is that a problem?"

I held the door to the building open for her. She lingered in the doorframe, glancing over her shoulder at me, her hair still windswept, a mark on her forehead where her helmet had been.

"Quite the opposite," she said as she resumed walking, and I was relieved she could not see the stumbling puddle I had become behind her.

I managed to regain my composure in the classroom. Classrooms are good places for me. It felt so good to be back in one, to hear the projector groan alive, the mechanical lowering of the screen, to plug in my laptop and project my desktop background of my neighbor's orange cat onto the wall.

Louise squealed when she saw the cat, which I was admittedly relieved about, for I had feared she might only be a dog person. And then she chuckled.

"What?" I asked self-consciously.

"It's nothing." But she was still smiling, attempting to cover it. I looked down to see if there was something on my shirt. I begged her to tell me.

"I just think it's cute that you're petting the cat's head with your cursor."

I stopped and immediately pulled up my terminal window to cover the cat. Petting her had become muscle memory. I avoided Louise's eyes, tried to salvage my dignity.

"What are you going to teach me, Professor?" She looked all too eager at her seat, hands clasped together, smiling wider than ever. The classroom was clearly a comfortable place for her too.

I took a breath, inhaling all the power the space would give me. My hands easily took their place on the keyboard. I told her I would be teaching git rebasing.

Her eyes fogged over.

"You'll like it," I promised. "Do you remember what git is?"

"From your video for the freshmen?" She leaned back in her chair. "It's for version control, right? Like every time you make a change to your code, you mark it with a git commit, and then you can always rewind and go back to that commit if you need to."

I was impressed. I had planned to go over everything in my video again, but she had retained it and was even able to explain it back to me. She noticed my pause and winked.

"I'm a good student. You'll have to try harder than that if you want to trip me up, Professor."

I had to look away from her again. It thrilled me to see this academic side of her that matched mine in a way that was so easy. I pulled up my lecture notes to remind myself how I wanted to start.

"Let's use an example," I said, opening a text editor. "Normally git is used for code, but really it can be used for any type of file. So today, let's use a regular text file and write a story. I'll start."

I typed out:

Once upon a time, there were two girls who went on an adventure.

I saved the file, then switched back to my terminal window to make the git commit.

"Commit messages are important because they tell you what the code you are introducing does, and, if it's a good message, why you are introducing the code. So we'll give this one a message of 'Add opening of a story.'"

I committed the message, then pulled up the git log. "Add opening of a story" was the only entry there, along with a timestamp and my name.

"Let's keep writing the story," I said. My hands were flying now, settled in and comfortable. "It's your turn."

She didn't have her computer, so I typed for her.

"Hm, alright," she said. "The first girl was kind and pretty. She had never been on an adventure before, but she was eager to go, especially with her friend by her side. She was a careful person and had all the bus routes and passes ready. And of course, she had her trusty steed, Bike."

"Is it a steed or a bike?"

"No, it's a steed named Bike. Her trusty steed, Bike."

"She has a steed, but there are also buses?"

"Yes."

I glanced from my laptop up at her. She was looking at me defiantly.

"Alright," I allowed. "Let's commit it. What should the message be?"

"'Introduce character based off of Monica,'" she said proudly.

I sighed and typed it in, trying not to fixate on the words *kind* and *pretty*. "My turn now."

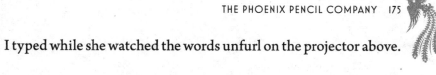

I typed while she watched the words unfurl on the projector above.

The second girl was tall and brave. There were rumors she
had some giants' blood in her, and perhaps some lion, too, for
her bravery was the talk of all the bus stops. Her only flaw was
that she was rather scared of her steed, Car, and so they set
off on their adventure both on Bike.

"Describe her more," Louise requested with dancing eyes. "What's
the relationship between the first and second girl?"

The blinking cursor challenged me.

The first girl really looked up to the second girl and deemed her a
perfect adventure buddy, I wrote, then paused. My fingers began to stick
to the keyboard. Typing was always easier than talking, so I continued.

She thought if they went on an adventure together, she'd work
up the courage to tell her how much she liked her new haircut.

I couldn't look at her, but heard her laugh, a beautiful sound that
made my hands tingle.

I gave it a commit message of "Introduce second character and establish relationship."

She did not need prompting to continue the story.

"They were on a quest to find the cutest dog in the land of Cambridge.
It would have floppy ears and be very derpy and would be wearing a fall-
themed bandana." She paused. "'Introduce character goals.'"

I continued.

Bike creaked under their weight. After all, the second girl was
part giant, and Bike was only used to carrying one rider. They
had seen many dogs, but none with quite the right bandana
or the proper amount of ear floppage. They were running low

on rations, and the first girl feared their adventure might not end in success.

I added a commit message of "Things get dire."

"Where are we going with this?" she asked, crossing her arms. "What's this rebasing thing you mentioned? Or are you just trying to show off your typing speed?"

It wasn't my intention, though I was pleased she noticed. I've always thought my typing speed quite formidable.

"Finish the story," I said.

"Fine. Just when all hope appeared lost—"

"Chad showed up," I interrupted.

"Who the fuck is Chad?"

I continued typing.

Chad came to the bus stop with his dog bouncing eagerly behind him. This dog had the floppiest ears either girl had ever seen.

I nodded for her to take over. She took a moment to think.

"The dog's tongue lolled out, and each of its paws had a little white sock. Best of all, Chad's dog wore a black bandana decorated with pumpkins. The two girls looked at each other and smiled. They had completed their quest of finding the cutest dog in Cambridge."

"That's a good ending." I smiled. "Commit message?"

"'Complete the quest against all odds.'"

I pulled up the git log again.

- Add opening of a story
- Introduce character based off of Monica
- Introduce second character and establish relationship
- Introduce character goals

- Things get dire
- Complete the quest against all odds

I asked her what she thought.

"It's decent, but you can't just deus-ex-machina Chad in."

I agreed. "Let's give him a proper introduction. So, who is Chad?" I scrolled back in the text editor to after the girls' introduction.

"The second girl had a neighbor named Chad," she said. "He was awkward and didn't really talk to anyone. He was quite shy, and reminded the second girl quite a bit of the first girl. The second girl happened to see a flyer for a dog adoption event hanging out of Chad's mailbox, and so an idea for a quest formed. Commit message: 'Inciting incident.'"

"Excellent," I said, though I wasn't sure how I felt about my character being compared to awkward Chad. "But now our git log isn't in order."

"That's okay. It preserves how the story was written."

"But what if my goal is a polished piece of software that anyone can pick up and take over? They wouldn't care that Chad was backfilled in. They'd rather have a clean history."

"Oh." Her eyes widened. My heart beat faster.

"So let's rebase. Rebasing can do a lot of things, but we'll focus on reordering these commits." I swapped the order using some well-practiced keyboard shortcuts. "Now the inciting incident is where it belongs, right after character introductions. A nice clean history."

"But not true to what actually happened."

"Right." I closed my laptop and unplugged it from the projector. "Did you enjoy the lesson?"

She was staring at me with an unreadable expression. Then she slowly stood up from her seat, slinging her daypack over her shoulders.

"You really were paying attention to all my digital archival talk," she said softly.

"I'm a good student." I grinned. "You'll have to try harder than that—"

She tossed her helmet at me, laughing. I caught it easily. Then she closed the distance between us so suddenly. I instinctively backed up against the wall, pinned by her body, the helmet the only thing separating us. Her fingers gripped the helmet on the other side, and for a moment we stood there, my breath becoming short as her face inched closer to mine, lowering to my level. I raised my hand, my fingers brushing the ends of her hair, right behind her neck.

"I like your haircut," I breathed, and she let out something between a laugh and a whimper.

But just as suddenly as she had approached me, she turned away, strapping the helmet back over her head. My one hand was still raised to where her hair had been moments earlier.

"Shall we go home?" she asked. She did not meet my eyes. "Your grandmother didn't want us biking in the dark."

"Sure," I said slowly, and packed up my computer.

Grandmother made an incredible dinner of lion's head meatballs, pea pod stems, and stir-fried bean curd. Grandfather made the soup—oxtail with daikon, and even cut one of the roast beef sandwiches into fourths so we could share it. But when I went to serve Louise a bowl of rice, she politely declined and said she was avoiding rice.

"You don't eat rice?" grandmother asked incredulously. It was the first time she had a vaguely negative reaction toward her.

Louise gave a sheepish smile. Then she pulled a packet of instant oatmeal from her bag.

"I break out pretty easily, so I stick with oatmeal. Can I microwave this?"

We all watched in wonder as she ate her oatmeal like we ate our rice, thick and watery and fiber-rich.

"Mm, so good!" Louise swooned at her first bite of the meatball. We gave her an extra plate so she would not have her meatball diluted in oatmeal water. "So much better fresh. And it was already delicious."

"The sauce is best on rice." Grandmother side-eyed.

"Next time," Louise said before slurping up the rest of her oatmeal.

Since it was late after dinner, grandmother and grandfather went straight to bed.

"What time is your game tomorrow?" I asked as I washed the dishes.

"It's in the afternoon. The team is getting brunch together, so I'll have to head out in the morning. Is that okay?"

"Of course," I said, even though I was disappointed. I'd thought we would have the morning together. Though maybe she did not want to spend more time with me.

But she had been the one who approached me. The one who pinned me to the wall, who moved her lips so close to mine. The one who pulled away and barely met my gaze afterward. Did I not react properly? Should I not have mentioned her hair? Or did some voice in her head remind her that she felt nothing toward me, that she had to turn around and leave at once?

"I'm going to sleep now," she said, and touched my wrist lightly with her hand. "I had a really amazing day. Thanks for everything."

And she went up the stairs, two at a time, to my father's room.

Later, as I lay in bed scrolling through my phone, I heard the whooshing sound of an email being sent from my grandparents' room. It was immediately followed by the buzzing of my own phone—an email from grandmother.

🐦 kuai dian 👲 😀 🍃

I looked at my phone in horror for a full second before tossing it away for the night. I tried to sleep but couldn't, and so now I'm staring into my computer screen, tapping at my keyboard, wondering what tomorrow might bring.

CHAPTER 18

From the Reforged pencil of Wong Yun

You would have hated Taiwan. I hated it before we even boarded the plane, hated it as we sat tightly against one another, wearing our winter jackets to save space in our suitcases, hated it when we landed, walked out, and there was only the humidity, as we removed layer after layer, sweating right through them.

Have you visited Taiwan? It is much nicer than it was back then. Monica says it is her favorite place in the world. We used to return every few years to see Torou's family before the journey was too long for me. We sent Monica to study Chinese while we played mahjong. She always came back with a snack for herself—a bag of fried popcorn chicken, skewers poking out, or a glistening cup of bubble tea, condensation forming as soon as it met the Taiwan humidity.

But instead of fast and clean trains or air-conditioned convenience stores on every block, Taiwan back then was a backwater island, just as your mother had said.

A military jeep picked us up. My father chatted with the driver, each exchanging names of other military men they knew, which ones had come to Taiwan, which to Hong Kong, which were still trying to stick it out on the mainland. The driver even knew Mr. Gao, called him a hotshot, though he was pleased to hear Mr. Gao had made it out, even if he had been sent to the south instead of the north, where we were headed.

Before reaching the city, we drove through sprawling encampments, barracks built for people like us, so many fleeing China during that time. The barracks were small and densely populated, a single dangling lightbulb for illumination. I dreaded finding out which one we would live in. But the driver took us straight past them and into the city.

"Not for you," he said, his jolly tone grating against my sour mood. "No, for your service, you'll have a proper house."

He looked not at my father, but into the rearview mirror, at my mother. I shrank farther into my seat. So they knew our secret here, too.

Though the house was nice, far nicer than the encampments we had passed, my father cursed as soon as we stepped inside. All of the doors were sliding, the flooring tatami, and the table and seating low to the ground. It disgusted him, to have spent so many years fighting the Japanese, only to live in a house of their style now.

If Mother was upset, she did not show it. You won't find it surprising that she immediately got to work. She and I walked around the neighborhood, scouting the market, the school, the public clinic, the parks, while my father stayed behind and brooded. We came back with bedrolls and a small bag of white rice.

"Ah," Mother sighed when she set the rice down. "I miss Ah-shin already."

I never realized that Mother did not know how to cook until those first few days in Taiwan. Our rice was hard, and our vegetables burned, though the raw ingredients were better than anything we had in Shanghai. I wondered what Ah-shin was scraping together for you and your mother, and wished I was at the table with all of you, even if our meal was only millet.

"We will be here a few months. That's all," my father insisted. He sat awkwardly on the tatami, as if his body could not properly relax on something made by the Japanese.

For those first few months, Mother and I did nothing. She, in particular, was bad at doing nothing. We did not have the materials to make pencils. Mother cleaned the house, again and again, while I wrote you letters. The letters were checked and censored. Of course, we knew how to work around that. I did not want to waste money buying paper, so I used our old trick, writing on the sheet of my bedroll, using only a hand width of space, layering the characters over one another. I complained about the weather and the mosquitoes and how I missed Ah-shin's cooking. I also mentioned the tension that even I, who barely left the house, sensed between the locals and the new arrivals. We were far from the only ones streaming into Taiwan during this time, far from the only ones from Shanghai. The locals called us waishengren, people from outside the province. They had recently been freed from Japanese rule, and now the Nationalists intended to rule over them.

I didn't know then that only a year earlier, around the time when you were struggling over whether to follow your boy to Hong Kong, the Nationalists in Taiwan had killed thousands of local demonstrators protesting what they saw as an incompetent, corrupt new regime. It kicked off martial law in Taiwan. There were whispers of the incident, though never loudly, and certainly not in the circles my father ran in. His circles talked only of returning to the mainland, of freeing China from what they saw as an incompetent, corrupt new Communist dictatorship.

Mother packed my pencil with a few packets of rice and shipped it back to Shanghai. We never knew if you received it.

"Just a few more months," my father said as he left for work, a new position given to him by the Nationalist government. It was again within the intelligence division. They were scrambling to find a weak point in the Communist regime as well as a way to keep the locals under control. "It might be good for you to meet some people. Make friends. You should really be looking for a husband."

"Why would I look for a husband here if we are leaving in a few months?" I glared at him the way you used to. He gave me only a passing glance before leaving us alone in the house again.

Those days blurred together, the only marker of time my father leaving and returning. Mother poured her energy into learning how to cook. I assisted halfheartedly. I could not help it. I would wake up wondering what you and your mother were doing in Shanghai, if you were safe. I spent every day in that little Japanese house, knowing each one would be the same, gray and dull, without my home, without you. I could not muster the energy to meet new people, convinced the locals hated us, and the others from China only saw us as competitors.

"Good news," my father said one day, returning from work.

"We are going back?" I asked, sitting up from where I had been lying down on the tatami. Mother straightened too, walking over from the kitchen.

"No." I deflated and almost did not hear what he said next. "The boss wants to open a pencil company here."

"In Taiwan?" Mother asked, eyes wide.

"Yes. Mr. Gao has been lobbying for it, even from the south. The government will pay for all expenses. They've found a few buildings they want me to choose from, but I said I needed to consult you two first." He stood behind me, placing his hands on my shoulders, and kissed my head. "Wouldn't you like that?" he asked. "To go back to making pencils?"

I wanted to yell at him. I wanted to tell him that he was missing the point, that it was not the pencils we missed. This island would never have the life of Shanghai. It would never have you, and no number of pencils would change that. But I was not a child anymore. I was twenty years old, and I knew he was trying his best, that he needed me to try as well, and the only thing I was good at was making pencils.

"That sounds great," I managed.

We began work on the Phoenix Pencil Company Taiwan branch. I helped Mother decorate the new store while the government bought equipment. The building had been left by the Japanese Mitsubishi company when they departed after the war. We tried to make it as similar to the Shanghai store as possible—the back contained all the equipment, the front a small counter, behind which would be a wall of pencil hearts. There was an extra nook to this place that we did not know what to do with, so Mother arranged a table and bench there and called it a study area.

I poured everything I had into reviving the pencil company. It started slow, but with each passing day, the building looked more and more like our home, and some of my energy returned. I chatted with neighbors, telling them what kind of store would be there soon, handing out sample pencils. I met others like us, straight from Shanghai, many who were familiar with our store. I took down their addresses, promised I would let them know when we opened.

By the time the store opened, we had been in Taiwan for a year. We still had not heard from you. The radio broadcasted news of persecutions and starvation on the mainland. They buried the news of the Communists taking Nanjing without a fight, followed swiftly by Shanghai. The day we opened the store was the first time I really suspected I would never return.

"Let's get to work," Mother said, and she hunched over her workstation, looking like she was home.

The reinvigoration lasted only a few weeks, during which we manufactured pencils, and I worked the storefront, trying to channel my father's way with people and your mother's easy charm. I had been good at it in Shanghai. In Taiwan my language faltered, everybody with such different dialects and attitudes toward people like us. My father invited his colleagues. They inspected our pencils, chatted with Mother, eyed me. I should have known where all this was headed from the moment my father said they were funding the company.

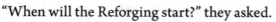

"When will the Reforging start?" they asked.

A few days later, we were back to Reforging, cutting ourselves open, bleeding out onto a page. In a way it was a return to our previous life and should have been a comfort. But our previous life was all about war and survival, and this time, too, was all war and survival, only without you.

It worked like this—we would sell our pencils, sometimes even give them away for free. We had what we called a recycling program. If someone brought their used pencils back to us, we would sell them new ones, heavily discounted. My father came up with the idea of crafting some with broken hearts inside. It would start off working fine, then suddenly there would be a gap in the heart, and the customer would return, complaining about their purchase. We'd take it back, replace it for free, and even throw in another one.

All the used pencils were Reforged. No matter the content, the Reforged text was passed on to my father's colleagues. Most of it was not incriminating, at least I did not think so. I did not know what became of the ones that criticized the government. I could only hope we were doing the right thing, that my father was right, and we needed a strong government to bring about stability, to muster a force large enough to take China back from the Communists and to take us home to Shanghai.

The days blurred even more than before. We were so tired, working the pencil company in the morning and Reforging at night. Mother often spent all day Reforging, as if she preferred the memories of strangers over her own. Despite the Taiwan heat, she was cold most of the time. She insisted it had nothing to do with the volume of Reforging she was doing, even as she rubbed her scars.

"Let me take on more of them," I said. "I'm not a child anymore."

"No." She wrapped a blanket around herself. "You know I hate working the storefront. Please just handle that."

"You're hurting yourself—"

"You should go make friends here," she interrupted. "Do not stay in this job long."

"What do you mean?" All my life, the only thing I had known for certain was that I would take over the Phoenix Pencil Company.

She looked down at her bleeding hand resting on a notebook.

"Don't rely on your Reforging skills. Or at least do not share them the way I have. Your grandmother was not wrong when she did not want me to teach you. It is a dangerous thing. If you can, find a different way to live."

She sliced her arm open once again.

I missed your mother the most then. She was the only one who could convince Mother to unburden herself. I wondered if Mother missed her the same way I missed you—in fleeting, biting moments, always with the undercurrent of dread that none of us would voice.

On the second anniversary of my grandmother's death, my father started a fire outside our home, in a metal cylinder. He methodically folded fake money and tossed it into the fire, pausing once in a while to bow his head and mutter beneath his breath. Mother tried to join him, but it was not a good day for her—she had Reforged too much the night before. She was pale and wrapped in blankets even in the tropical heat. She handed me a pencil and nodded to the flame. I joined my father and tossed it in for her.

Halfway through, it began to rain. It happened often on the island, sudden downpours on an otherwise clear day. My father cursed, trying to protect the flame with his body while I ran inside for an umbrella. By the time I returned, the fire was gasping for breath. I held the umbrella overhead and my father threw in bundles of dry paper money, coaxing the reluctant fire back to life. We winced when the wind blew the smoke right at us, stinging our eyes. He tossed the remaining paper money into the cylinder. The fire was extinguished, some of the money unburnt, tears ran down my father's face. He quickly wiped them away, blaming the smoke, the rain, the island. He sat in front of the house, head in his hands, attempting to wipe the smoke's sting from his eyes.

I didn't ask what he was thinking. If he regretted coming here, if he missed home, his friends, the time when his wife was healthy and his daughter happy. I didn't ask if he regretted making Mother cry—she cried not from moving or from Reforging or even from his temper, but from the fact that he made her craft broken pencils when she used to take so much pride in her work. I didn't ask if he thought our burnt paper money could even reach his mother from here, or if she would be looking for us in Shanghai. Instead, I closed the umbrella, retreated into the house, and worked on the next batch of pencils.

The clientele at the Taiwan branch was not as far-reaching as the one in Shanghai. For the most part, only university students were interested. They were my age, and yet they seemed a world apart, improving themselves through education, often with the goal of leaving Taiwan. And nobody dreamed of that goal, or was closer to reaching it, than Torou.

The Anti-Communist and Resist Russia Union hosted community events, an effort by the government to garner support for the military. They held free movie nights, organized tree plantings and social gatherings where they would, with each bowl of rice, hand out pamphlets showcasing all the good they were doing for the island. It was at one of these events where I met Torou.

I only went because my parents forced me out of the house. I had started playing mahjong with a group of women, sometimes for entire afternoons. Once, they invited me to come with them to one of these gatherings. Everybody would be my age, they promised, although I would be the odd one out, since I was not in university.

The event was held on campus at the local university. Thankfully it was winter, so the heat was not as oppressive. Most of the people there knew one another from class. I only knew the woman who invited me, who quickly abandoned me after seeing her classmates. I made a show of looking at the tent of meager refreshments. In the end, I sat on the outskirts of the crowd, next to a boy drinking, of all things, soup.

"Soup?" he asked, raising a spoonful.

"No thank you."

When I faced him, he recognized me.

"You're the pencil girl" were his exact words. "You work at the Phoenix Pencil Company."

"I do." I looked at him more closely, but I did not recognize him. I was the one working the storefront in those days, and so I knew most of the customers. "Do you get your pencils there?" If so, I likely would have Reforged his words before.

"No. My sister does though." He pointed at one of the women in the gathering closest to us. "She raves about them."

I wanted to warn him, let him know anything his sister wrote could one day be used against her, that our pencils were not safe. But I barely knew him, and so I said, "That's nice."

"I love communication," he blurted out, which was such an odd thing to say. He put his soup down and looked at me intently. He was much thinner back then, but the intensity in his eyes was the same. "That's what I study," he said quickly. "Communication."

"Oh."

"Your pencils are a means of communication, too, aren't they? The way all writing is."

"They're just pencils." I shrugged, even though they very much were not just pencils. I took one of ours out of my bag. I always had at least one with me. I twirled it expertly between my fingers, hoping to distract him.

"You must know all about how people communicate," he said almost dreamily.

We were getting into uncomfortable territory. "What do you study about communication?" I asked to turn the conversation away from me.

"How to secure it," he said.

"What does that mean?"

"Well, in wars there is always a necessity to send secure messages. That's what I study. How you secure a message."

The topic had somehow turned even more uncomfortable.

"So do you go to this university?" I asked, another attempt to change the subject.

"I take a lot of classes here," he said. "But I'm not technically a student. What do you do?"

I shrugged.

"All I do is play mahjong and make pencils."

"I bet there's more to you than that. Here." He took off his watch and turned its face to me. "Talk for five minutes. I won't interrupt or say a thing."

Five minutes did not sound long, and I had nobody else to talk to, so I agreed. I spoke in halting sentences at first. I did not hide the fact that my father was a proud Nationalist, though most locals did not take kindly to that. If Torou cared, he did not show it. I told him we came from Shanghai. That we ran a pencil company there. That we were reestablishing it here. That I left behind my aunt and cousin. When I began to talk about you, the words came easily. I talked about how we used to compete to settle the accounts, how we wrote a story together, how we slept in the same room every night for ten years, whispering deep into the night through our mosquito nets. I told him about Shanghai and startled myself with the longing in my voice, for the home we had left.

"You sound like you really miss your cousin," he said. I glanced at his watch. I had talked for more than ten minutes, and he had stayed silent the whole time.

"I guess I do." I tried not to think about how I had received no news from you or your mother since we arrived.

"I'd write a story with you," he offered.

I laughed.

"Our stories were silly," I said, and yet I ached for those nights all the same.

"What were they about?"

"Girls with special powers who fought the Japanese."

"I like that," he said. "But you're right, I probably wouldn't be very good at writing that. If there's anything else you and your cousin did, I could help you with that instead."

It was such a startlingly nice gesture that I did not know how to respond.

"Or maybe we could go see a movie or something." I remember he stared intently at his empty soup bowl as he said it.

"How old are you?" I asked. He looked young compared to the rest of the crowd.

"Almost eighteen," he said. He was three years younger than me, which at that age made me think him impossibly young. No wonder he was not officially a university student.

"Maybe in a few years, then," I said lightly.

"I won't be here in a few years," he sighed.

"Oh? Where will you be?"

"America. I'm going to study engineering at MIT. Have you heard of it?"

"You've already gotten in?"

"No." His face turned red. "But I will." He sighed again. "I don't want to live here anymore. It's occupation after occupation here. America though. That's the place to be free."

I shifted. Any pain he was going through likely had something to do with my father, who worked for the government, with Mother, who passed along messages for them. And with me, for helping make their operations more efficient, more secretive. Martial law was in full force. The Nationalists did not allow anyone to speak out against them, particularly the locals.

"Can I at least come by the pencil company sometime?" he asked.

"Sure," I said. "I'm Yun."

"Torou."

It was a Japanese name. But I could tell from his accent that he was a local. His family had likely given all of their children Japanese names, a practice during occupation to gain favor with the Japanese officials. Even after occupation ended, many kids were so used to having Japanese names that they never reverted to their Chinese or Taiwanese names.

"See you soon, then," he said, and left, soup bowl in hand.

My friend was the one who brought him up again, the next time we played mahjong.

"How did you enjoy talking to the Tsai son?" she asked. I knew that even if she was interested in our conversation, she was also trying to distract me from my tiles, to make me slip up in the game.

"He talks a lot."

"You two looked good together."

I glanced around the table, trying to figure out if the tile I wanted to throw out would be safe.

"He's too young."

"Lots of girls are interested in him though. He's the most likely to get to America. Very smart. Maybe he's tired of girls his age and wants an older woman."

The whole table laughed at that.

"Why don't you ask him out, then?" I suggested. My hand was a bad one. I knew I would not win this round.

"He's never talked to any of us. It was a surprise to see him talking to you."

"Maybe he pities you," one of the other women suggested, which really was a rather mean thing to say. But I had been thinking the same. I had been standing alone. And even though there were so many others like me, transplants from Shanghai, somehow I was still different from all of them.

"Well, I'm not interested in him."

I lost badly that day.

CHAPTER 19

From the diary of Monica Tsai,
backed up on three servers spanning
two continents

October 29, 2018 (2018-10-29T23:52:26.651987)
loc: Cambridge, Massachusetts. United States of America
(42.3721865,71.1117091)

I don't know what will happen next—none of us do—but I am grateful, so grateful, to have been able to experience a day like today. My grandparents enjoying themselves, and Louise, just a little clearer to me. Maybe even a little closer.

By the time I woke up, they were all having breakfast downstairs. Grandfather had made congee. A few small plates of various pickled goods lay out on the table.

"Louise invited us to her volleyball game this afternoon," grandfather said as I sat down. He scooped some preserved radishes into my bowl.

I asked if we were going. I had never known either of them to be into watching sports, save for the occasional Olympic figure skating event, and the gymnasium would be a very unfamiliar spot for grandmother.

"Of course we are!" grandmother exclaimed. "That is how you support your friends."

I winced, and Louise laughed.

"It's an away game for us, so it'll be nice to have some fans," she said.

"I don't know how loud we can be," I mumbled.

"Of course we can!" grandfather said, hitting the table. Louise and I both jumped.

"Haven't you heard grandfather in front of the television during the news? You think that isn't loud?" grandmother said. She glanced at my bowl, still laden with pickled radish, and scooped in some pork floss.

"Yeah, but I can't imagine him getting as fired up over a volleyball game."

"Hey! Volleyball is intense. You'll see."

"Monica, don't insult other people's sports."

"That's not what I meant—"

"No problem. I have to head out to brunch with my teammates now. Thank you for the prebrunch breakfast though. I'll see you later at the game?"

She did not meet my eyes even as she smiled.

After she left, I retrieved a long roll of paper from my room, a remnant from some high school project. I spread it out on the kitchen table, inviting grandmother over, asking if she would help me.

I passed her a pencil, and together we began to draw.

When we got to the gymnasium, grandmother and grandfather laid down the cushions they'd detached from our kitchen table chairs, placed them on the bleachers. I told them I didn't need one, and soon regretted it, sitting directly on the cold bench. We were in the second row even though I was normally a back-of-the-room type.

I didn't know the first thing about volleyball. I filled the time before the game reading about the positions and rules, rattling them off to my grandparents, who sat on either side of me. Eventually the gymnasium filled up, and even though I kept explaining the roles of each position, I was sure they could not hear me anymore over the bustle.

"Oh!" grandmother exclaimed when the players started jogging out. "They're all so tall!"

"Oh!" she exclaimed again, her hand rapidly tapping my shoulder. "There's Louise!"

"Louise, look!" grandfather said, pointing, having not heard grandmother.

I waved to her. She was average height compared to the rest of the team. They wore orange-accented shirts, and their black short shorts made them appear even taller. She smiled widely and waved back.

"Why doesn't Louise hit any?" grandfather asked as the teams warmed up. Most of the team was running up to the net, jumping, and spiking the ball, while Louise tossed the balls in the air.

"I think she's a setter," I said, resorting to English and searching for volleyball warm-up roles.

"Is that an important role?"

"It seems really important."

"Nice, Louise!" grandfather bellowed. The few people in front of us turned around, startled, and the spiker Louise had tossed to completely missed the ball.

"Maybe save that for between points," I suggested.

"Told you he could be loud," grandmother said proudly.

"Louise loves it!" grandfather insisted. And it did seem like Louise's smile was wider than ever.

Once the game started, I fielded questions from either side of me. Often, I answered the same one, just facing a different direction. It was clear Louise was indeed the setter. It was also clear the Harvard team had a much larger fan base than Louise's team did here in Cambridge.

"Don't worry," grandfather said. He removed his jacket and cap. His white hair was wild underneath. "I am experienced at cheering against Harvard."

"Quickly, open the banner!" grandmother urged, rapidly tapping my shoulder again.

I passed one end of the banner to grandfather and the other to grandmother. Each side was held up by long sticks grandfather used to keep his plants upright.

"Yes! Yes!" grandfather bellowed when Louise set the ball to her teammate on the far right who spiked it into the opponent's court. Grandmother cheered too, in a way that could only be described as ululating. I helped them raise the banner. They shook it wildly, their movements rippling the huge tiger we had drawn, its body stretching and lunging above our heads, its tail pointed, its head in the beginning of a snarl.

It seemed like the entire gymnasium quieted. I wanted to quiet down, too, seeing everybody staring at us. Grandmother and grandfather continued their banner waving and cheering, and I would not abandon them. Still, my stomach twisted, wishing people would look away. But Louise's team gathered, pointed to us, and cheered right back.

Louise stood in the middle of them all. Her eyes were wide, her lips just barely parted before breaking into a smile. Both her hands came to her mouth and then extended outward, a kiss blown in our direction. I wanted to shrink away, now for a different reason. I was delighted and would rather have harbored this feeling of joy alone for a moment.

The game ended not long after, with Louise's team winning in straight sets. Grandfather's voice was hoarse, and grandmother had not stopped waving her end of the banner, even when it was lowered by our feet.

Louise jogged over afterward. Grandmother began cheering all over again, her hands waving as if a celebrity were approaching. Louise took her hand in both of hers.

"You all are amazing," she laughed, looking between the three of us. Then she looked only at me. "Thank you."

"It was all them," I murmured. "I'm not very loud."

"Oh, come on." I could see the sweat along her forehead. "It was your idea, wasn't it?"

"I—" Grandmother nudged me with her elbow. "Yeah, I guess so. Grandmother did the drawing though, I just outlined it. And grandfather—"

"Take the credit, Monica," grandfather huffed.

"Yeah!" Louise crossed her arms. "You're always doing such nice things for me. I don't know why you'd bother."

Another nudge from grandmother.

"I—well, I like you," I managed.

She tilted her head. I tried to make it sound casual. Had she seen right through me, though? Would she talk about me with her teammates afterward, and would they all laugh at me?

"I like you too," she said gently. "I'll grab my stuff, and then we can head back together?"

"You're not going to celebrate with your teammates?" I asked.

"Nah, I already spend too much time with them." She ran off, waving behind her.

"She likes you!" grandmother exclaimed in a whisper that everybody around us definitely heard.

"We're friends," I mumbled.

"Hmmmm."

On our way home, grandmother and grandfather swiped their senior passes on the bus scanner with gusto. They asked Louise questions about plays they saw earlier in the night—my answers had clearly been unsatisfactory. There was a lot of pantomiming of volleyball moves, praise for Louise's clever thinking, and curses for the opposing team, who grandfather was convinced had played dirty.

"Ah, Monica!" Grandmother tried to draw me into the conversation. "Maybe you can learn to play volleyball too!"

"I don't think I'm tall enough." I smiled.

"Ah, you are probably right." Grandmother sighed. "Louise is much taller than you are. Louise is like an asparagus. And you . . . you are more like a button mushroom."

"I—I'm not that short!"

"Mm, I love mushrooms, though!" Louise grinned.

"They all have their strengths," grandfather placated right before pressing the button for our stop.

When we were outside of the house, Louise tugged my jacket sleeve.

"Want to walk a bit more?"

"We'll go in first and prepare dinner," grandmother said awfully quickly. Grandfather followed grandmother dutifully, fumbled in his jacket for the keys before they both disappeared inside the house.

"Where did you want to go?" I asked.

"Anywhere."

We headed toward the river. The neighborhood from our house to the Charles River is a quiet one. The only other people out were dog walkers and the occasional passing car. After we walked in silence for a block, I could not hold it in any longer. I asked if she was feeling alright.

"Huh?" The sun was setting, and she looked so soft in the light. It hurt, how she glowed. I questioned every one of my own feelings. "Yes, of course. I'm really quite happy."

I swallowed. "I just feel like things got weird between us after our git rebasing."

"Ah. That's—" She threw her volleyball up and caught it deftly. She did this a few more times before answering. "That's not your fault. I was thinking too much."

It took me another block of colonial brick buildings to make myself press for more.

"About what?" I asked.

She, too, took her time. Throwing her volleyball up again, the same way I would tap at my keyboard.

"About you, I suppose."

"What about me?" I braved.

She paused again. We had made it to the riverbank, the Boston skyline shining. She set her volleyball on the ground and perched on top of it. She gave me her gym bag to sit on.

"About how different your family is from mine," she said finally.

I was disappointed. I was also certain, even from the few in-person interactions we'd had together, that she was lying. "My family is quite different from most people's, I think."

"But it's so loving. It's such a . . . family." Then she told me about her older brothers, who were both doctors, and how her parents had expected the same from her. "What a cliché," she laughed. When she was in elementary school and only scored the average on math and science tests, her parents had begun to lose hope.

"I actually think maybe I'm not bad at math," she said. "But for pretty much all my life I thought I was worse than my brothers. My parents instilled that story in me, whether they meant to or not, and just like that I didn't believe I could do many things."

"Is that why you didn't want to tell them about your change in majors?" I asked.

"Yeah." She began to rock on top of the volleyball. "They still don't know. They're going to freak out. They've settled for economist. But your grandparents never told you there was something you couldn't do, right? They seem so supportive. And that's why I'm struggling to understand you. Someone who has had that much love and affirmation—I guess I'd expect you to be more . . . confident. Arrogant, even. More like the white boys in salmon shorts at Princeton."

"I didn't get into Princeton," I said seriously, and she laughed.

"That's not a problem. We met regardless."

I hugged my knees.

"My parents left when I was really young. I think that messed with my self-esteem." I had never really talked to anyone about my parents' situation before. When people asked about them, there were always assumptions involved. That my parents must be so proud, how could they miss this, why did my mother never volunteer for school activities, it seemed a little harsh that my grandparents were shoveling snow? But in the quiet of the setting sun with only her to listen, it was easy to talk about.

"My mom left first, and my dad went to Shanghai to work when the stock market crashed here. He rarely comes back. I guess that's why I'd do anything for my grandparents." I nestled my chin between my knees. "They didn't have to raise me and treat me so well."

Louise turned to me suddenly.

"Let me try reframing your story."

"What does that mean?"

"There's some research that shows if you change the way you see your own story, there can be profound benefits. Therapists sometimes use this technique to help patients dealing with trauma see their own life differently, to help them come to peace with their past. Reframing is one way to put it, you might also see it called story editing, or—"

"Or git rebasing?"

She laughed. "I think only you would call it git rebasing. But yes, you know what? You're right. Let's git rebase your commit history. Actually, scratch that. I'll reframe my story. Then you reframe yours. It'll be a good exercise, you'll see." She cleared her throat.

"My original story: I was never as good at anything as my brothers. I didn't win any of the awards they won. I only got into Princeton because they both went there. I'm going to disappoint my parents even more once they find out I've changed majors. They're going to say I'm wasting their money. But I'm the helpless youngest child, so they'll grudgingly continue paying for my degree, as long as they can still tell their friends that all of their children went to Princeton."

"Can I rebase your story?" I asked suddenly. I hated hearing all the ways she talked herself down.

"Oh, yes. Please do."

"Your new story: You weren't as good at math or science as your brothers, but you were good at talking to people and making friends. You won awards for volunteering and for your essays in history class." The words came easily. "You got into Princeton not because of your brothers, but because you were interesting—you had a drive for story-telling and uniting people, and you could join the volleyball team to boot. Your parents were confused when they found out about your change in major, but it made sense to them since you were always asking for stories. They were reluctant to show it, then they became interested in these stories and new histories you're uncovering and archiving, and it helped them learn more about themselves too."

She did not say anything for a while. By then, it was too dark to make out her expression, so I stared at the river. The wind of the late October evening was picking up, but I wasn't cold, not next to her.

"You're good at this," she said eventually, a softness to her voice that wasn't there before. "Thank you. Now let me try you. Tell me your story."

I struggled to start. She had rattled hers off so easily. But it was not so different from writing a journal entry.

"My mom left before I can remember, and no one has ever told me exactly why," I began. "I think she didn't get along with my grandparents. I do remember my dad leaving. He and my grandfather fought terribly. So it was just me and my grandparents. I guess I did wonder if my parents didn't care enough about me to even visit. It's not like they're dead, they're just living their lives elsewhere. But I didn't wonder that much. My grandparents were always more than enough.

"I worked hard in school, but I didn't have many friends. I always felt like I should be helping my grandparents, since they're getting old and sometimes their English falters. I studied computer science because that seemed like the quickest way to make money without a graduate degree. I wanted to make sure they wouldn't have any financial problems. Now my grandmother is losing her memory, so I'm trying to spend more time with her, to help my grandfather, but also to understand her better, before it's too late. I've spent my whole life with them and yet I barely know anything about them. And part of me is scared to ask."

She placed her hand on mine and squeezed.

"Alright," she said, taking a breath. In the dark, there was only her voice, soft and assured. "Here's your rebase message: You grew up beloved by all of your family except for the selfish ones who ran off for their own purposes. Your grandparents were hurt by your parents' leaving, but they will never stop thanking the day they were left with you. They delighted in how quickly you learned everything and how you helped them embrace modern technology in a way that made all their friends jealous. Whenever they pulled out a phone and sent off a text message, their friends would exclaim, 'Wow, you know how to use one of those doohickeys?' and they would say, prouder than any parent, 'Yes! My granddaughter makes sure we keep up to date and that we are protected from malware.' It was no surprise to them when you got into one of the best colleges in the country and studied computer science, something you've always had a natural inclination toward. You didn't have many friends because your concerns didn't align with most high schoolers, who cared only about popularity while you cared about your family.

"In college you found people you could call your friends all while continuing to make your grandparents proud. Technology is still something you love, and you can't wait to work in a burgeoning field where you can quickly make a difference. You want to use your skills to help. You already have, by using your project to reunite your grandmother with her cousin. You have always been about help and support, first to your grandparents, then to your friends. And your friends, even if there may not be many, are so grateful.

"But wait, there's more!" she exclaimed when I tried to interrupt her. "You understand the value of stories, and maybe that is because it is in your very blood. You come from a long line of pencil makers, and though nobody in the family makes pencils anymore, you have taken over the mantle in some way. Isn't technology—typing, writing, blogging—the new pencil?"

"That's a bit of a stretch," I finally managed to interrupt.

"I'm still going! Tech is a means to connect with others, and you did not want your grandparents to be left behind. You are the latest in a series of story preservers and sharers and enablers, and you are carrying that on whether you know it or not. Does that scare you?"

I sighed.

"It does." My voice shook, taking me by surprise. "I'm scared because I know they won't live all that much longer. And with grandmother it will be even sooner. Even if she is alive, it won't be long before she can't remember. Today was a really good day for her. But most days . . . Soon she might not even remember me. I guess I should be grateful for what they have already given me. I know they're older than many people live to be."

When she did not say anything, I glanced over at her. I could just make out her smile.

"What?" I asked, replaying what I had said.

"You accepted your reframed story. That's a huge step."

"Is that what happened?"

"Totally!" She threw her hands in the air. "But I was tricky about it. I reframed your story and then asked you a question that you could only answer if you had accepted the story as yours. Clever, right?"

I hid my smile in my knees.

"Yes, very clever. But I'm not convinced that believing in my story is going to change how I go about things."

"I can send you the research papers. Or rather, let me give you an example." The energy in her voice was palpable. "I used to be really mediocre at volleyball, or at least that's what I thought. But then one day, before a big game, I overheard one of the older girls talking about the team. She said, 'The underclassmen are either athletic and lazy, or diligent and not athletic. Except Louise. She is both athletic and diligent—we'll need to keep an eye on her.' And I'm telling you the truth—before that point, I really did not think I was good at any part of volleyball except showing up to every practice. Once I realized somebody was seeing my story in that way, the confidence boost was incredible. We won every game that season."

"That sounds great," I said. "But I don't think that has happened to me before."

"Just wait."

"Can I tell you something?"

"Of course."

"I'm afraid of what I might learn about my grandmother," I admitted. "That's why I haven't tried to learn to Reforge. Whether I learn about it through pencils or EMBRS or you asking for her story—I'm afraid."

"That's not unusual," she said gently. "But perhaps another question you can ask yourself is, will you regret not learning about her?"

I didn't know the answer to that. At one point, even a few months ago, I would have responded yes, of course. But for the first time, I was questioning the need to know everything. Questioning even EMBRS and its need for data, questioning Prof. Logan's radical sharing philosophy. Not everything needed to be shared, did it? Or was it merely blissful ignorance I chased?

"I would give anything to know about my grandparents," she said quietly. "Even if it was horrible. That's how we learn to be better, isn't it? And I think you would want to hear her side of the story, wouldn't you?"

She had a way of making things seem so logical, obvious. I was about to tell her so when my phone buzzed.

😒😑😀😊 🀄️!!!快點回來 🏠🏃

"We have to go home." I stood and picked up her gym bag.

"Is everything okay?"

"I think grandmother just realized we have four people here."

"Is that bad luck or something?"

"It means we have the right number of people for mahjong. Have you played before?"

"No." She stood up and kicked the volleyball into her hands. "My parents told us to stay away, since it's gambling."

I grinned, suddenly eager to not be the straitlaced one.

"C'mon. I'll teach you. Or rather, my grandparents will teach you by winning all of your money. It's okay! They'll let you use Monopoly money for now. It's rare that there are two other people around for them to play."

"I don't know." Even so, we began to walk back. "What if I become addicted?"

"It's good for keeping your mind active. They always say that's how they're still sharp at their age. All their former mahjong partners have passed away over the last few years."

"Ah, you're cruel to bring that up! Fine, let's go."

After dinner, we played deep into the night, grandmother insisting on playing a full set. The game moved slowly at first, as they explained the rules to Louise, but after the first round, tiles were flying.

Louise ended up with only a minor loss, while grandfather and I both lost a significant chunk. Grandmother came out on top, her stack of neon Monopoly money piling up throughout the night.

"I was so close to winning that last round!" Louise sighed.

"We can play again tomorrow," grandmother said smugly, counting her fake money.

"Yes!"

"You're not addicted, are you?" I asked.

She cast me a sly grin.

"Your fault if I am."

"You two can play together when you're old," grandfather said. "Keeps your mind sharp. Mr. and Mrs. Lee stopped playing with us, and that's why they died so soon."

"They died in a car accident!" I exclaimed.

"Because their minds couldn't think fast enough when it happened," grandfather insisted. "Mahjong prevents that."

"Well, I'll look forward to that when we're old, Monica." Louise grinned, finding my hand under the table.

Now here I am trying to record all that has happened before I forget a single detail, my head full of stories. What they mean and how they can change, even the ones from the past. How we rewrite and revise, how we see ourselves, how EMBRS might see me. My head is full of a girl who has worked her way into my closed-off life and somehow pried it open, one who can be the fourth leg of our mahjong table, one who I cannot stop thinking about, who pulls me in and pushes me away in the span of a smile. And it's full of simple gratitude, for grandfather's cheers, and the way grandmother comes into my room and says good night, it was a good day today wasn't it, sleep well, my little mushroom.

CHAPTER 20

From the Reforged pencil of Wong Yun

I find myself reflecting on those early days when I first met Torou. There is not much else I care to recall from my years in Taiwan. Even the time spent with Torou, when he kept his promise and visited the pencil company, my parents peering curiously, the two of us sitting closer and closer—I hesitated to share this with you. It is trivial compared to everything else that was happening around us: martial law in Taiwan, families fleeing Shanghai. It didn't seem important by comparison.

But seeing Monica and Louise together this week—oh, my heart soars. I was worried at first (when have I not been worried for Monica?). They are kind to each other and care for each other in a way that makes my heart ease, just a little. It is not only seeing their interactions. It is seeing them *exist*, thriving and laughing, at the same age when you and I were fleeing, hiding, and betraying. This letter is my attempt to explain myself and all of my wrongdoing, and yet I cannot help highlight this: Monica is happy and she is a good person, and that is my greatest achievement.

And so I have been thinking a lot about love these days, and how I could not possibly have known then how much that boy who came to visit would stay with me. We would leave homes, adjust to new ones, fail in parenting but succeed in grandparenting—and how he would stay with me even now, when I am falling apart. How can you ever expect someone to do all of that with you, for you? How can you know when you're young and sad and vulnerable how to choose someone to share your life with? And how can you know when you're old and weak and vulnerable that someone will be kind to your granddaughter, long after you are gone?

In those days, when business was slow, I would read in the nook, out of sight of the customers, and work on my English. Everybody knew that to really escape war after war, hunger after hunger, displacement after displacement, you had to go to America.

And one day not long after the picnic, I found Torou sitting in my nook, two textbooks and a notebook opened before him. He had kept his promise.

"Hi," he said, looking up from his notebook. "Your mother said I could study here."

"You talked to my mother?"

"Yes. She was very kind."

I had been in the back with Mother, and she had mentioned no such thing. I think she preferred to see how our relationship might develop without her meddling.

"Do you mind moving over a bit, then?" I asked.

"Of course."

The desk was pushed against the wall, only one side of it suitable for sitting. We sat on the same bench, him scratching at his notebook as I opened my books to read.

Like him, I had two books in front of me: one an English text, the other a Chinese translation, and a notebook where I wrote out new words in pencil. I was convinced the words I Reforged were easier to remember. So at night, I Reforged everything I wrote and in that way committed the translation to memory. I was sure English would be my way out.

We sat side by side for most of that first day, not speaking. There was a calmness to our pencils scratching at paper, pages flipping. It was the closest I felt to the days you and I used to spend reviewing the accounts, though without that same urgent competitiveness we used to share.

He came nearly every afternoon after that. I only joined him sometimes. I was too busy, either in the back, Reforging, or in the front, showing off our pencils to the customers. I would turn on my father's charm and everything I learned from your mother. I was good at it, I think, though each interaction left me drained. I often caught Torou watching me. With each pencil I handed out, I wondered when it would come back, mutate with my blood, and reveal all of their secrets. Gone were the days when I enthusiastically demonstrated their smoothness, balanced weight, and customizability. They were excellent pencils on their own. Only we knew the power they possessed.

No longer were we Reforging cryptic work orders or military commands. Now we Reforged the words of ordinary citizens, and worse, their secrets and personal stories, stories full of anger at the current political situation or their hope for the future. Their words coursed through me, and I felt their full meaning, suffered with them—the Taiwanese people, freed from Japanese occupation, believing things would be better under the Chinese, only to discover occupation always looks the same. No matter how hopeful their words, as soon as they were bleeding out of my body, it was over for them. I didn't know it then. But I do now. The government had these people arrested, disappeared, labeled Communist sympathizers. They were exiled to small surrounding islands. At the time it was only a hushed rumor. If you had been there, maybe we would have had the courage to ask questions, to rebel, like the characters we wrote. But it was only me, and I was trying to help my parents, who were trying to survive and who really believed this the best course of action for their family and the nation. At least through our pencils we could do something when we had always been powerless.

Then there was the day I found Torou using one of our pencils. Before I could think better of it, I snatched it out of his hand.

He had been in the middle of writing an equation, his hand still shaped to hold the pencil as he looked up at me, baffled.

"I didn't steal it," he said immediately.

"I didn't think you did," I said, suddenly guilty.

"It was sitting on the table. I thought I'd try it out. How could I resist, after the way you describe them to the customers?"

"They're not . . . I didn't think you would like them." I tucked the pencil into my apron.

"Are you kidding? I understand what my sister was going on about now." He frowned. "They write beautifully. I can afford it if that's what you are worried about."

"It's not."

"I feel like I should be supporting your business with all the time I spend here."

"Mother doesn't care about that kind of thing."

His expression turned dark. "Is it because you don't want locals using your pencils?"

I was able to cut off that line of reasoning quickly.

"You know I have sold to plenty of locals."

He crossed his arms.

"Then why not to me?"

"Because—" I tried to weigh the risk in my head. The powerful thing about a pencil was that almost always, one of the first things a person wrote was their name. Then no matter what else they wrote with it, we could always trace it back to them, even if they lost it and somebody else began to use it. I knew Torou did not hold kind feelings for the Nationalist government. If they ever suspected him of dissidence, or simply did not want him to succeed for whatever reason, they would only need to find his pencil and twist his Reforged words to send him away. Maybe he would write only calculus equations. But his conviction that he would go to America and finally live his freedom—that was not worth the risk.

"Please trust me," I said. I could not tell him the truth or even think of a suitable excuse to convince him never to buy one of our pencils.

"Fine. Then come see a movie with me."

"What? That has nothing to do with pencils."

"They're both things I want." He smiled. "Surely you can do that much?"

I fidgeted. He was right. There was no harm in going to a movie with him. I was not planning on falling in love with him, after all.

"Alright."

That night, I quizzed Mother.

"Is there any way to make a pencil heart that cannot be Reforged?"

She was almost always rubbing her wrist in those days. It is only now I understand that feeling. I cannot imagine Reforging at the volume she did at her age.

"There are pencils that harm us when we Reforge them," she said. "Ones with cheap and impure hearts."

"But what about ones that don't hurt us? If we try to Reforge them, and we don't get any words?"

She tilted her head and stared at me.

"But why would we do that?"

"You mentioned it was dangerous. That's because people don't know we can collect their words and use them against them, right?"

"Quiet down," she ordered. "That is true. But we are sharing truths. That is noble, isn't it?"

Her question was genuine. I think she really believed she was helping create a better China, and who am I to say that she wasn't?

It was 1950, a new decade, and yet nothing had changed. We were coming up on our second year in Taiwan. My father's promise of a few months seemed a lifetime ago. I didn't care for the Nationalists or the Communists. I wanted to be free of it all, the same as Torou, and you only wanted a place to call home, regardless of who was governing it. Our mothers longed for stability and the most straightforward way to achieve that was to support the government. If the Nationalists could not form a unified front, there would be no hope of driving out the Communists, or returning to China, returning to you.

What little news we received from Shanghai was dire. We heard about the forced confessions of business owners, how everyone was once again paranoid, trying to sniff out any capitalist leanings among their neighbors. That in itself was frightening. But then there was the matter of the pencils. They were uniquely suited for this kind of work, spying and revealing. It was possible you were doing the same thing we were doing here. You would have an opinion, I knew, about whether it was noble. You would not merely acquiesce as I did. You would take action.

I dreaded Reforging Torou's pencil, worried it would be like that time I stole your boy's pencil and Reforged it, saw and felt those things that were not meant for me. Torou might reveal some truth he felt about me—that he hated me or, even worse, that he loved me. Both options terrified me. But I had to do it so there was no chance his words could ever be discovered.

It turned out I was self-absorbed even in my paranoia. He wrote nothing about me, only math equations. A slanted, efficient handwriting, numbers and symbols that I could not begin to understand. He wrote with a mix of care and excitement and—at the very end—a fullness, a satisfaction, an appreciation that could only be described as love.

Afterward, I lay on my bed and raised my hand toward the dark-paneled Japanese-style ceiling. My phoenix black against my skin, the way it was after Reforging, made vivid by his words. For that moment, I let myself admire the minimal lines, the way his heart filled in my scar. I wrapped both arms around myself. That was what his love felt like, I thought, smiling.

Torou and I finally went to our movie. He took me to Ximending, perhaps the closest in terms of bustling city life that Taipei had to offer. It was the largest shopping district and home to several movie theaters, including a Peking opera house my parents enjoyed. I cannot recall the name of the film we saw. I even asked Torou, just now, and all he could remember was the way the movie stopped in the middle for some Nationalist propaganda. Nothing happened between us during the movie or afterward. He told me he had a test the next week and so he would not be stopping by the pencil company.

"I thought you studied well there." I was disappointed. I told myself it was not because of any soft feelings for him, only that I longed for the minimal amount of comfort he provided.

He laughed.

"I never said that. I always end up too distracted by you."

"By me? I'm just reading."

"It's one of the only times you look happy."

Only through remembering the things he used to say to me can I recall the depth of my unhappiness during those years. A shadow of what you must have felt when you came to live with us in Shanghai, though maybe I flatter myself by believing my being there helped you adjust. In Taiwan, I had no one, and I shut out even those who wanted to be close to me.

"I think you should see that boy more," Mother told me after a few days passed with no visit from Torou. "The Tsai son."

"He has to study."

"Oh, Yun." Mother looked at me, rubbing her hands together to stay warm, her eyes lined with her weariness. "You have not been the same since we left Shanghai. You used to love life. You wanted everything from it. Remember the qipaos you used to admire? The dances you wanted to attend? The drawings you used to make?"

It did not even sound like she was referring to my life.

"Well, we're not in Shanghai anymore," I said. "Shanghai was alive and real and home."

"Find the boy again," she suggested. "Do not forget there is still pleasure in this life."

The next time I found Torou studying at the corner desk, I joined him with my books. He slid a package over to me. I opened it. Inside were two more books—an English novel and its Chinese translation.

"These aren't cheap," I said, because I could think of nothing else to say.

"Of course not." He turned back to his work. "Stories are priceless."

"How was your test?"

"Good. I think I can afford to goof off a bit now."

Even so, we both opened our books and began to study. Somewhere along the way, I realized he had inched closer, or was it possible I had shifted nearer to him? Our thighs touched. Neither of us moved away.

As I finished the page I was working on, I felt his eyes on me. I considered asking if he should be studying and not staring at me or if there was something in my hair, or closing my book and moving away. Something would change, I knew, if I turned to face him. Mother's words made the decision for me. I chose pleasure.

The kiss was simple, the barest touch of our lips before I pulled away. We returned to our books. I struggled to concentrate, though, too focused on the way his leg moved against mine, his furiously tapping foot.

The next time, a few days later, lasted longer. Each time, a bit longer than that, our hands slowly exploring each other's bodies, both of us hoping no customers would walk in or that Mother would decide to make a rare appearance. We would have heard someone approaching, I was sure of it, but there were also times when the rest of the world seemed to fade away entirely except for his arms.

Even then—and I find it difficult to convince myself of this, so I wonder if it is possible to convince you—I did not like him much more than any other person I might have dated. You know I married him, that things worked out. But in those days, I hardly felt anything other than adrift. His arms locked me in place, slowed my descent. I chased those feelings and kissed him deeper, felt more of his body each time.

One day, after I had locked the front door and my parents had left to meet their friends, and only Torou and I remained, we went even further. We lay on the bench, him on top of me, the bench hard against my back, his body warm and welcoming.

His hand ventured beneath my shirt, working its way up to my breasts, which was not new. But on this day, I wanted more. I let him touch me as he pleased, his cold hand in stark contrast to his warm lips and breath. I slowly raised myself upright, pushing him until we were both sitting. I moved so I could face him, so I could straddle him with my legs and wrap my knees around his waist.

I rubbed my body against his, and as I did, my mind circled back to you and your boy. How once, you had done something just like this, and how you never shared those details with me, and now I could see why. The reactions of my body, new and foreign and intoxicating. I wanted only him to witness it. His hand began to lift my skirt.

He stroked me and I shuddered into him. I reached for his belt. He took my hand with his free one, held it in place on the bench. My left hand still held his Reforging—I had not wanted to bleed it out yet. My mind briefly wandered to the work I still had to complete, the pencils I needed to Reforge, all the stories to which I had grown numb. He teased a finger below my underwear, pulling the fabric to the side, and all those stray thoughts disappeared.

I pressed harder into him. His finger remained an obstacle between us. It moved slowly, lazily, tracing corners not even I had explored, slick. Then it slid right into me. I shuddered, again, a soft moan against his neck. I could feel his smile. His finger continued to explore, to thrust. My left hand protested weakly against his, though his grip was firm. I wanted more. I even told him so. He quieted me with a laugh, traced his lips over my neck, and that sent the first wave through me.

It was a wonder to feel this way. My body had only produced pain before—words bleeding out on the page, knives to skin, monthly blood, the helplessness of wartime—and to now feel this glow, this euphoria. I bucked against him, barely registered his hand trying to keep up with my movement. I gasped and squeezed my eyes shut as he sent wave after wave through me until I finally fell against his chest.

For a moment, right as I thought I was coming to my senses, the world disappeared. Not even Torou was there, or at least, not the version of him that should have been. Instead, I experienced the silent and studious Torou, the one who smiled at his mathematics, and though I had no hope of understanding his numbers and logic, something about his posture, his warmth, made me want to try regardless. It was like I had Reforged a more vivid version of his pencil heart—and I realized that was exactly what had happened.

"Hey." His voice came from a distance. "Yun? You still there?"

I was back at the pencil company, still sitting on top of him. His hand brushing my cheek, so startlingly intimate that I recoiled even when I didn't want to, not really.

"Are you alright?" he asked, full of concern.

I scrambled off him and rolled up my sleeve, too caught in the moment to worry he might see my scar. But it didn't matter. The dark glow that his words had formed on my skin and that I had privately enjoyed these last weeks, was gone. The phoenix was barely visible, pale as it would have been if I had bled out his words. His story was lost to the world, as you had said.

"Sorry," I said quickly, trying to understand. "I'm okay."

"Are you sure? It was like you were . . . gone. I mean, I don't have much experience with this, but I don't think that's normal."

"I'm sick," I blurted out, a sudden lie I could not control. I needed time to think, to understand myself and my body, run back through our mothers' warnings, our past conversations. I had finally caught up to you. I had all the missing pieces, and still, I could not quite see what it meant.

His expression shifted.

"How so?"

"My body is—weird. It's not normal. That's why I . . . disappeared for a bit." He kept trying to look into my eyes. I twisted away from him.

"Does it affect your health?"

"I don't know."

"Should we go to a doctor?"

I had to place a hand on his knee to stop him from rising. "I don't think a doctor could help me."

"Why not?"

"It's something that runs in my family."

"Let me help you." His earnestness would one day save me, but that day it wrenched.

"My mother wouldn't want me to tell you."

"Why is that?"

"Family secret."

He frowned.

"Would I get to know if we married?"

"We aren't marrying." I nearly laughed. It was too much, all at once. This riddle of Reforging, finally an answer within reach, something to do with pleasure instead of pain. I mourned that we hadn't been able to puzzle it out together. We had spent our last year feuding. To know that you were experiencing something like this with your boy, that this, of all things, was what we had fought over. "We're—we're only enjoying each other."

He leaned back, his eyes wide. My words had hurt him, I realized, the first time they had done so, even as I had continually brushed him off for weeks.

"But I—" he began. Then he shook his head and packed up his books, stuffed them into his bag.

"Wait." Something had gone wrong, something I had not intended. The pleasure I was chasing, those moments of happiness, was leaving.

"I need to focus on studying," he mumbled. "I've wasted too much time."

He stood. I was in his way, between him and the door. I continued to sit, looking up at him, at a complete loss for words.

"You're not coming back?" I asked weakly.

"I'm going to America. Maybe I'll see you there."

I moved aside. He left the pencil company, the door clicking closed behind him. I wished he had slammed it. It might have woken me from whatever stupor I was in right then. I had been relying on him to help me.

I picked up the nearest pencil and traced it across my notebook. Each stroke deepened as I tried to rub the heart deeper into the paper, turn it into nothing more than a nub. My fingers turned white from the pressure. Then the heart snapped. The tip rolled away. I stared into the hollow of the wood.

Heartbroken. It could not have been more obvious.

CHAPTER 21

From the diary of Monica Tsai,
backed up on three servers spanning
two continents

October 30, 2018 (2018-10-30T19:10:16.747097)
loc: Cambridge, Massachusetts. United States of America
(42.3721865,71.1117091)

Louise has left, and the house is quiet once more. Things didn't go the way I hoped for her last day. There's nothing I can do about that now though. She had a train to catch. She's back on her path, and I'm back on mine. That's how these things go, I guess.

I had planned to wake up early to make us breakfast. So when I heard footsteps behind me, I assumed it was grandfather, usually the earliest riser. I jumped when it was Louise's voice behind me, her mouth right next to my ear.

"How can I help?"

"Don't!" I exclaimed. I had never felt more like grandmother than in that instant, wanting to drive her out of the kitchen and yell at her for sneaking up on me, while also strangely pleased she was there.

She peered over my shoulder at the still-rising dough and asked what I was making. I told her it was a secret, that she should go back to bed.

"Can't sleep. Keep seeing mahjong tiles in my head." She glanced around the kitchen. "I was hoping your grandmother would be awake so I could interview her before I left."

I told her grandmother always sleeps in after mahjong nights. I tried to focus on the dough. Rolling and brushing on sesame oil paste, rolling again, layering, Louise's gaze warm on me. Grandmother had taught me the recipe a few weeks ago. Hers had turned out perfectly rectangular while mine were looking more trapezoidal. I flattened each trapezoid into a plate of white and black sesame seeds.

"You're making shaobing," Louise said, still behind me.

"Stop peeking."

"I need a spoon for my oatmeal."

I was indeed blocking the spoon drawer. Right as I was about to back up to open it, I felt two light touches on either side of my waist, followed by the gentlest of nudges. I stepped aside, clearing the way. Even so, Louise's hands lingered. I opened my mouth to say something but could think of absolutely nothing to say. Her hands left my waist and opened the drawer, pulled out a spoon, and popped it in her mouth. She smiled, teeth reflecting off the metal surface, her eyes crinkled.

"Your shaobing?" she reminded me, taking the spoon out of her mouth and plopping it into her bowl.

I turned back to my raw dough.

"Maybe you should stay another day," I said, clearing my throat and turning away. Only the heat from the open oven door was able to match the heat in my face. "My grandparents seem to enjoy having you around."

"Just your grandparents?" Louise leaned over the counter, stirring her oatmeal. I had never felt so much desire this close to oatmeal before.

I managed to avoid answering by shoving the tray of shaobing into the oven.

"I wish I could," Louise sighed. "But my parents weren't happy about me spending this much of my fall break away from them."

"Ah, of course." I wished I had never blurted out such a request. Of course she would be in high demand, and of course her parents had priority.

Louise sat at the kitchen table with her cereal as I tried to cut the soy-sauce-braised beef. Grandmother had been braising it for days—probably longer than she intended to—and it would be all the more delicious. Typically, we only ate the beef with rice. On special occasions, though, grandmother would rise early and make shaobing from scratch, flaky flatbread that wraps around the cold beef perfectly. It was not long before grandmother came into the kitchen, as if she could sense there was some bad knifework going on, and shooed me away from the cutting board. She took over. Something about using a knife seems embedded in her muscle memory, and she cut us perfectly thin slices.

By the time grandfather came down, the room smelled like warm bread. He took a few deep breaths, opened the window, and declared it perfect soup weather. He pulled out the leftover soup from the night before and stirred some eggs into it.

The shaobing came out perfectly. All different shapes, yes, thanks to my amateur rolling pin skills, but their coloring was beautifully golden and the smell of the toasted sesame irresistible.

We ate at the table, warm bread, cool salted meat, cutting the shaobing open with a pair of kitchen scissors, washing it down with grandfather's tomato and egg drop soup.

Louise let out a contented sigh.

"I never want to leave."

"What plans do you have today?" grandmother asked.

Louise glanced at me, then back to grandmother.

"I was hoping I could spend some time interviewing you," she began. "About your time in Shanghai during the war. And afterward."

Grandmother took her time answering. I tensed. She was chewing in a harsh way, perhaps fiddling with her dentures.

"Did you hear Louise's question?" I asked, hoping she had not, that she would agree without an argument.

Grandmother nodded.

"Why do you wish to know about that time? About Shanghai?" grandmother asked. She always said "Shanghai" a little differently, a remnant of her Shanghainese she could not abandon entirely.

"It's a fascinating time period," Louise said, sitting up straighter. "And there aren't many people around who lived through it that can still remember."

"Maybe they don't want to remember," grandmother suggested.

Louise swallowed. "It's one of the greatest migrations in human history. When so many people fled Shanghai. With all the ... immigration issues we're facing today, I think we would be able to learn ... from that time period—"

She was speaking in Chinese, and for the first time, I heard the faults in it, the imperfections from not having grown up entirely in the language. It was still better than mine. She faltered, though, and made what should have been an impassioned argument seem clumsy.

"I'm sorry. I would rather not share." Grandmother finished her soup and handed her bowl to me.

"But you said you would be okay with it earlier," I reminded her.

"Did I?"

So she did not remember our conversation or she had changed her mind. I took the bowl and stacked it on top of my own empty bowl. I bit my lip.

"Maybe the retelling would be good for your memory," I ventured.

"There is nothing that can help my memory now." She said it in a way that made clear the argument was over.

But Louise did not have that same experience reading her.

"Meng shared with me. She said she thought you would too."

Grandmother frowned.

"If Meng told you her story, then you know mine as well."

"Everyone has their own story—"

Grandfather cut in.

"Monica, why don't you take Louise to find some Boston souvenirs to bring home to her parents before her train?" He took the bowls to the sink. "Maybe some, ah, what do you call them, with the cream?"

"Cannoli," I said automatically.

Grandmother took that moment to leave the kitchen. Grandfather stacked the other dishes in the sink and followed her out.

"Oh fuck," Louise breathed once they were out of earshot. "I really messed that up."

"It's alright," I said. "She'll forget about it soon enough." I had meant it as an offhanded comment, not anything specific to her disease, and only realized the weight of my words after I spoke.

Louise groaned, covering her face. I did not know how to reassure her, so I grabbed the dishrag from the sink and wiped all the stray sesame seeds from the table.

"Oh fuck," she said, and looked away, pushing out her chair. She wiped her eyes with the back of her sleeve.

"Don't worry about it," I attempted, limp dishrag in hand. "Really. They like you."

"Surely not anymore."

"Yes, they do. You gave them so many good memories in the last few days. I don't think I ever saw them as excited as they were at your game, not for a long time. And then you played mahjong with them. That's their favorite."

"That was before I messed everything up. There's no reason they would still like me now."

"Yes, there is. They still like you because I like you."

"You still like me?" Her face was unreadable.

"Yeah. You've really helped me this semester." I paused, fidget-ing with the rag. "Your prying may have bothered grandmother just now, but without you, I would be going through all of this by myself. You're . . . you're the only one I've opened up to, the only one I've wanted to open up to."

Louise sighed, stuffing her hands in her pockets.

"You're so kind."

I shrugged and retreated to the sink.

"Should we get some cannoli, then?" I asked.

"Is it close?"

"Yeah. Can't go a mile here without running into a place that sells cannoli."

She gave me a weak smile.

An hour before her train was set to depart, she hauled her duffel bag and cooler of cannoli to the front door. I called for grandmother and grandfather even as Louise protested. They came down to say their goodbyes, hunched over by the door, hands behind their backs, smiling.

"Come again whenever you like," grandfather said, attempting to help Louise with the bag before she grabbed it herself, thanking him profusely.

"Yes, please do," grandmother echoed.

Louise blinked at her, then broke into a smile.

"Thank you all so much for having me. I had the best time."

"Let's go, then," I said quickly, ushering Louise out the door. I did not want her to realize grandmother was in one of those states where she didn't actually know what was happening and was merely following grandfather to be polite.

"Ah!" Louise cried as the door closed behind us. "We didn't take their senior cards to use."

In that moment, I knew that whatever was happening between us, whatever I had been fantasizing about or hoping for, was real. That I hadn't, in my isolation, invented this longing or somehow overglorified her virtues. That even if I were a lost network packet, and grandmother and grandfather were too, that she, at least, was looking for us, remembered and cared for us. I wanted to wrap my arms around her, to touch the cheeks that were beginning to redden in the cold, and savor how they might feel against my fingers, how soft her hair must be, bunched against her scarf.

She was turning back when I reached for her shoulder and stopped her.

"I bet they're already in my pocket," I said and fumbled inside my jacket. Sure enough, two senior cards with grandmother's and grandfather's smiling faces came out in my hand.

Louise shook her head, smiling.

"I'm in awe of their hustle."

"We have to hustle now too," I said regretfully.

It was only a short subway ride to the train station. I fought with myself the whole time. I should tell her how I feel, but the very thought of it sent my heart hammering. Or I could at least show her how I feel. It wouldn't be so weird to take her hand, or place a hand on her knee—no, something that intimate should involve explicit consent, I scolded myself, partly in relief. Perhaps I could ask her first—ah, then what kind of moment would that be? And what if she said no, or worse, asked why? She was silent throughout my internal crisis, staring out the window as our train crossed the river.

When we arrived at the station, the terminal was already announced and passengers boarding. Louise fished out her phone and pulled up her ticket.

At the same time, my phone buzzed. Once I saw the message, I quickly pocketed it again.

"Your grandparents okay?" Louise asked.

I nodded, touched that she had figured out what I was doing.

"Please tell them I'm sorry." Louise pulled at her sleeve. "I just—I really wanted to know—"

"It's fine. She's already forgiven you."

"I don't believe you. Asian mothers hold grudges like none other."

"That's true. But I can prove that she's forgiven you. If you really want." I reddened even thinking about it. I could not bear to see her torture herself. My heart beat painfully fast.

Louise glanced at the clock on the wall. Her train was set to depart in a few minutes. She locked eyes with me.

"Alright, what's the proof?"

I unlocked my phone and opened it to the latest message from grandmother. I held my phone out in front of me, screen facing her, heart bursting. If I could not muster the courage to say something, this would be the next best thing.

It took Louise forever to read the message. If grandmother had written it in Chinese characters, there would have been a chance she wouldn't be able to read it, a chance we could revert to normal. But grandmother had written in her usual combination of not quite pinyin, scattered English, and emojis.

zui hou yi ge chance 👲 📝 👲 ‼️

Louise stared at it for a long time.

Then she smiled, a smile that widened so slowly until it became impossibly large.

"Does she ship us?" she laughed, a hand covering her mouth.

"I—yeah, I guess she does," I murmured. I locked the phone and stashed it away.

"That is the cutest thing I have ever seen."

I cleared my throat.

"Well. Anyway. She would never have said something like that if she didn't like you."

A last call for boarding. Louise glanced at the train tracks and began to move toward them backward, still facing me.

"How can you know me so well?" She shook her head. She was backing away faster now, hands gripping the shoulder of her duffel bag, twisting its strap. "Thank you."

And just like at the volleyball game, she brought both her hands to her lips and blew me a kiss. She hopped onto the train, seconds before the doors closed. I lingered, watching her leave on the well-traveled tracks.

Even now, she is cryptic, and I wonder if I'll ever fully understand her. For the first time, though, it doesn't bother me. A few months ago, I would have asked EMBRS to show me everything it could find about her, to understand all we might have in common. But now? I don't really know. It hasn't been entirely joyful, discovering her, unearthing her truths, and seeing her tears. But there has also been joy, and that's what I cling to as I try to frame this into a story that feels true.

CHAPTER 22

From the Reforged pencil of Wong Yun

1 can't avoid fulfilling my agreement with Monica much longer. I didn't think she'd really hold up her end of the deal and invite that girl over. It is time to Reforge your pencil. I have decided to ask Monica to do it. The wisdom she can learn from your words, feeling them in her blood, that is the best way for her to understand the power and danger of our ability.

As much as I want to feel your words run through me again, I must concede that I am not the best receiver for them. More and more of my days are blank. Torou tells me I keep asking him when he's leaving for work even though he has been retired for years—and more troubling, Monica told me I mistook Louise for you the other night, briefly, during mahjong. I do not remember these things. I have no idea what it was about Louise that made even an addled me trust her to the point I would mistake her for you, the closest friend I ever had. There is clearly something about her though. She drew you in and Monica as well. I fear she may not be all that she appears.

What do we really know about her? She is the one Monica loves, or at least is beginning to love. I don't know how you feel about a woman loving another woman, but I will always support Monica. Torou even finds it preferable. He is terrified of what a boy might do to her, though I wonder how he can see it in such simplistic terms after the way I treated him back then.

I did not see or hear from him for months after he stormed out of the pencil company. The next time I heard of him was from my father, who called me into his office.

"The Tsai son," he said without any introduction. "I thought you two were close."

"He came to study a few times." I tried not to think about his warm breath at my neck or his fingers tracing my skin.

"Hm." My father folded the newspaper. "I've heard he is going to America."

"Oh?" I could not say anything else.

"To MIT." He enunciated each of the three letters. "The only one from Taiwan accepted this year."

"He must have studied well, then."

He slammed his newspaper down on the table.

"Your mother said he was interested in you."

"He might have been."

"You could have been packing for America by now. Did you scare him away with all your talking?"

"I can't say we talked much," I said, a joke with myself, since in those last few days, there really had not been much, our mouths otherwise occupied.

"There it is again. That quick tongue of yours was charming when you were young, but how will we be able to marry you off talking like that? The Tsai son might have been remarkable for his academics, but also in that he took an interest in you. Now what will we do with you?"

"I can keep working at the pencil company with Mother."

"Your mother will have you, but don't think she is pleased about it. She and her sister coddled you and your cousin far too much while I was away. Neither of you will be able to carry on their family line."

"You've heard from Meng?" I said, my tone sharp.

His eyes darkened. He returned to his newspaper.

"Last night. She has ruined everything your mother built. Go ask her."

I was grabbing my shoes, ready to run next door, when I saw Mother at the dining table.

"You haven't left yet?"

She was normally at the pencil company long before it opened. Instead, she sat kneeling at the table, writing, her pencil scratching against paper.

"A letter from your aunt came last night."

"What did she say? Was there anything from Meng?"

"There was." She was frowning in concentration as she wrote. The frown remained even when she stopped to look at me. To my horror, there were tears in her eyes.

"Are they—"

"They're fine," she assured me quickly, then wiped her eyes with a sleeve. "It's just . . . you can read for yourself."

She pointed to a piece of paper with neat handwriting on the table. Underneath it sat another stack of papers, the characters bleeding in a way I knew meant they had been Reforged. And next to both, a short pencil.

The letter on top was your mother's writing. It was marked from an unfamiliar address and name, a disguise on your mother's part, since maintaining a Nationalist relationship was reason for persecution. She wrote about how well the pencil company was doing, how the gangs were finally leaving Shanghai, how it was safer than it had ever been and you were staying active and healthy, though if we had some rice to spare, that would be lovely. She was including a pencil to prove to her older sister that the quality of the pencils was as high as ever.

I can imagine you glowering behind your mother as she wrote this, watching each motion of her pencil as the characters emerged. We knew other families who had received letters from China with large portions blacked out. Your mother's had none of this. Her message appeared pristine, in stark contrast to the bleeding characters in the second letter.

The second told us the truth that could not be censored. Mother burned it after I read it so there would be no proof. I can only recount it as I remember it, with this doctor-certified faulty memory of mine. I remember the first lines—*Meng burned down the pencil company. This may be our last honest communication with you.*

Burned it down! You always had a flair for the dramatic. Your mother was doing much of the same work Mr. Gao had tasked her with during the war, only now for the Communists. The same work we were doing in Taiwan for the Nationalists. That you and I ended up on opposite sides of the war—it did not make sense to me. How could we be on opposite sides of something as significant as war, when we ourselves were not opposing at all?

You were the one who decided to rebel. You made it look like an accident, of course, cutting off their supply of pencil hearts. More could be made in time, but that was my mother's specific skill and any Reforging would have to wait.

Your mother's anger was clear even in the Reforged characters. She called it a youthful symbolic rebellion—I believe those were her words—for we could still Reforge pencils that were not our own. It would only hurt us more. The Communists did not yet know you could

Reforge other pencils. Your mother was sure they would find out soon enough. She feared they might hear rumors about our Reforging in Taiwan, and how Mother could Reforge any pencil. She ended the note saying to reply under a pseudonym, all their mail was screened, and any connection to the Nationalists could result in public denouncement, ostracization, even a pencil might not be safe, not when they knew what they could contain.

I looked at Mother. She was writing furiously. Her tears were for the company, I realized, the one she had built, nurtured, and that was suddenly, thanks to you, gone. I did not feel the same sense of loss she did.

You cut off a means for the Chinese officials to spy on its people, at least temporarily. I was in awe of you, as I always have been. All I had done in my time away was ruin a relationship and dutifully aid the Nationalist cause.

"I saved that pencil for you," Mother told me. "That one is Meng's."

I wasted no time Reforging it. You wrote that you and your mother were feuding, that she had changed since we left. She had fully embraced Communism and that whenever people were around, she spoke endlessly about your father and his sacrifice for the Communist party, even though she had hardly talked about him when he was alive. You said she had come to believe in her work helping to uncover insurgents. You did not believe they were really insurgents though. The Chinese government had flagged three things as signs: corruption, waste, bureaucracy. But anybody's words could be twisted and labeled as these, you argued.

How I wish I could have kept your letter to show Monica. You framed the problem and the gift of the pencils so clearly. They can unearth lost stories. They can breach privacy. They allow an intimate connection between the Reforger and the writer. They can revive something that never wanted to be revived. It was the kind of thing we never thought about when we were young and Reforging felt like a superpower.

The note ended with a sentence I will never forget.

Come back for me.

It hurts me to write those words, because we both know that I never did, even though in that moment, I absolutely resolved to, you must believe me. I knew that if you wanted me to save you—you who so desperately longed to be rooted in place—and had resorted to burning down the home we both loved, it meant the situation was dire. Words concealed within our already concealed words.

It was as if a fog had lifted. I could see the situation clearly, practically, and everything told me I needed to leave. But the only voice I could hear was Torou's, saying America was the place to be free. China would not welcome us back, and Taiwan would not accept you and your mother. America was the only place we could all be together.

Should I swallow my pride and beg Torou to take me with him? I cringed even thinking about it, reaching out to him only because I knew he was going to America.

Maybe I should have. Knowing what I know about him now, I am sure he would have taken pity on me. Torou has always favored quiet, careful people. That is why he looks out for Monica in a way he never did with Edward. He would not have liked me had we met back in Shanghai when I was more brazen and teasing. But had I gone begging to him then, our marriage would never have been equal, we might never have survived those most difficult years when we raised Edward.

And yet how much pain I might have avoided!

That afternoon, I began to plan. The Nationalists needed help if they were to have any chance of regaining control of the mainland. Now exiled to Taiwan, their greatest hope was the American military. We heard the Generalissimo's wife was camped out in America, working her charm on the American senators, urging them to fund the Nationalists, to not let a nation as large as China be lost to Communism. I helped

Mother decode enough notes to understand their desperation. It made the Nationalists rule with terror in Taiwan, fearing anyone who might stand against them.

Meanwhile, America, formerly severe in how many citizens were allowed in from Asia, was loosening its rules. They passed bills permitting an increase in immigrants in order to help those fleeing Communism. This could apply to me. The rule also applied to the war in Korea—yet another war against Communism that America forced itself into.

The key to my plan was Mr. Gao. We rarely saw him except when he came north for business. He would spend long nights with my father, reminiscing about Shanghai.

He happened to visit shortly after your pencil arrived.

"A letter from Chi-ling," my father explained. He showed Mr. Gao the letter—not the Reforged one, the one that said everything was going well.

Mr. Gao took his time reading it.

"All lies, yes?" he said, folding the letter and handing it back.

"It is good you left her," my father assured him. It did not sound like the first time he had said so. Mr. Gao had risen quickly through the ranks since his arrival in Taiwan, which my father attributed to him no longer being distracted by your mother. "Apparently, she has gone full Communist. You'll find someone more suitable here."

Mr. Gao had changed since Shanghai. His face, while still serious and severe, was softened a bit by facial hair. It suited him. He turned to me then, his gaze lingering. I sat up straighter. He blinked, as if seeing me for the first time—and I knew then he would give me what I wanted.

I know what you are thinking. I can see you narrowing your eyes. You knew how infatuated I was with your mother, the striking image of her on Mr. Gao's arm, how elegant they were, as if from another time entirely. You think I wanted myself in that picture, that I would stoop so low as to seduce the man your mother once loved. The thought occurred to me, I must admit. But I did not think I could compare to your mother. My self-esteem was terribly low at the time. The only thing I was confident in was my Reforging.

I volunteered to walk Mr. Gao to the train station when he left to return south. He offered me his arm, and I took it.

"Work must be difficult for you these days," I said. The Nationalists had been all but driven out of China.

"Yes," he answered. "We are unfortunately reliant on the Americans."

"What can we do to get them to support us?"

"Madame Chiang is doing everything she can. It is difficult to know what the Americans are thinking. It is too much for a young woman like you to worry about."

I ignored his condescending tone.

"But I do worry about it. I want Mother and Father to retire at home, in Shanghai. I want to see my family again." I paused, then took a breath. "Send me to America."

"You?"

"Yes," I said. "Let me start a pencil company there. Mother can handle everything here. You said it was difficult to know what the Americans are thinking. I could tell you. I could share the truth with the Americans, stories of people like us who have lost our homes and the people we love."

For a long time, he did not reply. We continued our walk. His arm was tense.

By the time we arrived, he still had not spoken.

"You have grown so much," he murmured, more to himself than me. His gaze lingered on me yet again, and I did not shrink from it.

"Let me consider it," he said, finally.

"Thank you." I spoke calmly, though my heart pounded.

And then he smiled, some of the handsomeness from his Shanghai years returning.

"And if you could go anywhere in America, where would you go?"

I hardly knew the names of any cities or states in America.

"Where is MIT?" I asked.

"The university?"

"Yes."

"Massachusetts, then." He fixed the collar of his coat and re-adjusted his hat. "I'll see what I can do."

When I summoned the courage to tell Mother what I had done, she was not furious as I thought she would be. She only looked tired.

"I was hoping to spare you from this life," she said. "But maybe it isn't time. Maybe, if you have a daughter someday, she can be spared."

I never had a daughter. Only Edward, who I never told anything about pencil hearts. He shone so brightly. I would not burden him with Reforging, and he would not have survived it anyway. But Monica? Monica, who I want to protect more than anyone in the world. Monica, who only learned about Reforging because I was looking for you, because Louise found you, because you told Louise about Reforging and Monica loves her now.

I wish for her to know only the joy of our power, the moments of connection. That it is not all pain, knives stabbing in your wrist. That it can be pleasure accompanied by wonder. I want her to Reforge from pleasure. Is it too much to hope for that? That the world is safe enough now? That if she were to write her story, it would be full of love and laughter and none of the war and betrayal of our own?

Mr. Gao made me work another year with Mother to prove I could run the business side of things as well as she could. At that point, I was better at Reforging than Mother, who was always exhausted. I took on more pencils to relieve her load. We cut our arms over and over, bleeding out the words from each pencil whether they wanted to see paper again or not.

And I wrote to you. I told you of my plan to go to America, and how once I was there, I would bring you over. I used a service that promised anonymity, routing through Hong Kong. I don't know if you ever received that note. I wrote that I would bring our mothers, too, and I would send you a message as soon as I reached the land of the free.

In the winter of 1952, Mr. Gao convinced his higher-ups to send me to America. I would be under strict orders. I did not mind. After three years on this island, I was finally leaving.

"I have found my own way to America. See? I did not need Torou," I could not help boasting to my father. I had not seen Torou before he left. He departed without saying goodbye, and when I found out, I cried. Now I was triumphant and, for the first time since leaving Shanghai, looking forward to the days ahead.

"Who?" my father asked gruffly.

"The Tsai son."

He snorted.

"I suppose you can be clever at times."

"Be careful," Mother said. "You'll be alone."

"They won't let anything happen to me," I said, confident in my value.

"Be careful of your mind," she corrected. The words chilled. She was thinner than ever, always bundled up in bed or in a blanket.

"I'll bring you to America," I promised, grasping her cold hands.

I was so sure, so stupidly certain, that America would fix all our problems. Their doctors would cure her. Their senators would welcome you. All I had to do was get there and leave everything else behind.

CHAPTER 23

From the diary of Monica Tsai,
backed up on three servers spanning
two continents

November 5, 2018 (2018-11-05T21:58:12.218777)
loc: Cambridge, Massachusetts. United States of America
(42.3721865,71.1117091)

There's been some good news on the work front lately. Apparently, Prof.
Logan spent fall break presenting EMBRS to potential investors, the
first step in turning it from a research project into something bigger.

I watched his pitch a few times—him onstage with a headset, large
banners of the name of the conference in the background. He wore a
T-shirt with the EMBRS logo (a doodle I made of a fire with sparkling
eyes and jazz hands) and emphasized his words in the way startup
founders do, all passion and drama. Behind him were his slides, and
suddenly the picture of Louise and Meng—Louise beaming, Meng
squinting at the camera—blown up for thousands to see.

He went on to explain how grandmother was looking for her cousin,
how they were separated during the Chinese Civil War, and were now
over ninety years old and had lost contact. His performance was a more
elaborate version of what I sent him—and at times, completely made
up. He talked about me, an engineer on his team who journaled about
her grandmother's wish in EMBRS, and how EMBRS connected me

via this photo. Then he showed my visualization of the data, the connections and algorithms that took place to make this happen. He did not include a conclusion, only the implied reunion.

"This program isn't just about sparking lost connections," he said, his voice deep with emotion. "It's about sharing enough of ourselves to form true, real connections. Never in the history of the world has there been as much information freely shared as there is now. Let us use it to spark connections in every part of our lives."

He flipped to the last slide. It was a picture of me and grandmother on her ninetieth birthday next to a tray of roast beef sandwiches. I had sent it to Prof. Logan along with the other EMBRS-related assets. I had never imagined he would end with it.

The room erupted in thunderous applause. Now there were some big-name investors who wanted to pour money into EMBRS.

He called me that night.

"Monica," he said warmly. "The one who ignited EMBRS to life."

"That's you," I corrected. "EMBRS was always your idea."

"Yes, but you were the one who successfully used it. You were the one who saw what it could do, even when it was a bunch of bash scripts cobbled together. You made it work, and that story about your grandmother *resonated*, let me tell you."

"I didn't actually use EMBRS as a journal though," I said, afraid I had somehow misled him. "I manually looked through its data."

"Well, it's the same thing, right?" he said breezily. "A proof of concept, with some manual processes, which EMBRS now automates. If you *had* journaled and EMBRS had been ready at the time, it would have turned up the same thing."

I agreed reluctantly and asked about the interested investors.

"They're all across the spectrum," he said vaguely. There was a faint background noise on his end, the sounds of a conference party in full swing. "But I need to know more. Your grandmother's story has piqued the interest of these investors. Not only the investors, it's also just a good story. People want to know what happened afterward."

"Afterward?"

"After they reconnected. In other words, how does their story end? We're humans, after all. Our lives are defined by stories, even if they're retroactively formed. People are invested in this now and want to hear a happy ending."

"I want a happy ending for their story, too."

"Of course. We all do. We're all involved now. So if there are any updates to their interactions, will you let me know? All of us would be thrilled, to celebrate this connection born from EMBRS."

"Sure," I said, strangely touched.

"And how about that other connection? Have you been in touch with the girl you met through EMBRS? The one in New Jersey?"

I thought about her weekend in Cambridge, the late-night mahjong, our story reframing by the river, how my heart ached as I watched her train leave. How she had read grandmother's all-too-revealing text message and seemed happy, thrilled even. Except now our messages had gone back to what they used to be—simple updates about our days. I wanted to see her again but couldn't think of a good excuse to ask her.

I must have paused for too long because he suddenly laughed.

"Oh, is it like that?"

"N—no," I said quickly. "I mean, I don't know what you're talking about. Yes, we've kept in touch, but—"

His gentle laugh interrupted.

"Sometimes I forget how young you are. It's refreshing, it really is. I'm glad you two have connected. Now, there's something I need to tell you." His voice changed from wistful to serious. "We have gotten more interest than you can imagine. I am probably going to leave teaching to pursue this full-time."

"Oh," I said, too surprised to say anything else.

"Come with me."

"What do you mean?"

"Come be one of the first engineers of EMBRS the company. I'll hire more experienced engineers too, of course. But you've got such potential and you already know the problem space so well. And you have a personal connection to it. I'd pay you a full-time salary with benefits and all of that. Equity, too, and as an early engineer, that could be a huge amount of money down the line. You can continue working remotely and be with your family, of course."

"So I would drop out of school?" I asked, the idea nearly unfathomable.

"I know you are a good student. But this is another option. You know those stories about college kids dropping out of school and becoming billionaires before they're even thirty? This might be one of those opportunities."

I could not think of anything to say.

"Think about it," he said gently. "You can always return to school. But I don't know where EMBRS as a product or a company will be by the time you graduate. And this way you won't have to pay college tuition. You'd just be making money. Anyway, I don't mean to pressure you. Take some time."

I've been seriously considering it. It's the logical decision, right? To ease the burden on my family—no more tuition fees, and I can stay working from home as grandmother's illness progresses, and potentially make a lot of money. The only downside would be not finishing college, though a lot of computer science students drop out these days, and they are still super successful. I never pictured myself as that kind of person—I've always stuck with the road map. But I haven't been on any road for a while now.

At least that was what I was thinking before I told Louise about it. I even sent her Prof. Logan's pitch.

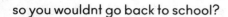

so you wouldnt go back to school?

                                        I guess not

but dont you like school?

                     I did. but this way I can stay with my
grandparents and help them out more

I mean, I can't say much since im still in college
too. but you know how everyone says its the best
time of their life? would you want to give that up?

    Suddenly, I was annoyed.

                     in an ideal world, no. but not all of us
are so fortunate to be able to spend
four years away from family

    I thought she would apologize. She was usually so good about re-
alizing her mistakes and correcting them, always ensuring she wasn't
hurting anyone. Instead, she replied:

okay, but working on EMBRS? is that really what
you want to do?

    The angle surprised me.

                              why wouldn't I?

because its kind of a creepy application, dont
you think?

That hurt more than anything else she had said. She followed up.

I watched your professor's pitch. it's cool, of
course, but how much data is it collecting
without anyone knowing? I certainly didn't know
when I uploaded that picture of me and Meng
that it would alert you. I mean, im glad it did. but
you couldve been anyone. it just seems like it
can be taken advantage of too easily

I avoided my phone after that. It was cowardly, yes, but I needed to re-treat. Because, to tell the truth, I had not only been seriously considering the offer, I had been excited about it. So much of this year has been out of my control—grandmother's health, Louise's responses—while EMBRS has been a steady presence. I am proud of my coding work. My former classmates will eventually have a degree as proof of how they spent their semester, a shiny bullet point on their résumés. I had EMBRS, the various commits to the codebase, a proud log of *look: this is what I was able to do even as my world fell apart.* And for it to become an actual product spread to more users, for other people to connect in our increasingly disconnected world—I had been really excited about that.

Louise's questions pricked. It wasn't my job to understand how the terms of service worked, or who the consumers were, or how unscrupulous actors might take advantage of EMBRS. I was an engineer trying to make money to support my grandparents. Who knows how long grandmother's illness will last, how long we can hold out with only me and grandfather as her caretakers, how long until I'm the caretaker for them both?

All of these questions are making me confront a separate, though equally uncomfortable, truth: If I really believe in EMBRS and radical sharing, it can only be a good thing to know more about grandmother, right? I should be able to tell her what I know, and we should be closer

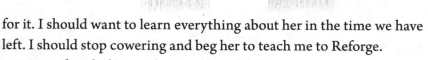

for it. I should want to learn everything about her in the time we have left. I should stop cowering and beg her to teach me to Reforge.

Armed with this resolve, I went to find her.

She was writing at the kitchen table. I sat next to her and peered over her shoulder.

"What's wrong?" she asked. The paper was lined with her Chinese characters. The computer makes characters very boxlike, but her handwriting has always been beautiful to me, flowing and precise, even if I can't read it.

Her pencil was dark; the wood somehow still shone after all these years. The tip appeared recently sharpened. Grandmother handsharpens her pencils, even now, even after I bought her an electric sharpener. The pencil heart drew my eye. Maybe there really was something in me that was organically drawn to it.

Grandmother noticed me staring at the pencil. She waited for me to answer her question. She was very aware of herself today. Those days are getting fewer and fewer. Grandfather had gone out to meet with a former student. There would not be many more opportunities like this one, where it was just me and her and she was fully present.

I took a breath and recited all the facts I knew.

"I know you lived in California and that your house burned down. I know pencils burned with it. I know the house was owned by a Taiwanese official. I know they were running a large surveillance network at the time."

The pencil betrayed the trembling of her hand. I told myself it was due to her age, not from any reaction my words might have caused. She would tell me I was misguided, to go to my room and stop with the wild theories. Instead, she whispered:

"Did I tell you that?"

The words crushed me. Both because of the implied admission and because she genuinely could not remember. She did not know what I knew about her or what she had told me, if anything.

"I found out from EMBRS," I said, trying to steady my voice. "My research project."

"Is it a spying tool?"

"No! No, it's a journaling tool. It's what helped us find Meng, remember?"

She shook her head.

I took another breath.

"And I want to learn how to Reforge," I said. "Please teach me. I was scared to learn before. But I want to understand you."

"Even now?" she asked, voice weaker than I had ever heard it.

"Yes," I said firmly. "I want to understand you as you understand yourself."

"Even if you may not like what you learn?"

I did not trust myself to convey certainty, not when I was wondering if I could pretend this conversation had never happened. I nodded.

I helped her stand. She took me to her room, to her bedside table. From the drawer, she retrieved a familiar pencil. The first thing Louise had given me.

"I'd like you to Reforge this," she said.

"Me? But it's for you. We had a deal."

"I can't," she said simply. There was no sadness to her voice. It was a statement of fact.

"But what if I mess up?" I asked.

"I'll teach you properly first. You seem distraught, maybe even lost. But I think you will find you are very much like your great-aunt."

"Really?" I took the pencil from her.

"Yes. And she did what I couldn't do."

"What was that?"

"You'll discover for yourself."

I couldn't help but feel she had somehow swindled me yet again. The interaction left me drained, though also hopeful. Maybe my questions will soon be answered. It was enough to make me forget about the argument with Louise. When I returned to my room, I unsuspectingly picked up my phone, only to find a series of missed calls.

I called her back.

"I'm sorry," she answered immediately. "I really shouldn't have insulted your work like that."

That was much more like the Louise I knew. I could not blissfully accept her apology, not without acknowledging the ways she had been right.

"I'm sorry too," I said. "I had a lot to think about. And you made some good points that I didn't want to consider. Not right now."

"I was jealous, to be honest."

"Really?"

"Yeah. I told my parents earlier today that I was changing majors and what I was going to do instead."

"Did they not take it well?"

"Not at all. They kept asking what I was going to do for money and if stories could pay, which of course I couldn't say yes to, and we had a huge spat while my doctor brother watched gleefully from the corner."

I winced. "You're not going to let that change your mind though, right?"

She paused.

"No. Not right now. I'm still hoping I get that grant. It's kind of a big deal. I think if I had that, they might take me seriously. Or maybe one day I'll end up crawling back to them because I really don't have any money." She gave a weak laugh. "It stinks that everything revolves around money. But hey, at least one of us will have it."

"I don't know if I'll actually sign on to the job," I said. "I need to think about it."

"Oh." She sounded relieved. "Well, good to know we are both at a crossroads, then."

I smiled. "It's not so bad with the right companion."

"Will you still say that when your companion is poor and unemployed?"

"Then I'll protect her even more fiercely."

She laughed. "I'm so relieved you called me back. I was really worried. I think—" She cut herself off.

"Hm?"

"Ah, nothing. Look at us. We've survived the first fight of our relationship! We should get ice cream."

What was our relationship even? What did she think it was? Did she count the number of fights she got into with all her friends? Or was that for romantic relationships only? I was more confused than ever.

"Come visit again, and I'll buy you ice cream," I nevertheless agreed. "And maybe I'll show you something else too."

"Oh?" Her tone was impossible to decipher.

"Something you'll really love."

"There . . . are a few things you could show me that I would really love."

The back of my neck tingled. The pause was unusual for her. Normally I was the one stuttering. Was it possible that I could have a similar effect on her?

"If my train had been a few minutes later," she continued, "would you have shown me then?"

"No," I said. "It's not something that I've learned yet." I could not just brush off the suggestion in her question. "But I do wish your train had been a bit later."

"I do too. But tell me what you are learning."

"Magic," I said.

"Really?" There was true awe in her voice. "Your grandmother is going to teach you?"

"Yes, starting tomorrow. I—I don't know. I've been wary of it. But I think you were right. That I would regret not learning. I'm so confused about so many things lately, and grandmother says Meng's pencil might help me sort my thoughts."

"Meng is very wise," she said earnestly. "I mean, her accent is strong, so I could only understand every other word she said. But every other word was a banger, so I imagine she's twice as wise as I think."

"I am excited to hear from her. But I don't know how it works. Will I hear her words in her accent and not be able to understand? Or will I only receive the written words and be able to understand even less?"

"I'm sure that's what your grandmother will teach you. Damn. Wow. Please tell me all about it. If you're allowed. I don't know what secrets there are around magic and all that."

"I will," I promised. "I'll tell you everything."

She had to leave for practice. I rewatched Prof. Logan's EMBRS pitch, the picture of Louise and Meng flashing on his PowerPoint in front of thousands of people, followed shortly by the one of me and grandmother. I scrubbed back to the picture of Louise and Meng, focusing on Meng this time.

She looked old and stern, like grandmother, really. She would have blended into any crowd in Asia. I've spent so long looking for her, and even now it feels like I've been circling around her. What did she do that grandmother apparently couldn't? What does grandmother want me to learn from her? And what will I learn about grandmother in the process?

I'm dreading it all.

CHAPTER 24

From the Reforged pencil of Wong Yun

I began teaching Monica how to Reforge today. It was easier for me to learn than it has been for her. Back then, I would have done anything to be your equal. I was surrounded by pencils. Monica, meanwhile, has barely used one outside of math class, and not even a good one at that. But she seems motivated to learn.

The first step is the easiest, if mentally the most challenging. The sinking of the heart into the wrist. She has always been strong mentally though. How else could she have studied so well after her parents left? To push a pencil heart into a wrist—well, you know the feeling. She winced when her skin broke, her eyes widening as her body absorbed my words. When she looked back up at me, we were both smiling.

The difficult part is the second phase. Like I said before, I do not want her to resort to the knife. So I asked her if she had ever pleasured herself, to which she faltered and stumbled and turned an incredible shade of red. I believe she must get this from Torou or from her mother's side. She pretended she did not know what I was talking about, but I came prepared with both the English and the Chinese and a description that could not be mistaken. Still, she stammered and looked away, as if she wanted to sink through the floor.

Eventually, she told me she had never done so. I was surprised, considering all the time she spends alone in her room. I guess she really is just using her computer. I almost hope she was lying to me. The next logical question was whether anybody had pleasured her before, to which she became even more red, something I did not think possible.

She eked out a no. That I was less surprised by, seeing how she has been pining after your girl and done absolutely nothing about it. I think of Louise as your girl now. Not only because she was the one who reconnected us. Having met her in person, I see ghosts of you in her. Oh, she is much happier, more joyful than you ever were, and I would not have seen the similarity had she not stood up to me the other day.

She offended me, as you once offended my father. She wants my story for reasons I cannot comprehend. Merely because there is a lack of stories from people who fled Shanghai, she thinks I should share mine with her? And then what? What difference would it make, and what would she gain? Maybe she plans to include it in some book no one will ever read that will sit on a dusty library shelf. Or worse, she wants to publish it on the internet, one of millions, billions of pages. The people of their generation—they have so many resources that they think they need to use them all. Perhaps some stories are not worth saving.

If she had told me it would help her personally in some way, I might have relented. I do like her, and it is easy to see Monica does as well, and I always try to do whatever I can to help Monica. But my story is not one I willingly share with just anyone.

Monica has already figured out much of it on her own. Though I desperately wish she hadn't, and I don't completely understand how she did, something about technology. I've done a lot of things I regret—bullying you, Reforging that boy's poems, being too hard on Edward, the list goes on and on—but I'd rank my time in California at the top of that list. I wish I could have told her about it myself.

And so I suppose it is time to write about the most difficult years of my life, which also happened to be the loneliest. I sent you a note before I left Taiwan. Every time I moved in the United States, I sent you another with my updated address. At least one of them must have reached you, since you did eventually write to me. But that would not be for many years.

They put me on a plane to California. When I looked at the map, I was stunned and disappointed to see how far it was from Boston. I would be looking at multiday bus itineraries I could not afford if I wanted to see the only other person I knew in the country.

In the summer of 1953, I landed in America. A colleague of Mr. Gao's collected me from the airport. We drove straight through San Francisco. He did not stop. The city might have been easier for me. The buildings we passed did not look so different from parts of the International Settlement, and there was a bustling Chinatown. But Mr. Gao was not interested in the city. He was interested in the universities around it, where the students gathered. He placed me in the most foreign situation possible—a suburban neighborhood.

I don't know if you've ever seen an American suburb. I only have two words to describe them—wide and isolating. I could not get over the wideness of the roads, how much space between the boxy vehicles, such a far cry from Shanghai's cramped streets filled with rickshaws and workers. Mr. Gao's men had bought a small house, and this, too, sat on a wide street. They could have fit another two houses between mine and the neighbor's. Can you imagine a place like this existing back then?

Eventually, the area would be known for its protests, its fight for free speech. But when I was there, it was quiet and, like the rest of the nation, paranoid. The university had recently required a loyalty oath from its staff members that they were not members of the Communist party. Anti-Communist sentiment was rampant. This worked well for us. We knew students from Taiwan were gathering to scrutinize martial law and viewed the Korean War with a skeptical eye too. It was this group that Mr. Gao wanted to control, before there was a chance of them drawing national attention to their cause.

Looking back, it was not only the students he wanted to control. It was me as well. I could die here, I realized, and no one would know, not until Mr. Gao thought to check on me. It was impossible for me to make my own connections. In San Francisco I might have blended in or found my way in Chinatown, even if I did not speak Cantonese. Not here, though. I could not even go to the grocery store on my own. It was too far. One of Mr. Gao's colleagues picked me up twice a week and monitored me as I shopped for ingredients.

Walking into my first American grocery store—the closest comparison might be the one and only time I went to Great World, that huge amusement arcade in Shanghai. It was before you came to live with us, before it was bombed, back when it was five floors of acrobats, dancers, magic mirrors, fortune tellers, and gangster hangout spots, designed to dazzle and overwhelm. The grocery store wasn't as crowded and didn't have any sort of entertainer, but I experienced that same overwhelming feeling, looking up at its high ceilings and unbelievably bright lights, food as far as the eye could see. The way they displayed their fish, cleaned and descaled, spread across the clearest ice, then another row of refrigerated meats, wrapped in cellophane so you might see the fat in each cut, practically run your hand across it. And my favorite part—they would give you stamps for your purchases, which you could collect and trade in for appliances. I collected meticulously.

Though the house seemed huge to me, I now know it was tiny by American standards. There was the first floor with a kitchen and a seating area, which I arranged to be a restaurant. Then there was the second floor, more of an attic, really, where I slept. The most remarkable thing was the refrigerator. I had never seen one.

That first night, I remember opening my suitcase in the cold, bare attic with its low, slanted ceiling. I took out my clothes and spread them across the floor. Then I pulled out the US dollars they had given me, rolled up in my sock, and placed them next to my clothes. The rest of the suitcase was filled with boxes of pencils.

"I'm here," I whispered in English, lying on top of my clothes, the strange smell of the US dollar seeping through the sweater I used as a pillow.

I had to become good at cooking, and fast. According to Mr. Gao's men, food would draw in the local immigrants, and they would share stories while eating, imagining my tiny home a haven from government surveillance. The men would help by having their spies recommend the restaurant. They wanted it operating at maximum capacity before the school year began, before the university students returned to campus and fostered any radical ideas. If I did not prove useful, they would send me back to Taiwan.

Mother had taught me two dishes before I left. They were pretty much the only two dishes she had picked up since moving away from Shanghai, away from Ah-shin.

One was a simple stir-fry of anything green.

"The more oil and salt you add, the better it will taste," she promised. "Garlic, too."

Once I was confident in my stir-fried greens, I progressed to beef noodle soup.

"American beef is very good," Mother told me.

I allowed myself a week to work on both recipes, most of the time experimenting with substitutes I found in the American grocery stores.

A noodle soup with meat and a side of vegetables. If I had leftover flour from the noodles, I would bake an apple pie, which I learned how to do from the bag of flour. Those were the only things on my menu, and once I ran out of food, I closed the store for the day. It was lucky that I did not need to make money. I could never have handled running an actual restaurant. I only needed customers who would talk.

Nobody came the first week. I was in a neighborhood surrounded by houses, far from street traffic. If the spies were directing people to me, they were not doing a good job. The second week, I drew up flyers, putting my drawing skills to use for the first time since we were children. I drew the soup, the vegetables, and the pie, included imitation calligraphy characters with my address. Then I wrote the name.

I called it Phoenix 708 after the restaurant's street number.

Nearly all the customers who eventually came were male. There was a time when I would have loved the idea of all those men coming to see me, paying me money, complimenting my mediocre food, if only because it was faintly reminiscent of meals they remembered from home. I would have looked forward to their visits, flirted, laughed, and entertained when they brought their friends. But even though it was my job to loosen their mouths, I mostly kept to myself. I tried to recall your mother's easy hospitality, her gentle, convincing nudges, channeled her as best as I could. It exhausted me though. By dinner most days, I was meek and quiet, much more like my mother than yours.

There were still men who stuck around and talked to me. Not because I was particularly charming or pretty. There were so few women from our home there, even fewer on their own, not accompanied by a husband or a brother. It would have made sense for me to find one with citizenship and marry him, to secure my place in the United States, then bring you and Mother over. Except I shrank from their touches and brushed off their attempts to spend time with me. I was there to betray them, not to love them.

Phoenix 708 balanced a fine line between drawing in enough customers and being an entirely illegal operation. I did not know how to become a certified restaurant, did not even know that was a requirement. When one of the neighbors came by, eyes narrowing at the small tables and men seated together eating vegetables, noodles, and pie, I assured her they were my family.

"I have a lot of cousins here." I smiled. I did my best to conjure some charm. "My family is very wealthy back home. Sent all of us here. The boys to study, and me to cook for them." And then I laughed, imitating your mother, leaning in, as if sharing a secret. "I really only know how to make a few dishes, but they're so desperate for any kind of food from home."

She squinted at the lot of them.

"Ah, yes," she said slowly. "I see the resemblance."

"Would you like some pie?" I offered.

She took a slice and left, mollified. I assure you my cooking was not good. Still, more people came, desperate for a passable meal and a place to talk. I swapped the small tables for two larger circular ones so everyone sat together. I told Mr. Gao it would encourage chatter, and he gladly paid for it, calling me very smart, just like my father.

"What did you do before you came here?" the men would ask.

"I made pencils."

"Pencils?" The surprise was always there. Most of them found it odd. The ones from Shanghai, though, and even those from Taipei, suddenly looked at me differently.

"The Phoenix Pencil Company was run by my mother," I would say to anyone who asked if the pencils of their youth were still available.

"Yes, I brought a few with me." I'd pretend there were not many, that it was a great kindness for me to let them buy from my small stash. In reality, Mr. Gao sent me Mother's latest offerings every month.

They were ready to pay twice the amount we used to charge for them. Your mother no doubt would have challenged me to see how much I could get them to pay. But I never charged them extra. The real price was their words, and those I would collect later.

Mr. Gao visited me twice while I was in California. When he first arrived and entered my attic, he insisted at once he must buy me a proper bed. It was then that I realized he had not bothered booking a hotel and assumed he would sleep with me.

I suppose I cannot lie to you any longer. I slept with him even back in Taiwan, though I told you earlier I had not. Why hide it? Or rather, why reveal the truth now? I am ashamed of it, so ashamed, most of all to tell you, when you hated him. I look back on those moments and wonder how I could have done it, when he was so much older and had been with your mother first.

I believe your girl has something to do with my sudden decision to share this truth. My story doesn't quite make sense otherwise—I would have happily married any of those men if it meant I might be able to bring you and Mother to America. But Mr. Gao would never have let me.

As my words skirted around his presence, I saw your girl's face. That wide mouth, bottom lip trembling, pleading for me to tell her my story. I didn't tell her anything. But I owe you, and I want you to understand me. So from here on out, I promise you the whole truth, and you can think of me however you like.

He never treated me the way he did your mother. Your mother he loved. I was a poor substitute, which was fine by me. Preferable, even. We were both using each other. There were times when he would reminisce about Shanghai and we would laugh, a small, sad laugh, for the home we once shared. Other times he was cruel, demanding to know why I did not have more pencils Reforged for him, calling me as lazy as your mother.

"I hope the Communists show her their true nature," he would say.

But as easily as he dismissed her, it was clear he missed her.

"I always wanted a child," he said once. "Did you know your aunt carried my child? No need for that alarmed look. You don't have another cousin running around. She aborted it before I ever knew."

I could not imagine how your mother had managed to hide something like that from us, where she could have even gone for an abortion in our occupied city, if my mother had known.

"I always hated her for that," he said, his wistful tone quickly disappearing.

He introduced me to two of his other pawns on that visit, his arm around my waist. They were closer to my age, students I recognized. I had seen them before at Phoenix 708. The government was paying them to be there, to spy on their classmates, and they did so, hoping it was their way into America. I saw myself in their eyes. We were the same.

They were responsible for befriending the men at the restaurant, for getting close enough to borrow or take their pencils and return them to me. I would then Reforge them and report to Mr. Gao. The pawns made sure to always replace the pencil so the owners never realized they had been stolen.

That night after we lay together, Mr. Gao showed me a pencil he had brought from Mother and insisted I Reforge it, saying I must miss her words. I told him I would Reforge it later. He demanded I do it in front of him. His arms pressed into my rib cage, his fingers trailing over my stomach. We were lying on the new bed he bought for me as I cut deeper into my skin than I ever had before, black blood spilling onto white paper spread across the gray sheets.

There was hardly any news. Perhaps she knew Mr. Gao would insist on reading. She spoke of how she and my father were in good health, how she had not heard from you or your mother, and business was going well.

"A lovely note," Mr. Gao said, kissing the back of my neck.

"Yes," I managed.

I buried my head in the new pillow. It smelled vaguely foreign, like the department store, a distorted version of the one your mother used to love. I breathed slowly, carefully, so he would not notice my shakiness or the tears gathering on my pillow. Tears for no longer having even the pencils to connect with Mother, tears for having lost touch with you, for the days when we bled our stories into each other, marveled at how the pencils could conceal. And now I was on the other side of the world, away from all of you, and without even this small power.

CHAPTER 25

From the diary of Monica Tsai,
backed up on three servers spanning
two continents

November 14, 2018 (2018-11-14T15:27:03.563753)
loc: Cambridge, Massachusetts. United States of America
(42.3721865,71.1117091)

I don't know where to begin. I don't even know if I can write this down. It's weird and embarrassing. But if there's one thing I need to process, it's the last few weeks. Starting with the horrifying conversation I had with grandmother, where she asked me if I had ever masturbated before.

She said I had to answer honestly if I was ever going to Reforge properly. I wanted to hide, if not physically, then to at least not have to speak my answer out loud. I was still recovering when Louise asked me how my training was going.

I stared at my phone, heart pounding, cursing myself for promising I would tell her everything. The truth was almost too strange to put into words.

When I pushed the pencil into my wrist, the world faded, set to a quarter opacity, an image of grandmother overlaid on top. She was writing with the pencil, and I felt a brief wave of sentiment—hopeful, whimsical—but did not catch exactly what she wrote. She had only written a few words. It was over too quickly, reality returning.

"It'll be clearer when you Reforge it," she said. "Come find me when you do."

After that, I had a phoenix on my arm. I would be coding and part of its wing or tail would catch my eye. I'd hold my arm up to the light, admiring the abstract, elegant lines. It seemed to almost pulse. It was bold, and I would even say—and I never thought I'd say this about myself—sexy. When I twisted my arm, the phoenix responded, glimmering, each angle striking. I wanted Louise to see it, I realized, to trace her finger along its curves and bends.

I braced myself.

> did meng tell you about the mechanics
> of reforging?

I knew it was after volleyball practice for her, when she would normally be hunkered down at her desk for some late-night studying before bed. Sure enough, she replied quickly.

I just know she ingests the pencil lead somehow
and then bleeds it out

I told her how grandmother didn't want me to bleed, that there was another way.

oh? what is it?

I closed my eyes and typed without looking.

to have sex. But that wasn't quite right either. I erased and retyped. to become really aroused. Was being aroused enough though? I didn't want to ask grandmother for all the details, and when she tried to tell me more, I shut her down. I only had one takeaway that grandmother insisted would work.

to have an orgasm

I sent it and stared at the message box. The indicator that she was typing came up, then went away again. Was she going through the same process I had, trying to find the right words? How do you even respond to something like that? Would she think it was my poor attempt at flirting?

Finally, she replied:

wow

I tried to come up with something witty to close the conversation. I didn't know what I had hoped to get out of it.

But then she was typing again. I held my breath as she started and stopped, started again. When she stopped for more than a few seconds, I shoved my phone under my pillow and went to the bathroom.

I came back to a stream of messages, all from her, links to websites I did not recognize. I had to scroll up through the links to find the reason she sent them.

here is some of my fav erotica, if that helps

I dropped my phone.

By then the messaging service we used would have indexed those links, if not tied them to her or my specific accounts, or if we were lucky, we were anonymized as links that young women, likely Asian, enjoyed, and shared. The contents of those articles had likely also been scraped, the sentences tokenized, topics determined—*lust, sex, perversions*—and added to the model of things the computer knew about me.

I picked up my phone again, scrolling through, more slowly this time. None of the domain names were terribly suspicious sounding.

Some of them were from magazines I had heard of before. Perhaps if I did not click on the link, the app would not bother trying to scrape it. A mark of disinterest.

But I was not disinterested. I combed through the slugs of each URL, heart beating faster as I realized I now had evidence of whatever it was that Louise enjoyed sexually. A hard lump formed in my throat. The slugs did not give enough information, almost always cutting off too early:

/2015/12/a-surprise-christmas-visitor-comes
/women/2016/the-hotel-balcony-and-the-hot
/lit/how-to-stop-screaming-for-the

It would be impossible not to read these. I crawled to my desk, rummaging through the bottom drawer until I found my first smart phone. I had wiped it clean years ago and intended to take it to electronic recycling but never got around to it. It didn't have an account associated with it anymore. The features were limited—pretty much only a web browser, which was all I needed.

While waiting for the old phone to charge, I tried to compose a response to Louise. I had been silent for too long.

wow, thanks!

Add something more, I told myself. The truth? Why not, since we're already this far in. If I could tell grandmother about my sexual experience, I could tell anyone.

I've never actually done this before. I've been trying this week but no luck . . .

She would probably see me as I am—sheltered, antisocial, with not even the most basic sexual experience. I assumed it was normal for people to have experimented with masturbation at my age, even earlier. But there had never been any time or desire on my end. High school was for studying and helping my grandparents. And college, what little of it I had experienced, had been for studying and trying to make friends.

whatve you been trying?

I typed slowly.

just touching myself. circular motions?
I think that's a thing

if your mind isnt in it youll never get there

you sound experienced

lol I dabble

Then another message:

try reading those links, see if it works for you.
then lemme know which ones you liked best

Try something a little flirty, I thought, just a hint, step out of your comfort zone. We were already in strange, new territory.

thanks for kickstarting my sex life!

I regretted sending it immediately. Luckily, her reply was quick.

anytime 😚

What followed was one of the strangest weeks of my life. I would wake up, work through the day, have dinner with my grandparents, during which grandmother would ask about my progress.

"Still working on it," I'd mumble as grandfather looked away, pretending he didn't know what we were talking about. Then I would lock myself in my bedroom and lie on my bed, pull out my old phone, open an incognito browser (even though I know incognito doesn't do much), and painstakingly retype one of the URLs Louise had sent.

I would read, pacing my breathing, my fingers trailing along my body.

make sure youre comfortable. keep your feet
warm. wear socks if theyre cold

Louise would send me these sorts of messages throughout the evening. I'd stare at the persistent gray lines on my wrist as my other hand grew tired and eventually gave up.

The links Louise sent did help. Sometimes I would feel something building, just like her stories described. And I would wonder if that was it—if I had done it. But always the phoenix was still there, and never did this so-called sense of release course through my body.

maybe you need to think of a real person.
someone you had a crush on before? or maybe
have one on now?

I thought of her long fingers tracing my body, her lips trailing down my stomach, her eyes glancing up, sly. A majority of the stories she sent took place in a hotel room. So I imagined us in a hotel room, nestled in clean sheets, the heat turned high so we would not need to wear our socks.

do you have a crush on anyone now?

yes, I managed to type, my breathing shallow. do you?

you haven't noticed?

Circular motions. My typing was slow with one hand, my thoughts muddled for other reasons.

no not really. you're always cool and collected

maybe only because you make me feel so comfortable . . . so like myself

I had begun to type, one letter at a time, when she beat me to another message.

are you touching yourself now?

I erased the sentence I had started. Not even the idea of a machine parsing our conversation and trying to learn more about us could have made me stop typing.

yes

k im gonna join you. which story are you reading?

What was happening? That was the only question I could think of as I read her text, half aware that I was supposed to reply. I glanced at the other phone I had pushed to the side and read the title.

ooh when she opens up the gift bag in the room
and there's fried chicken in there . . . unff

She didn't bring up the other unmentionables in the bag.

I picked up where I left off in the story, my mind hardly on it anymore. There was only a seed of a thought, one planted when she said she would join me.

mm, I needed this

For the first time, I was able to block out my childhood bedroom, the thought of my grandparents right downstairs. I imagined my hands not on my own body, but on hers instead, after a long day where she was tired or sad and this was what she needed, what my hands, my body could provide for her. I increased the pressure and varied the motion, speeding up.

are you close?

What was happening?

I wish I was with you right now. id get that
reforging right out of you no problem

It started off—and this is going to sound lame, but I'll say it anyway—not so different from a coding high. Then it kept building, like all the stories said it would, and suddenly it surpassed anything coding-related at all, and she was part of it too, her coaxing words, her teasing ways. I could almost feel her next to me, smiling at me with that wide mouth, doing more with that mouth. Wave after wave of pleasure.

I certainly had not felt this before, did not know there could be anything like it. I dropped the phone and was gripping my sheets. I could not clench my fist hard enough.

Eventually, my limbs relaxed, my mind slowed. The stories often described a relaxation afterward, partners holding one another, safe in each other's arms. I became aware of my bed again, my room. Just when it felt like my mind was returning, when I thought to check my arm for the phoenix, the room faded again. My arm pulsed once. But this time I was back with grandmother, who was writing at grandfather's table.

She wrote in Chinese, in the script I couldn't read. It didn't matter, because I felt her words in a way that reading alone would never have allowed, and the feeling transcended all languages—Chinese, English, emojis—an overwhelming love and pride, and finally I could see the words she had written—*let's get ice cream*—and I smiled and was pulled back into my room and curled into myself, hugging my arm close to my heart.

Eventually, I picked up my phone and typed carefully. did you only say that to push me over the edge?

Her response was slow.

did it work?

I took a picture of my arm. The dark etching was gone, though the pale lines were still there, if you really looked. I swiped between the before and after picture, the phoenix fading, then reappearing, over and over. I sent her both images.

incredible

And a few seconds later, one more message:

can't wait to help you with your next one

What was happening? I still don't know, still don't understand what our relationship is exactly. I thought rewriting the events might help me figure it out. But I am left more confused, and also now flushed, lightheaded, craving—not just her, that rush of feeling, the intensity, the flash of pleasure followed by the surge of power from having grandmother's words so close to my heart.

I ran my hand over my new scars, a ghost compared to grandmother's. I thought back to the moment of Reforging. There had been a lot of other distracting thoughts at the time, but there had also been grandmother's clear voice. For a brief moment—how to explain? I felt like I really, truly, understood her.

Words are so difficult to parse, so imprecise. I'm starting to think they're a ridiculous form of communication. Totally unlike computers, which can understand one another perfectly via APIs and established network protocols. But humans are so different from one another, all with our own stories and interpretations. Especially grandmother— the careful phrases she has adopted to cross our language barrier, massaged to make sense across generations. Even me and Louise, both of similar backgrounds and age. I constantly wonder how she will interpret my words, worry if they will make the impression I want.

And yet, when I Reforged, I felt close to truly understanding. If the goal is to totally, completely know someone as they want to be known, the way computers can know one another, Reforging is it. Grandmother's words were right there, as if lifted from my own head. And even though she had written the one sentence, somehow I felt all the hope she pinned on it, that she pinned on me. This is what EMBRS also strives for, to share totally and completely, forge a real connection. But EMBRS is a poor imitation of what I felt.

I went downstairs. Grandfather was nodding off on the sofa, his chin drooped onto his chest. Grandmother was next to him, watching television. She lowered the volume when she saw me.

"Let's get ice cream," I said.

And even though it was mid-November, and the meteorologists were threatening another snowy Boston winter, grandmother's entire face lit up. She shook grandfather awake, and we all pulled on our jackets and scarves and marched to the grocery store, grandmother's arm looped through mine.

To understand somebody else so thoroughly, no matter how briefly—it truly is magic.

CHAPTER 26

From the Reforged pencil of Wong Yun

Even now I have trouble thinking of my time in California. They were some of the worst days of my life, days spent standing, working the customers at the restaurant, Reforging all through the night, collapsing in my attic room. I haven't been back since—skipped Torou's conferences, begged Edward not to apply to any schools there, shot down Monica's vacation suggestions a bit too forcefully. She says there are beautiful forests and thousand-year-old trees. Somehow, I missed all of that.

Within a month of Mr. Gao's departure, the other pawns started bringing me even more pencils. I replaced the ones they brought with new ones straight from Mother's factory, shaved down to the same length.

I Reforged the stolen pencils alone in my attic, the blood dripping from my wrist onto loose paper. As I pressed the pencil heart into my skin, I could feel their excitement and optimism.

It was as if they were all in the room with me, hovering above. I remembered them, vaguely, young men who had visited the restaurant before, one who had even tried to court me, his eyes shining.

I pressed my bleeding wrist to my forehead. I was betraying them, as planned, and yet it hurt more than any other time before that.

They were writing to organize protests around the disappearing of people in Taiwan. One was writing flyers, the other a manifesto. It was as incriminating as it could get.

I held up their Reforged words to dry, blowing on them gently even as my breathing turned ragged. I wiped the blood off my forehead.

It is moments like this I cannot bring myself to share with someone like your girl. She and others her age—they're so hopeful nowadays, so set on what they think is morally right. Preserving stories, raising voices, yes, all that sounds great. Their words so closely echo those I Reforged and systematically betrayed, and maybe that is what makes me recoil now. I would have betrayed her, too, if I had met her then. It helped that there was a rising fervor in America, so staunchly anti-Communist, anti-China. The news was filled with details about that couple they executed for spying on behalf of the Soviet Union. Catch the Communists, save the world. America and Taiwan were both saying the same thing. I could have turned anybody in during that time. I was doing this for you and for Mother. At least that is what I told myself, even as I began to acquire more food, more possessions. My fastidious stamp collecting even won me a toaster. I delighted in these things.

I sealed their Reforged words in an envelope with all the premium postage required to send them overseas, straight into the hands of Mr. Gao.

I don't know what happened to those students. I never saw them at the restaurant again. I never heard news of any protests. I don't know what became of all the others I betrayed. I think that was part of Mr. Gao's plan. To keep me unaware. It worked. As long as I could not see the harm I was doing, I continued without complaint.

But now I know the truth, and you do too, don't you? There was a famous case, that professor who taught at the prestigious American university and criticized the Nationalists, who returned to Taiwan on vacation. They captured and interrogated him, his body later found, the authorities claiming it was an unfortunate fall. That was long after I quit Reforging, but I am sure the same people were behind it, Mr. Gao's team. Could I have sent those students to their deaths?

Taiwan eventually changed course and condemned that period of their history. Looking back, I can't help wondering if I made the Nationalists' reign worse? It is impossible to say. But then I see Monica lounging at our home in the United States, tapping away at her computer, without any of our fear, and I cannot regret what I did. I would not sacrifice her for the lives of those men. But then again, I was always the selfish one.

The next time Mr. Gao visited, I planned to ask what it would take to bring Mother here. I was prepared to cite my productivity, the number of incriminating reports I had uncovered, insist I needed her by my side so I might have a steady stream of pencils. We could establish a new company. Pencils were widely used, even in America.

I now followed the news carefully like my grandmother had back in Shanghai. I knew of Madame Chiang Kai-Shek's prolonged stay on the East Coast, how she was trying to win US senators over to Taiwan's cause. The sentiment of the American people could sway the outcome back home. I remembered so clearly the day we had learned the war was over. How we stared into each other's eyes and even my grandmother praised the Americans, who rolled into our city days later with their huge tanks and white teeth. America would save us again, I was sure of it.

Mr. Gao arrived with a large suitcase. In my attic room, he unloaded box after box of pencils, fresh from Mother's workshop. A good sign, I thought—he must want to expand our operation.

Then he sat on my bed and told me Mother was dead.

"We wanted to bring you back to Taiwan to take over," he said, staring at his hands. I stared at them, too, the slender, calloused fingers. My wrist pulsed. I could not speak.

"But your father pulled every string he had to convince them you should remain." He sighed. "I would have liked to have you back on the island."

The news my father had done something like that for me somehow registered before Mother's death. Maybe it was more believable or easier to process, though I had recognized my mother's weakness, seen her shaking hands.

I glanced over at the boxes of pencils. He noticed.

"Those are all the reserves your mother made. They are useless to us back home without someone to Reforge them, so I brought them here."

That was when I began to cry. He had called her pencils, her life's work, useless. When he, more than anyone, should have known how special they were. They possessed an unexpected power, one Mother had kept from me until she believed it could help. I first knew our pencils as just that—implements that were a delight to use, with which I could draw and write and even bully you. Mother had sought to better them not for Reforging, but for writing. The people who had bought them, whose eyes widened even in this foreign land when I mentioned I still had some in my possession, who ordered them in bulk when we were children running around Shanghai, had loved them for their comfort and craftsmanship. They were the finest pencils, and that should have been enough.

He patted me on the shoulder, rubbed my back, then left me alone. I wanted him to leave me alone forever, desperately, but even so, this country was so far away from where Mother would be buried, where my father still worked, and even farther from the place I called home, and I was devastatingly lonely. I fell onto my bed, buried my head in the pillow. It no longer smelled like that clean department store. It smelled like me, and I did not like it.

I wrote you a letter that same day sharing the news. I don't know if you ever received it. I thought of you more than usual that night, wondered if you sensed Mother's absence in the world. You would have understood what it meant to lose her. You would have understood what it was like to be in a home that was not yours.

That was when I Reforged your pencil. The one with the end of our story, the one you had given me in Shanghai, and that I had carried with me always, knowing I would need your voice someday.

I hadn't thought of our story in years. I remembered the broad strokes of it, the antics of our characters, but Reforging even just the ending, I was stunned by its darkness, how much the war had warped us. I was only a few years removed from the reality of war, and I could hardly reconcile the violence as something we once thought so commonplace.

More than the bloodshed, which was overdramatic and unrealistic, I was stunned by the joy. In that moment, alone in the attic, reeling from Mother's death, I felt you with me as your pencil melted into my wrist, as your words came to life once again. The joy we shared in those evenings as we wrote, giving ourselves the power to face the world.

There was joy in stories, too, I reminded myself, as you had always reminded me. There was pleasure, as Mother said.

I drew a phoenix that night. It looked like the one that used to adorn our front door, an abstract set of lines coming together in flames and wings. Mr. Gao complimented it. He even tacked it to the wall of the dining area downstairs. He said it looked regal. I said it looked lonely. He asked if I wanted him to stay longer. I declined.

I had been profoundly stupid, I realized. You had warned me. Your situation in Shanghai was the same as mine. You had recognized the danger of the pencils, and I had somehow interpreted your message as meaning I had to get to America through any means possible. And so I leveraged Reforging and pencils, the very things you burned away, and now I was far from home and Mother was gone.

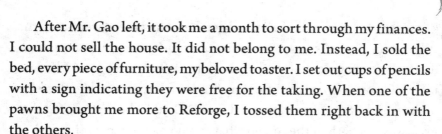

After Mr. Gao left, it took me a month to sort through my finances. I could not sell the house. It did not belong to me. Instead, I sold the bed, every piece of furniture, my beloved toaster. I set out cups of pencils with a sign indicating they were free for the taking. When one of the pawns brought me more to Reforge, I tossed them right back in with the others.

It was not enough. Mother had made so many. She had given her life to the pencils.

I ended up leaving with only the belongings I had arrived with, the small amount of money I had saved, and a handful of her pencils. The rest I stashed in a wooden box.

I bought a bus ticket that would take me out of California, as far away as I could think of while still being in America. I checked it again, double-checked the date and time and destination.

I knew what I had to do, but my hands trembled all the same. You had made it so obvious. Did you hesitate when it was time? Was it strange or inevitable that my life came to mirror yours?

I turned on the gas stove, the flame flickering reliably alive. Then I tossed in the drawing of the phoenix. The edges curled, burning, before disappearing altogether. I used the flame to light four sticks of incense—one for my grandmother, one for Mother, and one each for you and your mother.

I thanked my grandmother for letting me learn the secret of our pencils. I even thanked her for her reluctance, told her I now understood, oh, how I understood. I cried for my mother, for there could not have been a better mother for me—her steadiness, her unfailing work ethic that kept us alive and sheltered, war after war, how much she sacrificed to attain that for us. She had deserved a life of pleasure, a life of happiness.

As for you and your mother, I prayed you were still alive even if I could not reach you by letter or pencil. I hoped your mother would never learn about my affair with Mr. Gao, and that if she did, she would know that for him, it had always been her. Now there were only the two of you, when there were once five of us gathered around my grandmother's roaring flame—and I was alone. Where were you? I had no idea. Did you ever feel the utter loneliness I felt then, on the other side of the world, so far from everyone I loved? Could it be that you felt that exactly as we both lit the fire on what should have been our homes?

I splashed some cooking oil around the stove and on the box of pencils. I poured the remaining oil into the pot I once used to make soup and added water.

I moved the pot to the flame. It would take a while for the oil to heat, to cause the water to splatter, to ignite the oil around the stove, the drawing, the pencils beneath. First the ancestors and gods would receive the drawing of the phoenix. Then Mother's pencils would come pouring in, a gift to give voice to those we couldn't hear anymore.

I used the time it took for the oil to heat to clear out of the house and begin my walk to the bus station. It was night. I crinkled the bus ticket in my pocket. A reminder this wasn't the end, even though it certainly felt like it. My last remaining connection to my family, my home, burned behind me.

Soon I was on a bus driving across the country I had hoped would save me, heading toward one of the only other cities I knew by name. My only requirement was that I end up far from the place where I had resurrected so many words that should have been left alone.

I had only the smallest sliver of hope that I would find Torou there.

CHAPTER 27

From the diary of Monica Tsai,
backed up on three servers spanning
two continents

November 23, 2018 (2018-11-23T09:49:14.489947)
loc: Cambridge, Massachusetts. United States of America
(42.3742289,71.133843)

I'm in a hospital waiting room. I can hear each tick of the clock. Time advances and I am frozen in place. It feels as if we have sped through the events of the last few days, and I must now make up for it by staying very still. Only my fingers can move. The sound of my tapping joins the clock's tick, urging it forward, or backward. I'm not sure which direction I'd prefer.

It's Thanksgiving weekend. For a few days, things were normal. Grandfather hates turkey, so I stocked up on our usual hot pot ingredients—thinly sliced pork, napa cabbage, enoki mushrooms, every kind of tofu I could find. The perfect meal for the chilly season. My father video called to check on me.

"Happy Thanksgiving, Monica," he said. He was in his office, windows bright, a hint at the busy world outside. He asked how grandmother and grandfather were doing, and I asked if he was still planning to come back before the end of the year.

"Ah, well, I have to take care of a few business opportunities, and it'd really be better for everyone—you included—if I stayed a bit longer."

I let the silence hang between us. I wanted his guilt to fester while I stared at him from behind his screen.

"You should start your spring semester though," he continued. "I will probably come back in the middle of it."

"That's months where grandmother and grandfather would be by themselves."

"A few months. They'll be fine. They have each other."

"You think they'll be fine because you haven't seen them in years."

"I can hire someone to check in on them," he said, running his hand through his still-dark hair. "A nurse to make sure they take their medicine. Someone to buy their groceries."

"If that is what you think is best." And I meant it, too. Who was I to say he should sacrifice his goals to take care of his parents? They would not want that any more than he did.

"Alright. I will think about it. It's late for you, isn't it? Get some sleep. Good night, my love."

I sat with the idea for a few minutes, returning to school, leaving grandmother and grandfather to strangers for a few months until my father could return. I hated it.

There was another option, the one Prof. Logan had offered me. It would solve all my problems. Staying home, making money, working on the kinds of coding projects I love. And yet I've never been less sure about EMBRS. Prof. Logan recently shared some of the investors' emails. They are enthusiastic about the potential. He was deep in talks about the business model. He wasn't worried that we'd lose our access to all the social media posts because of our status as an academic project. The journal entries were data gold, he explained, and though I wondered what he meant by that, I didn't press.

It was too easy to just keep working, so that's what I did.

Grandmother told me she was confident I could now Reforge Meng's pencil, and that it would help me sort through some of these feelings.

"Whenever you are ready," grandmother had said.

I planned to do it the very next day, since I had off from work.

I had my usual chat with Louise that night. Our conversations since my Reforging had been chaste, easy, comfortable. We recounted what was 😞 and 😄 about our days. And then I went to bed.

I woke up when my whole room shook. My eyes opened, my body would not move. Something had fallen, something much larger than a picture frame. My room was next to the stairs.

It was a pure Schrödinger's cat problem. As I lay there in bed, there was a chance that once I got up and looked, my life would never be the same, and I would think back to this moment, with my head buried against the pillow, my heart pounding, when everything was still okay. I squeezed my eyes shut, then threw off the blanket.

I peered out my door, still the dead of the night, and I could just make out her body, crumpled at the base of the stairs. When I knelt beside her, she made no sound. Her neck was bent forward at an alarming angle.

I have trouble remembering what happened after that. I probably stammered something, gathered that she was alive if unable to speak. Somewhere along the way I woke grandfather, who creaked out of bed so slowly yet as fast as he could, and then we were at the hospital, grandmother carted off while we waited in the lobby.

I was shaking badly. I had forgotten to grab a jacket, and winter was descending. Grandfather looked sharp in his overcoat, even in his pajama pants, sitting stately while I trembled in the chair next to his, trying to warm up.

"Are you scared?" I asked when I could no longer stand the silence.

He gave only a small nod. "But we have been through worse."

I started to pace, to work some blood through my limbs. Sure, he could stay calm and collected because he was right—they had been through worse as immigrants. They had lost their home and their families. But I had not.

He shrugged off his overcoat. Though he was a tall man, he looked so small sitting in the blue padded chair of the ER in his threadbare pajamas. He handed his coat to me.

"Get some fresh air," he said.

"What if they come back with an update?"

"I can talk to them."

"No, I need to be here too—"

"You won't be of any help in your state. Go outside."

I took his coat.

Outside, the air cut into my lungs. I leaned against the wall. There was somebody else there, not too far down, doing the same, smoking. I buried my head in grandfather's coat, breathing in the sandalwood scent of him, attempting to override the smell of cigarette smoke.

"You okay?" the smoker asked.

"Yeah," I said automatically, a stupid answer, since I was obviously very much not okay.

"You have someone you can talk to?"

How very Boston of him, I thought, to suggest a solution that did not involve himself. He was right though. He could not talk me through anything, but perhaps a friend could.

are you awake?

Immediately after sending the message, I regretted it. It was well past midnight. She would not see it until she woke the next day, and she would see my desperation.

And then my phone was ringing.

"Are you okay?" she asked.

"Why are you awake?" My breath puffed in front of me, even if my voice did not shake this time.

"My brother and my mom are fighting downstairs. I was eaves-dropping. Is something wrong?"

I swallowed. I caught the smoker glancing at me and buried my face farther in grandfather's jacket.

"Monica?"

"I'm at the hospital," I said finally.

"What? What happened? Your grandparents—"

"She fell down the stairs. Her neck was bent. She couldn't speak. We're waiting. I can't take all of this waiting. I need to know if she will be okay or if I will be alone. I need her to be okay, because I can't be alone—I can't—"

"You're not alone—"

"I am!" My nails dug into my palm, clenched together in grand-father's oversized pocket. "I'm not like you. I don't have siblings or even parents. I only have them, and if they're gone, then I'll have nothing. And you'd think I'd be better prepared because they're so old, that I should be prepared when any day I could wake up and find them dead. But they are all I've ever known, and how can anyone be ready for their whole world to fall apart around them, even if they are warned? What's that noise? Are you listening to me?" My hands were shaking even worse than when I had no coat.

"I am. I'm just grabbing some things—"

"Never mind." I closed my eyes. "Forget I said anything. I'm—I'm being overdramatic."

I hung up before she could respond. For a while I stared at my phone, hoping she would call or at least text me back. Neither came. The smoker walked past me, heading inside. He stopped to offer me a cigarette. I took it even though I have never smoked in my life. A small bit of kindness that made me cry after he left me alone outside.

It was then that I realized who would be awake. Who would have to listen to me, even if he did not want to. Who owed me, at least that much.

"Grandmother is in the hospital," I said as soon as my father picked up. "We are all here. Except for you."

"What happened?" he asked, his voice through the phone sounding so far away.

"You left," I said, even though it was obvious that was not what he was asking. I wanted him to hurt, to feel even a fraction of what I was feeling. "You left even though my mother had already left. You left and didn't come back, not even now when grandmother is sick. You left them to take care of your child, and now you've left me to take care of your parents. And I never hated you because I trusted you had your reasons to leave, and I love them, you have no idea how much I love them—"

"Monica—"

"I never hated you," I repeated. "Until now."

I gave him a chance to say something. When it was only silence from the other end, I hung up.

I turned off my phone. I did not want to talk to anyone. I did not want even my service provider or whatever apps running on my phone to know I was at a hospital, to know I was facing something I might not be able to handle. And then I thought of grandfather, alone in the waiting room in his faded pajamas, and began to cry all over again.

I returned to the waiting room to find grandfather dozing. I draped his coat over him. He shook his head awake. He looked at me and his face fell. I turned away to try to hide the streaks of tears. It was too late.

"Go home," he said softly. "I'm worried we left the stove on."

"There is no way the stove is on." I almost laughed. It was grandmother's job to fret about the stove being left on. How many times had we circled back to the house to confirm it was indeed off? "We had hot pot for dinner."

"But then grandmother used the stove to braise eggs. Please go check. It is really worrying me."

"I'm not going to leave you by yourself—"

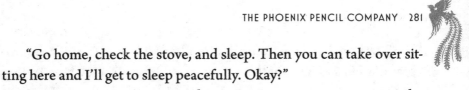

"Go home, check the stove, and sleep. Then you can take over sitting here and I'll get to sleep peacefully. Okay?"

He was trying to get me to leave. It was too easy to imagine the worst here. Even he knew I was weak. I crumpled in the seat next to him.

"Okay," I said finally because I was tired, because I was afraid, and because I thought it might be the last time I could act like a child, like their grandchild, shielded and loved. He handed me his T pass.

I was the only one on the bus. The house was dark when I got home.

The stove was off. I twisted the knobs again to give my hands something to do. I turned the knobs on, off, on, off, watching the flame flicker alive and wipe back to darkness just as quickly. Sudden memories came—grandmother cooking, arranging a little altar. I don't know the occasion, but pictures of family I never knew would sometimes appear on the dining table, fruits laid out on red plates before them. A cushion from our couch on the floor. Incense burning on either side of the frames. She and grandfather would take turns kneeling on the cushion, bowing to the portraits. Not all of them had been captured by a camera. A few were pencil sketches done by grandmother. I knelt beside them, even though I didn't understand what I was doing. The memory was so vivid: grandmother digging through the drawer searching for a lighter and instead sticking a bundle of incense directly into the stove's flame before whisking them to the altar.

Without quite realizing what I was doing, I went to search for the altar. The portraits were stacked above the bookshelf. The incense in the same drawer as the lighter, their holders in the glass cabinet with my high school math trophies. I lined the portraits along the dining table, lit the incense, and threw a couch cushion on the floor.

I had done this same ceremony in Taiwan, deep in the mountains, where grandfather had relatives buried. We built a large fire for burning paper money, separate fires for ancestors and for gods. Here all we had was incense and these portraits of people I did not know.

The sketches were from grandmother's side, and the pictures from grandfather's. Their mothers, fathers, siblings? Somewhere in there were people who knew my grandmother, how strong she could be, who could lend me the conviction that she would not leave me, not now, not when I was just beginning to understand her, flaws and all.

"Please," I whispered to the empty house. A clump of burnt incense fell onto the table. I gripped the corner of the cushion, bunching the fabric between my fingers. I don't know who I was addressing—one of grandfather's relatives, or maybe grandmother's mother, or her aunt, or maybe even her own grandmother.

"Please," I whispered again, my voice shaking as the tears came, thinking of grandmother alone in an unfamiliar room, hurt and terrified, and grandfather alone in the hospital waiting room, waiting for news of his lifelong companion, wearing his fraying pajamas. And to think only a few days earlier, I had been so confident that I would have time to connect with grandmother, believing the pencil and whatever Meng had to say would solve my problems. To think I had basked in the strength of a Reforged word, believed I could claim this small advantage against the world. The power was ultimately useless when it mattered. Instead of all that time spent learning about pencils, or working on EMBRS, perhaps the right thing to do had been to talk to her. Pencils and technology—could they really be a substitute for human connection?

I bowed my head to the cushion, my forehead meeting the cool fabric. My tears fell in heavy drops.

"Please don't leave us alone," I whispered.

I did manage to sleep, the tears tiring me out. I woke to the sun shining into my room. It could have been late morning. The sooner I got out of bed, the better. But it was another case of confirming reality, so instead I lay there staring up at the ceiling.

The worst possibility was the doctors were not able to save her, that she was dead. Grandfather would be heartbroken. I would take over cooking. Maybe my father would return. I would take the next semester off. Grandfather could be convinced to move to a smaller place with no stairs. I would take the job with Prof. Logan so I could stay home with grandfather, to ensure he wouldn't be alone.

I thought mechanically, logistics only. It was all I could manage. Prepared for the worst, I reached for my phone, fingers tapping the carpet, coming back with nothing. I leaned over to find the place where my phone normally sat empty.

I remembered turning it off after calling my father. I ran to my laptop to check the time. Seven in the morning. I had not slept as long as I thought. Still, it had to be enough. I had to get back to the hospital.

Grabbing a coat this time, I ran out of the house, then ran back in to double-check the stove and to grab grandfather's T pass. As I began the walk to the bus stop, a car horn blared.

It came in stuttered intervals after that, clearly trying to get some-one's attention, as if they had just realized it was early in the morning on a holiday weekend. I kept my head down, frankly, embarrassed for them, and increased my speed. The car horn eventually stopped, to my relief.

I was nearly at the bus stop when a car slowed down beside me. I sped up again, heart hammering. I had always thought seven in the morning a safe time from kidnappers.

"Get in here, you doofus."

I barely recognized her through the half-rolled-down window. Her hair was pulled into a messy bun, her eyes framed by glasses I never knew she needed, and the car—a rust-red hatchback, paint flaking—so antithetical to her usual polish.

"You're not supposed to be here," I said stupidly.

"Just get in already."

She had to lean over to manually unlock the passenger side door. The car smelled like herbal medicine. She cranked her window back up. Then she tilted her head toward me, eyes meeting mine, and gave a tired smile.

"Hi."

"Hi."

I fumbled with grandfather's T pass.

"Put in the hospital name?" She handed me her phone. I set the destination. The phone was plugged into a battery pack. It was probably too much to ask this car to drive and have a port to charge a phone at the same time. She began to drive.

"You hate driving," I mumbled.

"Sure do."

I gripped the door handle as she switched lanes barely in time to manage a left turn.

"You drove all night?" I looked out the window, or else I knew the tears would start again.

"Yeah. Luckily my brother was still distracting my parents. Turns out he was having an affair and told us he's getting divorced." She took one hand off the wheel to drink her coffee. I braced as the car swerved. She quickly righted it. "So my parents were furious, and nobody noticed when I slipped out of the house with the only car they let me drive."

"You could have told me you were coming."

She slammed the brake as soon as the light turned yellow. We lurched forward.

"You're the one who hung up on me. And then blocked all of my calls afterward."

"I didn't . . ." Then I remembered turning off my phone. "I didn't mean to." But maybe I had.

"Well, what did you expect me to do? You were in pain, going through something terrible. You thought you were alone. And your phone—have you ever not had it on you before? I was freaking out."

"I think I left it in grandfather's coat. He's still at the hospital."

She turned smoothly into the hospital parking lot. Only after she parked was it noticeable just how loud the car had been. The quiet morning enveloped us. The sun shone brightly through the windshield.

"Thank you for coming," I said, staring straight out the window, at the hospital door, where some sort of fate awaited me—and then I stopped trying to keep the tears at bay. I let them roll freely and drop onto the ripped cushion of her passenger seat. I thought about her driving all night long, at least five hours, just for us, veering off her Ivy League path to this little side road where we had ended up, otherwise forgotten. I felt a bit less alone, and that made all the difference.

"I think this is the nicest thing anyone has ever done for me," I said.

Whatever anger she held against me for abandoning my phone vanished.

"Of course," she said gently.

I unbuckled my seat belt, and we climbed out of the car. At the entrance to the hospital, she waited for me to enter first. I paused far enough away the automatic doors didn't detect me, not yet.

"I'm here with you," she promised.

And then the doors opened for us.

CHAPTER 28

From the Reforged pencil of Wong Yun

1 am writing through a fog, writing until my mind clears again. The fog will pass. It always does. Until one day it won't. The surrounding is entirely unfamiliar. A woman came in my room earlier.

"Your husband wanted you to have this." Her voice was gentle, her words in Chinese. I probably reminded her of her mother or grandmother as she reminded me of Monica, if Monica were older and confident and where was Monica? Where was I? Where was this husband the woman mentioned? Who was this husband?

She handed me a bundle of paper wrapped around a single black pencil. I pulled out the pencil, the feeling of its solid wood against my fingers the only familiar thing. Each paper was blank. What kind of husband did I have, who would give me blank paper?

"The doctor is coming to see you again. Your granddaughter is waiting to see you, too. We'll let her in after the doctor."

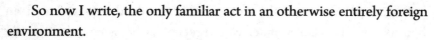

So now I write, the only familiar act in an otherwise entirely foreign environment.

The fog is beginning to pass. I am in a hospital, I understand now, scribbling on blank paper. Torou likely thought this would comfort me. He was right, of course he was.

I am beginning to remember falling down those stairs Monica always warned us about—and I am remembering that I am writing to you, Meng, and that was related to the fall. I had woken up in a fog. Not the worst since I knew I was home, Torou next to me, but I suddenly could not remember where you were. It was almost as if I were living two lives. Part of me knew Monica was in the room next door, and yet another was convinced I had just received your letter, that you were still waiting for my response, except that was before Monica even existed, before even Edward.

I did not reply to you when you needed me most. Maybe that's why I wear this pencil down now, to apologize for all these years. And maybe that's why I stirred awake, thinking I still had time to reply, that you were alone and lost in Shanghai. The letter you sent is tucked away downstairs, underneath all the boxes of tea we've received throughout the years, in the bottommost drawer of the cabinet farthest from the oven. I never wanted to unearth it before—probably why we never drank the gifted teas.

I can only say that the time has come, that even my harried mind can sense it, where we must iron out our misunderstandings.

The doctor just left. He barely spoke to me, whether it was because he did not think I would understand English or because he did not think I would understand any language due to my memory loss, I do not know. At last, he brought Monica to my room, my sweet, precious Monica, and told her I had a fractured hip and would need surgery, but that I would be able to go home soon.

When she looked at me, I wanted to cry. She would always be, to me, the small, quiet girl whose hair I tied into a bun each morning before school; who wore the same green vest every day to kindergarten because I worried her stomach would get cold, who, when others on the playground asked her to play, said no thanks, and sat quietly reading by herself. Her eyes did not accuse. Still, I understood. She had thought she would be left alone in a world we had never let her be alone in.

"I scared you, didn't I?" I asked.

She nodded, her jaw tight.

"Did Grandfather go home?"

Another nod.

"He was very tired," she said stiffly. After a pause—"Louise drove him home."

"Oh." And even though I could tell she wanted to move on, I could not help lingering over this. "She must be in love with you."

Her cheeks, predictably, flushed.

"That's—there's no reason for that to be the conclusion—"

"Either that or she really loves driving."

"She doesn't," she murmured, looking away.

"Ah."

She shook her head and changed the subject. "How are you feeling?"

"I can't feel much of anything right now," I said honestly.

"Do you remember why you were going down the stairs?"

It was my turn to look away. I knew I had to tell her because it was likely the next time I had an accident of this sort, I would not recover, and I would rather her find out from me than from your pencil or from her software.

"There is something I need you to know about me and Meng." I nodded to the chair next to the bed so she would stop standing and fidgeting. Instead, she sat and fidgeted.

"You don't have to tell me."

"I will tell you the important part." It took me a moment to gather the words. "When she needed me most, I ignored her." That is true, isn't it? "Because I wanted to move on from our past, even if it meant moving on from her." In that moment, I could almost see you there in the room with us, how you were when I left, when we thought we would only be separated a few months, only to have it turn into the rest of our lives. You were a ghost, floating by the door, lying down, chin propped up in your hands, the same as you were when we wrote our story at night. I could never tell, back then, if you enjoyed my additions, your face a mask of concentration. It was the same as I explained myself to Monica. I could not tell if you would forgive me.

I told her about the letter you sent, the first one I had received from you since I arrived in America. By then Torou and I were married. It was my fourth year in this country, eight since I left Shanghai. And I was, this is important, carrying Edward. I need you to know this because it is the only bit of information that might excuse my actions. You sent a pencil, no other note, and I told myself it would be too dangerous to Reforge it with Edward growing inside of me. Our mothers had never told us if that was the case. I did not want to risk his little life, even though I knew you would only write to me if you desperately needed help. There was nobody else who could Reforge it, so I kept your pencil locked away until Edward was born.

Even then, I delayed. I can partially blame being a new mother. Torou was working late all the time, doing all he could to attain a tenured position, and Edward wasn't a happy baby. I convinced myself you did not need my help anymore, that it had been months since you sent the pencil, that you would have figured out a way, as you always did. And I had not Reforged in years, had sworn off it, was terrified to do so again. It was not until Edward was a year old that the guilt overcame me, and I Reforged your pencil. The note was short, so simple, it would have been nothing to bleed it back out, probably would not have affected Edward. I can still see the words now.

Mother has died. Will you please come back? I am alone.

Why did you not just write it on a piece of paper? There were no incriminating words that would have been censored. So there had to be somebody after you, somebody who would take advantage of knowing you were alone and without your mother. Your mother would not have been old by then. How had both of our mothers died so young? Our greatest defenders, our greatest teachers, who danced and gambled and then left us to fend for ourselves after their lives burned out too soon.

You did not say what happened to your mother. Was it not safe even for the hearts of our pencils to carry? In a way I did not need to know. Your words—*I am alone*—were enough to tell me you had reached your lowest point, as I had in California.

I imagined you alone, and it was the same image of Monica sitting before me now, not quite looking at me, not quite accusing, though not absolving either.

And as I told her all of this, she tried to defend me.

"It was unlucky timing," she said. "You were pregnant when you got the pencil."

Then I told her my true mistake, the one that still haunts me, the one that makes you a ghost listening in on my conversations even now.

"I never replied."

At first, I told myself I would eventually. Even after I had stashed the letter away, deep inside the cabinet drawer. I was afraid I would write, and you would be dead, and I would never hear from you again. I was afraid I would write, and you would be alive, and you would ask me to return to Shanghai.

I feared Shanghai by then. I feared the ghost of our home, tensing at the passing footsteps of soldiers, the shadows of neighbors slipping away after spying on us. The memories of family meals and Ah-shin's cooking and when I teased you in school were gone. It was the late fifties. The American news reported that China had become a country of famine and poverty under Communist rule. I did not want to see what my home had become, to witness what I was lucky enough to escape, what you were unlucky enough to have to live through. Did not want to see how famine changed you, as I wandered through luxurious super-markets, carefully selecting the freshest bok choy and the choicest cut of beef. Did not want you to see this blessed life I had somehow built on top of all the lives whose words I had betrayed.

Even if we could have made our way there, even if all of the officials in China overlooked my flight to Taiwan, my father the Nationalist, and if I somehow made it back to America afterward, somebody would have accused us of being Communists, enemies of America, enemies of Taiwan. Footsteps around the house, neighbors spying, again, even in America. If it wasn't famine in China, it was the Red Scare or the Cold War here. Torou would never have been able to keep his job. We could not lose our home, I told myself, not now, not after Edward's birth, not when he could have a life free from occupation after occupation.

Excuses piled on excuses. Convenient reasons to leave my past behind, to leave you behind.

"I don't think it was unfair of you," Monica said. Always so careful with her words.

"And of course, you already know about the pencils I betrayed in California," I said.

She gave the smallest of nods.

"I wish you hadn't found out that way," I said. "But even if I could explain it myself, I don't think I could do so in a way that would make it forgivable."

"It was a different time," she said. "And I should have waited for you to tell me. If and when you wanted to."

"That's why I wanted you to Reforge Meng's pencil. She did not make the same mistakes I did."

She shook her head.

"I don't know Meng. And I don't know exactly what it is you did, what it was like living through those wars. All I can say is what I know of you now, and that for all my life, I have never had a reason to doubt you. I would forgive you for anything."

I wanted to hold her close, wished she was once again small enough where I could place her on my lap and squeeze. I wanted nothing to touch her belief in me.

"But I could have written back," I said.

"You could have written back," she agreed eventually.

I always believed it was too late. Until Monica taught me how to use the computer, until she told me about what it could do, until she said maybe she would be able to find you.

Your girl came into the room then, led by a nurse. She gave me all of the proper greetings and well wishes. Either her parents rammed this etiquette into her, or she could not bear to be seen as out of touch with a culture that elevated elders above all. She looked different this time—hair unkempt, glasses smudged. My heart softened for her, driving all the way here, shepherding my little family back and forth to see me. And if that hadn't softened me to her, the way Monica straightened, brightened, even, as soon as she came in, would have made me partial to anyone.

"There's no point staying," I said. "Go home. I think I may have left the stove on."

"We can keep you company," your girl offered.

"I'd like to be alone." I was itching to get back to my writing, the urgency pressing ever since my fall.

"Alright," Monica said. She stood and reached for my hand. I gave it a short squeeze, my promise not to scare her in such a way again, a promise I would not be able to keep forever. "I'm going to use the bathroom first." She glanced between me and your girl, gave a small smile, then hurried out.

"Thank you for driving all this way," I said at the same time as she said, "I'm glad to see you're feeling well."

A light laugh to brush off the collision of our words.

"Were you scared?" she asked, her eyes finding mine. Thick glasses—no wonder she normally wore contacts.

"Not really," I admitted. "When you get to be my age . . ." Once I had recovered from the shock of landing at the bottom of the stairs, I had even felt a bit of relief. That I would be finally free of my guilt over my choices and over you.

"Monica was scared," your girl said softly. "She called me in the middle of the night, and I could barely get through to her."

"Thank you for driving all this way," I said again.

"I—" She glanced at the door, then back to me. "It wasn't only for Monica that I came." Her words came out very fast. "I was worried for you. And for your story."

You swirled above her, your chin on her head, gazing down at me with lazy eyes.

"My story?" I repeated.

"Yes." Another glance at the door. "I know we disagreed about this the last time we spoke. But I thought maybe now, after your close call, after you saw how much Monica was shaken, you would be more willing to share your story."

"Stop—"

"What are you going to leave Monica with once you're gone?" Her voice was strained. You tilted your head. "You can leave her all the money in the world, but it won't be what she needs. She will always want to know more about you and the life you led, and if you don't share it now, it may be too late—"

"Stop." It hurt to raise my voice. I thought only Edward could make me do so. "What right do you have to my story?" By then I was looking above her, right at you, when you were twenty. "Why should I relive all of that just to share it with you? It was not a kind time. I don't—I can't—"

"You are writing it all down anyway, aren't you?" She gestured at my pencil, at the paper. "You are reliving it, so please, please let me archive it—"

"Did you come here," I said suddenly, the thought constricting itself around my heart, which had so recently softened for her. "Did you drive all this way for Monica or for me?"

"For you," she said without hesitation. You vanished as soon as I tore my eyes away from her. I looked to my worn-out hands, wishing they could be strong and capable again instead of wrinkled and frail, to give myself something, anything, to make me feel like I could still protect Monica.

"Please leave," I whispered.

"I just mean—of course I came here for Monica too. But she would have been fine whether I came or not. She's stronger than she thinks. But your story—"

"Leave."

"Please. I'm begging you not to just give it up."

"I think we should leave Grandmother now."

Even I had not noticed her, though I was facing the door and used to her quiet ways. Her face gave away nothing as to how long she had been there. It was calm, just as it had been when each of her parents left.

"This—" your girl stammered. She looked between me and Monica. "This wasn't how I wanted this to go."

"Monica," I began, even though I did not know how I would finish the sentence.

"You should rest now," Monica said. "I'll come see you again tomorrow."

She nodded at the door. Your girl looked at me. You were back to floating alongside her, eyes accusing me. The two of you turned slowly toward the door and walked out, Monica following behind.

I stared at the closed door. I think a fog must have hit me at some point after they left, because the next time I felt like myself again, it was dark and the pencil Torou left me was gripped tightly in my hand.

Another truth: one of the only reasons I told Monica to start looking for you again was to clear my conscience. I thought there was nothing you could do to me that would hurt me anymore, not at my age. But clearly there was, and I see I am now facing the punishment I deserve, a vengeance for what I did to you, the severity of which could only be matched by hurting Monica. I let her leave the hospital with someone who could hurt her worse than any of the scenarios I had ever imagined—car accidents, thieves, bullies. What damage could they do compared to a broken heart, and one I helped facilitate?

I'm afraid there is a world where you and I never understand each other again, where even all the words in the world cannot right what the decades have wrought on us.

CHAPTER 29

From the diary of Monica Tsai,
backed up on three servers spanning
two continents

November 24, 2018 (2018-11-24T17:24:29.420083)
loc: Cambridge, Massachusetts. United States of America
(42.3721865,71.1117091)

*There's a state of calm I can sometimes enter. Yesterday the calm was no-*where to be found because there were too many unknowns. But when everything is laid out, the panic subsides, replaced by logic. For me it's the same feeling as coding once all the specifications are in place. The problem is clear. All that is left is to address it.

After we left the hospital, Louise drove me home. She had not driven all the way here out of any sense of love for me. She came to get grandmother's story. Otherwise, she feared it would be lost forever. She cared more about collecting stories than for the people at the heart of them. In this calm state, I didn't even feel that bad for myself. I felt worse knowing grandmother's hopes must have deflated.

We were silent the whole ride, her hands tight on the steering wheel. The cramped brick houses of Cambridge lurched past. We remained silent even after her fourth attempt at parallel parking, when she finally managed it, the car sticking out only a little bit. She turned the engine off, and our silence was amplified.

"Listen," she said as I continued to stare out the window. "I know I've messed up somewhere. And I probably owe both you and your grandmother an apology."

I told her she didn't.

"I do. I think." She shook her head. "But I'm so tired. I'm not thinking properly. I didn't sleep at all last night. So I'm going to find a hotel or something and get out of your hair."

I sighed and told her to sleep in the guest room.

"No, that doesn't feel right—"

"No matter how much you insulted grandmother, she would find it even more insulting if you paid for a hotel."

I opened the car door to show I was done arguing. For a moment, as I walked toward our home, I thought she would drive away. She finally climbed out of the car.

"You know where the room is," I said as we took off our shoes. I headed to my room. I heard her follow me up the stairs.

"Monica."

I had avoided looking at her since the hospital. Her shaking voice forced me to face her now. She stood in my doorway. I could hear grandfather's snores from the room next door.

"Yes?"

When she did not say anything, only continued to stare at me, opening her mouth, then closing it again, I turned away from her. I opened the top drawer of my desk and pulled out the pencil that had started it all.

I had almost all the facts. How Louise truly felt. Why grandmother felt so guilty over Meng. There was just one part of this story I had not heard yet, one point of view whose lens was the last one I needed to make a rational decision.

I pressed Meng's heart into my wrist.

All I could see was white, my room gone, replaced by a lack of vision and a spiking pain. The other pencil heart had not felt remotely like this. Grandmother had warned they could be painful. Even so, I had not expected this much. There was something piercing in my head, as if a high-pitched scream, and my fingers were in my hair, clenching, grabbing. The scream contained words, I eventually sensed, too high and garbled for me to comprehend, for me to do any more than to catch a few here and there when the ache did not overwhelm.

Gradually, as the pain subsided, I could see my room again, registered the pink carpet rubbing against my cheek, recognized Louise kneeling beside me, her hand on my back, as I regained control of my breathing.

The words were clearer now. It was something about Shanghai, something about—could it be?—my father, and finally, in a flash of light, Louise, so clear that I could not tell if the Reforging had ended right as I saw the real Louise in front of me.

"Was I screaming?" I asked.

"More like whimpering," she said. "I closed your door so your grandfather wouldn't wake up."

"Thank you. I'm fine. You can go to sleep now."

"Don't you need to Reforge?"

"I can do it while you're sleeping."

"I . . . could help you though."

I sat up. The room became clearer still. Our eyes met, and I could see each red vein in hers, the dark circles around them.

The calm fled at this point. She was confusing everything I thought I knew. Perhaps she did care for me, after all? Then she glanced at my arm, at the darkened phoenix, ready for its rebirth, and everything clicked.

"You just want to help me so you can get Meng's story."

Her eyes widened.

"No, no, that's not—"

My whole body trembled, leaning away from her. "You've only ever tried to get close to me so you could learn about their magic—"

"Monica, please, I would—"

"You would, you would what? Get me off if it meant you might be able to claim an old woman's story for your collection? What kind of person are you?"

"Meng already told me her story!" Louise nearly yelled. "And even if she hadn't, I wouldn't—I wouldn't do that to you. I offered because I wanted to, alright? I've wanted to for so long now, and oh god, none of this is going how I wanted it to—"

The world quieted and slowed. Her bloodshot eyes filled my field of view, though she was still an arm's length away. I wanted her closer, I wanted her farther.

I jerked my head away and locked my eyes on the doorknob. That was safe, dull, and mundane and promised an exit.

"How could you think that of me?" she whispered.

"I heard what you said to my grandmother. How is that any different?" I ran my thumb over the phoenix's head. The way she had dragged me along—it was a dull imitation of the pain that poured out of Meng's heart. "You tried to force grandmother's story out of her while she was in a hospital bed, when she already told you she didn't want to share it with you."

"I didn't handle it well," she conceded. "But I would not have tried to take advantage of you—"

"Haven't you already?" The doorknob began to blur, tears forming. "As soon as we met, all you wanted was to meet my grandmother. And you must have figured out how I felt about you because I couldn't hide it. You knew I would have done anything for you." I brought my knees to my chest. "Anything except hurt grandmother."

"I wasn't trying to hurt her." Her voice was hard now, urgent. "I was trying to help her."

"You can't force people to share things with you that they don't want to—"

And then she knocked the wind out of me.

"Oh?" The change in her voice made me flinch. "Is that true, scraper of the internet? I don't think someone who makes money from gathering data on users without them even realizing can have anything to say about that."

I couldn't speak. She picked at my guilt, the vulnerability I had revealed to her, twisted it. I closed my eyes. Not even the doorknob was safe anymore.

"That's different," I stumbled. "That's to connect people. To connect people like grandmother and Meng—"

"And that's what I'm trying to do too." There was a desperation to her voice I had never heard before. She needed me to understand, and I needed her to understand, but we were too far past each other.

"I'm sorry," I said even though I really was not.

She exhaled.

"I am too," she said eventually. "I'll see myself out."

"Get some sleep first." I somehow could not stop caring for her, even now.

The floor creaked as she stood. My door opened then closed, gently. I kept my eyes shut, listening to her footsteps, wondering if she would go to the guest room, collapse on the bed, and wail into the pillow the way I wanted to. Instead, the front door clicked open and closed. Her long stride tapped down the sidewalk. I convinced myself I heard her car door wrenched open and the ancient engine stuttering alive.

I opened my eyes and stared at my phoenix. It was the pencil that had begun our relationship, the pencil she had slid over to me at the frozen yogurt shop with a smile, the pencil that had built the relationship between the four of us—her, grandmother, Meng, and me—the pencil that I still can't understand, even though its heart is aligned with my own.

I don't even know why I'm bothering to write all this down, why I'm reliving these awful conversations when every keystroke hurts. After all, what has this journal done for me? I thought it'd help me work through the trauma of grandmother's illness. I thought it'd help me figure out Louise's cryptic signals. There's no way I'll share this with EMBRS or anything or anyone. Yet I can't stop writing, trying to make my life make some sort of sense. But maybe there isn't any sense to be made and this is just how life goes, and any endeavor to turn it into a coherent story is futile, an attempt to make a path out of nothing. I can hardly even type anymore because my arm hurts. The phoenix is pulsing. My wrist is on fire.

CHAPTER 30

From the Reforged pencil of Chen Meng

I will keep this concise because I know you are longwinded.

First thing, I am not mad at you. I haven't been, for a long time. But also for a long time, I was. You have reason to be mad at me too. I knew you were alive. You see, I met Edward, maybe ten years ago now. He told me all about you, and I asked him to tell you nothing about me. My impression was that you two were not talking much, and so I did not think it a difficult task for him.

Edward looks like your father. That was my first thought when we met shortly after he moved to Shanghai. He would have been around the same age as your father the last time I saw him, the last time I saw you.

Edward was in an awful state. I won't go into detail, except that he seemed lost in many ways—far from home with few friends, unsure where home was anymore. I was a last resort. He was so pitiful that even though I thought I had long moved on from you, I decided to help him.

I hated your father—do you know that? The times when he was away during the war were the most stable of my life. As soon as he came back, everything went wrong. Mr. Gao spent more time at the house. A new war began. And of course, he took you away. The circumstances were dire, I know that now. But at the time, I absolutely hated him.

Yet for some reason, I kept his pencil. You left it here, do you remember? You were mad at him and threw it across the room that first night he suggested leaving. I found it months later, under my bed, and recognized it for what it was if only because it was one of the older designs, ones that would have only been made when our mothers were young. I kept it. I thought you might want it back if we ever met again. In a way, I kept it hoping it would allow that to happen.

Instead, Edward showed up, looking so much like your father and reminding me that I still had his pencil. Edward told me he had never met his grandfather, that by the time your family was able to return to Taiwan, he had already passed, that he only knew him from a tombstone on a mountain where he'd burned paper and hadn't known what to say.

But I still had his pencil. And when Edward came, I Reforged it.

It was the first I had Reforged in decades. I had sworn off it. It was easy to avoid after I burned down the company. Mother was furious with me all the time. She continued to Reforge, but the pencils weren't ours, and she was sick more often than not. I know that is my fault; her death is on my hands. I was devastated when I learned your mother had died. I looked up to her more than my own mother even. I didn't hear about it until decades later. There was a small bit of relief, though, too. Your mother still became ill, Reforging our own pencils. It made me think that maybe I was not entirely to blame for my mother's illness.

Pencils and this power we possess ruined my life. I think it may have ruined yours, too. Yet when Edward came, I realized I might have something that could help him, and so reached for the pencil again.

You know how close you feel to someone once you Reforge their words. I didn't want to feel close to your father, and yet it happened anyway. The pencil was from when he was young and full of hope for himself and his family, and for China. He described your mother with such admiration. He loved her, he really did, and I realized you can both love someone and hurt them irreparably, as he did when he made your mother continue Reforging, even after it was clear it was killing her. I did the same when I burned down the company. As maybe you did, when you pushed Edward toward your own dreams and watched him fail.

I gave the Reforged message to Edward, told him it was written by his grandfather, for his grandmother. I told him there was nobody I respected more in the world than his grandmother. I told him he might be unsure about himself and where he comes from, but that I knew, and there was nothing to fear.

He cried into me like a child. I never had children. I never wanted them. But when he buried his head in me, I thought—so this is the feeling. This is the reason. Why people have children, why people share their stories. These small moments of connection. We used to know that, didn't we? Back when we wrote our own.

Edward kept in touch. He began to find his footing here. He updated me on his life, and once things were stable for him, I saw him less and less. I haven't seen him for years now. I don't mind. I am happy for him, that he has found himself. He does not know this, but I will tell you because I think you may need to hear it—seeing his reaction to your father's letter helped me too.

To really understand someone I once hated, in such an intimate way, to see their words help someone they never could have imagined. The few stories your father told in his letter grounded your son, gave him a sliver of connection to his history, his family. To watch him interpret your father's story for himself.

Most people will never understand or experience a story the way you and I can. And yet they're always trying, and there's something beautiful in that we can help them. What I thought of as a curse for so long maybe—when the world is not consuming itself in war and betrayal—is not so bad after all.

That was the state of mind I was in when that eager girl showed up. My god, they grow so tall these days, don't they? We got along, which surprised me, given that I have not had a conversation with someone her age in years. Looking back, it was not so surprising. You see, she was a lot like you. Let me explain in a way that even you will not be able to deny.

There was that brief period of our lives when I knew about Reforging and you didn't. You knew there was something we were hiding from you, and how furious you were in those days! I would have told you in a heartbeat, but Mother warned that your grandmother was the last person we wanted to cross, that we only had a home because she agreed we could stay. You probably don't even remember how much you threatened me, how much you lied to both of our mothers to try to get more information. You were so desperate to have this family link. The day your mother finally said you could learn was the best of your life.

Still not convinced? Then how about when only you did not know the other way of Reforging? We were so young then, even our mothers, and we had no idea how to talk about sex or pleasure. And when we wouldn't share this knowledge with you—how easily you set fire to our relationship, the final weeks of our time together.

That tall, eager girl was much the same. She was so desperate for a connection to something, anything, really, to feel a part of her own history and family. And I saw how Edward had changed from having a story of his own to hold on to. Nobody was around to tell me I couldn't, so I told her our secret. I figured she might take it for the babbling of an old woman, but that if it could help her, she would latch on to it. You cannot imagine my surprise when, right before she was due to head home, she told me your granddaughter had contacted her. It was fate, it seems, some string that has always tied us together across decades and continents.

And so I write this note for you, using one of the few Phoenix Pencil Company pencils I have left. I'm not interested in filling you in on all that has happened since we parted. It would be too painful. But I needed to tell you about these two—your son and this girl. They don't know each other, don't even know the other exists, and yet they came to me with the same look in their eyes, and it was your look, the one that wanted to belong to our family so desperately.

I had thought of Reforging as nothing but pain after years of war and separation. Then I witnessed your son's transformation, and I let myself hope again. And when that girl gushed about the power of stories and how she wanted to dedicate her life to preserving the history of ordinary lives—it was hard to drown in the darkness of that pain when her light shone so bright.

All that to say, my oldest friend, though we may never see each other again, though you may have closed your heart to our stories the way I did, I hope you will at least take this one. I hope you can see that perhaps this world is less cruel than the one we grew up in. We made hard choices, wrong ones, because we had no other way. But these girls, growing up now, will have a better life, will make better choices, and you played a part in making that happen. Perhaps their story can reignite the hope we once had.

—*Chen Meng*

CHAPTER 31

From the Reforged pencil of Wong Yun

onica has Reforged your pencil. She brought your words to me in a convenience store notebook. There was a poorly applied bandage on her arm, lopsided and peeling. That she had cut herself to Reforge your words—it was the one thing I had wanted her to avoid. I know the dangerous places it can lead. I tried to ask her about it, how she had felt, if it hurt. She was reluctant with her words, distant in a way that squeezed my heart tight. There is a sadness to her I have never seen before. I asked if it had to do with your words, if they changed the way she thought about me.

"I will always love you," she said, with a serious melancholy that ached more than my hip, more than the nights alone in the hospital.

When I asked if your girl had hurt her, she turned quickly away, changed the topic to the logistics of my surgery and recovery instead. She forced a smile upon her face, though I could still see the stain of her tears, no matter how she tried to hide them.

"Did Meng . . . ?" I began.

She knew what I was going to ask.

"She forgave you," she said. Those were the words I wanted to hear for so long. And yet, to have Monica deliver them, to see her like this—I hated myself all over again. Monica left at some point, I don't remember, and there was nothing I could do for her, not here in a hospital, not with my mind like this. But she is strong in her own way, and I must believe that she will find a way.

I've now read your words. That you met Edward, that my father's words helped him—that alone will take me a while to process. And now that I've read your letter—well, I'm a little embarrassed by how long mine is in comparison. There is unfortunately more to my story that I haven't gotten to yet. I know, I can see you rolling your eyes. I know your patience is thin. But I am finally starting to form the message I'd like to leave you with, now that I understand how you view the world.

I went to Boston because it was one of the few cities in the United States I could name, the only one where I knew someone. He would still be in his program, I calculated, since I had come not long after he left. I did not really think I would find him. I merely thought it would be useful to be able to say I knew somebody at the university. If Torou had made it to Boston, I thought it likely others from China and Taiwan had as well, that maybe I could find people who understood where I came from.

I found my job and my lodging the same way. Our mothers would be proud. I asked around Chinatown for mahjong gatherings. I ended up more than once in basements surrounded by mostly men. I would lie and claim I had a husband.

"He's a student at MIT," I would say. Most of the time we conversed in English, since the majority of Chinatown's residents spoke Cantonese. The name MIT, at least, meant something to everybody there.

"You're very good at mahjong," a woman said to me during one of the early days. Her English name was Linda. I had been trying to sit at her table. I heard she ran a restaurant. She was a rarity—most restaurant workers were men. Women were seamstresses. I had spent all my life making pencils. I was good with my hands, yet I had never learned to sew, so I thought working in a restaurant would suit me better.

"I played a lot back in Shanghai," I said, because I knew she, too, was from Shanghai. After all, millions of us had fled in those years.

"Oh?"

It was not long until we were speaking in Shanghainese, when I dropped the hint I was looking for work, a place to stay, and she welcomed me to her restaurant and gave me the address of a group of women who needed another person to live with them and split their rent.

"What did your family do in Shanghai?" she asked.

I tensed, then told her the truth.

"My mother ran the Phoenix Pencil Company."

"The Phoenix Pencil Company!" Linda pulled her hands from the tiles in the center. The rest of us continued shuffling. She looked away from the game and stared at me.

"You know it?" I asked as casually as I could.

"But your surname is not Chen."

She evidently only knew the company after you and your mother had taken over using your father's name.

"That would be my mother's sister," I explained carefully. "And my cousin." I pulled down my sleeve. Few people knew of our Reforging. Still, I suddenly did not want her to see my wrist.

She drew her tiles. Her playing was messy after that—she matched on tiles that had already been played earlier, tossed rare ones that resulted in losses for her.

"You seem unsettled." I decided to confront the matter.

She slammed her tiles down when one of the other players called mahjong.

"My father loved your pencils." I focused on the tiles, dreading what she would say next. "Your aunt set up the largest surveillance system in Shanghai. We left soon after my father was killed. I'm sorry, but you are no longer welcome at the restaurant."

"I left Shanghai before any of that," I said. We were both playing sloppily now. "My father was with the Nationalists. We went to Taiwan. I haven't talked to my aunt since we left. Please. Give me a chance. I was only a child when I knew her."

Of course, I did not tell her about the small surveillance system I had established in California before coming to Boston. I was more than happy to denounce your mother if it meant I would have a job and a place to stay. I knew in a way you had denounced her, too, when you set the company ablaze.

In the end, it was not my charm that won her over. It was her own soft heart. We would be lifelong friends, though we never spoke about Shanghai again.

The restaurant Linda ran was well known, having once been featured in the *Boston Globe* as serving tastier food than any that could be found in China, where the Communists did not know how to cook anymore.

"Do you get MIT students here?" I asked during my first week.

"Oh yes." Linda grinned. "Looking for a husband?"

"I wouldn't say no."

After that, she made an effort to have me wait on all of the young men reading thick books.

"You're not interested yourself?" I asked. She had gotten over our initial confrontation. I think she was lonely and had the idea, like we all did, that those from Shanghai were above others from our country, and she was waiting for someone of a similar background, someone who was more suitable.

She shook her head with a wink. It would be another few months before I met her lover, a rich white woman who financed much of the restaurant's initial costs. Their story would have perhaps been more interesting to tell you than mine.

I wrote to you during that time, at least once a month. I wrote often but did not send my letters, knowing they were unlikely to reach you and might cast suspicion on me, sending messages to red China, which at that point was thoroughly closed off from the world. But you were all I was living for then. Mother was gone, and I longed to bring you and your mother to America. There was a freedom to living in Boston I had never known before, comparable only to the brief period between wars, when we believed Shanghai was truly ours. The freedom relaxed me, the job helped me live, and the mahjong even made me some friends. But inside I was hollow except for my wish to find you again and the ghost of the thought that maybe I would find Torou.

When his eyes peered over his textbook as I placed his pork and radish soup down in front of him, I was not surprised. I had hoped for this meeting for too long. He was there at an odd hour, which was not surprising, nor the fact that he had ordered soup. If anything, he should have been surprised to find me there, for I'd had no prospects of leaving Taiwan the last we spoke. Instead, he smiled.

"The pencil girl." His first words to me after years apart.

"The soup boy." I tried to stay calm, to maintain his level of casualness even as I thought back to the time at the pencil company when our bodies were entwined.

He raised a spoonful of soup to me. "I haven't changed."

"I have," I said.

"Tell me how." Then he unstrapped his watch and placed it at the seat across from him. "Ten minutes?" he asked in a way I found infuriatingly presumptuous and yet irresistible.

He was no taller, even if he was not as scrawny as he had been in Taiwan. The full American meals had filled him out and enhanced the confidence in his eyes. He always had some semblance of it, accustomed to being the smartest, but now that he had made it to America and worked through a top institution, his confidence had soared. A few months would pass before I witnessed the way that certainty would shed off him when he was around his white classmates and professors—how quickly the gleam left him, replaced by wide eyes trying to hang on.

"I'm still working," I said, and made to leave.

"Wait," he called. "Who did you marry?"

"Nobody," I said. It was true there were not many other ways a woman my age could have made it to America. "I need to get back to work now."

"When will you be done?"

I pretended not to hear him. When I returned to the kitchen, Linda scolded me.

"You'll never find a husband if you're so cold."

"I knew him from Taiwan."

"Oh? Old enemies?"

I remembered how his fingers trailed along my legs beneath the table at the pencil company, how I had ached for him after he left.

"Something like that."

I left my shift depressed, Linda's words ringing true as my own cut into me, wondering how I could alienate him in a world where I was already so alone. She and I left the restaurant together.

"Cheer up, now." She jabbed me with her elbow. I was staring at my worn-out shoes, pitying the way I could almost feel the uneven floor beneath me and how I could not afford to replace them, when she jabbed me again. "Maybe he likes the cold type."

Only then did I look up and spot him, leaning against the side of the restaurant, angling his book toward the neighboring restaurant's light.

"Did you wait here for me?" I stammered. Linda gave my arm a squeeze before continuing on, leaving me alone with him.

"I was at a good part in the book." In fact, he did not even look up from the page. I could just make out the title—*The Mathematical*

Theory of Communication—and could not help smiling, remembering the awkward boy who once blurted out that he loved communication.

For a moment, I stood in front of him, smelling of garlic and oil, while he did nothing but read.

"Who did you marry?" I asked to get him to look up. A part of me feared his answer.

"No one." He finally closed his book. "Though my parents are actively looking in Taiwan."

"You don't care who they find?"

"I asked them to find you."

"I don't believe you," I said automatically. It was so much easier to believe there was nobody who cared if I disappeared. His words were incomprehensible.

"They told me you had gone to America, though nobody seemed to know where, or why. They told me your mother passed. I was sorry to hear that. She was so kind to me. I assumed you found someone and they brought you here."

He was not wrong. But I was not ready to tell him the truth of how I had wormed my way across the ocean.

"I never understood why you took an interest in me."

He shrugged. The shrug was so familiar, something I had not thought about for years, yet which brought him back forcefully, even more than seeing him again after so long.

"I think at first it was only because you worked at the pencil company and were mysterious. I wanted to know your secrets. I love a good puzzle." He smiled, and I did not smile back. "But then it became clear you weren't something for me to solve. As I sought to unravel you, all I peeled back was layer after layer of sadness I could not comprehend. So when you pushed me away, I left. I guess I've still maintained that same curiosity about you though."

"I don't think you would like what you'd find."

"Hard to say if I don't know."

"I made it to America by sleeping with a man and then burning his house down." And that wasn't even the worst of my crimes! I wanted to shock him, to convince him to turn against me now rather than later. "How does that make you feel?"

If he had a visible reaction, it was too dark to tell.

"Mostly jealous," he said eventually.

"Of my path to America?" If a child in Taiwan could architect their own life, it would follow the path Torou's had taken—accepted into America at a prestigious university through merit alone. It was impossible he could be jealous of me.

"Of the man who got to have you, if only for a while."

"You're insufferable." Linda's accusation of being cold hit me again. Being with him was a constant cycle of wanting him closer and needing to push him away. I did not like the person I had become, and I could not stand when he flattered, sure he was only telling me lies.

"May I see you again tomorrow?"

I did not deserve his persistence. I did not deserve this life in America, won from embracing the very worst our pencils could offer. But I could hear your voice and Linda's voice in my head, the scolding I would get if I rejected him again.

"Yes," I said, letting a bit of light into my dark, lonely world.

CHAPTER 32

From the diary of Monica Tsai

November 30, 2018

I've had more time to think about grandmother's words, and Meng's. A number of things became clear to me after I bled out Meng's pencil heart. First, I stopped feeling quite so bad for myself. I made myself get up and go to the hospital. Grandmother's surgery went well. Still, it is alarming how quickly she's fading. Maybe it's the unfamiliar environment or the fact that she is writing less and less, or the pain is getting to her. She is only present half the time when I visit.

The day after her surgery, she was remarkably lucid. She smiled when grandfather said he was going to help himself to more of the cafeteria's General Tso's chicken to support their diversity initiatives. And she complimented the lion's head meatballs I made for her, even though they were flat and dry.

I asked her what kept her writing. Her pencil is so short now. One of the nurses asked me if grandmother was writing a novel, to which I could only say no, I didn't think so, and really, I had no idea what she was writing. Could she have that much to say to Meng?

"It's not only for Meng," she said. She tapped her pencil against her chin. "I suppose it is for me, too."

"Your memory?" I asked. I pictured her as Penelope, weaving her shroud each day, unraveling it each night to keep the suitors at bay. Grandmother was writing to keep the fog away, and once she allowed herself to finish, she would be lost.

She denied it, though, insisted it wasn't to help her memory. "To make myself more palatable. To start forgiving myself."

It's made me rethink all this journaling that I've been doing. At first, I journaled for EMBRS, thinking it would help me form connections in the future. I guess I never really thought about just having this for myself. To help me reframe my story as something more palatable. One where I'm strong and independent and not a heartbroken recluse. One where I'm more like Meng and grandmother, capable of surviving so much.

"There's nothing to forgive," I said. "Not anymore. You left the pencils behind."

"But what of all the lives and stories I betrayed?"

I didn't know what to say to that. It reminded me of the articles Prof. Logan sent around, the big tech employees wondering what role they played in our fractured democracy, our polarized political body, and media, when they had believed they were regular people with a particular talent, something unique to offer.

"I don't know about their stories," I said. "But you made mine better than I could have ever asked for."

Her eyes went soft for a moment, then faded into blankness. I held her hand for a bit longer. She idly traced the scar Meng's words had left on my arm. I told her I would be back, that I had to speak to my professor, and she gave a confused nod.

After the fight with Louise, I had returned to EMBRS, hoping I could drown myself in code. Instead, I ended up digging through Prof.

Logan's internal documents. You can't say he's a total hypocrite—he even shares these kinds of sensitive investor business plans freely with the team. I was just never brave enough to look.

They confirmed what I already suspected and wouldn't let myself really consider. The plan to make EMBRS profitable was simple. It followed every other tech product model. Offer the tool for free. Let users experience the wondrous connections it could make. Then sell the journal data, the richest kind of data there is—stories of how we perceive ourselves, perfect for targeting ads, for language models, for letting us think we've automated something as important as human connection.

Since grandmother's fall, Prof. Logan messaged a few times, telling me to take it easy, to only log back on once everything had settled down. He even sent flowers. In so many ways, he and EMBRS saved me this past semester. Not only the money, or the mentorship, or even having something productive to work on, to keep my mind busy. But all the journaling he so wholeheartedly recommended is finally making things clear. It became too obvious what I had to do.

It took me the whole afternoon to devise what I wanted to say in the first and only journal entry I would submit to EMBRS. I wrote that I was an EMBRS engineer, the one with the grandmother. I wrote the truth about how Louise and I had connected, how it had all been through social media data and quite a bit of luck, how there hadn't been a journaling component at all. How that data was technically private and not something EMBRS would have access to after it went for-profit. How Prof. Logan's pitch was built on a lie. How my father had found Meng years ago without using any new-age technology.

I submitted the entry, then hard-coded other branches to ensure EMBRS matched my entry to all the investors who were testing the product. I had to commit the code to deploy it. My commit message: *I'm sorry.*

I only had to wait eight minutes before he called me.

"Monica." His voice was strained, the complete opposite from his smooth presenter voice. "What have you done?"

"I'm sorry," I said, and I meant it. It was not his fault, really, not entirely. I had gone along for so long. "I know you and the team mean well. But I don't believe in it anymore."

"So you'd burn us to the ground?" he asked in a way that made me flinch.

"EMBRS was only ever supposed to share between two people. Not data brokers and, and—"

He made a strangled sound. "Don't you see data selling is the only kind of business model that works these days? A critical mass of people will only use EMBRS if it's free. Otherwise, there aren't enough nodes to make meaningful connections, like you're paying for a telephone that no one else uses. But someone needs to pay. The server costs alone are huge. This was the trade-off. The connections formed are priceless. I thought you understood."

It was so practiced. I wondered how many times he had told himself these very same words.

"I understand," I said. "But that doesn't mean I'll continue working on it. You could just go in and delete my entry."

"You and I both know data is never really deleted on the internet," he said. "Those investors received notifications as soon as you linked your entry. If I delete now, they'll find it even more suspicious."

"Maybe they'll still back you."

"Well, you've made it really fucking hard now, haven't you? After all I have done for you?"

He had saved me from a semester of languishing, believed in me and my abilities when I could have easily been cast aside and forgotten. Had really been nothing except kind, looking out for my future when I did not believe I had one.

Was this how Meng felt when she started the fire that burned down the Phoenix Pencil Company? Did she hesitate to burn her family's legacy once she recognized its danger? Her pain echoed. Of course it hurt. As her mother screamed at her, trying to run into the building, and Meng held her back, wrapping her arms around her mother's flailing body, until the flames were all-consuming and her mother turned limp in her arms, as if Meng had destroyed her, and not a building.

My actions were trivial in comparison. Still, it hurt. To set fire to everything I had built the last year, to burn this bridge with him.

"I'm grateful. Really, I am." It was all I could say.

He gave a shaky sigh, bordering on a laugh.

"I knew it was a mistake to work with idealist undergrads."

"I am sorry things turned out this way."

"I'm mad, Monica. In fact, I'm furious. Part of it is because I know you are at least partially right, and I can't stand it. Do me a favor. If you come back next semester, don't sign up for any of my classes."

"Yes, Professor."

He hung up. When I tried to refresh EMBRS again, I received an access-denied page.

For a while, I sat at my desk, trembling. I even spiraled a bit, thinking of Prof. Logan's many connections, wondering if he would tarnish my name, turn the other professors against me, place me on a do-not-hire list. I now realize it was the first time I had truly taken a risk in sharing how I felt. With grandmother, I had only done so when she forced the truth out of my pencil—and with Louise, it was only after I learned her motivations and I had nothing left to lose. I shuddered, and wondered what she would think of me now.

But it doesn't matter what she thinks, does it? She tried to call me, text me, until I told her to please stop, not right now, I need time, I need to take care of grandmother, and she had gone silent.

That night was grandmother's last in the hospital. Grandfather was already asleep, and I still didn't want to talk to Louise. I was tired and drained after my call with Prof. Logan, but found I wanted, needed, to talk to someone. Meng's message made the answer obvious. I called my father.

One of the most surprising things I learned was that he had spoken with Meng. We always knew she was likely in the same city, but it was a large city, and he did not care enough for his family here, so why would he seek out this distant relative? That I could have called him, that he could have simply told me how to reach Meng—compared to the way I went about searching, setting up internet scrapers, driving to meet Louise, retrieving Meng's pencil from her, learning how to Reforge, having my heart broken—it was almost laughable, the simplicity of the alternative. But maybe that's just the way of the women in our family, for everything to involve a pencil and a broken heart.

"Monica!" he exclaimed, genuinely surprised. We had not spoken since I called him from the hospital. He had written a few emails to me, which I had skimmed, then ignored. "Is everything okay? Grandmother should be coming home soon, right?"

"Yeah," I said. "No, she's fine. I just . . . I wanted to see how you were doing."

He blinked. Then he told me things were going well, he would be able to wrap up loose ends more quickly than he thought. He didn't realize until hearing about grandmother's fall how bad things had gotten, and he would try to get home as soon as possible.

"In fact, I should be able to return before your spring semester. So you can go back to school."

"That's wonderful," I said, surprising myself with how much I meant it. Even if I had to avoid Prof. Logan, I wanted to go back to school, to keep learning.

"But how about you come to Shanghai first? While I still live here. You can come before your semester starts, and I can show you around. I think you'd like it here." For the first time, I heard the pleading in his voice.

"I can't just leave grandmother and grandfather here."

"Well, why don't you ask them? I think they might like the idea of you coming here."

I said I would, though I did not actually intend to. Still, it was difficult not to envision myself in Shanghai, walking along that same skyline that had been in Meng and Louise's picture.

"Do you have Meng's contact info?" I asked suddenly.

"Who?"

"Grandmother's cousin's."

"Oh! I—I would need to look for it. I probably lost it though, I'm sorry to say."

"That's alright." It was such a typical answer from him that I was not even disappointed. "But how did you find her in the first place?" I could not help asking.

"Oh. I met her in a mahjong hall. She's a fiend."

I smiled. "Of course she is."

We talked for a little longer, mostly about logistics—when grandmother was coming home, when my spring semester was starting, what flights he should look into. And it was nice, to be able to speak to him normally, to begin to allow some of the old resentment to fade.

The next day, grandfather and I went to the hospital to take grandmother home. We rented the nicest car we could afford. Grandmother came out in a wheelchair. She will need it for a while. Grandfather insisted on tying a balloon to the arm even though the first thing we did, once grandmother was safely in the car, was collapse the chair and throw it in the trunk. But when we got home and opened the trunk, the balloon eagerly floated to attention, and grandmother laughed in delight. She was not totally present, but it was wonderful to see her happy, to see her at home.

I had a whole setup waiting in the living room, which we had converted into her bedroom. We helped her onto her bed, and I gave her an old tablet. I showed her how to navigate through the apps, as grandfather booted up his desktop. And once grandmother was set up,

I grabbed my laptop, and we all signed in to the mahjong app. A mah-jong LAN party.

We needed the app so that our fourth player could be the computer. But it took both grandmother and grandfather a while to understand how the game worked in a virtual setting, and it didn't help that the rules were slightly different from the variant we played. The computer would play its tile immediately, but grandmother and grandfather played slowly, so different from their usual cavalier tossing of tiles. The patterns on the tiles were different than ours and grandfather had a hard time discerning the flower tiles from the wind tiles, and grandmother would pause for long periods. I would go over to help, explaining how to play a tile and reach for one a player threw out, but it never seemed to stick, and by the end I knew her whole hand.

We had a few good rounds, even if grandmother was never fully present.

"Maybe we try again another day," grandfather suggested gently. Grandmother looked relieved when I took the tablet out of her hands.

That was when everything caught up to me. A nurse will be coming by for the next few weeks to aid grandmother in her recovery. It felt like the last day it would be only us. I had wanted it to be special. But the weight of the previous weeks, Meng's letter, grandmother's fall, confronting Prof. Logan, Louise's betrayal, and now grandmother, home but barely remembering, all came crashing down. I hung my head and tried not to let them see. But of course, they noticed.

"Oh, it's okay to cry, 寶貝," grandfather said immediately. He rested his hands on my shoulders, and we sat with grandmother on the bed. "It has been such a hard semester for you, hasn't it? But you have been so strong and good."

Grandmother nodded. She wasn't fully present, I knew, but even this version of herself that could not remember where she was, or maybe even who I was, still frowned, a pained arch to her eyebrow, as she saw my tears.

I swallowed.

"What hurts?" she asked.

Everything hurts, I thought. I wanted, more than anything, someone to talk to, someone other than them, someone who would listen to the highs and lows of my day and help me process this slow, cruel loss.

"What about that girl?" grandmother suddenly asked. "You were so happy when that girl was here. Invite her back."

I managed a shaky laugh. I tried to catch grandfather's eye, to have a moment where we could agree she was talking nonsense. Instead, he looked as sincere as she did.

"You don't remember how she hurt you?" I asked.

Grandmother shrugged.

"I forgive," she said, as if it were the simplest thing to do.

And maybe it was, for her. She, who had wanted Meng's forgiveness for so long and who now finally had it.

"Grandmother and I talked earlier today," grandfather said, "and we want you to go to Shanghai."

"Shanghai? But I can't leave you two here."

"We'll have the nurse. And it might only get harder for you to leave us. Grandmother wants to give her pencil to Meng. She wants you to meet her."

"Are you done writing?" I asked grandmother.

She picked a pencil up from her bedside table. It was always with her, the one possession she never forgot. She held it out on the palms of her hands. I took it gingerly.

At night, I found a box to store it. I wondered about the story inside and how it ended. What kind of ending would grandmother write for herself?

I closed the box and tucked it in my suitcase. I drafted a message I knew I would not send:

😄: grandmother is finally home!

☹: she is getting worse and I miss
you but I don't know if I should and it's
only going to get harder here. she can
barely move on her own and I miss her,
even though she's still here, and I have
never been surer of myself yet also
more alone

I deleted the draft. Then I began looking up flights to Shanghai.

CHAPTER 33

From the Reforged pencil of Wong Yun

1 set out to explain myself to you. To tell you my story from my perspective in the hope that you would forgive me. Now that I have your forgiveness, I find myself unsure of how to end this letter to you.

I was surprised though also relieved to hear the optimism in your message and what you saw in both Edward and Louise, that perhaps these stories may have a use, after all. So let me leave you with a bit of optimism, and my own message for you, which really comes from Torou, the man who is the greatest fortune I did not deserve, the awkward soup boy turned best grandfather, and in the middle, the steadfast partner who helped me in every way.

There was an afternoon when it was just me and him in the hospital. He was nibbling on a cookie, and I was trying to write. Neither of us found our tasks satisfying, so we ended up staring out the window, at the lamppost in the emptying parking lot, already dark, the sun setting so early in these Boston winters.

I took his hand. After all these years, he still wears a watch every day. I unclasped it from his wrist.

"Four oh-five," I said. "You have until four fifteen to tell me everything you're thinking."

He laughed, shaking his head. But he obliged. He told me about all the preparations Monica was doing at home. At 4:07 he told me that Edward was coming back. He asked if we had been too hard on him, a question we've asked each other so many times. At 4:09 he told me he did not think Edward would return if it were not for me. Not because of my illness, but because I was the one he loved. He insisted Edward had left because of him, the difficult father, and that he would do better this time. He was grateful for this second chance.

At 4:12 he said the sun really sets too early these days. But that there is nothing quite like a New England sunset in the winter.

And at 4:14 he said that for all of our suffering in this life, he hoped to still find me in our next one.

Finally, at 4:15, I could speak again. I told him I had brought him enough misfortune for one lifetime, let alone all that was yet to come, that it hurt to even think about what he and Monica and Edward would have to go through. He shook his head and waved his hand.

"The only thing I would change about our next lives," he said, "is that we choose a house without stairs."

And we both laughed until tears came, and my body ached, all too aware of the truth of his words, my whole body grateful for him, for everything about him.

When I began my relationship with Torou the second time, I made sure he knew the truth, for it was my hiding that had driven him away initially, all the way to America. He did not press me to reveal my secrets to him. I wished to anyway. Above all, without you or Mother in my life, I was feeling very lonely in this power.

But there was the complicated matter of my having disappeared from the Nationalists' watch, having unceremoniously burned down their house. If Torou were to even mention to his parents he was seeing me, word would no doubt spread through that small Taiwan community and eventually into the ears of Mr. Gao. So I told him he could not let anyone from home know he had found me and, ideally, nobody in America either.

"Tell me what you have to hide," he said when I made this request.

And I was ready to tell him. I had it all planned out—a ridiculous series of events, really, now that I think back on it. The plan combined the truth by making it more palatable, or so I hoped, via seduction.

"Take me to your room first," I said.

He lived in a small dormitory room with a bed for one.

"This is what I bleed," I told him, holding up a new Phoenix Pencil Company pencil. He smiled at first, thinking it a metaphor. Then I kissed him and pushed him onto the bed.

I still had the pencil in my hand even as my legs wrapped around him, even as our breathing quickened, and he traced his lips along my neck. When I pushed the pencil into his hand, he broke away from me.

"What do I do with this?"

"Write something."

"Write what?"

"Whatever you're feeling."

"Can it wait?"

"No."

He fumbled with a notebook on his bedside table, distractedly flipping it open as I turned his face back to me. As he entered me, the scratching of the pencil heart against paper thundered, the paper crinkled, and I almost forgot what the next step was supposed to be.

"Press it into me," I remembered.

"Mm."

"I mean the pencil."

"What?"

"Into my wrist. Don't worry. Just push it in."

He was too tentative. I guided his hand, pushing the heart deep into my wrist, watching the vein along my arm turn black. For a moment I could feel his thoughts as he had been writing, could see myself the way he saw me. I held him tight.

"What is happening?" he breathed, tracing my arm. The phoenix glowed.

I raised my hips and he moaned, all other thoughts gone. The phoenix lightened, fading from dark to gray as he rocked into me. His notebook fell to the linoleum with a clatter. We were as connected as two people could be. Our bodies pressed against each other, his thoughts coursing through my blood. My body Reforged his words eagerly, the most pleasurable Reforging I ever had.

I closed my eyes and let the Reforging take over. There we were, on his bed. The last time I had Reforged his pencil was six years earlier, a lifetime and a continent ago, when I saw him working on his math and felt a hint of his love. But this time I felt all of it, or what I thought was all of it. I basked in its warmth, its safety, having no idea how much it could grow through the decades, how far-reaching it could be. I saw him fumble with the pencil I had given him, watched him write nothing but scribbles in his notebook.

I recovered to find him propped up on an elbow, looking at me curiously.

"I asked you to write something, not just scribble," I laughed, tracing a hand along his cheek.

"It's very difficult for me to think properly in certain circumstances," he offered.

"And I thought you were the brightest in Taiwan!"

"Hardly. But even if I was, you have always been my weakness."

He reached his hand out, and I gave him mine. Pulling me back into him, he ran his fingers along my wrist, traced the dormant phoenix.

"But how did you know I scribbled?" The notebook was still on the ground, untouched. "Tell me what happened to that pencil heart."

I told him the truth. And the truth started with you—from the day you came to Shanghai, how I bullied you and you struck back, how you lorded the knowledge of Reforging over me until Mother finally allowed me to learn. I told him how Mr. Gao worked our mothers, and the secret network he established thanks to their ability. I told him how mostly we Reforged through bleeding, the words bled back out, but there was this second method where only the Reforger would experience the words, no one else, and that was what I had just done. I even told him what we were doing in Taiwan, how we were working against locals like him. I told him Linda had shared what your mother did in Shanghai. And I told him every detail of what I had done in California, even though I knew it would hurt him, knew it would hurt to know about Mr. Gao and the types of people I had betrayed. But I had to tell him the whole truth. If he was to turn me away, I had to make it now. I could not bear spending more time with him knowing he could still leave me because of the pencils.

He sat up and ran his hand through his hair.

"How remarkable," he murmured. His intrigue did not carry any anger. I nearly cried. "All this time, I was studying how we communicate. The age-old problem: How do you send a message to somebody else only they can read? And here you were the whole time."

"Pencils can't be the only solution," I said.

"Yes, but the other solutions are not as . . . elegant. The Egyptians had a way of substituting hieroglyphs by altering every few symbols. But it was guessable by anyone who had enough time to sit down and take a deep look. The Greeks had a neat one, too—they wrapped papyrus in a ribbon around a staff, then would write their message down the length of the staff. They would then unwind the papyrus, which would be nonsensical without the staff. Two pieces were needed to form the message. Do you see how it is a difficult problem?"

"But it's been so long since the Greeks and Egyptians. Somebody must have come up with a better solution by now."

"Not an unbreakable one. America had a good one, during the Great War. They had Native Americans transmit messages in their tribal languages. I have told you already how sorry I was to hear of your mother's passing. I am even more sorry to hear how she was used. But the world has a history of exploiting people like you, people like your mother, people like the Native Americans, for their language and abilities, and then casting them aside.

"Now we have machines that can do all sorts of math, so we can formulate codes that are harder and harder to crack. But the other side has good machines, too, that can crack our math." He shook his head and laughed. "And here you are." He ran his hand along my arm.

I found myself leaning away from him, gathering the sheets around myself again, the barest bit of separation possible. He noticed immediately.

"I wouldn't make you do anything for me." In that moment he was the boy alone at the party again, eyes wide, drinking soup. "Even if it completed my thesis. Even if it landed me a professorship."

When he opened his arms, I crawled into them and let my head rest on his chest. I felt, for the first time since leaving Shanghai, finally safe.

But if the community in Taiwan was small, the community of immigrants from Taiwan to Boston was even smaller. I knew how to avoid the ones who might be Nationalist spies—I had worked with enough of their type in California to pick them out. Typically, straight backed, slicked hair, wealthy in Taiwan, trying not to show their struggle in America. Torou, however, did not have the same instincts. He was always curious, always meeting new people. I doubt he told anyone my name or even that I came from Taiwan. Torou, or maybe even Linda, one of them must have mentioned me, then I was likely followed and figured out. I knew their ways, and still, I could not beat them.

One of these men grabbed my wrist when I placed a bowl of noodle soup at his table.

"A gift for you, from Mr. Gao," he said. He pressed a pencil into my hand. As soon as he released me, I swept the pencil into my pocket and retreated to the kitchen. The next time I came out, the man was gone.

In Torou's dormitory, I sharpened the pencil. Its black was a rare thing now. With Mother gone and the Shanghai company burned to the ground and me hiding in America, there was nobody left making these pencils. I held in my hands likely one of the last Mother ever made. I had to Reforge it, even if I feared the message it contained.

Torou was bent over his desk, angling his light on his textbook. He paid me no attention, did not even notice I was Reforging. Only when I sucked in a breath from the cut did he turn around. It had been a while since the last time. I had forgotten the pain of it.

"What's that?" he asked.

Mr. Gao's characters formed slowly across the page—so slowly, did it always take so long? I already knew what it would say.

He was sending his men to take me back to Taiwan. I could no longer be trusted in America. I would work for him, take over for Mother, until I could repay him for the house I burned and for my betrayal.

Torou crumpled the note.

"Leave the state for a month or so," he said as if it were the simplest thing. "They have no real power here."

"They will take you in to find out where I have gone. Or they will threaten my father back home."

I could tell he did not believe me. He had been coddled—he was what they wanted, the star student who would prove to the Americans that there were worthwhile people in Taiwan. He might have been more familiar with their ways once, but here, I knew them much better. I had been one of them.

I was cornered. I was also ready to gnaw off my own arm before leaving this little life I had built with Torou. He would graduate before long, find a job, gain citizenship, and we would marry and, eventually, I would have citizenship too, and then I would bring you over. It was a long process, I knew, but it was the first time I was remotely close to realizing this dream.

"I'll think of something," I said.

I paced the long corridors of MIT while Torou was in class. Nobody stopped me. I peered into classrooms, mulling the idea I had posed to Mother before I had left Taiwan: Was it possible to make a pencil that could not be Reforged? That was the key, I believed, or rather the lock—a lock on this ability.

Torou winced when he heard my idea. It would be painful, mostly for me. But he saw I would not change my mind and connected me with his friend who had access to a kiln on campus.

I worked at the restaurant during the day, ending my shift after midnight, and then I would go to the kiln. I dredged up all the theory Mother had taught us. Torou helped me research, lending his always curious mind to material science. By then I loved him, though I still ached for your presence. Your mind would have easily solved this problem or would have at least sparked more thought on my behalf, more competition.

I would prototype a pencil heart, stab it into my wrist. Each time, Torou flinched. I was looking for a heart that would not melt into my wrist at all. I tried every percentage combination of graphite and clay, and every one still Reforged. So I began to mix in different elements, whatever I could get my hands on. The heart still needed to be able to write. It needed to still be a pencil. And I only had until Mr. Gao's men made it to Boston. My only comfort was that Boston took much longer to reach than California.

And eventually, we did it. It was a mixture of a whole host of elements, along with graphite and clay, but no matter how I angled the heart at my wrist, my body would not accept it.

Torou smiled, eyes tired.

"It hurts me to lose this method of secure communication," he teased.

"I am securing it for everybody," I said. "Between a person and their paper, and no one else." I carved our phoenix into it.

I was ready to face whatever men Mr. Gao sent. Never did I imagine that he, himself, would show up.

I almost ran at the sight of his crisp western suit, the slicked-back hair, the familiar air of confidence. He had aged, of course, though he still sat straight, appearing far too high-class for our dingy restaurant. Had I actually meant something to him, for him to come all this way? Or had I merely injured his pride?

I took deep breaths in the kitchen, clutching the stack of pencils I had made. It was all that I had. Under the guise of politeness, he escorted me out of the restaurant and to a small office on the corner of the block.

"Yun," he sighed. We sat across from each other at a desk. The lines around his eyes had become more severe. Around us, his men stood in a suited line against the wall. Of everyone who had been a part of our lives in Shanghai, at the end, it should have been me and you here. It was a distortion, a sign that something had gone horribly wrong, how instead, at the end, it was me and him. "Did you think I would not find you?"

"I can't go back," I told him. "You should save the money on my airplane ticket."

He practically rolled his eyes.

"We need you in Taiwan. And you owe us terribly. Your father would be happy to see you."

The mention of my father was a threat. Though we had never been close, the thought of him alone in Taiwan still hurt.

"I can't Reforge anymore," I said.

"What?" he asked. Though his voice was calm, I recognized his anger.

"I lost the ability," I said, heart beating fast, clutching the pencils behind my back.

"How could you have lost the ability?" he demanded. His eyes, which had known me since I was a child, had seen everything my body had to offer, drilled into me. I gripped the arm of my chair so tightly I could not feel my fingers anymore. A sudden sinking feeling—I had practiced this scenario with Torou, but never had Torou's kindness remotely resembled Mr. Gao.

"After I lost your child," I invented wildly.

You were right—when we were young, I was always lying. Lying to trick my grandmother into telling me more about Reforging, lying to have Mother do the same. It was like his eyes stripped me down to my essence, to the only skill I had been born with, my most outstanding trait, and I lied and lied to save myself.

"What?" he said again, this time darkly. The men around the room began to shift.

"Yes. You slept with me and then left. My blood didn't come that next month. And I was alone here, carrying your child, running a restaurant and your surveillance network. But I Reforged too much. It was in my blood. In the baby's blood. The baby didn't even make it a few months in my body before the pencils killed it. And when I lost the baby, I lost my Reforging too."

"That's . . ." He had gone pale. "That's not possible. Your aunt never said . . ."

"Did you ever think that maybe she didn't lose your child on purpose?" I was treading on thin ice. I recognized this weak point, knew this was where I needed to twist. "That maybe the same thing that happened to me happened to her?"

"Don't—"

"You made us Reforge, over and over. You killed us."

"Your aunt never lost the ability to Reforge."

"You just didn't know Meng and I were doing them all."

His jaw tightened. "But you Reforged my pencil. A few weeks ago."

"I did not. I guessed what you had to say. Do you want me to prove it? You, who made us go through this?" My voice became shrill. I pulled out a pencil, one whose heart I made with Torou and which I had encased carefully in the darkest wood I could get my hands on. "You, who promised me your heart, then left, whose child took away my one power? Took away my aunt's? I'll show you, let me show you—"

I stood tall in front of him, pulling up my sleeve, the phoenix pale. I stabbed it with the pencil.

It gouged my skin and I shrieked. He stepped back and the men stepped forward.

"Stop her," Mr. Gao said weakly.

A man tried to grab me from behind. I threw him off and stabbed my wrist again. The tip of the pencil was red and gleaming, blood trickled down my phoenix, pure red without any ink in sight. I stabbed again and again, screaming, and crying, thinking of you and your mother and my mother and all of the wars and countries we fled, until two men were able to separate my arms and I was weeping, really, truly, weeping, from the pain, and from so much more.

"Clean her up," Mr. Gao commanded from what sounded very far away. "She is useless to us."

The men were kind about removing the pencil from my hand, wiping my blood from the ground, from my arm, then bandaging it. Maybe they really did feel for me. One of them walked me back to the restaurant, even bowing before departing.

Torou was there, waiting for me, pale next to Linda. He took my hand, my arm, and pulled me into him.

"I'm fine," I breathed, holding on to him tight. "It's over."

And then he told me something I thought I would never forget. I will forget it, I know that now, but maybe if I pass it on to you, you can remember for me, and maybe the world can remember that there was once a man like him, who somehow managed to love me through all I have put him through.

"So many messages, sent through you," he murmured into my hair.

I want to share his words with you, for your life and my life have always been intertwined.

"But you have a story, too, and you deserve to live it."

How many stories passed through us? Combined with our mothers, it must be in the thousands. Stories Reforged in our bodies and bled back to life, whether we wanted it or not, whether or not the authors wanted it. I don't know if we have done enough good in the world for all the harm we have caused.

But I understand. Finally, I feel you close once more. I understand and I forgive. Neither of us had an easy time, made worse by our abilities. Perhaps my grandmother was right, all those years ago, to not want me to learn. But that would mean I would not have been able to feel at one with you.

Perhaps you are right, and in this world, which is kinder than the one we grew up in, it would be okay to share my story.

Oh, don't wave your hand and pretend like this isn't a big deal for us, or that you don't still care for me, after all these years. I know what you have done for Monica. Knew as soon as the pencil-shaped package showed up in the mail with Louise's name on the return address. Where else would your girl get one of our pencils but from you? Thank you, truly.

I've asked Monica to go to Shanghai to give you this last pencil heart of mine. Edward has already invited her. I will likely never see you again—who knew, at our young age, that would be the case. Traveling would disorient me too much, and the version you would see likely would not be a version I would want you to see.

Take my words, take my heart, they are yours always. Even as my mind fades, I give my story to you, you who know in the same way that

I know, their power. I have lived mine, and you have lived yours. That our stories can be together now, for this moment in time, is a gift. That they can help another two girls move forward with their lives—that is the greatest power of all.

—Wong Yun

CHAPTER 34

From the Reforged pencil of Louise Sun

Monica—
     Can you feel the false starts too? How long it takes me to write these words? The weight of each one? How much each word does not want to be wrong, the way all of my other words have been?
     The thing is that I
     I'm really sorry for how
     Let me back up.
     You know that stories are important to me. I really think that people are not made of atoms. We are made of stories. And I've spent so long looking for mine, in America and in Shanghai. And then I met you.
     You were remarkable to me, from the very beginning. You were hesitant and unsure of everything and yet you had a firm history. Of helping your grandparents. No matter what.
     I wanted that. I wanted that so badly. But my relationship to my own family, to my own history, what little I know of it, is difficult, to say the least.

You must be wondering how I got my hands on one of your family's pencils. The truth is, after Thanksgiving, I was feeling so lost and confused and nothing was helping—not talking with my advisor, my therapist, my teammates. I knew the only thing that would make me feel better was if I could somehow convince you to forgive me. Or perhaps speak to your grandmother, get on my knees and beg her to forgive me. But you said you needed time, and I had no way to get in touch with your grandmother. So I turned to the one other person I thought might be able to help me.

I still had her contact on my phone. I messaged and asked if I could call her. To my relief, she said yes.

We hadn't talked since the summer. But that day, we video chatted. Her eyes squinted the whole time, and she held the phone so close to her face I could only see the top half of her head, the brows furrowed, staring into the bright screen.

Without any introduction, I told her everything. Your first message to me. How we met and I gave you her pencil. How even from that first encounter I wanted to know you more, yet I felt you pushing me away. How we still became close, how I told you about my project and you, in turn, told me about yours. How you gushed about your grandparents in a way that made me ache for all I did not have. How you invited me to your home and brought me to your grandfather's old classroom, how I almost kissed you right then because you got me in a way no one else ever has.

But I didn't. And then I messed everything up. Like I always knew I would. Because in that moment, in that classroom, only the two of us, the thought that stopped me was how would I ever be able to live with myself if I broke your heart?

I guess more than any romantic partner or friend, I wanted most in the world to know that I belonged somewhere, to know my place in history so I could navigate a path through the chaos of the world we live in. You have that—you know who you are and that you can do anything you put your mind to. I wanted that so badly. I thought you could help me get there, that your grandparents' story might help me better understand myself and who I'm supposed to be now. That if I gathered enough stories, I could make that into my own, that I could create a map of the chaos around me, and something might make sense. And I knew I would give anything for that, maybe even you.

I told Meng all of this while looking at her scrunched-up forehead. At some point I started to cry, and she said, I kid you not—

"Oh, stop crying."

So I did, ashamed.

She rubbed her forehead, as if mulling something over.

"Why did you call me?" she asked finally.

I almost hung up then, afraid I was wasting her time, that I had angered yet another one of your family members. Eventually, I came to an answer.

"Why did you tell me about Reforging?" I asked. It felt so long ago that we were eating noodles together, and I was telling her what I wanted to do with archiving, and she told me to be careful, and I asked what made her say that, and she invited me home with her, and shared this great secret.

She sighed.

"Because you were so much like us. Because I thought you would understand the dangers." She paused. "But it sounds like you were no better than we were."

I was crushed.

"How do I ask for forgiveness?" I asked.

It must have been a question she has pondered many times herself. Her answer was quick and without hesitation.

"You get on your knees and you spill your heart out."

"And if that doesn't work?"

"Then you must move on. You have to remove yourself from their story."

I swallowed.

"How do I spill my heart out?"

That was when she told me to send her my address and hung up. Two weeks later, I received a small box in the mail, no letter or anything accompanying it. A customs form was taped to the top, from Shanghai. Inside was, of course, this pencil.

After I spoke to Meng, I felt calmer, like I could take on the world again. I even talked to my brother, the one who had the affair. I guess we both realized we were losers and finally had something in common. He suggested I take the next semester off. Is this something that's trending? He didn't know anything about you. But after he suggested it, it felt right. He said he'd help convince our parents. He even said he'd loan me money if I didn't have enough saved from my campus library job (which I definitely do not).

I still have some research funds from last year, though, so I've decided—I'm going to take the next semester and go to Shanghai. I won't bother Meng again, not unless she wants to see me. In fact, I don't think I'll bother anyone. I need to spend some time examining my own life before I can begin trying to archive that of others.

I've given up on the grant I was telling you about. I thought if I had some big name and big money behind my work, my parents might be okay with me and my choices, that they might even be proud of me, talk about me the way they do my brothers. But it's okay. I'll find my own path.

Something you said offhandedly once really stuck with me. You told me how data is stored in servers, but how that data is owned by these big tech companies. So if they find you've violated a rule, they can go and delete your data, or at least make it inaccessible to you. Or if you haven't used your account for a while, they may just delete it. And how even though our generation has more data saved than any other, we may actually leave the least behind.

That terrified me. I thought I needed that data, needed it to give myself a sense of reality.

But then you laughed.

"Do you know the actual best way to preserve data? If all humans were wiped out and eons passed, what data would survive and be interpretable?"

And I did know the answer to that one.

"That carved on rocks," I answered.

And you laughed again, even though I thought it should have terrified you, to have your work in all its technical glory deemed less useful than a carving on a rock, the most primitive of all technology.

"It's incredible the lengths we go to try to make meaning of the world," you said in wonder. "To try to make a story out of it all."

I didn't get it at the time. Now I think I do. In a world so full of hate and war, violence and betrayal, how can our stories not be all tragedies? But if there's truly no pattern, if our stories will be lost, no matter how hard we try to preserve them, then the only thing that really matters is the people in our lives, and how we treat them in this moment in time.

That weekend I spent in Cambridge with you was one of the happiest of my life.

I want to keep talking to you. I want to reframe your story and to have you reframe mine. I want you to always know how incredible you are. I want to be the one to tell you. I want to be entwined in your story, a critical seam of the binding. I want to hold you together even when you think you are alone. I want to be the fourth player at your mahjong table.

If you'll have me.

Until then, I'll be in Shanghai, figuring myself out. If you happen to be in Shanghai, too

Well

I hope to see you soon.

Love always,

L

CHAPTER 35

From the diary of Monica Tsai

December 29, 2018

Oh man, it's been a while, hasn't it? It's not that I've given up journaling. I actually appreciate it more than ever. But there was a lot going on, and for the first time I felt like I could handle it without all the constant reflection.

I can hardly believe the events that led to me being here in Shanghai. I guess it started with my father's invitation. Then grandmother asked me to go, and since my father lost Meng's contact details, it turned out the only person who knew how to get in touch with her was, of all people, Louise.

I composed and recomposed a message to Louise. Sometimes they were heartfelt; others, a few basic lines asking if I could have Meng's information. By then, it was almost Christmas.

And then her pencil arrived. Grandmother was the one who brought the package inside, passed me the pencil just as I had given her Meng's all those months ago.

"How did she get one of these?" I asked when I saw the unmistakable black of the Phoenix Pencil Company. "Did you . . . ?"

"Not me," she said. Then she looked at me pointedly. I stared right back at her. I did not want to miss any of these moments with her, no matter how she might glare at me. There were fewer with each passing day. Her recovery has not been easy, but I don't want to write about that. I want to write about how she looked between me and the pencil with a clear mind and how she nodded, as if it was something I was always meant to take.

"I'll Reforge it," I said, and she nodded approvingly.

When I was alone, I took a breath and melted the heart into my wrist.

I felt way too many things, afterward. She was going to be in Shanghai. She was sorry. I felt it, the truth behind her words. I felt her confusion, also her determination to lift herself out of it, and I felt strangely proud of her.

I called her that night. It was a simple call, really. I was prepared to offer only kindness, yet even so, I was guarded, at least a little, until her first words melted all of that away.

"Hi," she said after the first ring. "I missed you."

"I missed you too."

"Did you get my pencil?"

"I did. And I Reforged it."

"Oh. I hope—I hope it made sense. I was kind of a wreck when I wrote it. I'd understand if you still don't want to—"

"It's okay," I said. Something unclenched in me as I said it. "I'm going back to school next semester."

"Really? No EMBRS?"

"I quit EMBRS." I paused. "Actually, I kind of ruined EMBRS, maybe just temporarily though. I'm pretty sure my professor hates me now. But you were right. It took too much data and was sneaky about it and it wanted even more data and I couldn't do it anymore."

"I get it," she said, that thoughtfulness I loved so much in her re-turning. "I did the same thing, didn't I? Wanted your family's story, tried to be sneaky about it, destroyed myself in the process."

"I forgive you, you know," I said. And I was pleased by how easy it was to say and how much I meant it. "Mine was worse, since the tech amplified it."

"But you burned it down." Her voice was a mixture of a sigh and a laugh. "Look at you, you rebel."

"A rebel?" I repeated. A rebel was pretty much the last word anyone would use to describe me.

"Totally!" Her old familiar enthusiasm kicked in. "Think of it as a new way of looking at yourself. Rebel you is skeptical of this sort of tech and won't be drawn to it in the future. Rebel you has a history of taking down this sort of thing. How cool is that? That's something to celebrate."

"Celebrate with me, then." I said it too fast, before I had thought it through. It felt right all the same.

"Nothing would make me happier," she said without missing a beat. "I'd even drive to come see you."

"Fly."

"Well, that's a bit expensive—"

"To Shanghai. I'll meet you there."

I heard her rearrange herself. Maybe she was on a bed, or a chair, her long legs folded beneath her, her phone switching hands, pressing against a cooler cheek.

"You'll be in Shanghai?"

I filled her in on grandmother's pencil, my father's offer.

"But until now, until I thought I might see you there, too, I wasn't really looking forward to it."

She laughed, a soft one, followed by a sniff.

"That's incredible." Her voice was warm with a trembling joy. "I will see you in Shanghai then."

Grandfather promised he could handle a week by himself. The nurse, to our relief, has been great with grandmother, and will stick around for a while longer. I stocked the fridge and freezer and thoroughly cleaned the entire house. I let our neighbors know too—it was weird to share this vulnerability, that my elderly grandparents would be alone for a week—and yet they were so kind about it, promised to check in on them, even admitted that they had been looking for a way to help us out after the many times I had cat-sat for them. Their cat rubbed fondly against my leg.

I said goodbye to my grandparents on the porch. Grandfather made me take grandmother's senior card, of course, since she can't really take public transportation anymore. Grandmother smiled blankly when I bent down to hug her.

My first day in Shanghai, my father picked me up from the airport. He was taller than I remembered, until I realized I also felt taller here. Not as wary of standing up straight, not here in this place where I can blend right in. We took the fancy maglev train out of the airport.

My father lives in a nice apartment, though it is far from the city center. He had the day off, and after dropping off my stuff at his place and calling grandfather to let him know I made it safely, he took me to the site where the Phoenix Pencil Company once stood. It's now a flashy convenience store, fluorescent lighting showing off all the bright packaging. I bought a notebook and wasabi-flavored chips I knew grandfather would find amusing.

It turned out my father never knew Meng's address. He had met her here, at this convenience store. She was still very mobile, he told me, and refused when he offered to buy her a treat from the store—a tea egg, a lunch box, a hot drink. She drank from her own thermos. Something medicinal, he guessed, crinkling his nose as he said it. They had gone to a small park nearby. They used to sit there and chat. It had been a while since he last saw her.

"The older generation has more of a community here than they do in the States," he said. "I used to ask to meet up, and half the time she would say she was too busy."

He took me to his favorite restaurant for dinner, right down the street from his apartment, small and homey. He ordered lion's head meatballs. They were huge and perfectly round, thick droplets of soy sauce gathered on bok choy.

"I think grandmother's are better," I said. The meatballs were awfully good, just not the same.

"I agree," my father said, and I wondered if he thought of home more than he let on.

On day two, he had to go into the office. Louise sent me Meng's contact information.

she'll understand you, Louise wrote. but you probably won't understand her

Louise was already in Shanghai. I told her I wanted to see my family before meeting up. I had to download China-specific apps in order to message and otherwise get around. I am not nearly as familiar with the data surveillance here as I am with America's, and in a way, it is a relief. I am sure it is happening, likely on a scale larger than I can imagine. But I am also leaving soon, merely a ghost passing through, an ephemeral packet of data.

Finally, I called Meng.

I stammered my way through it, made sure to pronounce grandmother's name slowly and carefully, speaking loudly in case she was hard of hearing like grandmother.

Meng's voice is higher. It's fast and clipped, and Louise was completely right—I could hardly understand her rapid Shanghainese. Even when she slowed down, even when she attempted Mandarin.

"I'm sorry." I was sweating, wishing I had asked my father to call instead. It felt like my responsibility. And I felt connected to her, through her Reforged words. It was only these real-life words that were hindering us.

She asked a question. I tried to say again that I'd like to meet her, maybe at the convenience store where the pencil company used to be. She repeated the same question, this time faster, repeated it again before I even had the chance to answer. Then she hung up.

I wished I had thought to record the call, so I could play it back, slow it down, and see what I had missed. Maybe I would have been able to send the audio recording to grandmother and have her translate it for me.

Then my phone vibrated.

我们在铅笔厂旁边的公园见面

Even as I scrambled to copy the text into my translating app, she sent another message.

🕐? I sent back.

👍

I had not even realized the emoji of the clock I sent had a time on it. Her eyes were sharp. I prepared my backpack, tucked grandmother's pencil into the side pocket, then ran out the door to ensure I would catch the train and make it there by the emoji time.

She was already at the park near the old pencil company when I arrived, sitting on a bench. She held a cane in front of her that appeared less to support her weight than to hold her posture upright. Her expression was far sterner than grandmother's.

"Hi," I said, instinctively in English, running over.

"Monica?"

She said my name carefully, like porcelain on her lips.

"It's really nice to meet you," I said in Chinese. Meng smiled. Her teeth were small and crooked. So she did understand me.

She gestured to the open space beside her, and I sat down.

She said something I only partially understood. It was a question, asking if I did something. Then she pulled out a pencil. She pointed first to herself, then to the pencil, then to my wrist. She spoke her words again.

"Yes," I said. I startled her with my excitement, understanding what she was trying to say. "I Reforged your pencil. Grandmother asked me to."

She asked something else. This time, I could recognize the word for "grandmother."

I took out grandmother's pencil and handed it to her. She looked at it for a long time before taking it.

"She spent a lot of time writing with that," I said. "She really wanted to find you again."

She held the pencil in both hands, cradled in her lap.

"Her memory is fading now." I had looked up how to explain her disease, practiced saying it. "And she had surgery on her hip."

Meng did not say anything, so I kept talking.

"It means she can't do all the things she used to do, like cook or even walk across the room without someone helping her. The doctor says that will take a toll on her memory, too, if she can't do things herself. Ever since she stopped writing, it's like she's fading faster and faster, and there's nothing we can do about it." It was rare that I could speak so freely in Chinese. Somehow it felt easier with her, knowing her responses would be slow and careful, that there was already a gap in our communication that would not be made worse if I couldn't find the right phrase. "But for now, I am grateful to have more time with her."

"You really love her," she said, the first complete sentence I understood.

I nodded.

"It's weird," I said. "Sometimes she will have these bursts of clarity. But there hasn't been one in a while. And I wonder—" I paused. It was my first time voicing this out loud. "I wonder if I've already had my last conversation with her."

She said something else, except this time I did not understand a word. She took out her phone. It was a huge one. She spoke into it then squinted her eyes at the screen. She showed the words to me.

"Can you send it to me?" I asked sheepishly. Whatever app she had used translated her Shanghainese into characters on the screen, though I could barely read them. Once they were on a message in my phone, I could copy it into my translation app. I tried to ignore all of the data I knew I was sharing just to be able to communicate with a family member.

Your grandmother tried many times to give people a place they could call home. I think she finally succeeded with you. You do not have the same drifting as your father.

In truth, during that meeting, I did not understand her words well at all, even after they were translated into English. But afterward, looking through my translation history again, I understand. Both my father and Louise had gone to Meng. In them, Meng saw people unmoored. Grandmother had been unable to offer Meng a home, to give my father the care he needed. But she had given me a cohesive story, something that made me firm in who I am. I am her granddaughter, and I come from a long line of pencil makers. She is the most resilient person I've ever known. I can only hope I learned that from her, too.

Then, to my surprise, Meng grabbed my wrist. I let her turn it and roll up my sleeve. She traced my phoenix, dark from where Louise's pencil heart still ran through my blood. She rolled up her sleeve and showed me her scar. It was even more defined than grandmother's.

She tapped my phoenix's head with a questioning look.

"It's Louise's pencil," I said. "She told me you gave her the pencil."

She nodded, pleased. Then she tapped at her own wrist.

"Have you ever wondered why there are two phases to Reforging? Two chances to understand another's heart?" She spoke the question to her phone. I took my time translating it on mine.

"I haven't," I admitted.

"The first time is for the Reforger," she said, articulating clearly. "The Reforger then has a chance to decide—should this story be shared? They can bleed it out and share it widely. Or they can keep it just for themselves."

She tapped again at my wrist. "What have you decided?"

I looked down at her hand on mine.

"I'm going to keep it near my heart," I said. "I want her words to be only for me."

She nodded approvingly.

"It is interesting when a Reforger gives another Reforger a story though," she continued, holding grandmother's pencil before her. "She knows she has given me a choice. Just as I gave her a choice, when I sent her my pencil."

"A choice?"

She took a knife out of her purse and began to sharpen grandmother's pencil.

"Here?" I asked, glancing around the park. It was chilly, though still comfortable. There were a few others around. I had expected she would take the pencil home and Reforge it when she was ready, as grandmother had.

"No sense in delaying," she said. She handed the pencil to me. "Reforge it," she said. "Hurry up, now."

"Me? But she meant it for you."

"And I want you to Reforge it."

"But—"

She pushed the pencil into my hand.

"You have not had your last conversation with her yet," she said.

I took the pencil.

If she had not been watching me so expectantly, I would have delayed. I would have held on to the pencil until I felt like I needed to hear grandmother's voice. But she was right. There was no sense in delaying.

I pushed it into my wrist.

The park faded, Meng faded, and it was just me and grandmother, her calm presence, confusion interspersed, but above all, her love, strong and unwavering. Her life scrolled before me—ten years old, bullying Meng. Fourteen years old, finally learning to Reforge, the joy of understanding her family. Nineteen, emotions high, one war leading into another and the beginning of a rift. A cruel separation, the dark times in Taiwan, the darker times in California. It was too much; I had to bend over. I felt Meng's arm around me as it continued. Grandmother meeting grandfather again in Boston. Creating a pencil that could not be Reforged. Meeting Louise, seeing us together, the happiness—

As the scenes faded, I returned to myself, crying into Meng as she rubbed my back gently.

"I didn't know," I whispered. I saw once again, grandmother spending all that time writing her story. Writing for us. "I didn't know how much someone could suffer."

"It is good you did not know," Meng said. "Your life has been a happy one."

"And I didn't know . . . how much she could love."

Meng's expression softened. Then she held my wrist. The phoenix glowed, grandmother's and Louise's hearts coursing through me.

"And what will you do with your grandmother's words?" she asked.

Keep them close to my heart, was my first thought. But then I saw the knife she had used to sharpen the pencil, and I knew what I had to do.

Grandmother had not wanted me to Reforge in any way other than through pleasure. But that was not realistic. Stories can bring both pleasure and pain. Somewhere along the way, I had learned how to handle it.

Meng did not protest when I took the knife from her, as if she knew I would all along. I've always been a coward about physical pain, but in that moment, having just felt how much grandmother had gone through, I sliced through my skin easily.

I bled into the notebook I had bought at the convenience store. Meng helped me, holding my arm steady, flipping the pages as needed. Grandmother had not been succinct. I felt her presence again between us, lived her life all over again, here in this park in Shanghai. This time, it was a hum, a comfort.

When I began to feel Louise's note begin, I nodded at Meng. She pulled the notebook away and made a clenching motion with her hand. I copied it. Louise's note sank back into my arm, and only a few regular drops of blood dripped from my cut.

Meng rummaged in her purse and pulled out a roll of bandages.

"Some things you always carry with you," she chuckled as she bandaged my wrist.

I watched grandmother's characters rematerialize in the notebook. I missed her deeply then.

"That's for you," I said, pointing to the notebook we had left open to dry in the sun.

She bowed her head deeply.

"I will cherish it," she said. I was able to understand her better at that point, more used to the deviations Shanghainese would take, or maybe she was adding more Mandarin. "This story she wrote . . . I am very glad to have it. But I have a feeling it was never meant for me. That's why I wanted you to Reforge it." She touched the notebook lightly and smiled. "We used to write stories for each other, did she mention that? But this time . . . somehow, we both ended up writing for you."

I began to cry again. It's so embarrassing, thinking about it now, how much I cried in front of this woman I hardly knew, who I could barely understand. I'm going to lose grandmother. I know I am. I have no greater certainty. I'm going to lose the woman who raised me, the one who built me a home that I never once resented. But with Meng's words, I felt as if grandmother were there with us, that these two women trusted me with their stories, and it would be the honor of my life to carry them on.

I asked if I could see her again, maybe with my father, or Louise. She said she would have to check her mahjong calendar. Then she winked and said of course. I rolled my eyes. She had the same sense of humor as grandmother. I asked if I could escort her home. She said it would be a waste of my train fare.

"My train fare is free," she cackled.

I hugged her, suddenly and tightly. I watched her walk away, carrying the notebook.

At night, I finally met up with Louise. We met at the Bund, what was once the International Settlement. The city lights reflected across the water of the bay. She stood out, a head above everybody else.

We hugged. It was a relief to speak English again, to have someone who understood exactly what I was saying.

I pulled a scarf out of my backpack. It was Princeton orange and black and had a few small holes in it, even a section that was narrower than the rest of it, misshapen from when grandmother's memory faltered as she knitted.

"A Christmas gift from grandmother," I said, and threw the scarf around her neck.

"Really?" she asked with huge eyes.

"Yeah. I kept telling her she didn't have to push herself, but she really wanted to knit a scarf for you. Knitting is one of the few things she can still do on her own. I think she really enjoyed making it."

She wrapped the scarf tightly around her neck and beamed.

"Can I take a picture of you to send to grandmother?" I asked.

"Only if you're in it too."

We found a spot with a good view of the water and the city.

"Here, you have longer arms," I said, and passed my phone to her.

She held the phone in front of us, and we smiled as she took the photo.

I sent it to both grandmother and Meng.

There are moments when I feel so lucky, feel like I am exactly where I should be, like I would not trade a single thing. We walked along the land our families had resided upon for generations. We had ended up so far away and this was not our home, not anymore, but there was a feeling to it, like it could come close to being a home. Like if grandmother and her mother, her father, her aunt, her grandmother, and everyone before them could see us, they would be happy, and maybe my happiness would infect them too, and make up even a little bit for the hardship they had to experience to see me to where I am now.

We sat down on a bench overlooking the water. It was like we were in Cambridge again, at the river. Though this one was so much bigger. People milling all around, stopping for pictures of the flashing tower across the way, the holiday lights. Nobody paid any attention to us. It was perfect.

"What are you going to do now?" she asked. "Once you're back in school?"

"I don't know," I admitted. "Maybe I'll change majors too. Something more in line with data policy or privacy—"

"Yes!" she exclaimed. "Join the social sciences. That reminds me, I brought you a gift."

She gave me a card. I had to hold it up, angling it toward the street-light to see what it said. It was a string of letters and numbers.

"It's an account number," she explained. "For one of those things where you can securely connect to a machine without being spied on." She began to speak much faster. "I know you probably already have one. But I figured it'd be really useful for you to get past sites that are blocked here. And you probably got a cheap one and hacked together your own thing to enhance it, so I ordered you the most expensive one I could find. They don't even have your email—that account number is all they have, so you can be truly anonymous. Something about how long it is makes it safe? You would know more about that than I would. The app has all sorts of buzzwords I'm sure you'd understand. End-to-end encryption, no logs, split tunneling? I don't know what that is, but—"

"Stop," I laughed. "No need for all this jargon. You've already seduced me."

I was stupidly pleased when she blushed, stupidly pleased that she had gotten me a gift so strange yet so perfect.

"You're only here for a week, right?" she asked.

"Yeah," I sighed.

"Okay. They actually have a thirty-day free trial. So I'm not really paying anything. But I want you to know that I absolutely would."

I laughed again.

"Grandmother would approve. Thank you. I love it."

I still send grandmother messages even though she doesn't reply anymore. Whether she has forgotten I am away, or how to type Chinese on the keyboard, or how to use her phone, I don't know. But I send them anyway, a sort of comfort to myself.

When I took out my phone to look at my one-sided conversation with grandmother, Louise noticed. She squeezed my hand. I rested my head on her shoulder and let out a shaky sigh.

"You know what she would say," Louise assured me. "How proud she is of you. How much she loves you."

I nodded. After Reforging grandmother's pencil, I knew her better than I ever thought possible, all her faults and mistakes, also her resilience and her love. And I knew that if her memory were not failing her, she would have had something fun to say, some funny emojis to send, probably two girls and a city skyline and a heart, for she had always been the greatest supporter of our relationship. She'd probably add something else, too, something in Chinese, a sly reminder not to forget that no matter how much Louise might like me, she would always be the one who loved me the most.

I sent her a message, continuing our one-sided conversation.

永遠不會忘記妳的愛 😊 😊 〰️ ∞

Louise squeezed my hand again.

"Thank you," I whispered.

I put my phone away, and for a moment we sat there, my head on her shoulder, her hand in mine, enjoying the city. Then I turned to her and kissed her.

"Finally." She smiled and kissed me back.

She said more than that, words that made my head light and my heart soar. But those words—

I think I will keep just between me and her.

NOTES AND ACKNOWLEDGMENTS

There isn't really an Arby's Monica could have biked to in 2018. But maybe in a world that is a little more magical than ours, there would have been.

The bronze lions outside the Shanghai HSBC bank that Meng makes a wish on were mysteriously never taken by the Japanese, despite other bronze statues being taken for scrap metal. The Japanese did, however, take the Hong Kong branch's lions (which were modeled after the Shanghai ones). The Hong Kong lions made it as far as a dock in Osaka before being spotted after the war and laboriously returned to Hong Kong. Remarkably, the Shanghai lions also survived the Cultural Revolution by being hidden in warehouses. They now hang out at the Shanghai History Museum.

This book owes much to books, both fiction and nonfiction—first and foremost Helen Zia's *Last Boat Out of Shanghai: The Epic Story of the Chinese Who Fled Mao's Revolution*, which sparked my interest in Shanghai in the first place. Other books that informed my understanding of Shanghai and Taiwan, which also happen to be wonderful reads, include *Shanghai: The Rise and Fall of a Decadent City 1842–1949* by Stella Dong; *Daughters of the Flower Fragrant Garden: Two Sisters Separated by China's Civil War* by Zhuqing Li; *Lust, Caution* by Eileen Chang, translated by Julia Lovell, and its corresponding movie directed by Ang Lee; *My Years as Chang Tsen: Two Wars, One Childhood* by Annabel Annuo Liu; *Remembering Shanghai: A Memoir of Socialites,*

Scholars and Scoundrels by Isabel Sun Chao and Claire Chao; *The Third Son* by Julie Wu; *Green Island* by Shawna Yang Ryan; and *The Boy from Clearwater* by Pei-Yun Yu, illustrated by Jian-Xin Zhou and translated by Lin King. Any mistakes are my own.

Vivian Wu's history of Boston Chinatown talk hosted by Panethnic Pourovers was wonderful and helped me set the scene for Yun's arrival in Boston.

Michelle Caswell's *Seeing Yourself in History: Community Archives and the Fight Against Symbolic Annihilation*; Jarrett M. Drake's *Liberatory Archives: Towards Belonging and Believing*; and Randall C. Jimerson's *Archives for All: Professional Responsibility and Social Justice* were excellent resources for helping me understand memory work.

Now—there is much thanks to give!

To my agent, Seth Fishman, for being fun and delightful, in addition to being a wonderful agent, of course. Thanks also to the rest of the team at the Gernert Company, especially Ellen Coughtrey, Jack Gernert, Rebecca Gardner, Nora Gonzalez, Will Roberts, and also to Shiv Doraiswami and Sean Berard at Grandview.

This book transformed under the eagle eyes of my editor Jessica Williams, who made pretty much everything make more sense, and also convinced me to give EMBRS a better name (maybe SparkLE will live on in another book . . .). Thanks for championing my book so wonderfully! Thanks also to Peter Kispert for being so wonderfully responsive and encouraging, and to the tireless efforts of others at HarperCollins: Laura Brady, Ana Deboo, Kyra DeVoe, Jennifer Hart, Jen McGuire, Kelsey Manning, Mumtaz Mustafa, Eliza Rosenberry, Nancy Singer, and Liate Stehlik. And to Will Staehle at Unusual Co. for such a wonderful cover!

Thanks to Kish Widyaratna at 4th Estate for bringing this book to the UK! And to everyone else who has worked to bring this book to new lands.

I have many colleagues from various software jobs to thank for themes that wormed their way into this book. First, my colleagues at Cortico for all things digital archival and what it means to build story-sharing software in partnership with communities. To my colleagues at Ethyca for teaching me more than I ever wanted to learn about data privacy. Building open-source software with you all also taught me the value of a good commit message, a good git rebase, and a good emoji :chefskiss:.

This book started as a short story, and I only had the confidence to make it into something longer thanks to the encouragement of Amy Johnson, the Dream Foundry writing contest, and my wonderful co-hort at Aspen Summer Words, led by the incomparable Fonda Lee.

Super special thanks go to the earliest readers of this book, back when it was rambling and rough: Constance Fay and Mike Meneses, the best writing group anyone could ask for! Thanks for all the love and silliness. In addition, Zhengyang Wang made sure I didn't make terrible gaffes in Chinese and pushed me to be more detailed on the historical portions. He also helped me chase down what exactly happened to those bronze lions. Sam Cordero, in addition to providing always valuable feedback, made sure Louise didn't give our heroes food poisoning by taking a five-hour bus ride without putting her food in a cooler. Sam also gets a special shout-out for making incredible egg-tart ice cream sandwiches in Monica's honor. Monica would have loved them.

I can't thank the team behind Reese's Book Club's LitUp fellowship enough—Dhonielle Clayton, Zoraida Córdova, Tessa Gratton, Natalie C. Parker, Melissa Seymour, and of course LitUp's fearless leader, Gretchen Schreiber. Thanks also to everyone else at both We Need Diverse Books and Madcap Retreats who made the fellowship possible! To my mentor Adrienne Young, for walks through Nashville and also for startling insights that paved the way for Mr. Gao to fully realize his sinister potential. Most of all, thanks to my fellow fellows Tolani Akinola, Margot Fisher, Ashley Jordan, and Bora Reed. Nobody could ask for a better group of people to go through publishing with!

To Eddy Yang and Iris Chan, who lent their medical insight into hip surgeries and hospital cafeteria food.

To my friends in the Boston area for making every day so fun and reminding me there's more to life than writing and coding—Claire, Elisabeth, Gaurav, Karl, Rathanak, Wendy, Yin. This book had some good jokes, right? Right . . . ?

This book is really about family, and I've got a top-tier one. Thanks to my aunts, uncles, and great-uncle, who taught me how to play mahjong and how to appreciate a good coupon. To Peach and Woody, who are, in my unbiased opinion, the cutest cat and dog in the land of Cambridge. To my brother, Jeffrey, for being a role model, but also for being silly. To Jimmy, whose support has made all the difference—all of Torou's best qualities are yours. To my father, who taught me to love technology. And to my mother, whose care for my grandparents at the end of their lives has shaped my definition of love.

To my cousin Lin King—Yun and Meng pass stories to each other because you and I did first. I can't wait to read what you write next.

And of course, to my grandparents, who raised me, fed me both fast food and the best home-cooked food, and told me stories of their home and of their pencil company. 謝謝外公外婆。永遠不會忘記你們的愛 🫶 ∞